M. L. WHITE

Shifter Sacrifice

First published by White Wolf Publishing LLC 2025

Copyright © 2025 by M. L. White

All rights reserved. No part of this publication may be reproduced, stored or transmitted in any form or by any means, electronic, mechanical, photocopying, recording, scanning, or otherwise without written permission from the publisher. It is illegal to copy this book, post it to a website, or distribute it by any other means without permission.

This novel is entirely a work of fiction. The names, characters and incidents portrayed in it are the work of the author's imagination. Any resemblance to actual persons, living or dead, events or localities is entirely coincidental.

M. L. White asserts the moral right to be identified as the author of this work.

M. L. White has no responsibility for the persistence or accuracy of URLs for external or third-party Internet Websites referred to in this publication and does not guarantee that any content on such Websites is, or will remain, accurate or appropriate.

Designations used by companies to distinguish their products are often claimed as trademarks. All brand names and product names used in this book and on its cover are trade names, service marks, trademarks and registered trademarks of their respective owners. The publishers and the book are not associated with any product or vendor mentioned in this book. None of the companies referenced within the book have endorsed the book.

First edition

ISBN (paperback): 9798899713330
ISBN (hardcover): 9798896926573

Cover art by SeventhStar Art

This book was professionally typeset on Reedsy.
Find out more at reedsy.com

To my brother Broc,
For all your constant love and support
even though you don't like to read.
I forgive you for that.
–M

Contents

Preface	iv
Chapter 1	1
Chapter 2	9
Chapter 3	19
Chapter 4	28
Chapter 5	40
Chapter 6	54
Chapter 7	72
Chapter 8	78
Chapter 9	84
Chapter 10	100
Chapter 11	108
Chapter 12	120
Chapter 13	125
Chapter 14	131
Chapter 15	138
Chapter 16	140
Chapter 17	144
Chapter 18	147
Chapter 19	152
Chapter 20	160
Chapter 21	162
Chapter 22	168
Chapter 23	176
Chapter 24	181
Chapter 25	189

Chapter 26	196
Chapter 27	209
Chapter 28	212
Chapter 29	225
Chapter 30	236
Chapter 31	239
Chapter 32	247
Chapter 33	249
Chapter 34	260
Chapter 35	265
Chapter 36	276
Chapter 37	283
Chapter 38	289
Chapter 39	297
Chapter 40	301
Chapter 41	312
Chapter 42	323
Chapter 43	328
Chapter 44	330
Chapter 45	344
Chapter 46	355
Chapter 47	357
Chapter 48	365
Chapter 49	380
Chapter 50	397
Chapter 51	406
Chapter 52	415
Chapter 53	431
Chapter 54	445
Chapter 55	453
Chapter 56	472
Epilogue	475
Series Order	503

Are you not ready to leave the Shifter Series?	504
Bonus Chapter	505
Bonus Chapter	511
About the Author	521
Also by M. L. White	523

Preface

*Wouldn't you sacrifice everything
to protect the ones you love?*

Yeah, me too.

Chapter 1

Cade sped towards the Den. With as big and bulky as his truck was, it sure could move.

My leg bounced nervously with every turn and winding of the road. *God, this was taking too long*, I thought as my stomach twisted inside. Caleb either disconnected the line or someone else did it for him, and with Patrick and his Division goons there, I wasn't taking any chances. My hand went to the handle as Cade pulled onto Main Street.

The second the truck pulled towards a parking space, I opened the door and stumbled out. The truck lurched to a stop as I fumbled forward and ran, but I managed not to pile it in.

"Shanely!" Bastian bellowed, grunting in pain, but I didn't stop. I *couldn't* stop. Caleb needed me, and I barreled towards the door. *It already took too long getting here as it was.* A thousand different scenarios went through my mind at what could have happened to Caleb in the amount of time it took to get here. Not knowing was killing me.

Bastian hollered again as I shoved the door open and stepped inside the dimly lit bar.

My eyes widened when I took in the scene. It seems I caught the end of a brawl as Patrick had Caleb pinned against the wall, his lip bloody. His new goons were arguing with Octavia on the other side of the room, and boy was she letting them have it. Searing heat filled my cheeks as I clenched my fists together.

I saw *red*.

I stormed towards Patrick and yanked his hand off Caleb.

"That is enough!" I cried out gruffly, crossing my arms in a huff.

Patrick's dark squinted eyes softened as they settled on me. A sly grin formed as his face lit up excitedly.

"Shanely? Well, what a nice surprise!" he said, grinning. "Wasn't expecting to see you today, beautiful."

My wolf snapped within me, and I shoved him, catching him off guard. Worry lined my brother's face as the two new douche bags hollered behind me, but my wolf was pleased. *Aggressive little thing.* I saw handcuffs from the corner of my eye, but Patrick's hand rose, stilling the men with him. *He had authority over them...* I thought.

"What in the world do you think you're doing, Patrick?!" I demanded, earning nothing but a low chuckle from him.

"Shanely, knock it off," Caleb muttered. His attempt to pull me behind him was pointless when I turned and glared my red eyes at him. It was hard to control my wolf when I'm angry, let alone when she's angry too, and he seemed to get that. He cocked his head to the side ever so slightly, exposing his neck, and I felt my wolf's temper settle some. I took a deep breath and pulled her back. *I can't shift now,* I thought to myself. *I. Can't. Shift. Now.* Blinking rapidly, my vision slowly returned to normal. Taking another deep breath for good measure, I turned back to Patrick.

"I asked you a question," I said firmly.

The prick looked nothing more than *amused* with me as he slowly looked me up and down. His sly grin grating on my ever loving nerves.

"It's cute when you get angry like this," he said, leaning back against one of the high tables.

Cute?!

My wolf roared beneath my skin, and it was a struggle to pull her back this time. Shifting would not be a smart idea, but now I totally understood why the fellas had issues with control. *She's a nasty bugger when she wants to be.*

The bar door slammed opened again, and Cade stormed inside. His icy glare said enough.

"Words, Shanely. You and I will be having words."

CHAPTER 1

Ignoring my Beta, I kept my glare on Patrick. Cade was seconds behind me anyways. It wasn't like I was truly alone here with Caleb and Octavia, but I knew I'd still be getting a lecture from my Beta *and* my husband later.

Patrick rolled his eyes as the last Fenrir triplet made his way to me. Cade looped his finger in my belt loop and tugged hard.

"I asked you a question!" I shouted again, scrambling to stay upright with Cade tugging on my pants. I shot him a glare.

"Let me go!"

"And listen to Bastian chew me out the whole way home? I don't think so. Besides, it's my job as your Beta to protect you, but I can't do that when you go jumping out of moving vehicles!"

I was never going to hear the end of this.

"We had a civil issue," Patrick said, pulling me from my conversation with Cade, "but don't worry, gorgeous. It's been taken care of. Hasn't it, Caleb?"

My brother pursed his lips together but said nothing. He held his tongue, giving me a knowing look, and I gritted my teeth.

"That's a lie," I said, putting my hands on my hips. I had given up on removing Cade's finger from my belt loop. "We both know you have a nasty habit of sticking your nose where you don't belong. Where you're not *wanted*."

Patrick's smile fell, and I held his ruthless glare. I struck a nerve as color stained his face.

"I think it's time for you to leave, Patrick," Cade snarled, turning to the others. "All of you."

"Cade Fenrir. Not surprised to see you following her around like the mutt you truly are, but this business is between Caleb and I. So why don't you take Shanely home and leave us be. We wouldn't want her getting hurt, now would we?" Patrick snapped back.

The blood pumped through my veins like fire, and I bounced on my feet. *God, I wish Cade would just let me go!*

"I'm not going anywhere," I shouted firmly. "You need to take your new friends and leave now!"

Anger flashed in Patrick's eyes as he said, "Shanely, I won't tell you again. I'm not leaving until my business with Caleb is done. Unless you want me to take you home in the cruiser. *That* I can definitely do."

"Yeah..." Bastian said in a menacing tone, "I don't think so."

Patrick *paled*.

He turned slowly to see my mate entering the bar with Elijah and Noah behind him. Bastian moved slow and casual, gliding his hands over every passing table, and hiding the pain I'm sure he was in. You'd never see it on his face though. He held his head high as he pushed past the new goons and came straight for me. I bit my lower lip when when his icy eyes met mine. *Yea... he's not happy with me.*

"What?" Bastian asked, turning back to Patrick and yanking me to his side. "Surprised to see me or something?"

Patrick stared hard at Bastian. He seemed lost for words and straightened the collar on his shirt.

"Why don't you tell me who your new friend is?" he asked, ignoring my mate's question. "I don't think I've met him before."

Noah had stopped in front of Patrick's new goons, keeping the two from advancing any further. He briefly looked to me before squaring his shoulders and glaring back at them. Pride filled my chest watching him. Noah had a good few inches on the rest and was just as scary as the rest of my family. *Must be a family trait*, I thought amusingly to myself.

Bastian's eyes drifted around the room, flaring his nostrils as he did, and his jaw ticked. I looked past Patrick, seeing a small crowd just watching, and I sucked in a deep breath.

Humans.

"Nah," Bastian said, leaning back against the counter, "not right now, but you can tell me why you're causing trouble for Caleb here. We both know it wasn't a civil dispute."

Patrick glared again, and I could see the tension in his brow as he just stared at the two of us. The silence was uncomfortable to say the least, but Patrick snapped out of whatever was going on, flashing me a fake grin.

"Just a misunderstanding," he said with ease. "My new guys can be a

CHAPTER 1

little *overzealous* sometimes. They thought Caleb was eavesdropping on our private conversation concerning police business. They simply wanted him to mind his own business, but we're all good now. Right?"

I scowled as his goons nodded slyly. *As if we'd believe such a stupid lie.* Anger pumped through my veins, and I lifted my foot...

"You so much as take one step towards that man, Shanely," Bastian snarled, *"and we will be having a very different conversation later."*

I snarled through our link, stomping my foot back down to the hardwood floor and straightened my shirt. *I can still yell from here*, I thought to myself.

"No, I don't think we are. You may be the police, but it doesn't give you right to treat us this way. You are *not* in control here. You are meant to serve *us*. I mean isn't that what the whole oath is about? To serve and protect," I snapped at Patrick before turning to the new guys. "Let me explain something to you since Patrick neglected to tell you anything useful. You do not rule the town of Diablo. In fact, there are areas where you simply aren't welcome. The Den is now one of them. You are no longer welcome in this bar, and I want you all to leave now!"

Patrick's stupid, cocky smile slowly returned to his face as he watched me yell at his friends. I don't know why, but that bothered me. I shouldn't care, but I do.

"You too, Patrick," I said, glaring at him. "Get out."

"I don't think you have the authority to do that, beautiful. No matter how fun it was to watch you try," he finally replied.

"But I do," Caleb said, stepping forward. "I own this bar, and I ban all of you. Get out!"

Patrick slowly drug his eyes back to Caleb. Anger flashed in them as he said, "You really don't want to do that, Caleb. You'll be creating problems here you don't want."

"No, you did by treating my brother like this in the first place. You better believe I will go above your head to get this corrected if I have to," I snarled, pointing my finger at him.

He laughed and mockingly asked, "What are you going to do? Tell Daddy on me?"

I shook my head firmly. "No, I'm going to go above him. The apple doesn't fall far from the tree so going to your dad is pointless."

Patrick narrowed his eyes at me. The wheels turning in his mind as he thought carefully of his next move. *Choose wisely*, I thought to myself as my wolf snapped her jaws angrily. Patrick's face twisted with anger, and he shoved off the table.

"Fine, but don't say I didn't warn you!" Patrick shouted as he stomped towards the door.

"And yet, we haven't truly begun to warn you. I'd be careful, Officer Patrick," Bastian said in an icy tone.

Patrick stilled at the door before grunting once and storming out the bar. His two goons followed closely behind, slamming the door as they left.

"Everyone out!" Caleb yelled loudly. "Don't worry about your tabs. Just go. We're closing early!"

Adrenaline pulsed through my arms, making them feel like jello, as I watched the humans gather their things and make their way out.

Bastian kept a firm grip on my waist the entire time. His wolf practically breathing down my neck as he stared at me, waiting for the room to clear. The lecture was coming. I knew that already, but my mind had drifted to the problems unraveling before us. Patrick was clearly not going away, and the situation with him needed to be handle, but we couldn't afford to go to war against the Division. *We also couldn't be a doormat either*, I thought as nerves twisted my stomach again. *God, my head hurt...*

Noah locked the door as the last person walked out, and Bastian flipped me around angrily. His wolf surged to the surface as he barred his teeth.

"What is the matter with you, Shanely?! You can't just bolt from a moving truck and square up against Patrick by yourself like that!"

"I'm sorry..."

Pain struck my head so violently, it snapped back, and my legs gave way. Bastian caught me before I hit the ground, and I groaned, clutching my head. My lungs constricted as the pounding in my head grew worse, splitting my skull in two. I shut my eyes tight, screaming for it to stop, but it only grew worse. *What is wrong with me?!*

CHAPTER 1

The pain traveled behind my eyes, burning the lids until I couldn't take it anymore. My eyes shot open, but instead of seeing the bar or my family, everything in my vision was white. I was stuck in a solid white room with nowhere to go. My heart thundered I tried to search for anything. Even my bonds felt blocked somehow. *This wasn't right.*

"Bastian!" I shouted down the bond.

Silence. Nothing but the sounds of my own screaming filled my ears. *Why can't he hear me?*

"Bastian!!"

The pain grew worse. To the point I started to sob uncontrollably. *Was this a warning?* I thought as I hunched over screaming again. *This wasn't the same as before.* I didn't understand and my chest heaved, struggling to fill air in my lungs. I was coherent. I was fully awake and groaning in pain, but I couldn't *see* anything.

And then suddenly <u>everything</u> changed.

Images flew across the white space in my vision so abruptly I stumbled back. My eyes were forced open as the pictures passed by, and it hurt so badly whenever I tried to shut them. I couldn't make out what was going on, but nothing prepared me for what I was about to see next.

Patrick. So many memories of that man flew before my mind's eye. Each one slowing down just enough for me to recognize before whisking away again.

The first day I met Patrick; his slimy smile slowly appearing as he asked to buy me a drink at the Den.

The time at the diner where he squared up to Bastian after finding out we were engaged. The envy on his face, the fear within me. I felt it all.

My mind blurred to the next memory of Patrick. To him feeling me up at my wedding reception. His hands trying to touch every inch of me, and the way he maneuvered everything to his advantage that night. The rage in Bastian's eyes when he broke the door down.

Every memory I've ever had with Patrick was coming to the forefront in vivid detail. My stomach churned as the emotions I felt during these interactions slammed into me. I could feel everything as if I was back in the memory again, only to move on to the next one. Like flipping a deck of cards, the images came and went so fast, and I was unable to stop it.

But soon I had run out of memories to watch. *It has to stop, right?* The warning had to free me now that I was at the end. I waited to drop back to reality but nothing happened.

"*There aren't anymore!*" I shouted into the void.

To my horror, more images came, and they picked up in speed. This time I could barely make them out as they flew by, and so much of them was blurry and out of focus. The sharp pain grew in my head, churning my stomach as I tried to focus on what lay before me. *This was my mind, my warning!* I screamed inside my head as I tried to slow down the pictures. Nothing work. In fact, I think I made it worse as they went by even faster. Image after image zoomed by, and my head pounded against my skull

There were so many, I thought to myself. *So many images...* I screamed as they went by faster and faster, each one a new memory. *No*, I thought as fear gripped my heart. *Not memories. They're not memories yet.*

This was my future. My very imminent future if I wasn't careful. I was about to have a great deal more interactions with Patrick if I couldn't stop this. I *had* to stop my warning from happening. *I have time*, I thought anxiously. *I can keep this from happening!*

Because whatever was going on between us, it was just getting started, and we were at the beginning of everything if I didn't stop it.

The images finally stopped, but the pain didn't. It just kept coming in waves. My stomach rolled, the world spun, and the pain in my head was too much to bear. I screamed in agony because I couldn't turn this warning off. Panic crept inside as I searched for a way out. I searched for my wolf but couldn't breathe as it just got worse. She was gone anyways.

The light inside my mind continued getting brighter and brighter until finally everything slammed to a stop, and I fell into darkness.

Chapter 2

"Shanely? C'mon baby, wake up."

"Has this happened before?!"

"More often then I'd like."

"Baby Girl? Wake up now. You're scaring us."

The room was filled with anxious voices as I slowly came to. Everyone was talking at once, and I tried to get my bearings. I tried sitting up, but my stomach churned again, and I waited till the feeling passed. A small part of me didn't want to move though. Everything just felt wrong inside my head, and I was clueless as to why. Both my wolf and bear were here still, and I released the breath I had been holding. *A small comfort at least,* I thought as the memory of what happened plagued me. *What in the world did it mean?* I wondered.

"Shanely..." Bastian said again, his tone shaky and uneven. *He was worried.* I could feel it down our bond, and I forced myself to move. To ease his pain.

My eyes fluttered open, but I immediately slammed them shut again. I slowly lifted my arm to my head, trying to block out the bright light above. *God, that light was really annoying.*

"Hey, she's awake!" Elijah blurted and two hands gently pulled me the rest of the way up.

"There's my girl. Are you okay?" Bastian asked as he rubbed my back.

I felt groggy as I opened my eyes like I had been drugged again or something. I was on the floor, and my mate looked as freaked out as I felt. I rubbed my head and asked, "Did you see what happened?"

"Not this time. I wasn't able to see this one. Can you tell us what you saw?" Bastian asked nervously. My eyebrows furrowed. Bastian and I have shared my warnings since the first time it happened. *Why did it stop now?*

"How long was I out for?" I groaned, rubbing the dull ache in my temples away.

"Just a few minutes, but we were starting to worry because you've never passed out like this before," Bastian replied.

"You were screaming," Cade said nervously. He grabbed my chin, moving my head back and forth to inspect me, sighing in relief.

"I think..." I said quietly, "I think it was my last one."

I gently pulled away from my Beta who frowned.

"What do you mean your last one?" Bastian asked. His eyes narrowed, and I sighed.

"I saw every memory I've ever had with Patrick like scenes on a roll of film," I said, knowing full well none of this would make sense. "As I got closer to the future, the images got faster and faster, until I couldn't even focus on them anymore. What's scaring me right now is how many I saw. I'm about to have a tremendous amount of interactions with that man unless we can stop it."

"And the ability?" Caleb asked, crossing his arms.

I shrugged. "My head feels different this time. Like the ability just feels... gone almost. It just feels done, I don't know."

The room grew quiet, and Bastian's worry traveled through our bond. It was hard to stomach between the two of us, and I laid my head in my hands. *What if my warnings come true? What if it all comes true no matter how hard I try to stop them?*

Uncle Cain's advice came to mind then. He always said there were ways to keep warnings from happening, and that was true before. I stopped having dreams and warnings for awhile when we merged with the bear clan, but I didn't know which way to go now. This wasn't as simple as mending issues between our people. We were up against the Government. *What if my actions only push me closer to Patrick and whatever he had planned? Or what if I do nothing and they happen anyways? What if there was no point to*

CHAPTER 2

any of this, and somehow I was just given <u>a heads up</u> to what's about to come.

"Caleb, close up for the night," Bastian commanded, startling me from my thoughts. "We need to go home now."

My mate pushed me to Cade, who helped me stand. Elijah moved towards my mate and tossed his arm under his shoulder. Bastian winced in pain as the two stood, worry etching his brow. It worried me too, but I said nothing and made sure I kept my emotions from traveling to him.

Bastian slowly stretched out his arms only to yank his injured limb back in. His nostrils flared, and I looked to Cade, who's eyes were firmly on his brother. *God, I hated he was in pain.* I wished more than anything I had shared my quick healing ability with him.

No one said a word as Bastian opened and closed his fist repeatedly. He shook out his arm and stretched again, getting a little further this time.

It still wasn't enough.

How could he protect himself when he's injured? Bastian was dead in my warnings before. My stomach twisted again, and I bit my lower lip to keep from throwing up dinner. *What if that injury was the reason why he's dead in my warnings?*

Bastian spoke, "Caleb, call Thomas and Daniel and get them to the lodge. I've already called for a pack meeting. Let's talk as a group before we get some much needed rest."

I nodded solemnly, following the Fenrir brothers out of the bar. Caleb was the last to leave, and he locked the door behind him. I waved softly to Octavia who's own smile was grim. She never did hide her feelings or opinion very well, and right now it was just another reminder as to how bad things were for us. She waved back and hopped into Caleb's truck.

I turned back to Cade's truck only to find all three triplets staring at me. Cade was in the driver's side, but Bastian and Elijah waited for me by the open door.

"What?" I asked, narrowing my eyes and jutting out my left hip. Elijah smirked when Bastian stepped forward and grabbed my elbow.

"Waiting for you to get in, Shanely," he said with a feral grin.

I rolled my eyes, pulling my arm out of reach. "I can sit on the end,

Bastian. You're the one who needs help..."

"Oh no," he said firmly, "I am *not* making that mistake again. Get in, Shanely."

"I promise I won't do that again," I said, giving him a pointed look. My wolf bristled at his command, swishing her tail at him in clear defiance. The slight curl in his lips told me he knew how she felt and the attitude she was giving him right now. *Now it was a challenge.*

"Oh, I know you won't because you are sitting between me and your Beta with Elijah behind you," he said, his eyes glowing as he stepped towards me. "Now get your sexy butt in my truck before I throw you in."

"Bastian!" I exclaimed sternly. "You're still healing! You cannot lift me..."

He growled low and took another step towards me. My breath caught in my chest, and I scurried to the truck's door. "Alright, alright, I'm moving!"

I hopped up and buckled myself into the middle seat, sticking my tongue out at Bastian, who just grinned wickedly back at me. My wolf turned her nose up before settling back down inside me, and I couldn't contain the smile that slowly formed on my face. *The stubborn man.*

My face fell when pain swept across his face. Reaching up to grab the handle in Cade's tall truck looked excruciating, but Elijah was swift in tossing another arm around to help his brother get in too. Bastian exhaled the breath he held, and I mouthed a thank you to his Beta. Elijah nodded and hopped in the back.

Cade doubled checked my seat belt before patting my leg and starting the truck. We made the quiet drive back home.

The closer we got to the lodge, the worse I felt. I couldn't get my mind off what I saw. I didn't have any answers to the questions plaguing my head. And now I was Queen of the Wolves. An unofficial Head to *all* shifters. Their lives depended on me being able to make the right decisions. *What if I make a mistake and get them all killed?*

The lodge came into view with plenty of cars and trucks already here. Wolves and bears were trickling out from the woods as well as Abraham and Bay, who waited at the step. They brought quite a few tigers enforcers with them as well, and overall we had a decent group here. But then everyone turned to look at me. My stomach was in knots as they waited for me to get out of the truck.

Bastian opened his door, but I just couldn't do it. I couldn't leave the truck. I just sat there like a coward because I didn't want to explain this to them. I didn't want to relive it. I watched as they shifted nervously on their feet, *needing me,* but it still wasn't enough to get me to move mine. Bastian closed the door again.

"You good, Baby Girl?" Cade asked, looking ahead instead of at me. None of the Fenrir triplets looked my way, knowing I didn't want anymore attention on me.

I shook my head saying, "Not at all."

"Just take a second," Bastian said, looking forward too. "You're overwhelmed and rightfully so. Just focus on your breathing, love. We can go when you're ready."

I gave a soft nod and continued to watch the pack from here. They talked amongst themselves, trying hard not to look at me. I knew they didn't understand or maybe they worried I was hurt too. We were their leaders, and we were hiding in the truck. Guilt ate at me again as I watched everyone.

Uncle Thomas had arrived with my father, pushing their way through the crowd to Caleb's truck. Dad went straight to my brother, checking his busted face before hugging him. Octavia had climbed out now, and I had no idea where Noah ran off to as the truck was empty. *Should I ask where he went? Probably. Am I going to? No.*

Thomas's loud angry voice made me jump as he shouted angrily for his enforcers to protect his daughters. It always surprised me how loud he truly was. He could be understood perfectly clear even with the doors closed.

I sighed heavily. My time was up the minute Dad's gaze found me hiding in Cade's truck. *He'll come for me next.* I thought to myself. Sighing, I motioned for the triplets to get out of the truck.

The pack grew quiet as we approached, and I tried to hold my head high, but even my wolf felt fear. She worried too, and it was hard enough to handle my own emotions let alone hers.

I slowed my steps as we climbed the porch steps. *I should speak. I should open my mouth and explain what happened.* Everyone waited for me to say something, but every time I tried, the words just wouldn't come out. My eyes drifted from one loved one to the next and tears quickly filled them. I tried blinking them away, but the longer I looked, more came.

I don't have a plan. I don't have any answers for them and...

The boys said nothing as I turned and scurried inside. I made my way over to the fireplace and collapsed on the couch, wiping my eyes before anyone else saw me break. I pulled my knees to my chest and watched the flames instead as Bastian's voice sounded through the door. *Coward,* I thought to myself.

"Long day?"

I jumped, seeing Emersyn coming down the stairs. She smiled softly, and I nodded before slumping back in my seat. *She's another issue I don't know the answer too.*

"Can I join you?" she asked softly.

I gestured my hand to the other couch and watched the panther get comfortable. I heard the pack snarl from here, and I groaned, knowing full well I bailed and dumped this all on Bastian. Guilt gnawed at me as I stared at the fire, watching the flames dance safely inside.

"You okay?" Emersyn asked, her voice ever so quiet.

I snorted. "Not really."

"Yeah," she said, rubbing her hands together, "that was kind of a dumb question."

A small chuckle escaped my lips, and I looked back to her. Her cheeks turned bright pink, and I felt a little bad. I shook my head saying, "Nah, you're okay. I'm just overwhelmed. It's been a lot ever since I moved to Diablo. Always seems like it's one thing after another, and that's just weighing on me lately."

She nodded slowly, pursing her thin lips together. "I can imagine, but I bet having a large family helps lighten the load. I mean, I can't even imagine what it was like having a tiger and a bear for brothers. At least that must have been fun."

CHAPTER 2

"It's interesting to say the least, but I'd give anything for things to just calm down," I replied, rubbing my face as our situation came to mind again.

"They will. You've got an impressive team here already, and I know more will come if you call," she replied, giving me a small smile, "which is pretty incredible, if I do say so. We've all had big issues with each other in the past, and now look at us."

"Yeah, it's been difficult, but we've come a long way," I muttered, looking at my soon to be sister-in-law. Everything about her was just sweet. I don't think I've ever heard a fowl word come from her mouth. She always wore a smile even when I know she was nervous and uncomfortable. She was just... Elijah's perfect mate.

This was something I could fix. I could make amends with the panthers and get my brother to accept his mate. Walking around pretending like what Liam did to their family never happened was wrong, and *hiding* from your mate because you're ashamed of your father's choices was wrong too.

"Look, I know this may not be my place," I said softly as I leaned forward on my knees, "but I just recently found out about what Liam did to your family, and I wanted to apologize for him. That is not how my pack deals with other shifters nor is that how any of the Fenrir brothers behave. It was wrong, and I am sorry."

Emersyn shrugged, giving me a soft, pained smile.

"I appreciate that, Shanely. I was so young when it all happened, I honestly don't remember much. It's my sister and dad that remember everything. It's hard to get them to trust anyone," she replied, pulling at the ends of her long hair.

"Well the McCoy pack made amends with the Bear clan, and I'd like to do that with your claw. Start fresh, ya know?"

A weight lifted off my chest as her smile widened.

"I'd really like that," she replied quietly.

"Maybe once this mess blows over, we can extend the invitation out to your father and the rest of the claw. I'd like to get to know you better too," I said to her. I trusted Elijah's wolf, and I wanted the two of us to be as close as blood sisters. We belonged to the triplets after all. There was *no* breaking that.

"That sounds wonderful!" she said before giggling. "You know it's funny. We've all heard about the famous White Wolf, who shook the mighty wolf shifters and brought the pompous leaders to their knees."

I chuckled. "And?"

"And it's funny to see you're really not much bigger than I am," she said, giggling again. Her eyes lit up with amusement, and I couldn't help but laugh.

"Did you expect a beast or something?"

"Well... kind of," Emersyn replied, her cheeks staining pink.

"Sorry to disappoint, but I'm more ordinary than people think," I replied as I leaned back in my chair again. "Although, I heard my mom was the same way. Tiny lady, massive wolf."

"I don't know, Shanely," she said, cocking her head to the side. "You seem to have it all. There really isn't much you can't do."

"Eh, I ain't that special, but I do have an amazing family. I was really lucky to find my mate so quickly, and he's wonderful. I'd be lost without him," I said as my mind drifted to that awful night not too long ago. Both my animals snarled within me as they remembered too. I took a deep breath, settling my wolf and bear within. Keeping them from shifting so they can find our mate and make sure he was alright was difficult. Having two to calm was tiring sometimes.

"I don't think I'll have that," she said quietly, and my attention snapped to her. Her lips tucked together in a tight frown as she fiddled with her long hair. My brows knitted as I scrambled to come up with a plan to push these two together.

I didn't like seeing them incomplete.

"Of course, you will! Everyone deserves a partner in life, and shifters have this amazing ability for fate to chose the best one for them," I said, trying to perk her back up. She just stared at the floor, and I sighed.

"Emmie," I said, using my wolf's power ever so slightly to get her attention. She looked up, and I gave a soft smile. "You're too sweet not to get a good one. Trust me."

CHAPTER 2

Her smile did not return, and my foot started tapping nervously as I watched her. The wheels seemed to be turning in her mind's eye, but whatever she was thinking wasn't enough to bring back that typical smile and good mood I had come to know about her.

"Tell me what you're thinking," I asked quietly, and she sighed.

"My family doesn't really even talk about finding mates anymore," she admitted. "It's rare for panthers to find their mate in the first place so most just marry someone they fall in love with. And there's no hope for me in that department."

My foot stopped.

"So, you don't know how it feels then when you find your mate?" I asked as my eyes widened. "You don't know how to make the bond?"

This was a problem.

Her mouth opened, but so did the door. She clamped it shut as the Fenrir brothers entered the room, commanding attention like they always did. I snorted as they strolled through the room with ease. *I don't think they even realize how they look when they're all together like this.*

Emmie's eyes were wide and completely glued to the triplets. A small smirk slowly appeared on my face. I didn't blame her. All three were incredible to look at.

Elijah's shoulders tensed slightly as he scented the room. His blue eyes turned to us sitting on the couch, and I raised an eyebrow when his eyes flashed. Worry etched his brow, but he said nothing before fleeing to the conference room down the hall.

I shook my head in frustration, noting how Emersyn's gaze followed his every step. Cade rolled his eyes and followed after him. Bastian, however, stepped towards the two of us.

"Feeling better?" he asked, extending out his hand. Warmth and love trickled down the bond, and I smiled.

I got to my feet and wrapped my arm around his. "I am. Thank you for taking over for me. I'm sorry I bailed."

His adorable grin appeared, and my heart melted again. "Anytime. It's why we do this together," he said, kissing my cheek. He turned to Emersyn then. "Care to walk with us, Emersyn?"

He jutted out his injured arm and waited. I leaned my head on his shoulder, melting with adoration and pride. Bastian's brothers *always* looked out for me, and now Bastian can finally return the favor.

"Especially when his brother is being a butt-head."

Bastian looked to me from the corner of his eye, and I covered my mouth giggling. I had projected that last thought.

Whoops.

Emersyn gave my mate a smile and slowly took his other arm. He had me on the right, and her on the left. My mate and I were grinning like banshees by the time we made our way to the conference room. Elijah would know *exactly* what Bastian was doing, and that was sort of funny. Bastian was making a statement, claiming our future sister-in-law, despite the stupid reservations his brother had. They were mates and were perfect for one another. No one else may understand what Bastian was doing, but Elijah would. He most certainly would.

And if it made him mad, well so be it. This was a good thing. Something we were in short supply of lately.

I was going to make sure it stuck.

Chapter 3

The double doors were wide open, giving the three of us plenty of room to walk through together.

I leaned over my mate and whispered to Emmie, "Come over tonight. You can stay at our place, and we can finish our conversation."

She gave me a nod, smiling as we walked through the door, and Elijah stiffened when he saw us. The others had barely acknowledged us as we walked to our seats but not him. He knew exactly what Bastian was doing, and the red haze in his eyes only proved it.

However, he was not the only one. Esme glared as we passed her chair to Emersyn's. Another problem that needed corrected.

Later. I'm too tired to add her to the mix.

Elijah's body went rigid as Bastian led Emersyn to her chair before walking me to mine. Bastian kept that smug smile on his face, matching Elijah blatant stare as he sat down. Cade snickered quietly to himself.

Elijah forcefully pulled his chair out, plopping down and continuing to glare at his older brother. Everyone slowly looked from Elijah to Bastian as they took their seats, and it was all Cade could do to not laugh. He covered his face with his hands, and I could see his shoulders shake ever so slightly.

I just shrugged casually. I wouldn't be the one to explain this to everyone. *Not if I wanted to keep my life, thank you very much.*

Bastian held Elijah's gaze until his brother finally dropped his eyes. It actually took a minute, which was surprising. Elijah and his wolf were good about showing respect, but I guess not today. I chuckled softly again. *He must be pissed,* I thought to myself.

"I think Elijah's mad at you," I whispered in Bastian's ear. He laughed and leaned into me.

"Yeah, he probably is," he whispered, "but he can get over it. The only one freaking out about this is him. He would have smacked me upside my head if I tried to avoid you when we first met, so at least I'm being nice about it."

Cade lost it again, and Bastian gave me a wink before turning to the others.

"Alrighty then. Now that everyone's caught up with what happened, I want to start this council meeting discussing safety measures for pack lands. I'd like to send the majority of the pack back to Summit Hall, mostly the women and kids. I don't want them in the carnage if this gets messy," Bastian said in his typical Alpha voice.

"And it will get messy," Caleb chimed in.

"Why not send them my way?" Abraham offered. He leaned his head on his hand.

"You want to take in the pack?" I asked, my bottom lip jutting out. *This was no small task.*

He nodded. "I have plenty of space, and my home is remote with two massive wall defenses. Plus, it's a location unknown to Patrick and his father if they make things worse for us. My land is south of the border, so I deal with a different Division Head. The Head for our area is older than dirt, so I don't see him as a threat."

"That could work, and then they wouldn't have to relocate so far away," I said as Bastian mulled it over.

"Alright, send the word," my mate said, "but the second we feel it's not safe, the entire pack and streak are to make their way to Summit Hall. Any that cannot or do not wish to fight goes. Agreed?"

"Agreed," the group said in unison. Abey immediately started texting on his phone.

"Moving on," Bastian said. "I want to prepare for an all out war. We can't say for sure who was behind the attack, but I know we're all thinking the same thing. McCoy Pack has a decent security force set up already, but we're not fighting against other shifters. This is all new territory for us, so I want more. I want to send word out to the rest of the wolf packs to recruit enforcers to build up our numbers. As long as they answer the call, we should be able to hold down the fort."

"They'll answer the call," Bay said firmly, her eyes settling on me as if she already knew the doubt creeping in my head. "They will."

Bastian gave a tight lip smile, squeezing my hand in reassurance. "Let's hope."

"We can reach out to our own people, but our numbers are small. If this war turns world-wide, then I need to go home to my family," James chimed in. "You understand, don't you?"

The mood in the room shifted, and I more than understood. If this was a issue for everyone on a global scale then I *wanted* them to protect their families.

"If this goes world-wide, then I order you to go home," Bastian said firmly. "I'd rather you protect your families like I'm trying to do with mine. If I'm alive and kicking, then I will assist your families as well."

James nodded respectfully as my heart seized. *If he's alive and kicking?* My warning flashed before my eyes again. *Does Bastian believe he won't make it through this?*

Everyone continued to debate further on how to proceed and what to do to stop my warnings from happening, but no matter what plan we made, I didn't feel good about it. I couldn't shake this awful feeling like nothing we did mattered anymore. That we were all destined to go through it, no matter what we tried to do to stop it. My head spun, trying to make sense of it all. I checked my watch. It had been too long since my last meal. I was getting low with the boys again.

"Now if this is because of Patrick," Bastian said, jabbing his finger on the table, "I doubt the rest of the Division even knows what he's been up to. We might not even need to go to war if we can go above Calvin's head. Question is; how?"

"I can look into that," I said, and Bastian gave me a grateful nod.

"That would be great if we can talk to someone that didn't have a few loose screws going on up top," Ryder said, chuckling at his own joke. He brushed his dirty blonde hair from his eyes.

"Getting a hold of anyone will be the issue," Caleb said. "I remember when Uncle Thomas tried. The machine prompts pissed his off so bad, he gave up."

"After he broke his phone," Octavia chimed in from the back. *Sounds like my uncle.*

"Well it's an avenue we can't overlook," Bastian said, crossing his arms. "If we can get those two removed from the picture, life can continue on the way it's been."

We all collectively agreed, but the weight of the task settled heavily on my chest. *I had* to figure this out.

The meeting went over with minor hiccups. We all had jobs to do, and my job was to figure out how to go above Calvin's head, while Bastian was going to set up patrols for the enforcers we had at the moment. Abe was taking in the pack and bear clan with Bay, and Caleb, Johnny, and Ryder were going to scout out the town and figure out if there were more Division men coming towards us. Everyone would be busy for the foreseeable future.

"Elijah," Bastian said as the meeting was coming to an end. "I need you to start reaching out to the other wolf packs. Tell them our situation and see how many they can send."

Elijah nodded once. "Can do, brother."

"Actually, you'll need help," Bastian went on. I gave him a look from the corner of my eye as he snapped his fingers, scanning the room in search of something. *What in the world is he doing?*

"Let's see…" he said, and my eyes lit up. "Ah! Emersyn, right? Can you assist my brother with this task?"

I looked to Cade who was all too amused right now, and we both looked to Elijah. Our brother looked ready to strangle Bastian, and I dropped my head on the table, covering my smile.

"I can handle it fine, Bastian," Elijah snapped. Bastian waved him off though.

"He's going to kill your mate," Cade said through the link.

CHAPTER 3

I grinned. *"Then make sure he doesn't, Beta."*

"Nonsense! You need help, and Shanely's already invited her over tonight. She can help you tomorrow at our house. You don't mind, do you hun?"

Emersyn's rosy cheeks reddened even more as she went back and forth from Bastian to Elijah. *Aww, I was too amused watching Elijah squirm that I didn't think to check on her.* She was clearly overwhelmed too.

"Umm... sure. I can help him," she said, her voice timid and small. I nudged my mate in his side.

"I see," he said to me.

"Great!" he said, slapping the table. "Well, I think that's it for now. Good work, everyone."

The group filed out, leaving a stewing panther in the corner. She shot up from her chair the moment the door shut.

"No, that's not great. My sister is staying here with me. She doesn't need to stay at your house. We came to help because of the alliance, but that doesn't include sleepovers," Esme countered, crossing her arms.

"Why don't you come too, Esme?" I suggested calmly. I gathered the file from the table for my mate. "You both can stay."

"We have a room here though," she said firmly. Her fist staying clenched together.

"I know, but since they're working on this project, it will just be easier to be all together," I replied. "Plus, it might be nice to get to know one another a bit more."

"Look, we're here to help. That should be good enough. We don't need to be best friends alright," she snapped before storming out.

Emersyn's rosy cheeks stayed as she meekly said, "I'm sorry. I should go to her."

"Certainly. I'll wait for you in the lobby," I said, giving her a look. I was *not* letting her back out of this. I was going to be their friend if it killed me.

And it seriously just might.

She nodded and quickly followed after her sister, and *that's* about when the room exploded.

"What in God's green earth is the matter with you two?! I thought I said to back off!" Elijah bellowed as he shot to his feet.

"Enough, Elijah! We heard your reasons, alright?" Bastian huffed. He took his time getting out of his chair, and my heart hurt.

Elijah tossed his hands in the air. "And?!"

"And they're stupid," Bastian replied, rolling his eyes when Elijah snarled. "Tell me I'm wrong."

My eyes widened when Elijah got in my mate's face. *He's never acted this way to his family before.* The veins on the sides of his face looked ready to pop, and I quickly rushed forward, placing both hands on their chest.

"Alright, let's just settle down, guys," I said, but Cade just hauled me away from them.

"Not now, Baby Girl. Let them get this out of their system," he said.

I rolled my eyes at all this testosterone building in the room but listened on the sidelines regardless. Cade watched closely, choosing to sit on the table, while the other two yelled at one another.

"They're not stupid! We have a rocky history with those panthers, and her dad will never approve. I mean, look at her sister! She hates us!" Elijah carried on angrily. His fists continued to tighten at his side.

"No, that's not it," Cade muttered.

"I think it's you, Elijah," Bastian yelled right back. "You're afraid to have a mate. Someone to protect and love and feel that insane sense of longing and protection. You're afraid to bond with her!"

Elijah roared, which Bastian promptly returned. *Someone was bound to come running back in here if they didn't knock it off,* I thought, shaking my head.

"Knock it off, you two!" Cade snapped.

Bout time, I thought as my Beta stepped forward.

"Look," Cade growled, "just admit it, Elijah. That girl is your mate. It will go so much easier for you if you just stop denying it."

I groaned when Elijah shoved Cade back. My Beta kept his footing though, and his eyes flashed red. *This was going to get so much worse.*

"Shut up!" Elijah bellowed. "You don't know what you're talking about!"

CHAPTER 3

My eyes widened when Cade snarled. *I have never heard his wolf sound like that before.* He must really be angry.

"Oh, really?" he snapped, shoving Elijah back. "I don't know what I'm talking about? Just because I don't have my mate doesn't mean I don't know what's happening. We're triplets! Which means I can feel what you all feel! You are driving yourself crazy pushing her away like this. You are afraid! You may be freaked out about her family, but the biggest thing you're scared of is her rejecting you. You're afraid she's going to choose her family over you and all of us by extension!"

The room stilled. Elijah's chest heaved as he held his brother's stare, but my heart just hurt. I didn't realize how deep this reservation went. I opened my mouth but shut it before anyone noticed. Clasping my hands together, I waited. *He needs them, not me.*

"What if she doesn't want me?" he finally asked. His voice so low, I *barely* heard him.

"How could you say that, brother?" Cade asked, clasping his hand on Elijah's shoulder. "She's going to be head over heels for you. That's your mate, and she's going to love you more than anything."

"She's probably your Fated Mate," Bastian chimed in, and Elijah's eyes went wide.

"You think we're Fated?" Elijah asked.

Bastian shrugged. "Shanely and I are, and we are triplets. We're bonded in ways other siblings are not. It's why we made the agreement we did long before we ever met Shanely."

"Wait, what agreement?" I asked curiously.

"The agreement with our mates," Cade said, turning to me. "Remember I mentioned it the night of the bonfire? We all feel the need to protect each others mates, so we agreed to be extensions of each other once we found you guys. It's why me and Elijah take care of you the way we do."

Ah... that makes sense.

"Make no mistake though," Bastian said, giving me his typical brooding stare. "You, Shanely, are solely *mine*. You're my mate only, but when I can't be around to protect you..."

"Or when you screw up," Cade muttered, and Bastian rolled his eyes.

"Then Cade and Elijah step in," my mate said. "That's our agreement."

"Yeah well..." Elijah muttered as he began to pace the floor, "what if that idea freaks Emersyn out?"

"It won't," Cade answered.

"You sure about that?" he replied sarcastically. "Because I don't feel that confident about it."

"Because you dimwhit," Cade snapped, earning a scowl from Elijah, "she's your mate. She was chosen as your perfect other half, so she has to be okay with it! With us, I mean."

"Look, why don't you just try to talk to her?" I chimed in.

Elijah finally stopped moving. His face softening as he studied me. "I don't know, Shanie."

"Just table the whole mate thing for tonight at least. She's coming over, and the two of you have a job to do," I said, crossing my arms. "Just focus on getting to know her. You might be surprised what you learn."

Elijah shifted on his feet before sighing loudly. He rubbed his face muttering, "Okay."

My brows lifted slightly. "Alright. I kind of thought I'd have to pull teeth to get you to agree, but this is good. Oh, and by the way, you all should know that she doesn't know what to expect with finding a mate. Her claw doesn't wait to find theirs. They just marry. She doesn't know anything so stop looking so pissed off around her, Elijah. She's going to think you hate her."

His mouth dropped. "Wait, she doesn't know *anything*?"

"No," I said, rolling my eyes, "it's why I'm having her over, ding dong."

Elijah ran his hands through his hair before covering his face. We watched him inhaled deeply before slowly releasing it. He did this a few times before Cade sighed, clasping his hands on Elijah's shoulders.

"C'mon, dude. Let's go find your woman," Cade said, pushing Elijah to the door.

He feet dragged against the carpet like they were made of lead. I chuckled watching the scary brute freak out over a girl close to my size. Bastian

CHAPTER 3

extended his arm out to me again, and I leaned into his embrace. *Well, this was not how I expected to end my night.*

A laugh escaped my lip, and Bastian's brow rose. I shrugged saying, "I honest to God thought you two were going to punch each other."

He smirked at me. "Like it would be a fair fight."

Elijah whipped his head around Cade, glaring at his older brother. "I heard that jerk! You're lucky you're still healing!"

Bastian gave me a wicked grin as he led me out of the room.

Chapter 4

I snooped around Cain's old office while we waited for Emersyn to make an appearance, and I found a number with a name in the back of a massive folder marked, *The Division. Short and sweet, Uncle Cain. Just how I like it. Quick, to the point, and easy to find.* Everything else in the folder was just passing evaluations from Calvin, which I tossed in the trash. *The stupid man.*

A phone number lay below this dude's name, but at least this guy was a member of the Division. Hank Cartwright. It would have been nice to know what department he belonged too or who he was, but it was someone other than Calvin, and I'd try anything. Cain had scribbled Hank's ID number at least, so I'd start there.

I tucked the paper in my pocket and meandered down the hall, looking for the boys. Elijah was long gone by the time I found the others, and Bastian muttered something about needing a run when I questioned him. So the three of us waited for her instead. It took awhile, and I'm sure Esme was the one holding everything up, but eventually Emersyn gracefully walked down the stairs, bag in hand.

Other than Cade's stomach, no one complained for how long it took her to come down, and I was grateful. Her rosy cheeks said enough about how she was feeling. Esme would be tricky panther to come around. *I'll have to think a bit more on that.*

The walk home didn't take us long, and we found Elijah in the kitchen when we walked in. I figured he'd be in his room already, but something we said must have stuck as he at least *acknowledged* Emersyn when he said

CHAPTER 4

goodnight to us all. I gave him a cheesy grin as he fled up the stairs to his room. The door never latched though. *Baby steps.*

Emersyn watched the Fenrir triplets closely as they said goodnight to me. I had hoped by staying with the pack she might be able to weed through some of the misconceptions about wolves and the triplets themselves. She seemed very curious about how they each treated me, and I took that as a good sign.

When the boys were finally gone, I guided Emersyn to the couch with hot chocolates. It was time for a girl's night.

"So, what do you know about mate bonds?" I asked, plopping down on my sofa. I grabbed Cade's gray blanket and draped it over my legs.

Emersyn sputtered on her drink, and I couldn't help but giggle.

"Sorry, I should have warned you," I said, taking a sip.

She laughed, wiping away the hot chocolate that hit her cheek. "No, it's okay. I just didn't expect that right away. I've been distracted, I suppose."

"Hmm... let me guess," I said playfully. "You're stuck on an overwhelming smell that has your cat going absolutely insane?"

Her eyes widened, and she set down her mug. Gripping her blanket she said, "Yeah, actually. I don't understand what's going on or why."

"Well..." I said, taking a peek towards the stairs. No one barked at me through the link, and no one bolted to stop me, so I guess that means I can tell her. "That's an indication that you've found your mate."

I took a sip as her world came crashing down. *And here we go*, I thought.

"What? No, it can't be that!" she stammered. Her mouth opened and shut rapidly like she didn't even know what to say. I only grinned.

"The only thing my dad said about mates was a distinctive bond snaps in place when you find them. No bond snapped in place, and he never said anything about a smell."

"It's true though. When I first scented Bastian, it smelled strong like the woods. It was musky and just intoxicating," I said, vividly remembering the first time I scented it. The way his scent coated my room when I opened the window. My heart warmed at the memory. "It still is honestly."

"I keep smelling the woods too," she replied as she stared at her feet.

29

"And not just when I'm outside. It's so strong, but there's also this strange scent of water mixed with it. Almost like what you'd smell when sitting by the creek near your house."

"Mmhmm. Sounds really similar to mine, don't ya think?" I said, smirking. I took another sip of my drink, knowing full well Elijah left his door open so he could listen in. Maybe this wasn't my place but finding your mate was something to celebrate, and with all the chaos happening right now, we needed a win. *If Elijah was too afraid to do it, then I would.*

"Do you know how panthers are able to start the bond?" I asked, setting my mug on the coffee table.

She shrugged, picking at a fuzz on her shirt. "Not really. I was never told anything about it before because it's so rare. How do wolves find their mate?"

"Well, we have it easy. Usually sight does the trick, and once you hit the appropriate age, then the bond snaps in place. Other shifters have it harder though. Bears need touch, tigers need to kiss. Not all are the same," I said, and the corners of her mouth rose.

"Wow. Imagine being a tiger, huh?"

I laughed. "I know, right? Can you imagine where you'd be if you're too afraid of your first kiss?"

She laughed loudly before putting her hands on her hips saying, "Excuse me handsome, but can I just check one thing real quick? I promise, you won't mind."

We lost it then, cackling up a storm like we were teenagers again, and man did it feel good to let loose. I didn't realize how wound up I've been lately, but this was a night I needed.

"Oh, the scandals I'm sure your brother has in his streak," she said chuckling.

"I bet panthers have their own way too," I chimed in, but she shrugged and grabbed her mug again.

"Well I've never been told," she said, drinking away. "We've checked out on a lot it seems."

My smile tightened. I knew that lost feeling all too well. "Why don't you tell me about yourself then? What's it like living in your claw?"

"There's not a whole lot to tell honestly. Our land is small, and there aren't a lot of us left. Panthers tend to stay in immediate family circles instead of banding together. My dad's the first to really start a group of us. We're basically just a few families living on a large farm."

"Nothing wrong with living in small circles," I said, giving her a grin. "What about you? What do you like to do for fun?"

"Well..." she said grinning, twirling the ends of her hair between her fingers. "I like to draw."

"Really?" I asked. "I've always wanted to learn, but I've never been any good."

"My mother left me her kit when she passed. It was full of supplies I needed to start, although I've used most of it up by now. It's what started my passion for art, and I've been drawing ever since," she replied, grinning wide. The familiar pain of losing a parent hit my chest, and I gave her a tight lipped smile.

"I'm sorry about your mother. I never knew mine, and I only met my father when I moved here," I said quietly.

"My mother died when I was four, so I don't remember very much. It was right after we moved to the states actually," she said, her eyes lost in whatever memory she was drifting into.

"I'd love to see some of your work," I said, pulling her back to the present. "We can see what supplies we have at the..."

A loud knock sounded from the back door. My brows furrowed as I glanced at the clock on the wall. *Who in the world would be stopping by at this hour?* I wondered as I got to my feet. Bastian's hovered in my head as I meandered to the door. Another knock sounded, and I said, "I'm coming!"

My eyes widened when I opened the door to find Esme standing there. Her hands in her pockets.

"Is my sister here?" she asked gruffly.

I opened the door wider and motioned behind me. "Yup. Are you planning on joining us too?"

Esme shifted on her feet as she stared at the open door. "I just don't like my sister being away from me."

"I get it," I replied, softening my tone. "Family is everything to us too. Why don't you just stay tonight? We're just getting to know one another with hot cocoa."

I opened the door wider as Emersyn approached. Esme sighed and slowly stepped inside.

"Never thought I'd be staying with a Fenrir," she mumbled as she made her way over to her sister.

"I didn't think you were coming," Emersyn said, and Esme shrugged her shoulders.

"Yeah, well..."

I closed the door, securing the locks in place again, and about jumped out of my skin when I saw Bastian standing at the top of the stairs, wearing nothing but pajama bottoms. He squinted one eye as he looked around the bright room, his hair a mess of tangles. A massive white bandage covered his wound, and he placed one hand on the railing.

"Everything okay?" he asked, and I snorted.

"Other than you scaring the daylights out of me," I replied, shaking my head, "everything's fine."

"Sorry, love. I heard the door and wanted to make sure it was all good," he said quietly. His sleepy eyes fluttered slightly. *My mate was exhausted.*

"Yeah, Esme changed her mind and came over is all. I locked up," I answered.

"Okay," he said, flashing the girls a smile, "well have fun tonight."

He waved before turning on his heels and disappearing in the dark.

"Your mate is really sweet," Emersyn said, plopping back down on the couch. Esme snorted as she sat immediately next to her sister, but I ignored her.

"He is. He was just making sure everything was good," I said, covering back up with Cade's blanket.

"A bit overprotective, don't you think?" Esme asked sarcastically.

"Actually no," I answered, forcing a smile to my lips, "and when you find your mate you'll get it. It's a bit more with the triplets though."

CHAPTER 4

"What do you mean?" Emersyn asked, her brow rising.

"Wait, are you saying the three brothers share you or something? Cuz if so, that's disturbing," Esme chimed in. She leaned forward and stole her sister's mug of hot cocoa.

"What?" I asked, laughing. "We're close, but not that close. I *only* belong to Bastian, but the triplets are in tune with one another more than most. Cade and Elijah take care of me like seriously over-protective brothers. We're all connected because of their bond, and when those two find their mates, it will be the same towards them too."

"That's bizarre," Esme said, rolling her eyes.

"No, it's not! I think it's great, Shanely. Having a mate on its own sounds wonderful, but now you have extra people who love and care for you too. It's incredibly sweet, if you ask me," Emersyn said, swooning slightly in her seat. *God, to be right all the time...*

"I love it. Two bonus best friends who love me no matter what. Then again it's three times the scolding. Like the other day, I pissed Cade off so bad, he yelled at me just like Bastian did!" I said, sputtering out a laugh. Emersyn giggled with me, but it didn't escape my notice that even Esme cracked a smile.

"He did not!" Emersyn giggled. "He couldn't yell at you. Cade's so nice!"

"Oh, he did," I replied. "Twice actually. Bastian didn't even need to yell at me because I already got an ear full!"

Emersyn giggled again. "Cade just seems great. Really laid back and just fun. Although, I really haven't spent much time with any of the Fenrir triplets."

"For good reason," Esme muttered, and I narrowed my eyes to her. My wolf snapped her jaw.

"Cade is one of the best, and he's also my Beta. Elijah is Bastian's Beta," I said, sipping on my lukewarm cocoa. I debated reheating it, but the look on Emersyn's face made me stay. *Chocolate was chocolate. It's still good.*

"That makes sense. Cade seems more your speed while Elijah and Bastian seem to fit well together," Emersyn said, pulling on her hair again. But then her lips pursed together so tightly I wondered what was going through that mind of hers.

"They seem the same to me," Esme said, finishing the hot cocoa.

"Emmie's right," I said firmly. I turned to the younger sister. "Everything okay? You seem like something's on your mind."

Esme narrowed her eyes as Emmie tugged on her hair. After a moment she sighed and asked, "Does your mate ever get jealous of his brothers? Like with how they treat you."

I shook my head softly. "Nah, because it's not the same. I belong to Bastian only. Bastian knows his brothers would never cross that line, and neither would I. His brothers are my brothers. It's hard to explain, and I'm sure sounds crazy, but for me it's the most natural thing in the world. It's just perfect."

Esme scowled. She curled her lips in disgust, but I ignored her again. Emersyn seemed to be letting the information sink in, and I wanted to drive it home.

"It's perfect, Emmie."

Emersyn gave me a wide grin, and I really hoped Elijah was listening right now.

"To me, it seems like it would just cause problems," Esme said, souring the mood, "but if y'all make it work, then good for you."

"What do you think Emersyn?" I asked coyly. "Do you think it's weird?"

Her head leaned against her hand as she thought about my question.

"It is though," Esme said, turning to her sister. "Right, Emersyn?"

"Actually Esme, I don't think it's weird," she finally answered. "I mean it's no different than with Shanely's biological brothers, right? Shanely just has a large family, which is something most people want. At least I know I do."

I grinned wide. She was perfect for my brother-in-law. *Ooh, I have grand plans to gloat to Elijah later. Grand plans! I was right, I was right, I was right!*

"Everyone knows Cade's great, but what about Elijah?" I asked unable to contain my wide grin. Esme frowned.

"Oh, I don't know," Emersyn replied, her rosy cheeks reddening even more. "He seems quiet and very serious."

CHAPTER 4

"Oh, he's not that serious! That'd be my man," I said, giggling again. Bastian's presence pushed into my mind.

"Very funny, mate."

"Go to bed, Bastian," I said through the link. *"This is girls night."*

I felt his laugh in my mind as if he were in the room with me. It warmed me to my core, pleasing both my wolf and bear. *They loved to hear him laugh.*

"Alright, alright, I'm gone."

I hated feeling him leave my mind. Every single time.

"I don't know, Shanely. He seems stern almost," she replied, pulling me back to the conversation. "I think tonight was the first time he's ever even spoken to me."

I did not like the frown that appeared on her face, and I sat up straighter in my seat. *Maybe I wasn't quite at the gloating part of this whole thing yet.*

"He's not normally like this, I promise you," I countered. "He's insanely smart and incredibly sweet. I think you'd really like him once you get to know him."

"Why should it matter what she thinks of him? Once this is done, we'll return home, and we'll go back to only seeing each other at the Summit," Esme replied, crossing her arms. Her short dark hair swaying around her face.

Emersyn looked dejected, but she didn't counter what her sister said. I sighed. *Definitely no gloating.*

"Well..." I said, rocking my head back and forth slightly. *I had to be delicate here.* "Elijah and Cade haven't found their mate..."

Esme sputtered out a laugh. "And what?" she snapped. "You think it's one of us?"

"Well... just one of you," I muttered. I took a massive gulp of my cold cocoa as the room exploded.

Esme shot to her feet yelling, "Absolutely not! Don't even think about insinuating my sister being mated to a Fenrir!"

"You think Elijah's my mate?" Emersyn asked, her eyes wide. It didn't escape my notice that I didn't specifically name Elijah. *She came to that*

35

conclusion all on her own, I thought to myself. The corners of her mouth rose slightly, but fell when Esme yelled again.

"Oh, don't you start!" she said, yanking her sister to her feet.

I rolled my eyes and got to my own feet. *This effected Emersyn,* I thought to myself. Not her sister, and I pointed right at her.

"I think you are *perfect* for him, Emersyn. You are calm and collected, incredibly sweet, and absolutely adorable. And you both can scent the other in a way that is driving your animals crazy! Look, I know that there's bad history between your families," I said, softening my tone as I sighed, "but how is it fair to condemn the boys for something they had no part in?"

"You're kidding, right?" Esme bellowed, glaring at me. My wolf was desperate to handle the disrespect, but I held her back. *I would get nowhere if I let her out now.*

"Do you honestly hear yourself?" Esme went on. "There's no way my dad and I will *ever* let her mate a Fenrir. The only reason we joined the alliance was because my dad felt ending the law would be beneficial to all shifters, and as it was brought out in *your* council meeting that we have to help out if we ever expect it in return. That is what your mate said, right?"

"I don't get this, Esme," I snapped angrily. My eyes flashed gold as I squared up to this annoying panther. "I am *sorry* about what Liam did to you and your family, but he is not our family anymore. The triplets and Bay were children when it happened! It wasn't their fault, and I've tried so many times to be kind and forge a new relationship between us. I don't understand why you won't meet me halfway!"

"Because I don't trust the Fenrirs! I thought I made that pretty clear!" she bellowed even louder, and a door slammed shut upstairs.

My eyes widened as I realized my mistake. *Oh, Elijah... I forgot he was listening.*

"What was that?" Emersyn asked nervously. She pulled on the ends of her hair, twisting it between her fingers tightly.

"That," I said softly, "was what little hope Elijah had that you might accept him, just fly out the window."

"I don't want to hurt his feelings, but Elijah doesn't even like me, Shanely.

CHAPTER 4

I think you have it all wrong anyways," she countered. Her face sullen and empty, and I just shook my head. I knew the truth, and deep down so did she. Esme was the reason she doubted, and my anger rose again. I chucked Cade's blanket back in its spot for Aerith to find in the morning and grabbed my mug.

"No. I'm not wrong, Emersyn. That scent you told me about," I said with a clipped tone, "the one that smells earthy and woodsy? That's the Fenrir's scent. Bastian's is the same, except he doesn't have the water scent with his. That's unique to Elijah alone, while Cade's smells like earth and smoke. And Emmie, Elijah likes you, but he's been going against his wolf ever since he found you. That's why he seems so tense and stern."

"If he's her mate, then why is he avoiding her?" Esme snapped. "That sounds like a real lovely mate right there."

My eyes turned red, and I let her feel my wolf rise to the surface. Rage burned against my skin, and my wolf snapped at me to let her go.

Esme stepped back, and I felt her panther come to the surface too. We stood there quietly watching the other, waiting to see if that next step would happened. I swallowed hard, clenching my fists together and feeling my claws sharpen.

"That's enough," I snarled. "He's been avoiding her because he's terrified he's going to get rejected. Elijah knows *exactly* how you feel about them, and he's afraid to make the bond only to have her reject him because of you and your family. He's *terrified,* and rightfully so because I can't even begin to try and explain the kind of pain that they would both be in if she rejected him once the bond was made. All because of a dad he disowned and hates. You just confirmed all his fears with your little outburst, and how dare you stand in the way of your own sister's happiness!"

I grabbed the extra blankets we kept in the chest and tossed them to her. I wanted more than anything to throw her out, but if I threw out Esme, Emersyn would go too, and Elijah was more important than that panther.

"Here Esme, you can crash on the couch. Emersyn, it's been great getting to know you. The guest room is down the hall on the left," I said, setting my mug on the counter. "If either of you need anything, please let me know. My room is upstairs, second door on the left."

"I'm sleeping on the couch?" Esme asked, her arms full of blankets. I shrugged.

"If Emersyn wants to share her room, that's up to her, but I only had one extra room. My cousin Noah is in the other," I said, not caring one bit if she slept outside. "If she don't want to share then tough. Goodnight, you two."

With that, I left them to figure out the rest for themselves. My steps were heavy as I scurried up the stairs in the dark, hesitating at Elijah's room. It was quiet on the otherside, but I knew he was awake, and my heart went out to him. I pushed everything tonight. He asked us to back off, and I didn't. I went the exact opposite and ended up hurting him. *All because I had to be right.* I sighed and took my hand off the handle.

"I love you, Elijah," I whispered, wishing I could give him a big hug and make it all better. *But nothing I'd do will make this better. No matter how I'd try.* I never wanted to hurt him or Cade, and tonight I definitely messed up.

Bastian had one arm over his eyes as I entered our room, but he peeked out when I closed the door.

"Hey baby," he whispered, opening up his arms. He pulled the blankets back, and I tossed my jeans aside. I crawled into bed and snuggled against his large frame. My body ached from exhaustion, but I was too riddled with guilt to fall asleep.

"He'll be okay," he whispered as he buried his face into the crook of my neck. My heart ached again.

"Did you hear everything too?" I asked quietly.

"The whole house heard Esme," he responded, his voice sounding sleepy.

I sighed loudly. "I don't know what to do, my love. I made everything worse tonight."

"Mending lifelong issues doesn't happen overnight," he said softly. "Remember the bear clan?"

He kissed my forehead and laid his head back down. His soft snores quickly became the only sound in our room, but his words weighed on me. I couldn't get them out of my head. Mending the problems with the clan was not simple, but this just felt worse somehow. I didn't know if Esme would ever forgive the Fenrir family.

I had dragged Elijah through the mud in the process of mending things between us and the panthers. Between him and her.

Could I really put him through that again?

My mind raced for hours as I tried to come up with a solution to this whole mess. Bastian snored blissfully away, while I struggled to come up with anything I could do to fix this without making it worse for Elijah.

But I was at a loss, and soon I fell asleep.

Chapter 5

I woke to a very awkward morning in the cabin. *Everyone* was just pissy. I meandered around the kitchen, getting my coffee and vitamins, and avoiding the panther in the room.

Esme has yet to speak to me since our disagreement last night. She sat awkwardly at the table with her sister and a plate of eggs, and Emersyn seemed awfully quiet too. She looked lost in her own thoughts, picking at her food, while Bastian helped Aerith get cereal. I expected him to be more of a grump than he was honestly. It was his own flesh and blood that was insulted again, but he kept his distance from the brooding panther. Not saying a word to her either.

Cade had left early to make some calls to the other packs. After listening to my conversation with the girls last night, he decided to take over for Elijah, giving his brother the morning off.

I sipped casually, while I waited for the middle Fenrir to make an appearance, but Elijah was nowhere to be found. The morning was quickly disappearing, and soon we'd all split in different directions for the day. My eyes drifted over to the two still at the table. Their eyes glowed gold, staring angrily at one another while they ate their breakfast. They would be heading back to the lodge, and I doubt they'd come over anytime soon after this whole thing. I needed to find him before they left or this whole thing is only going to get worse. I set my coffee mug down and looked to my mate.

"Where is Elijah, baby?"

Bastian looked grim as he pointed upstairs. I gave him a sad smile and

CHAPTER 5

sauntered up the stairs. I knocked softly on his door, but no one responded. His bulky weights clanked around from the other side, so I knew he was in there. He was in there, ignoring anyone and everyone it seems.

"Elijah? It's just Shanie."

I heard the bar clank before shuffling of feet sounded from the other side. *At least he was letting me in,* I thought to myself.

Elijah opened the door, and boy did he looked haggard. His hair was a sweaty mess, and those dark circles under his eyes didn't help anything. His chest was already gleaming with sweat, and I sighed. He'd been at the weights awhile, it seemed. *My poor Elijah,* I thought to myself. He stepped aside, letting me in.

"Elijah..."

He waved me off before grabbing the bar again. "Don't worry about it, Shanie. It isn't what I was already thinking anyways."

I sat down on his bed and watched as he lifted the bar and brought it down to his chest. My mind felt muddled as I tried to think of something positive to say. Even my wolf whined within me. She didn't like seeing him like this, and frankly neither did I.

I looked around his room lost in thought. It was clean as a whistle, looking rather nice like always. I always loved how he decorated his room here. Soft blues and browns, everything was simple and organized. His bed was pushed into the corner next to his weights, with a nice desk on the other side and a very expensive computer sitting on it. A place for everything, and everything in it's place. It matched the way his brain operated. He was brilliant and so knowledgeable when it came to computer stuff. Cade's room was always a mess, with clothes tossed in a jumble heap and food wrappers scattered about, but that's because Cade was carefree. He was goofy and always moving, but Elijah had a place for everything. He was cool and calculated all the time and seeing him come undone like this was rough.

The bar clattered on the bench, and he added more weight to it. *He's our rock yet he was falling apart.* Unless we could figure out a way to fix this, I wasn't sure if I'd ever see my brother the same again.

"Elijah, have you eaten yet?"

"Nope."

"Can I make you something?"

"I'm okay, Shanie."

"Are you sure?"

"Yup."

I sighed. This wasn't getting us anywhere. I leaned back against the wall as he adjusted the weight on the bar and started again.

"Has Bastian talked to you at all?"

"He knocked," he said, grunting as he lifted the bar, "but I really wasn't in the mood to talk."

I counted each rep, noting the serious weight on the bar. After he hit 25 reps, I sighed again.

"You let me in though," I replied, and he set the bar down. He sat up and wiped his face with his towel. His face was red and the veins in his arm looked ready to burst. *He's overdoing it.*

"Yeah, well you're you," he said. "No one shuts out Shanie."

That made me smile.

"Alrighty, since you put it that way," I said, scooching closer. "I want to say something, and you can't be mad at me when I do. Okay?"

He gave me a pointed look before grabbing the weights sitting on the floor. "Shanie..."

"No," I said, scurrying over to him. I placed my hand on the weight before he started up again, "listen to me. Don't let the first conversation blind you to what still can be a good thing. You knew it was going to be shut down immediately when we attempted to fix things, especially from Esme. You can't expect to fix years of hatred in one conversation, but one thing to think about is that Emmie didn't say a thing like her sister did."

Elijah's brows furrowed as he listened to me. I pursed my lips, placing my hands over his.

"She barely knows anything about mate bonds, Elijah," I said softly, "but one thing she did say about you was that you seemed tense. She doesn't even think you like her, so to her it feels impossible to be mates."

CHAPTER 5

His eyes widened. He opened his mouth but quickly snapped it shut. I gave his hand a gentle squeeze.

"Think about that, Elijah. You aren't mated to her sister, so the only person you need to concern yourself with right now is Emersyn. The rest will fall into place, but maybe try wooing her for now. See how fast their impression of you changes," I said with a soft smile. His eyes softened, and I hoped I helped him feel a little better about the situation.

I stood, giving him time to sort this out himself and placed my hand on the door handle. I started to leave but turned. He just looked so lost. Like he truly didn't know what to do, and my heart broke. I couldn't help the pity that warmed my eyes. I *hated* seeing him like this.

"You are worthy of amazing things, Elijah. Don't let the best one slip through your fingers because you didn't try. Imagine what you'd tell Bastian if he was you, and then take your own advice."

Elijah looked to his feet, taking a deep breath, and setting down the weights. His leg began to bounce as he said, "I don't know how to do this, Shanie. I can deal with most thing thrown my way, but she... She *terrifies* me."

"Elijah, you do know how to do this. You've been coaching and helping Bastian since he found me. It's your turn now," I replied and opened the door. As I stepped through, I couldn't help but wonder something else. I peeked my head back in asking, "I am curious though; what does she smell like to you?"

He smiled softly. "Like wild daises."

I grinned, thinking how adorable that was. Bastian always said I scented like honey, and Emersyn's scent was wild daises. If Cade's mate smells anything bee related, I think I would laugh hysterically.

"Oh," I said, and he slowly looked up to me, "one last thing, brother. She seemed to think it's really sweet how you all care for me."

I smiled, leaving him to finish his workout in peace. I've reached out and gave my opinion. I've tried to help, but he has to make the choice to go for it. I've pushed far more than I probably should have, but I couldn't help it. These were my boys, and I wanted to care for them the way they did me.

I took two steps at a time until I was back in the kitchen with everyone else. Bastian intercepted me on my way back to the coffee pot and kissed me hard. My heart fluttered as his hands gripped my cheek. He slowly pulled away.

"I love you, Shanely," he whispered softly. His too perfect lips gently kissed my cheek, and my smile grew wide.

"I love you too, Bastian. What was that for?" I asked. I could already feel the blush creeping up my cheeks.

"I heard everything. I tried talking to him earlier, but he wouldn't let me in. You, however manage to get through to him, and everything you said was just perfect. It was exactly what he needed. You amaze me, Shanely," he whispered softly. His warm breath on my neck sent chills down my spine.

"God, I missed him. To have just a moment of time..."

Cade suddenly bounded on the deck in his wolf form, startling me from my scandalous thoughts. My cheeks blushed again, earning a smack on the backside from Bastian. The corners of my mouth rose when I realized I projected that thought.

Cade shook out his fur before walking through the door. My brow rose as I slowly put my hand on my hip, and he halted, backing up slowly and wiping his paws on my rug.

I grinned. *After nearly six months of hollering at Cade, this was as close to remembering as I was going to get with him.*

Aerith squealed before jumping on Cade's back. He yipped and trotted around our island, with her clinging for dear life. I chuckled, watching the two goof off again. *Now this was the typical mornings I was used too.* Loud roughhousing and loads of giggles.

As I scurried out of their way, a flutter rushed across my belly, and I halted in my tracks as the corners of my mouth rose. One hand slowly drifted to my stomach as I yanked on Bastian's shirt.

My babies were kicking.

I lifted my shirt and placed his hand on the center.

"Our babies, Bastian."

CHAPTER 5

Bastian's warm smile melted my heart as he searched to feel the flutter. I wish more than anything it was the right time for that.

"I wish I could feel, baby," he said softly.

"You will," I said, leaning up to kiss him again. "I promise."

Cade's large wolf pushed his brother out of the way like an incessant toddler. I laughed as he sniffed my stomach with that wet snout of his before placing his ear against it. I grinned, waiting patiently to tell me they were doing just fine. *Gotta love those ears,* I thought.

He paused for a moment before yipping loudly.

"Thanks Beta," I said gratefully, but then he *licked* my stomach. I shrieked, and Cade took off upstairs before I could throw anything at him.

Bastian laughed deeply and helped wipe the slobber off my stomach.

"I'll get you for that!" I shouted, hearing his stupid wolf chortled from his room.

"Are your mornings always like this?" Esme asked, and I quickly turned, my cheeks reddening slightly. I forgot the sisters were still sitting at the table. They merely watched with wide eyes, but I was surprised to find Esme more curious than anything.

Bastian gave me a look and went to the sink to clean up breakfast, letting me deal with the panther. I straightened my shirt and made my way over.

"You mean full of love and family happiness?" I asked with a cheesy grin. "Then yes. Yes, they are."

Esme's face reddened, and the awkward silence continued. I wasn't going to be the one to start first though. I was done extending my hand only to get bit. Esme behaved more like a viper than panther, and I crossed my arms to wait.

"Listen," Emersyn said softly, "about last night. I... well, *we* wanted to apologize. Right, Esme?"

Esme crossed her arms, shifting in her seat nervously, and refusing to look me in the eye. My brow rose, waiting for the actually apology. It took a minute, and after a gentle nudge from her sister, she finally said, "I'm sorry, Shanely."

"We didn't mean to insult anyone. Especially someone who's working so hard to help out shifters," Emersyn said with a genuine smile. "Us included."

"Thank you. Apology accepted. We can just pretend it never happened," I replied. My wolf snapped her jaws at me, irritated I was letting the disrespect go like this, but seeing the look of utter relief on Emersyn's face, I knew it was the right call. My wolf and I may still be pissed, but for Elijah and Emersyn's sake, pretending it was over was better.

"I'd like that," Emersyn replied, squeezing my hand gently.

"That means everything though. I don't feel comfortable with someone pushing a mate bond on my sister," Esme said coldly.

Emersyn glared at Esme, their eyes flashing gold as they argued through the link. *This must not be what they rehearsed,* I thought to myself.

"No one would make you girls do anything you don't want to. We're not those kind of men," Bastian said sternly. He walked towards the three of us, leaning his hands on the counter, and staring intensely at the girls. They shifted uncomfortably in their seat, making me smirk. A glare from an Alpha wasn't fun, but I didn't blame him for wanting to get his point across.

"Us Fenrir brothers are complete gentleman, I promise you. You are safe with us," Cade chimed in as he raced down the stairs. He grabbed his jacket, winking at them before hopping on the counter next to Bastian.

The energy in the room shifted when Emersyn took a deep breath. She went still as heavy footsteps slowly made their way down the stairs.

"But to be clear," Elijah said, stopping on the last step, "we treat mates as sacred and treasured. When a mate bond happens to one of us, it happens to all of us, and we love fiercely. We *do not* walk away from what belongs to us."

The corners of my mouth rose as I went back and forth between the two. Their attention was entirely locked on one another, and I honestly had a hard time choosing who to watch more. Elijah with his sultry eyes or Emersyn with her deer-in-headlights look. I quickly covered my mouth when Cade caught my attention. He wiggled his eyebrows, and it was all I could do not to laugh. Elijah finally dropped his gaze and moved to the

CHAPTER 5

fridge to grab a drink. Emersyn swallowed hard.

Dang Elijah! I thought to myself. *He did good.*

"Hey," I said as I turned to my mate, *"you think you can talk like that to me sometime?"*

Bastian slowly dragged his eyes away from the girls to me. He did not look amused, and my grin widened. Until his look turned wild, and I felt his wolf rise to the surface.

"Does my little mate want something from me?"

Heat flushed my cheeks, and the corners of his mouth rose to a wicked smile. *God, he was breathtaking. My mate is dropped dead gorgeous.* I bit my lower lip as my thoughts ran amuck, and he winked at me. Bastian grabbed Aerith's bowl and went back to the sink. *Oh two can play at this game,* I thought.

"I do," I said through the link. *"I want you and all your possessive, dominating traits."*

Bastian turned slightly, looking back at me from the corner of his eye. He smirked as Cade and Elijah stepped past and headed outside. It was time to get to work, and my fun was about to end.

"You are mine when I'm finally healed, mate."

I grinned wide. *"Yes, daddy."*

Bastian's eyes widened, and he ran his hands over his face. "I'm going to take a cold shower," he muttered quietly before booking it up the stairs.

The girls gave me a funny look, but I waved them off. This wasn't any of their business, and we weren't that sort of friends.

"Check mate," I said, grinning. Bastian's amusement trickled through the bond, but other than that he stayed radio silent.

"Are they always that intense?" Esme asked.

I nodded. "They're possessive dominating Alpha males, so yes. They may be overprotective, and somewhat controlling, but you get used to it."

I put the last of the dishes in the dishwasher and hollered up to Aerith to get dressed. I slipped on my flats as the girls put their shoes on too. Emersyn just looked so broken though. *This isn't fair...*

"The thing you need to understand about the Fenrir brothers is that they are the opposite of their father," I said, and they both stopped what they were doing. "They are complete gentlemen, and they genuinely care about others. Did you know both Cade and Elijah almost died saving my life?"

Esme cocked her head to the side while Emersyn shook her head no.

"When mixers were nothing more than a death sentence," I said quietly, "Elijah risked his life to protect me from a large grizzly. It broke his back and arm, but he *still* tried protecting me despite that. Go ahead and ask to see his scar sometime. It's still there. And when I was taken by Derek, it was Cade and Elijah who ended up finding me. Elijah ran miles to find my mate in the dead of winter, while Cade delivered my baby and then ran carrying me and Aerith while mountain lions chased us. He fought them until my mate could get there. They saved me more than once, and I could never thank them enough for it. And if you're curious, it was my mate who ended up killing both the bear and the lions. He may have been minutes behind, but he <u>*always*</u> found me. There isn't anything he wouldn't do to save me and our kids. That's who the Fenrir brothers are. They are fierce, strong, and loyal. Any female would be lucky to have them for a mate. I know I am."

I walked to my backdoor and stepped outside for a bit, leaving them to sort out what I said. I hoped more than anything it swayed Esme's mind about them being different. If this wasn't enough, I don't know what would.

A cool breeze touched my skin as I walked out, and when I closed the door, I turned around to find Cade and Elijah grinning from ear to ear.

"What?"

Cade laughed and yanked me towards him. "Aww, I didn't know you loved us that much, Baby Girl!"

I playfully slapped him as I shoved away. "Oh, let go! You both know I love you! I was merely trying to..."

"It's okay," Cade cut in. "We are pretty great after all."

Elijah laughed and gave me a gentler hug. "Thank you, Shanely. I needed to hear... well everything you said today."

He gave me a pointed look, and I knew what he meant. It made my wolf

CHAPTER 5

feel good that we made a difference for him.

"You're welcome," I said softly, leaning against his shoulder.

Cade asked, "Where's our elderly brother now? We've got stuff to do."

"Taking a cold shower," I replied with a devilish grin.

Elijah raised an eyebrow. "A cold shower?"

I laughed. "I may have been a little ornery earlier."

"Nope! I don't need to know! Just tell him to meet me at the lodge!" Cade said and quickly shifted to his wolf. The two of us chuckled as he disappeared in the woods.

"He'll get it when he finds his own mate," Elijah said.

"I think that's the first time you've even hinted at having a mate without freaking out," I said, grinning.

He grunted. "Yeah well, baby steps."

I stuck my tongue out at him. "What are you up to today?"

"Making some calls, and I need to run to town."

I straightened. "You sure about that? You shouldn't go alone."

"I'll be okay. I just need to get a few things," he said as he headed around the house to where the trucks were parked.

"Elijah..."

"Don't worry, Shanie," he said, giving me the same devilish grin Bastian always did when he was up to no good. "I'll be in and out."

With that, he bolted around the house as the back door opened. I tossed my hands in the air. *They never let me do stuff like this?!*

"Hey," Emmie said softly, "we're heading back to grab some new clothes at the lodge for Esme. We'll be back in a while, if that's okay?"

"Sure," I said, shaking my head, "today's going to be a slow day making calls mostly. I'll be here so..."

"Where did Cade and Elijah go?" she asked.

"Cade's at the lodge, and Elijah went into town," I replied in a huff. *We were definitely going to have words later.*

"Alone?"

"Yup. Did I mention the brothers can be stupid sometimes? Because this is a prime example!"

Esme barked out a laugh before slamming her hand over her mouth. A slow grin formed on my face as her cheeks reddened. She quickly turned and shot down the porch steps. *Hide all you like,* I thought to myself. *I am winning this stupid stubborn fight of yours.*

"C'mon Emersyn," Esme said sternly. "We'll be back soon."

They shifted and made their way back to the lodge. Their panthers were very cool to see in the daylight. They were near invisible at night with their jet black fur, but in the daylight they stood out like a sore thumb. Esme was slightly larger than Emersyn, but other than that they were identical. I watched until they disappeared through the treeline.

On the list of things to do today, cleaning was near the top of the list. The house had gotten out of hand since being away so much, and I went ahead and started a load of laundry. I made the smoothie the Summit Hall doctor instructed me to take, cleaning up that mess before making my way upstairs. Aerith was busy playing with her Barbie dolls in her room, and I left her in her happy little bubble. Bastian had just bought her the Vet Barbie, complete with the clinic and golden retriever. She has yet to put them down.

Bastian was still in the bathroom as I entered our room. I noticed my jeans were still tossed on the floor, and I remembered Hank. Sighing, I dug through the pockets of my jeans and pulled out the now crumpled strip of paper.

I grabbed my cell phone and dialed the number. *Caleb wasn't kidding,* I thought as the ridiculous government message played on a loop. I rolled my eyes and pushed #29187 when it asked for the extension. It seemed to ring for an eternity, and my heart skittered inside as I waited. It was enough that I felt Bastian's presence in the back of my mind, hovering to make sure I was okay.

"This is the office of Hank Cartwright, Head of International and Internal Affairs. I am away from my office at the moment. Please leave your name and number, and I will try to get back to you in a timely matter."

I sighed heavily as the voicemail message played out. "Hello, Mr. Cartwright. This is Shanely Fenrir. If you would please give me a call

CHAPTER 5

back as soon as possible, I would appreciate it. I have a very urgent matter I need to discuss with you. Thank you."

I set my phone on the bed, feeling defeated once more. *How is this the only way to reach anyone at the Division?* I grabbed Bastian's laptop and typed *The Division* in the search bar. Nothing came up.

Frowning, I searched for our state's website, scrolling through an abundance of information that I didn't need. It was daunting trying to sort through the many pages of laws or taxes. None of it made any sense. I was about to close the laptop when something caught my eye. At the very bottom of the page, in the departments section, was the Division's logo. I dragged the mouse over the icon and clicked but nothing happened. I clicked again and again, feeling more and more agitated when the screen stayed the same. The site wouldn't load, and I slammed the laptop down in frustration.

My eyes drifted back to the paper. *Maybe I just need to try a different department. Someone had to talk to me. Right?*

I dialed the number again, but this time I listened to the prompts. Four different areas, four different departments. I let the prompt continue playing out and was surprised to hear they had an option for complaints. I pushed 9.

"This the the Division's complaint department established for shifters to speak when issues arise. Please leave your name and number and a detailed message after the tone and someone from International and Internal Affairs will get back to you. By leaving a message, you admit that what you say is true and accurate under perjury of law. Any false statements will be sought out, and the maximum punishment will be dealt out. Thank you, and have a nice day."

I froze as the dial tone sounded. Despite the warning bells going off in my head, I gave my name and number and said I had a problem that needed addressed. I left no other details than that. Just in case.

I blew out another breath as I looked at my phone. It was getting really annoying not being able to reach someone though. I bit my lower lip before pushing redial. The phone rang again, playing that ridiculous prompt as

I grabbed my smoothie and made my way back to the kitchen. This time I selected the Homeland Security Department. *I mean this sorta applied, didn't it?*

"This is Division's Homeland Security. How may I direct your call?"

I sagged in relief on the kitchen stool. *An actual person!* "Hi! This is Shanely Fenrir. I have an issue that I need to speak to someone about. Can you help connect me to someone in charge?"

"Well, that depends," the woman said. "What sort of issues are you having?"

"The Division Head over my pack has been causing problems for me and my family," I replied. "We've tried to make amends but..."

"Ah... you're a shifter."

I frowned. "Yes, I am Alpha..."

"You really should be talking to someone in Internal affairs then," she said firmly. "I can transfer you."

"No please!" I begged, and she paused. "I've already tried, and no one answers. I need this problem taken care of now."

"Ma'am," she said with irritation. "This is a government agency. Not a place you can snap your fingers and demand results. This department is run by Lieutenant General Dennis Hemingway. We handle massive amounts of conflict, not little issues within a pack. Now please hold, and I will direct your call."

"Wait!"

But it was too late. I heard the same stupid jingle before that complaint message began to replay. I hung up.

"God, I finally manage to get a hold of someone and this happens," I muttered to myself. I ran my fingers through my hair, trying to gain some resemblance of control before I called her back. I didn't want to bite her head off. At least not until I fixed this problem. *One thing at a time, Shanely.*

Taking a deep breath, I went to push the button to dial again when a truck's door slammed shut outside. My eye narrowed, and I set my phone down. I made my way to the front door, but before I could open it, Noah barged inside sniffing like crazy. He bolted around the living room,

CHAPTER 5

following his nose like he was tracking something.

"Noah?" I said, but he didn't answer me. My eyes narrowed. *It was like he didn't even see me standing in the middle of the room right now.* Suddenly, he was in my face scenting me. I shoved him off. "Noah!"

I jerked my arm away as Caleb finally walked in with an annoyed look on his face.

"Dude! You didn't even put it in park!" my brother snapped. "I wrenched my back to stop the truck from hitting the house!"

Noah didn't answer. He just kept sniffing everything. From the pile of blankets to the mugs in the sink. Bastian walked in dressed in new clothes from his shower earlier. He rubbed a towel against his head to dry his hair.

"What is going on here?" he asked.

I shrugged, not knowing what to even say. Noah was rambling nonsense in Russian, so that was absolutely no help.

"Noah, stop! Just tell us what is going on?" I begged, and his eyes finally focused on mine.

"Where is she?" he demanded.

"Who?"

"My mate," he snapped. "The one that smells like wild daisies. *Where. Is. She?*"

My eyes widened. Bastian and I looked at one another as Caleb's mouth dropped.

This was not happening.

Chapter 6

"Your what?" Bastian asked, his eyes wide.

I stood frozen in disbelief. I couldn't get my mouth to close, I was so dumbfounded by what he just said. *Emmie smells like wild daisies... God, this couldn't happen, could it?* I thought anxiously as I turned to Bastian. Noah started pacing the house again.

"I need to find her, Shanely," he demanded. His eyes were gold already. "Who was here, and where has she gone?"

"Other than Aerith and I," I stammered, "it's only been us, Emersyn, and..."

Noah was suddenly in my face, and I stumbled backward. His bear was hyper focused on me, and my heart started pounding in my chest.

"Emersyn," he said quietly, "She's the panther, isn't she? She scents like daises, correct?"

Crap.

"Yes, but we might have a problem," I replied, but he shoved away from me.

Noah was scenting the house again and found his way into the guest room, where Emersyn slept the night before.

I turned to my mate and brother.

"Oh God, Bastian. We have a serious problem here!" I said in a hushed tone. "How is this even happening?"

He looked as panicked as I felt. "Don't look at me! I've never heard of this happening before!"

"What are you talking about?" Caleb asked, his eyes narrowing.

CHAPTER 6

"Elijah already scents her as his mate," I whispered quietly. A snarl rattled the walls.

"He said what?" Noah demanded as he stormed over to me.

Caleb swore as Bastian stepped in front of me. "Noah, calm down. There must be some sort of misunderstanding, okay? We will figure it all out, I promise, but you cannot snarl at my mate. I won't allow that!"

Noah snarled again, storming away in a huff.

"It's okay, my love. It's just his bear talking," I replied, kissing his cheek.

"I know," Bastian said, watching my brute of a cousin pace the living room, "but he's got to rein it in. He's going to shift in our living room if he's not careful."

"Good lord, why is *this* all happening right now?!" Caleb asked, joining our little huddle again.

I shrugged as Noah stormed back towards us.

"This is driving me crazy! Where is she?!" he demanded.

"Whoa there, buddy. You can't actually find her right now!" I said, tossing my hands against his chest, blocking him from the door. "You're not totally in control right now, and she knows very little of the whole mate bond thing. Besides it's not fair to Elijah, and we should..."

Noah roared, shaking the walls, and I staggered backwards. Noah barred his teeth at me growling as he asked, "Are you choosing Elijah over me, Shanely? Are you changing the fates now?!"

Bastian shoved him away, tucking me safely behind him. Noah began yelling in Russian. *Calling me every name in the book, I'm sure.*

My mate's Alpha power poured into the room, striking Noah in the chest. Noah winced as he stumbled on his feet. He barred his teeth as my mate stepped towards him.

Bastian yelled, "Noah, I'm warning you to calm down right now! My daughter's in the room right above us! Until we figure this out, you aren't going anywhere."

Another wave of Alpha power struck my cousin. Noah shook where he stood, his eyes still shifter gold as he glared at my mate, and a sickening feeling hit my gut. Cade burst through the back door then.

"What's going on?! I can feel your guy's panic," he said as he approached. "You guys okay?"

Bastian eased up, letting Noah breathe, and I hoped it was enough to get him to settle down to discuss everything. I would never choose one over the other, but there was no way they both were mated to Emersyn. To my dismay, Noah glared at the newcomer and stormed over to Cade shouting, "I want what's mine!"

"Whoa, what's he talking about?" Cade asked. His hands raised slowly as he looked to me from the corner of his eye.

"Noah's scenting his mate. He thinks it's Emersyn," I replied.

Cade swore as another truck door sounded.

"Oh no," I whispered, but it was too late. Noah flew through the door, and I couldn't catch him. *For barely fitting in this house, he was fast!*

Elijah hopped out of the truck with a bag from the convenience store. "Told you, Shanie! In and out..."

Noah snarled in Elijah's face. Elijah stepped back saying, "Whoa dude, what's your problem??"

"I'll tell you my problem, Fenrir. They said you are trying to take Emersyn as your mate! I'm here to tell you that she's *mine!*" Noah growled.

Elijah's eyes widened as the words sunk in, and his hands clenched into fists around the bag he carried. "Excuse me? What did you just say?"

"You heard me. Emersyn *is mine*, but if you're too dumb to understand, I can always say it in another language if that will help get it through your thick head!"

Elijah's eyes flashed with murderous rage, turning from a bright gold to his Alpha red. *This was going from bad to worse,* I thought as Cade and Bastian stepped towards the two.

"Guys," Bastian said as he slowly approached, "let's take a deep breath now."

Noah roared loudly. His bear pulled through his voice, grounding the boys to a halt.

"Oh no," I muttered, when the front door swung open. The panther sisters stepped out looking entirely alarmed. Esme's nails had already shifted into her sharp claws. Her eyes roaming to assess the situation.

"What is going on?! We heard the commotion and..."

Emersyn's voice trailed off as her eyes settled on the brooding males before her. They widened into fear as Elijah and Noah scented the air at the same time and slowly turned to face her. *Like a predator who's found its prey*, I thought to myself.

"Crap, crap, crap," I muttered, scurrying over to her. I wrapped my arms around her and pulled her back.

Noah took a step towards us, and Elijah snapped. And I do mean *snapped*. My cool, calm, and calculated brother grabbed the back of my cousin's shirt and slammed him into his truck. The truck jolted from the hit, and Elijah snarled in Noah's face.

"DON'T YOU TOUCH HER!"

My eyes nearly popped out of my head as I stared at my brute of a brother-in-law. I have *never* seen Elijah lose his temper like this. For the first time since I've known him, he acted feral, with his hand on Noah's throat, digging in hard enough to draw blood. I forget how much of an Alpha he really is, and I truly didn't know how to diffuse this situation.

Noah shoved Elijah off him, revealing a dent in the truck's body as he got to his feet. The scent of blood filled the air, flowing down Noah's neck where Elijah's hand had been, but not enough for me to truly worry. *Not yet at least.*

But then Noah shifted.

His massive reddish-brown grizzly with a dark underbelly roared angrily, and Elijah didn't hesitate in shifting with him. They were at each other's throats in seconds, snarling and snapping their jaws at one another like they were the enemy. *God, we don't hurt our allies!* I thought, tossing my hands in the air. *Unbonded males, I swear!*

I staggered down the steps after my mate, who was already trying to get in between the two again. I barely caught him by his collar, pulling him backwards to me.

"Don't even think about it, Bastian!" I snapped, pointing my finger in his face. "Gun shot wound! You are healing from a gun shot wound!"

He barred his teeth as Cade and Caleb shifted and tumbled with the two currently destroying my front lawn. I rolled my eyes in a huff. *Again.*

"Why are they fighting! What happened?!" Emersyn asked nervously. Her fingers were entangled in the ends of her hair as she watched the brutes fight.

"It's a long story," I said, sighing heavily and tightening my grip on Bastian, "but they both scent you as their mate and..."

"What?! That's not possible!" she stammered, reaching for Esme who stared intently at the scene ahead. Her brows furrowed, blatantly judging my family's behavior, and to make matters worse, I didn't *blame* her! All the convincing I had done to get her to see how wonderful my family was had just gone out the window. *They just had to go do something like this.* Noah's roar shook the trees, and I took a deep breath to calm my wolf. *The boneheaded Alpha males!*

"Hey, it's okay," I said, mustering a smile in hopes of calming them both. The snarling only grew louder behind me. *I was going to kill them.* "They're loud and emotional right now, but you don't need to be afraid of them."

"You promise?" Emmie asked, and I raised my hand.

"Scout's honor," I said, when I suddenly stumbled backwards. Bastian had started forward again, dragging my butt with him.

"Bastian!" I hollered as I tugged him back.

"Shanely, let go!" he shouted as he took another step. "This clearly isn't working. They need an Alpha."

I looked past him, seeing Cade and Caleb getting nowhere with the two boneheads. I rolled my eyes as Bastian started for them again.

"Down boy!" I shouted, and he barred his teeth at me. I barred mine right back. "Oh, don't you start now!"

I had just about enough of this, I thought to myself. *They were being loud and dramatic and giant pains in my butt!* I shifted into my white wolf and howled loudly. I let my Alpha power out in full force, and the four shifters dropped to the ground. I slowly walked over to the two at fault, snarling at their behavior and inability to have a simple conversation with one another.

Like grown adults.

CHAPTER 6

My wolf was just as irritated as I was, especially with Noah who lost control in the first place. She hovered over his head, barring her teeth for far longer than Elijah. They all knew better, and they weren't pups or cubs anymore. They were *grown* men, and they needed more control than this! Especially with what we're up against.

"Show off," my mate muttered behind me.

I swished my tail in a huff, giving him a pretty view of my backside, and heard his low growl from his wolf. Bastian shook his head as I trotted over back to him. I let the four go as I shifted back. They all visibly relaxed, and I rolled my shoulders, ready to give them a further lashing.

"I'm giving you all this command to shift back right now!" I hollered loudly.

Noah and Caleb forcefully shifted.

"Ow, Shanely! You could have just asked!" Caleb said, stepping aside and rubbing his chest. Noah straightened himself still glaring at Elijah, who's wolf barred his teeth. I swore under my breath.

I had forgotten I had released the brothers from Alpha commands. I had no sway over them anymore, and the two stayed in their wolf forms despite what I commanded.

"Elijah..." I said sternly. I crossed my arms and waited. Elijah wasn't budging, and he snarled again at Noah.

Noah took a step forward, his hands curling into fists, and I scoffed.

"Knock it off, you two!" I snapped.

But Noah ignored me, snapping his arms and shaking out the tingling feeling that came with a forced shift. I nearly slapped my own forehead. *Good God, these boys were thick headed sometimes.*

"Guys!" Bastian said, his voice low and commanding. There was a warning behind that one word, and Noah stopped in his tracks. *Oh sure,* I thought. *Listen to him.*

Cade shifted first, staying close to Elijah just in case. The middle Fenrir took his sweet time but finally shifted back to his human form, and I sighed in relief. His lip was busted and Noah still bled, but no one looked to have serious injuries thankfully. *Last thing we needed was more shifters down and out due to stupidity.*

"Oh, so they listen to you," I said, giving my mate a pointed look. Bastian wiggled his eyebrows before turning back to the guys.

"Don't move!" Bastian shouted, crossing his arms as he stared hard at the two just itching to fight again. "If either one of you takes a step right now, then the fight will continue because of your lack of control."

"Alrighty boys," I said, clasping my hands together, "lets just fix this. There has to be a logical explanation for whatever is going on, and we can figure it out with a clear head. What I won't accept, is you two killing one another over something like this! We are family!"

"I want my mate," Noah said firmly. His voice still deep and raspy from merging with his bear.

"And I want mine!" Elijah clapped back, and the snarling continued.

"Guys! Good lord, let's just see who she is drawn to! Alright? You stubborn, possessive, animals..." I said irritatedly before stomping back to the girls.

Cade covered his mouth, stifling a laugh.

"You tell them, Baby Girl!" he shouted, making Bastian roll his eyes. *He was having way too much fun with this.* Elijah and Noah, however, never took their eyes off one another.

"Emersyn," I said as I approached, "this isn't conventional, but can you please help us out. I just need you to go to the one who's scent is intoxicating. Like it's the best thing in the whole world, and you crave getting to scent it again."

Esme's eyes went wide as terror stretched across her sister's face. I didn't have time to explain everything though as the two behind me were still fuming mad and growling.

"What?" Emersyn asked shakily.

I held my hand out to her, and after a moment, she accepted it. I helped her down the steps and put my arm around her. "Just inhale their scents, and move your feet. Follow your cat's instincts."

She gave me a look, and I nodded my head to her. She looked back to the boys and took a step carefully.

CHAPTER 6

Both boys instinctively turned to her, frightening her, and she stopped in her tracks.

"Go on, Emmie," I said with a smile. "They won't take a step, I promise."

My brow rose to the males before me. *"Take one step towards her, and I will fight you myself,"* I snarled in warning.

Emersyn inhaled deeply, closing her eyes and concentrating hard at their scents. She slowly opened them, turning to give me one last look, and I nodded reassuringly again.

"They won't hurt you," I said, quietly nudging her forward.

Emersyn looked uneasy as she turned to face them again. She took a step, and then another, and soon found herself standing in front of Elijah. He stiffened when she reached up to touch him, and I had never seen him so vulnerable before. He radiated tension as he stood before her, waiting for her to claim him. He was scruffy from not shaving lately, and exhausted from the lack of sleep, but his muscles relaxed as soon as she put her hand to his cheek.

Noah's shoulders dropped, and my heart filled with pity. His brows furrowed slightly, and I pursed my lips together. *This wasn't fair to him either.*

I had barely taken a step to console my cousin when he bolted towards Emersyn. Elijah gripped her waist, pulling her in and behind him, but Noah only frowned. He didn't touch her, but his brows knitted in... *Was that confusion?* Suddenly, he leaned in, scenting Emersyn, and Elijah gave him a low warning growl.

"No," Noah muttered, "this isn't right."

"Noah," I said, stepping forward, "she chose who calls her."

I looked to my mate, who scratched the back of his head. It was clear neither one of us knew what to do here, but my cousin wouldn't leave. He wasn't accepting the choice made.

"Noah..." Elijah warned again.

Noah moved then, scenting the air like he had in my house.

"This isn't my girl," he said softly, following his nose as he turned back to the porch. "She smells similar, but it's off."

My eyes widened, and we all turned to look at Esme. She had rubbed her chest raw, staring at my brute of a cousin, with wide petrified eyes.

"Oh, my God," I muttered.

Noah bolted. With one swift motion, he yanked her towards him and kissed her. Emersyn gripped her chest and fell against Elijah in shock.

Noah clung to Esme like she was his salvation. He was needy, and the longer he held her, the more she relaxed. She looked complete, and dare I say *happy*. Esme was half the size of my massive cousin, but I had to admit, the two looked good together.

I turned to Bastian who stared up at the sky in relief. He winked at me before grabbing my waist and pulling me in.

"You..." Noah said softly once he finally pulled away. Their heads resting against the other, "you are the one I've been looking for."

Esme was at a loss for words. For the first time since I've known her, she didn't know what to say. *It was rather nice, if I was being honest.* Noah smiled softly, kissing her lips again.

"I didn't know what was happening to me when I got here," she finally said, "so I just pushed it aside. I didn't understand any of it, but I'm so sorry. I thought I smelled something unique this morning, but I thought I was just going crazy. I just... I don't even know your name."

"Yeah, well apparently he doesn't know your name either," Cade muttered as he joined me by my side. I shushed him.

"My name is Noah Medvedev, and I'm the one who should be sorry. I jumped to conclusions, my love. Shanely said Emersyn, and I thought it was your name," he said bashfully.

"Hey, I tried to say Esme too, but your bear is a stubborn jerk when he wants to be!" I shouted, making Esme grin.

"So, he didn't want me?" Emersyn asked quietly.

Elijah tensed by her side before realizing he still held onto her and quickly let her go. My face fell when I saw the protective wall return. He took a step back, and I noticed her face fell too.

"No, they were each fighting to protect their own girl," I said softly. "Elijah was fighting for you."

CHAPTER 6

I walked over and pushed him back towards her. Heat rose to his cheeks as he rubbed the back of his head nervously, but I just gave him a cheesy smile.

"Go on, Elijah," I said softly through our link, and he sighed.

"Hang on," Elijah muttered as he rushed to the truck. He grabbed the bag he dropped earlier and slowly approached his girl again. She watched his every move, shifting back and forth on her feet nervously. I chuckled softly to myself. I just wanted to rip the Band-aid off and declare them mates already. *Gosh, these two...*

"I wanted you to have something fun to do while you stayed with us," he mumbled, handing her the bag. "I'm sorry I lost my temper in front of you and frightened you. If it feels like you ended up with the wrong mate, then I am really sorry to disappoint you there too. No matter how you feel about me or the bond, I still want you to have this."

She looked inside, pulling out drawing pencils and a sketch pad. My heart melted just a tiny bit, and I gently slapped Bastian and Cade as I watched them. I couldn't pull my eyes off them. *They were the cutest thing ever.* I didn't care that Bastian and Cade were giving me odd looks. I just waved them off.

What Elijah did was incredibly sweet! He remembered something she loved to do and went out and bought supplies for her. I've always loved all this romantic stuff, and I was so proud of him.

Emersyn studied them for a moment. She didn't say anything as she looked at the art supplies in the bag.

I felt bad as Elijah suddenly began stammering, "I wasn't sure what all you'd need, and the store didn't have a lot to chose from anyways, but I don't know. I just thought it would be a good start, and maybe..."

Emersyn flew into his arms, dropping the bag on the ground. She kissed him abruptly, startling everyone who watched the whole thing unfold. Bastian, Cade, and I all felt the new bond hit us square in the chest. A strong connection formed to Emersyn now. Esme and Noah felt the same thing.

"Did we just witness a double mating?" I whispered to Bastian, rubbing my chest as the sensation wore off, and he just grinned.

Elijah pulled back slightly, a grin slowly forming on his face as he gently moved her hair away from her eyes. She smiled back before noticing everyone staring at them, and her rosy cheeks heated again.

"I... ah... yeah," she fumbled with her words. "I was just... umm...."

We chuckled as Noah approached dragging Esme with him. Elijah was the first to extend his hand.

"I'm sorry, man," he said.

Noah gladly accepted. "It was my fault, Elijah. I lost control in the house, and I didn't realize I had the wrong name. I apologize as well."

Elijah nodded before his eyes dropped to the woman standing by Noah's side. She looked a little uncomfortable, but surprisingly she extended her hand out to him.

"I'm sorry for the things I said about your family and about you," she blurted. "I was wrong, I can see that now, and I think you will be good for Emersyn. You seem capable enough to keep her safe, which is all my father and I really wanted for her anyways."

My brows rose, and I looked to my mate. He pursed his lips together and shrugged his shoulders. This was a new side to the panther, but I was grateful to see it finally. *We had enough stress in our life than to keep dealing with petty stuff like this.*

Elijah's face soften, and he wrapped his arms around Esme. He whispered something in her ear, and she nodded as he pulled away. The four stood together, forever bound with one another, just like I was with the triplets. We will always have our own thing, but now so will they. It was really cool to see.

Emersyn shifted on her feet as she asked, "So, how does it all work? This is all new to us."

"You need to seal your bond now," I said nonchalantly.

Bastian muttered, "Yeah, then I get to win a bet about them being Fated."

I nudged him slightly. "You seal your bond and then live your lives happily together. Noah has transferred from his Russian clan to the clan here. He's supposed to eventually take over for his father as he's the

CHAPTER 6

rightful heir, and Elijah is Bastian's Beta, as well as a member of our Council."

"Meaning?" Esme asked with less sarcasm and more curiosity. It was still strange not to hear venom spew from her mouth though.

"Meaning, I live here, and Noah lives just over there," Elijah answered, pointing in the direction of the clan. He gently bit his lower lip as the girls realized what he meant.

"We have to move here?" Emersyn asked quietly, grabbing her hair again. "Don't we?"

Elijah nodded slowly. Bastian gave me a worried look.

"Nothing but stress and tension coming down the bond from my brother," he said through our link.

"This is the moment he's been stressing about," Cade chimed in, giving me a grim look as well.

I sighed. The bond has been made with the kiss apparently, but now was time to decide to complete it or not. I didn't see them walking away, but I understood being afraid. I understood not wanting to leave your home and family behind.

"And leave our dad," Esme continued lost in thought.

The girls looked distraught. An awkward silence filled the air, tipping the good mood into a depressing one. *They needed this. They needed to cement the bond before this whole crap with Division got worse.* I couldn't bare the thought of any of them losing their lives because of an incomplete bond distracting them.

I stepped towards the four with an idea. I'll figure out the rest later.

"For right now, it's better that your dad is farther away," I said to the girls. "We can figure everything out when the time comes, but let's just make sure your bond is complete for now. All this is new and exciting, and it's meant to be celebrated. In fact, that's exactly what we're going to do."

"What do you mean?" Esme asked, and I flashed her a smile.

"We're going to celebrate this," I answered. "We'll have a joint party for the four of you, and when all this is said and done with the Division, we can throw something bigger! A wedding if you want."

"Are you sure it's wise to throw a party right now?" Elijah asked, and I gave him a reassuring smile.

"It's just a mini one! Look, we haven't even spoken to Calvin yet, and I will not let the Division keep us from our traditions and happiness. We can't stop living, right?" I countered as everyone mulled over my plan.

It's a good one though, I thought to myself, and I trusted my wolf. She seemed to whole-heartedly agree, so I walked in the middle of the boys and grabbed both girls.

Noah and Elijah snapped to attention, narrowing their eyes and tightening their grip on the girl's hand. I tugged again, rolling my eyes when they still didn't let go.

"Oh my lanta, you two. Let go, and I promise to stay where you can at least see us!" I said firmly. Noah growled, and I scoffed. "Babe!"

Bastian laughed as he approached the fellas. He put his arm around Elijah's shoulder and started pulling back to help me. "Remember how you two made fun of me when I first mated Shanely? It's not as easy as you think, is it?"

Elijah gave him a pointed look but slowly let Emersyn go. Caleb stepped closer to Noah, who barred his teeth.

"God, Noah. Relax some. No one's taking her away like that," Caleb said, laughing. Noah grumbled but finally let go too.

"Where are we going?" Esme asked as I pushed the girls to the porch. I looked back and both boys were staring directly at us with longing in their eyes. When I turned back to the panthers, I noticed they looked just as desperate as the boys. *New mates,* I thought to myself smiling.

"I need to give you a heads up. I figured it all out slowly and sort of along the way, but since you two don't know much about how this works, I thought I'd explain. First off, congratulations on finding your own possessive Alpha!"

Esme stuck her tongue at me as I clapped my hands, and Emersyn giggled, covering her mouth.

"I heard that, Shanie!" Elijah shouted.

"Oh c'mon, you guys," I bellowed. "Give us a minute!"

CHAPTER 6

Bastian, Cade, and Caleb laughed as they pushed the guys behind the truck to give us some privacy. As I turned back to my new family members, I realized something. My family was growing again and becoming extremely diversified. We had a plethora of different shifter kinds now, and I couldn't contain my grin.

"I am really glad I invited you guys to the Summit. Now, I have an even bigger family," I said before hugging them both. Tears filled my eyes, and I furiously tried to blink them away.

"Are we technically related now?" Esme asked, and I rolled my eyes.

"Yes. Your giant brute of a mate is my cousin," I replied, laughing. "Remember, white bear?"

"Oh, yeah. I actually forgot about that," she said, smirking. "You usually use your wolf."

"It's because my wolf is stronger and more dominate within me, but she's there. I promise you," I said, putting my hands on my hips. "Look, you two have officially made the bond. There is no going back, although I doubt your cats would want to at this point."

They looked to one another before matching sly grins appeared on their cheeks. I chuckled.

"That's what I thought. Okay, so here's something that will be the same for you both. Don't be alarmed because it really doesn't hurt that bad, but in order to complete the bond, you mark your mate and vice versa."

"What does marking mean?" Esme asked hesitantly. Her doe eyes looked nervously to the large man behind the truck, trying desperate not to look this way.

"You bite one another," I answered plainly.

"What!" Emersyn shouted.

Elijah bolted around the truck, and I put my hands up, halting him dead in his tracks.

"Oh no," I said, shooing him away. "She's fine, lover boy! Just hang on!"

Elijah gritted his teeth as Cade forcefully pulled him back, grinning the whole way. I straightened my shirt.

"He's going to bite me?" she asked quieter.

I laughed, pulling my hair aside to show them my mark. "Twice actually. Once in his human form, and then again in his wolf form or bear for you, Esme. It solidifies the bond then, and that's where I think your bonds will differ."

"How so?" Esme asked. She leaned into her sister, placing her arms on her shoulders protectively.

"Bastian and I are Fated Mates. We have special abilities along with the White Wolf stuff, and what you have you share with your mate. I gave Bastian his very own bear, changing him into a mixer," I answered.

Emersyn's eyes widened at the tidbit of information. She tugged at the ends of her hair, and I gave her a soft smile.

"Now, you won't have that Emersyn because Elijah is 100% wolf," I said firmly, and she relaxed a little," but the triplets share things closely. Remember when I explained how they care for me? Cade and Elijah love me, but it is different than how Bastian loves me. Cade and Bastian will step in and protect you when Elijah cannot. You and I officially share all three boys now. That will *never* change, so get use to having three Alpha males bossing you around instead of just one."

Esme laughed loudly as Emersyn relaxed against her sister's arms. The corners of her mouth rose as I felt Elijah hover in my mind. When I felt his eyes boring into my soul because he was agitated, I sighed heavily.

New Freaking Mates.

"Let me be clear though, because I can feel Elijah burning holes in the back of my head, you belong *solely* to him," I said, rolling my eyes.

"Happy now?"

"Immensely," he said, and I spat out a laugh.

"Anyways because Bastian and I are Fated, we think you guys will be too. When you mark one another, you're going to feel a stronger connection than Esme will. You're also going to feel his heart beating inside your chest, and it's the same for him."

Emersyn put her hand to her chest. "Really? You feel Bastian's heart beating right now?"

CHAPTER 6

I nodded. "It's how I stayed as calm as I did when he was shot. I could feel it beating the whole time. You are also going to feel what he feels. His anger, panic, jealousy, and pure joy. It's all going to come through, and he will be in tune with you too. Now the last thing, which I don't know if it's a White Wolf thing or a Fated Mate thing, but Bastian and I have been able to touch or kiss one another through the bond, even if we're nowhere near each other."

"Whoa," Emersyn said in awe.

"That can't be!" Esme scowled. I shrugged, turning around to face the boys, who now stood by the tailgate of the truck.

"Watch," I said.

I hadn't done this too often, but I focused on kissing Bastian's cheek through our bond. He startled before slowly looking my way. I smiled as he winked, sticking his tongue at me before turning back to Noah.

"All I see is him looking at you," Esme said, and I rolled my eyes.

"Well you won't see the kiss, but you'll have to trust me, I guess. The point is," I said, turning back to the girls, "this is all normal and honestly rare. I just want you girls to feel happy and enjoy this because finding your mate is an amazing thing."

"What are we going to do though? I can't leave my dad, Shanely. He's not doing that well," Esme said quietly. Her eyes glistened with unshed tears, and my heart broke for them.

"I don't want to make you guys choose between your mate or your dad, but I think you both can feel the answer in your heart. Those two are your other halves, and the idea of leaving them kills you, doesn't it?"

"But so does leaving our father," Emersyn said softly. Her face fell, and Esme wrapped her arms around her sister.

The boys suddenly stopped talking, turning to look at us with concern in their eyes.

"Wow, you weren't kidding," Esme said quietly, and I laughed.

"You get used to it. Look, let me figure out how to deal with your dad. You two just go get your men!"

I gently pushed them forward, but Esme dug in her heels.

"How are you going to fix this though?"

"Not sure," I answered truthfully, "but if there's a way to move your dad closer then I'd like to try. Then you wouldn't have to leave him behind."

A genuine smile rose on her face. "Thank you, Shanely. I'm glad I was wrong about you guys."

I nodded as they turned back to the fellas. Bastian, Cade, and Caleb stepped aside, freeing the two who gave the girls hungry looks. It was borderline wild with their eyes glowing gold and their teeth barred.

The girls stilled, while I struggled to muffle a laugh. I didn't know if it was an Alpha thing or what, but Noah and Elijah both stood in the exact same way, with their arms folded across their chest and their feet spread slightly apart. I decided to give them one last bit of advice.

"Remember girls," I shouted with a ornery smile, "Alpha's love a chase."

I gestured to the woods, and the girls got the idea.

They gave me a wicked smile before shifting perfectly in time with one another. Elijah bounced on his feet, acting more like Cade than ever before, as he waited for Emersyn to make a move. To chase after the girl of his dreams and catch his mate.

The girls moved slowly in sync with one another before they took off in opposite directions. The boys wasted no time in shifting and going after them. Elijah's howl grew quieter as he chased after Emersyn in the woods away from the cabin. Esme had chosen the woods going to the clan's land funny enough. Despite being larger, Noah could really move in his bear form, and soon they were all out of sight. The four of us relaxed then.

"Oh, good lord. That worked out nicely!" Cade said, leaning against the truck.

Caleb ran his hand through his hair, looking at the dent Noah's massive body left. He touched the side of the truck with his eyes wide. "I was in absolute panic when we thought they somehow bonded with the same girl!"

"I know, and this one was trying to get in the middle!" I said, pointing to my mate. "You are still healing by the way! No shifting for at least a couple more days. Remember, the doctor's orders?"

He smiled sheepishly. "Yeah well, my brother needed me."

"Well, I need you too! You need to be completely healed…"

"Oh right!" he interrupted, his eyes glowing as he perked up. "Forget my brother! I'll make sure to heal up as quick as I can for you, baby."

Cade snorted. "Good lord, not this again. C'mon, you two! We need to get to the lodge. I made progress with the other packs, and I was waiting for Bastian before all this started."

I giggled as Bastian glared at the back of his brother's head. He held out his hand, pulling me in. "C'mon baby. Let's follow the fun sucker then."

Cade whipped his head around so fast, glaring at Bastian. No sassy remarks though, and I laughed harder. *Just wait till he finds his mate.*

"You know," I said softly, "Elijah and Noah deserve something grand for this. I know we have too much going on to plan anything major, but it isn't fair to rob them of their celebration just because all this is going on. I don't want to be the reason they miss out."

Bastian rocked his head back and forth thinking. "I know, baby. I like what you're thinking though. Give them something small now, and then we can give them a proper wedding later."

The five of us, including Aerith, made our way to the lodge. Nothing would come close to the news of a new mating, but I was ready to hear some good news when it came to the whole Division thing.

It was seriously stressing me out.

Chapter 7

The projection screen was already down as we strolled into the conference room once more. Angry voices sounded, and I realized we were on a call already. I shot Cade a look.

"My apologies, Alphas," my Beta said as he walked around the table. "We had a small issue that needed to be addressed right away."

"With Calvin?" a deep voice asked as I took my seat. I looked at the screen to find 10 Alphas all sitting and waiting for me and my mate. I recognized a few but narrowed my eyes on some I had no idea who they were. My lips pursed together in a tight line. *I should know this.*

"No, Finn," Cade answered, "just a pack related problem, but the Alphas are here now, and we have some things to discuss."

"That we do," another Alpha said, crossing his arms in a huff. "The Division has gotten out of control, and that was before we knew about your Head and what he's been doing."

"We're sick of being under their thumb anyways," Finn said as the others grumbled in agreement. "They are puny, insignificant humans. Yet we answer to them? I don't think so."

The Alphas all began to speak at once, and I shot Bastian a nervous glance. I hadn't realized there was so much tension with the Division from the other packs. *Have I been so consumed with my own problems that I neglected the packs?*

"What exactly are you dealing with?" Bastian asked. The Alphas quieted down as my stomach twisted in knots.

A tall Alpha with crystal clear blue eyes snorted, and I cocked my head to

CHAPTER 7

the side. I vaguely remembered him from the first Summit. *What was his name? Dan? Dylan? Or was it Dominic? It started with a D.*

"The Division Head for our area is an arrogant fool," he went on, his accent a thick southern drawl. "The condescending tone and derogatory remarks are the least of what my pack deals with, but he demands to walk through my entire land."

Cade's brows furrowed as he asked, "What in the world for? Do you let him, Dylan?"

Dylan! I thought to myself. *I was right!* Dylan looked annoyed as he tossed his hands in the air.

"What else do I do?" Dylan asked with a clipped tone. "He threatens to send in a team if we don't comply. According to him, he's making sure the pack doesn't own anything he deems illegal. He uses that threat for anything he wants really."

"Ours too!" another Alpha bellowed. "To the point that he's using my shifters for his own personal agenda. Just last week, I had to send four men to his home to clear trees that fell in his driveway!"

Bastian emitted a low growl as they all started talking at once again. Tension was strong amongst the Alphas, and I didn't blame them. I'd be pissed too, but something wasn't sitting right with me either. I couldn't shake the fear from the pit of my stomach as I listened to the Alphas vent. I tried pulling on my wolf's instincts, but all I could feel was *worry*. *Was that normal?*

"We should just flat refuse!" Dylan bellowed loudly. "They have no pull over us if we simply stop obeying them."

"We don't need them anyways," another said. "We don't answer to human laws."

"We don't answer to humans!"

The others hollered in agreement, but my eyes widened. My wolf was alert and begging to be let out. *What they wanted... what they were going to do...*

"We can't go to war with them!" I cried out, silencing the room. My hands slammed on the table, and every Alpha turned to me. "You have no idea the damage you will bring to your pack if you do."

Silence filled the room.

"What do you expect us to do, *Queen?*" Finn asked in a clipped tone. "Alpha Bastian was nearly killed, and we all can assume it was the Division. Should we just sit back and wait until they destroy us all?"

My eyes flashed red.

"Careful," Bastian said in a icy tone. "No one is saying we do nothing, but Shanely is right. If we don't do this correctly, then many of our people will die. That's not a risk I want to take."

Everyone dropped their eyes in respect as I gave Bastian a grateful smile. I turned back to Alpha Finn. "There must be another way. I am attempting to go over Patrick and Calvin's head to a man in charge, but it's been difficult to get through to anyone."

"Why do we even need them? Would it be so bad if humans actually knew about us?" a female Alpha asked. *I wish I knew her name.*

"You want to expose shifters to everyone?" Cade asked nervously.

"Just asking," she replied casually. "Personally, I don't see it being a bad thing. Then we wouldn't have a need for the Division at all."

"You have no idea the repercussions of exposing shifter kind to humans would be," Bastian said firmly. "That would be catastrophic to us all."

"So, what *do* we do Alpha," Dylan asked. " We can't just let this go, so how do we fix this?"

I sighed, leaning back in my chair and placing my hand under my chin. *He was right.* We couldn't do nothing, but I was barely figuring out how to handle my issues with Patrick and Calvin. *How can I fight a war on so many fronts?*

"The laws need changed," I said firmly, "but I genuinely feel that it is wise to continue to stay hidden from humans. The issues that would come from it would put us all at risk."

"Until we are able to speak with this Hank guy, I suggest we continue down the path we are on and wait," Bastian continued.

"So we do nothing?!" Finn asked, his eyes widening.

"Look at what I'm dealing with at my pack with Patrick and Shanely,"

CHAPTER 7

Bastian went on as anger laced his tone. "Do you really want to have wars on multiple fronts here? I have a genuine concern that my pack is in danger, that *my mate* is in danger, but I cannot have multiple packs fighting at the same time. I can't be everywhere at once."

Fear wrapped around my heart, twisting into agonizing pain at the thought of Bastian *enlisting*. I don't think I'd survive without him. My father may have the strength to go on, but there was no way I'd live without Bastian.

I looked up to the Alphas again. I opened the mental box I kept of my wolves and pulled on their connections. It was strong, pure. Dylan was down in Alabama. Finn in the U.K. They were all here. All connected to me.

"And the whole point is to try and avoid war," Cade countered.

Suddenly, I felt one of my connections snap in two. I grabbed the ribbon, seeing one of my beloved wolves fade away. Henrick. Age 71. Died in his sleep from old age. And then he was suddenly just gone, leaving the empty spot where his connection should be. My wolf whined within me as tears filled my eyes. Bastian looked my way as I shoved that mental box close. *This is why I don't keep it open all the time.* Loosing a connection was too painful. *If we go to war...*

"I am connected to each and every one of you," I said, silencing the group again. I quickly wiped my cheek, breathing slowly to gain my composure. "The pain I feel when something happened... I don't..."

I closed my eyes as my voice trailed off. Now that I had this power, this control, I couldn't stand the thought of any of my wolves dying.

I had to find Hank.

"What do you need from us?" Dylan asked in a quieter tone. My eyes drifted over to the over-sized Alpha, who was watching me with a hint of sorrow in his eyes. I blinked, appreciating what he was doing.

"We need recruits," Cade answered for me. "We're almost positive it was Patrick who shot Bastian, but we can't prove it. Somehow, Summit Hall was attacked by a lot of people with guns. I fully expect the war to come here. We *must* protect our White Wolf."

"Aye," the Alphas said in unison. My eyes glistened again, and Bastian gave my hand a gentle squeeze.

"Our goal is to avoid war," Bastian said to the group, "but let me be clear. We *will* answer the call if war is what they want."

"Then we will send all we can spare," Finn went on. The other Alphas nodded their head in agreement.

"Thank you," I said, giving them each a grateful smile. "I cannot tell you how much I appreciate everything you are sacrificing for my family. I promise, we will figure this all out and return the favor."

Every Alpha lowered their head in respect before the screen went blank. I sighed, leaning on my husband's shoulder.

"Good work Cade," Bastian said as he rubbed my arm. "It will be wonderful to have the added numbers. Something to keep the Division off my land."

"I just hope they get here in time," Caleb muttered. I felt a little bad, I had forgotten he was here as he stayed utterly silent against the wall. "We have a decent amount with the pack and clan, but everyone has children and families to think about too. Are you really thinking we'll be fighting here? On pack lands."

My heart seized. I can't sacrifice my own pack or clan, especially the ones with families. I couldn't force anyone to take a stand.

I turned to Bastian. "We need volunteers. Not recruits."

Bastian nodded his head in understanding before turning to Cade. "Send word to everyone. The men who wish to volunteer to protect Shanely and this pack, come to the bunkhouse. Those who wish to relocate until this has settled are free to go. I understand needing to protect your mate and children first. All enforcers are getting drafted. This is what they signed up for, and we need them. My *hope* is to reach out to Hank and have Patrick and Calvin removed amongst the other Heads causing trouble, but if this turns into a fight then I want to be prepared."

Cade gave us a swift nod before bolting from the conference room. I dropped my head in my hands, feeling the stress of everything. *This was too much. I wasn't ready for war. I wasn't ready to deal with this kind of responsibility, and with Aerith and the twins in my belly, I don't want any of it.*

CHAPTER 7

Bastian gently rubbed my back, going up and down slowly just like I always liked. It eased the tension building, and I groaned, leaning further into him. He chuckled softly before I felt his warm lips against the side of my head.

"It will be okay, Shanely," he said softly. "I promise you, we will figure this out. We have extra help and more is on the way. They will see they cannot push us over like they think they can, and *no one* is touching you."

I leaned back in my seat and sighed. "But how many of our pack will die protecting me. It feels wrong and..."

My voice trailed off as another tear slid down my cheek. I buried my face once more feeling overwhelmed and exhausted.

"No one is going to die sis," Caleb said firmly. "We will find Hank and work this out. We will figure everything out, and those babies will grow up happy and safe right here at home."

I gave him a weak smile from the corner of my eye, praying he was right. We have to get this sorted because I don't know how much more I could take.

I stood, giving my mate a pat on the back and made my way to the door.

"Where are you going, love?" he asked.

Placing my hand on the door, I said, "To continue making calls. I'm bound to get through at some point."

He gave me a soft smile as I left the room.

Chapter 8

Lieutenant General Hemingway

"Sir?" Amelia said, knocking once on my door.

I set down the file I was reading, giving her a long frustrated look. This secretary had been with me for years. She knew when I didn't want to be disturbed, yet here she stood. *Might have to get a new one.*

Her cheeks reddened as she cleared her throat. "That shifter I told you about is calling again. She wants to talk to you."

I snorted and raised the file once more. "Transfer her to Hank."

"I have sir," Amelia answered, rubbing her hands together nervously. My lip curled in disgust.

"Multiple times," she said nervously, "but Hank is across the sea, and everyone knows how the complaint department operates. She's getting... troublesome."

I rolled my eyes, sinking further into my luxurious cushioned office chair and looking out my massive window. The Colorado mountains weren't too far away, giving me a nice view outside my window. I had moved my department closer to the Research and Development team decades ago, not knowing how much I would come to love this place. I was right at home, but growing weaker by the second. Age was a tiresome thing to deal with as was the shifter who *continued* to annoy me.

"Just transfer her again," I finally answered with a clipped tone. "She'll stop eventually. They all do."

"She doesn't seem like the others sir," Amelia said, and I slowly turned towards her. "She said multiple Alphas have become upset with their

CHAPTER 8

Heads. There's a growing discontentment amongst their kind, sir. I think you should take the call."

My eyes narrowed on the petite woman. Her blonde hair and blue eyes, that were once a bright beautiful color, were now dulling with time. *Another perk of the job, I suppose.* But she was a tough nut, which is why I hired her in the first place. To sort through the endless annoying calls to my department. *If she was worried...*

"Patch her through," I said, rubbing my face. Amelia stepped outside the door, and soon my phone rang.

"This is Dennis Hemingway," I said with a gruff voice. I fully expected an older male's voice to come through the line, but what I did not expect was such a sweet, angelic voice to be on the other end.

"Hello Mr. Hemingway! Thank you for taking the time to speak with me. I'm Shanely Fenrir," she said sweetly. "You are a difficult man to get a hold of."

"Well, you are a persistent person, Miss Fenrir," I said, leaning back in my chair. "What exactly do you need from me?"

"I've tried reaching out to Hank, but no one from that department is answering my calls," Shanely said firmly. "We have a growing problem between us, Mr. Hemingway, and I do not know how to fix this."

"Lieutenant General Hemingway. What's the problem?" I asked. The fainest sigh sounded through the phone.

"Our Heads, *Lieutenant General*," she replied, and I picked up the irritation in her tone. The corners of my mouth rose as she went on, "I've spoken to many Alphas already, and they're all saying the same thing. The Heads assigned to our areas have become difficult and demanding. Threatening to annihilate us if we do not comply. We also have reason to believe that one of your teams attacked us for no reason too."

I frowned, sitting forward in my seat. *If the Alphas were already communicating with one another over this...*

"Do you have proof of this, Miss Shanely?"

"Well no, but..."

I rolled my eyes, plopping backwards again. *And here I thought war was coming.* "Miss Shanely, I am a very busy man, and stuff like this is not even apart of my department. I don't have time for *assumptions*. I only deal with war."

"Lieutenant General Hemingway, I can assure you this is not just an assumption," she said frustratedly, "and if we do not find a solution, I'm afraid war *will* come. While I do not have exact proof of who shot my husband and pack, I can tell you that your Head for Diablo, Washington is way out of line! He's demanding monthly visits instead of yearly and insists that he..."

"Wait, you're the Alpha in Diablo?" I said, my brows knitting in confusion. *That can't be right. I've never heard of a female Alpha before.* I pulled open a metal drawer next to my desk and started searching for the file on Washington state.

"I'm more than just Alpha to the McCoy pack. I'm the White Wolf, head over all wolf shifters," Shanely replied angrily, and my eyes widened, "and I don't appreciate what Calvin's been doing to my pack and family. I don't appreciate hearing what *your* people are doing to the other Alphas either, and I certainly don't agree with the rules we currently have in place. It's time for change."

The White Wolf? Wait, Calvin... That name rings a bell. I flipped through the file quickly while this woman continued to talk, setting the phone on the desk so I wouldn't have to hear her incessant rambling. Last known Alpha to the pack in Diablo was Cain McCoy. Calvin Jennings is the assigned Head. *Ya-da, ya-da, ya...*

I quickly opened the next drawer and searched for his file while she continued to complain about one thing or another. I flipped through Calvin's file, which held everything about the man. From his training results and recommendation from his previous Commander to his yearly evaluations. Basic info really. Behind that was a stack of security measures granted to the man because he's Head for the largest pack in Northern America, and he governs the Bear clan. My eyes widened at the total. *The man charged us a fortune...*

But then I saw a handful of photos underneath all that paperwork, and I

CHAPTER 8

stilled.

"Sir? Are you hearing what I am saying?" Shanely demanded as I stared hard at the photo on top. It was of the annual banquet I had gotten rid of when I assumed Command. Calvin was smiling next to one of the previous Heads, but the woman in the photo with him...

"We need help!" she bellowed in my ear.

My brows knitted in irritation. She was the last person I wanted to deal with right now, but if she was telling the truth, and she was indeed powerful enough to be Head over them all, *then I needed her.*

"The White Wolf you say," I mutter somewhat lost in thought. I had to be careful with how I went about this. I nearly didn't get away with it last time. "Well I'll be honest my dear, that term doesn't really mean anything to me nor would it matter to the rest of the Heads. Now, I'm sure Calvin is handling things the way he should, and any issues should be brought before him. Not me."

"But he's the problem!" she bellowed again, and I turned to look out my window. The Research and Development building was a five minute walk from here. *This could work. It could work, and maybe this time not be spoiled by arrogant do-gooders.*

I slowly extended out my hand, seeing my wrinkled skin stretch and ache. *Arthritis struck me hard, but if I could make this work...*

"Alright Miss," I said, turning back around and smiling, "I'll see what I can do."

Her silence didn't concern me in the slightest. She was thinking, processing everything like the cunning wolf I assume her to be. If she was indeed Head over all the wolves, then her power is what I needed. I would become strong again. The United States Army would become invincible, and *my men* would lead the charge. This couldn't have come at a better time too. *We needed a leg up on the world. On the monsters who live here.*

"Thank you," she finally said, and I smiled wide.

"Absolutely," I answered. "Now, I will reach out if I need anymore information. Take care now."

I hung up on the shifter before she could say anything more. I picked up the file once more and dialed another number. On the fourth ring, he answered.

"This is Calvin Jennings."

"Calvin!" I said cheerfully. "This is Lieutenant General Dennis Hemingway. How are you doing today?"

He paused. I grinned wide, enjoying that I caught the man off guard. I could hear a shuffling of papers in the background as he gained his composure.

"Hello sir," he said, clearing his throat. "I didn't expect a call from you. We don't report in for another week."

"Yes, yes, I realize that, but you have a very large area to maintain," I said still smiling. "I just like to check in, especially when I receive calls from shifters in your area, complaining over the way you are handling things."

Silence. Absolute silence as the man scrambled to figure out what to say. I just let him stew. I could care less about the complaints, but I needed to light a fire under the man. He's obviously doing something to piss off the locals. I just needed grounds to go in, and this man was going to give it to me. Although, I'd doubt he'd do anything for me if he knew the truth.

"How did they even manage to reach you?" he finally asked.

"Does that little detail really matter, Calvin?"

"No sir," he said with a sigh. "I have handled everything the way I've been directed."

"Oh, I don't doubt that, my boy!" I replied. "However, I don't appreciate getting house calls. My division is busy enough keeping our nation safe from shifters and humans alike. Whatever is going on in Washington must be dealt with and quickly."

"What would you like me to do then?" he asked. I could hear the irritation in his voice. The disrespect he was trying so hard to keep to himself. Calvin was a good solider. Always had been. The fact that he never knew what happened with his wife was comical to say the least, but he was going to help me finish her work. I was finally going to get what I wanted all along. *What this country needed.*

CHAPTER 8

"Investigate the McCoy pack. Use the drones, the ornithopters you ordered in that last request, whatever you need to see what's going on down there. I don't care how you do it, just get me the information I need or I'll send a team if you can't. That shifter mentioned war, and I need to know if this is an issue that needs taken care of or not. I want a detailed report sent to me right away, and you will check in with me daily until this is resolved. We cannot let the shifters run amuck. Do we understand?"

"I do sir," he said quietly. "Can I ask who in the McCoy pack called you?"

I leaned back in my chair again. *It wouldn't hurt, I suppose. It's not like he knows how important she is to me.*

"Shanely Fenrir. Claims to be the Alpha," I answered with a clipped tone, "which was news to me."

He got my point as he sighed into the receiver.

"Consider it done, sir. I promise you, she will *not* be bothering you again."

"Just get me answers, Calvin," I commanded. "I don't care about the rest."

"Yes, sir."

I hung up on the Head and dialed one last person. *Everything was coming together rather nicely, I had to admit.* They didn't take long to answer, and I turned my chair to face the Research building once more.

"We may have an opportunity."

Chapter 9

Shanely

"You've done everything you could, baby," Bastian said as we ended another disappointing conference call with more disgruntled Alphas. Our entire council was here, other than Abey and Bay, but everyone seemed to be in the same mood as I was. "Unless Hank calls back, we just got to wait for that Dennis to get to the bottom of everything."

I sighed heavily. It had only been a few days since my conversation with one of the top people in the Division, but I couldn't shake that awful feeling in the pit of my stomach. I chalked it up to the stress of everything, but that man gave me the creeps.

"There must be something more we can do," I said, looking to my mate.

"What else is there?" Cade asked. "We've already received the first batch of enforcers. Bay and Abraham have been discretely guiding the pack to their home already, and we continue to run constant patrols around the lodge and cabin."

I sighed again. "I don't know. I just... I feel like..."

"You're antsy," Bastian said with a grin. "You need to just focus on something positive, Shanely. Like the party."

I perked up then. "Oh right... We've got a lot to do before tomorrow."

"You guys seriously don't have to throw us anything," Elijah said, blushing. "We've got enough to deal with. It can wait."

"No," I protested, jutting out my bottom lip, "I want to! Besides, we fully plan to give you a proper reception once this has been sorted, but this is special! We can't do nothing, Elijah."

CHAPTER 9

"Yeah but..."

"No buts," Bastian said, patting his brother on his back. "You and Emmie deserve this, and besides, this gives Shanely something positive to do. It's taking her mind off all this stressful crap, which is better for her and the twins. Just say thank you, and let it go."

I grinned wide as Elijah rolled his eyes.

"Well thank you, Shanie," he said, and I got up to hug him.

"Of course!" I said, squeezing him tightly. "We wouldn't miss this for the world!"

"Calvin's inbound."

The four of us stilled.

"Was that Brody?" I asked as Bastian pulled me towards the door.

"Is he alone?"

Bastian's voice boomed through the pack in a hive message. Everyone was listening in now.

"He is," Brody answered. *"In an unmarked police cruiser. I'm tailing him now."*

"Good work, Brody. Stay with him. I want another team in the surrounding woods, and someone get the group from Summit Hall. Send them to me at the lodge. I'll wait for him there."

"Yes, sir." A collective answer came through the link as the enforcers did what they were told. I wish the rest of the wolves would arrive already. There was safety in numbers, and I hated not feeling like we had enough.

We stepped out onto the porch just as a small car came into view down the long drive. My mate was already angry and kept his hand on the belt loop of my pants.

"It isn't a scheduled visit," Elijah said nervously. "What could he possibly want now?"

Bastian's icy glare stared straight down the drive. The fact that he left that question unanswered made me nervous. Bastian always knew what to do. Always knew what to say or how to handle things, but he didn't answer his brother.

The car's tire crunched against the gravel drive as Calvin's Corolla slowly parked before us. I watched the lanky man open his door and step in front of his vehicle. No one said a word for a moment. Even the forest fell silent as if waiting for the worst to happen. My heart slowly began to race.

"We need to talk, Bastian," Calvin finally said.

"Not really sure what's left to say, Calvin," my mate replied, taking a step down the stairs. He stopped on the last step.

"Oh, there's plenty, my boy!" Calvin said with an icky smile. "Starting with why you felt the need to go over my head and talk to my boss."

I snorted. *This is what he's pissed about?*

"Well," I said, stepping towards my mate, "talking to you is just pointless, isn't it?"

Calvin slowly dragged his eyes to mine. "That wasn't a very smart thing to do, Shanely. I've been rather lenient with you all, but now I've got to change everything. My boss is very interested in the McCoy pack now, and I've been asked to investigate further. Dennis is very *concerned* with the lot of you because you threatened war."

My heart sunk. "But I…"

My voice trailed as I looked to my feet. I scrambled to go back over every detail of the conversation again in my head. *I didn't… I mean I didn't mean to… Oh, God. This was all my fault, wasn't it?* My face paled as I looked to my mate.

"I'm so sorry," I said through the link. *"This is my fault. I didn't mean to, but he's right. I did say war would come."*

Bastian stepped in front of me protectively, growling low at our guest. "There is nothing to worry about when it comes to my pack. You cannot continue to bend the laws to benefit you, Calvin. You are abusing my wolves, and I have had enough!"

"Nothing to worry about?" Calvin challenged. "I've noticed a lot of new faces around here, Bastian. More and more continue to trickle in as well, coming in through the backside to avoid town. You've changed your patrols up too, and even the bears are behaving differently. That's enough to cause concern for our Lieutenant General. Care to explain why you seem to be building a small army?"

CHAPTER 9

My husband stilled. Surprise filled my core briefly as my mate processed everything. I slowly looked to the rest standing with us. They looked ready to shift and fight, and fear gripped my heart. I don't want anyone to get hurt. I slowly looked back to my mate.

"Not unless you can tell me how you seem to know what's always happening on my land. Like you said, we haven't been parading anyone around town," Bastian snidely responded, and my eyes widened. *I didn't even think of that. How did Calvin know?*

"And what our Alpha demands of his wolves are of no concern to you," Elijah chimed in with a low growl.

"So what exactly have you been doing, Calvin? How have you been keeping tabs on us?" Cade asked, stepping closer to me.

The triplets stood protectively around me, while my stomach twisted in knots. *How does he know so much? Oh God... What else does he know?*

Calvin stared at them for a moment. "How we keep tabs on you people is our business. By law, I don't have to tell you anything. Ever since you two came into power, you've been nothing but trouble, and the Division doesn't like that."

"We've done nothing against the law," Bastian said firmly. "It's you and your son that's the problem!"

Calvin glared. "You have no proof of anything. You're the one recruiting shifters and building an army, and she's the one who threatened war against our Lieutenant General! All this is happening because of you."

"That's a lie, and you know it!" Cade shouted angrily.

Everyone began shouting at once then. Some barely holding back the shift as they yelled at Calvin. He didn't seem fazed, but my heart raced. This had gone from bad to worse. War didn't just seem like a possibility anymore. It seemed imminent.

I took Bastian's hand in mine and squeezed. I know he could feel the trepidation coming through the bond from me. I couldn't keep my panic from trickling over to him even if I tried, and even my wolf seemed quiet inside me. Bastian just seemed the total opposite of me. I got nothing through the bond from him, and I wondered how in the world he could do this? *How can he handle this without freaking out?*

My mate raised his hand, silencing the group at once. No one spoke for a moment, and I gripped Bastian's hand tighter.

"Care to explain where Patrick was a couple weeks ago?" Bastian asked calmly.

Calvin's eye narrowed. "He was training with me. Had him on a training exercise near Bellingham."

Cade threw his hands up as everyone snarled.

"Yeah... We don't believe you," Bastian replied, pulling his shirt to the side and showing the bandage.

Calvin's lips pursed together, and I saw the wheels turning in his mind.

"Looks painful, Bastian. You really should learn to be more careful," Calvin said with a sly grin.

Elijah growled. "Your douche of a son shot my brother!"

My wolves snarled angrily, stepping closer to the lanky human. Calvin staggered back, raising his hands defensively. "I won't allow you to blame my son for an injury he didn't cause! I'm starting to feel a little threatened and..."

"Not yet, you aren't," Bastian snarled, letting me go and stepping off the porch. "You haven't begun to feel truly threatened by me."

My mate rolled his shoulders, clenching his fists together tightly as he stalked towards the man who had been a thorn in our side since the beginning. *He might just kill him,* I thought anxiously as I looked to my mate.

"You don't want to go down this road with me, Bastian Fenrir!" Calvin shouted nervously as he rushed backwards to his car door. Fear gripped my heart as the dark fur of Bastian's wolf appeared on his forearms.

"Actually, I kinda do," Bastian growled, when a deep voice startled us.

"Now Calvin," Uncle Cain said as he walked around the corner, "you and I both know how dumb your son can be."

The group stilled as our old Alphas returned, and I sagged in relief. Cassia was right behind him followed by my Uncle Ash and Aunt Deidre. They all had dark circles under their eyes, and my heart hurt. *I should have been*

CHAPTER 9

there for them too.

Ash's eyes flashed bright gold, and he looked outright feral as he stared at Calvin. I think the only thing keeping his wolf in check was his mate. She was holding his hand with a death grip.

"Cain," Calvin said, letting go of the car handle. "I didn't expect to see you today."

"Yeah well..." Cain said, looking to his mate and Ash, "we've had some personal things to attend too."

"Like the burial of my brother and his mate," Ash snarled, his wolf pulling through his voice heavily. My eyes widened slightly.

"I've got him, Shanely," Aunt Deidre said through the link. I gave her a grateful nod.

"I didn't know he died," Calvin said quietly. "My condolences."

Bastian's anger flooded my veins, and I quietly stepped down to meet him. I took his hand in mine again, hoping to keep him from shifting. I gave him a firm look.

"We need everyone to calm themselves while we sort this out, and that starts with us," I said through the link. His eyes drifted to mine. *"Please, Bastian."*

His deep sigh was the only response I got, but his eyes shifted back to normal. I kissed his hand before turning back to Calvin, but he no longer seemed interested in talking to us. He had practically turned his back to my mate and I to talk to Uncle Cain.

My wolf didn't like that one bit.

"Cain, we need to discuss some things. The Division has not been happy with the McCoy pack lately, and there has been quite a bit of talk of taking care of the problem. I think everyone here knows what that means too. I came here myself to see if we can strike a deal, but there's no reasoning with these two. I've gotten nothing but threats and accusations. However, I am willing to overlook that and help you all out *if* you agree to my terms."

Everyone froze.

"A deal?" I asked my mate nervously, but he didn't answer. He simply glared at Calvin as my mind began to run amuck with all the possible things he could want from us, but when Bastian's anxiety trickled into me, my whole body began to panic. Even my wolf whined within me.

"Are you telling me war is coming?" Cain asked gruffly.

Calvin simple shrugged, gaining his confidence again. "I cannot confirm nor deny anything, you know that. We both know how these things go, especially since that one over there called Dennis directly. She told him *all* about the disgruntled Alphas who are pissed with their Heads and threatened war. He's asked me to investigate, Cain."

"What exactly do you want?" Bastian asked. His grip on my hand tightening to the point it hurt.

Calvin shifted on his feet as the stale stench of fear filled the air. I wrinkled my nose, realizing it was coming from Calvin. He inhaled deeply, squaring his jaw and trying to seem more confident than he was. *This was bad. Whatever he wanted was bad.*

"Now I want you all to seriously think about the consequences of what will happen without my help," he said firmly as he adjusted the sleeves on his shirt, "and I will *only* help if I get what I want. Or rather what my son wants."

I blinked. *He wasn't asking what I thought he was, was he?* I stepped backwards in disbelief. Both my bear and my wolf were instantly alert and on edge and nobody said a word.

"My son has this crazy fixation with that one," he said, pointing to me, and my heart sunk. "Give her up, and I make sure Dennis and the Division goes away. Otherwise, you can all be slaughtered for all I care."

Silence filled the air as my heart raced. Either give myself up or send my people to war. *Those were the only two options I had?!*

Bastian suddenly roared, yanking his hand away from mine as he stormed towards Calvin. Cade and Elijah rushed after him, grabbing Bastian by the collar and struggling to keep him back.

"You are demanding that I give up my wife to your prick of a son, or you'll kill my pack!? Is that what I'm hearing?!" Bastian bellowed. Cade and Elijah slid further in the dirt as Bastian pulled harder.

"I don't know why, but he wants her," Calvin went on. "The Division knows all about the laws you've broken, and they're ready to do something about it. Now I can fix this boy, but you have to let her go right now."

"You can't be serious!" Cade snarled back.

"We haven't broken any laws! And do not forget Patrick is human! It's against your own law for him to even be with Shanely!" Cain shouted viciously.

"That's not what my reports show," Calvin said casually. "I'd think long and hard about this one fellas. Dennis is a pit bull, and he's gotten himself involved now. He's a military man first and foremost, and he has no issues slaughtering someone *who gets in his way.* Because of Shanely's phone call, he doesn't trust wolf shifters anymore. Especially when their so called Alpha mentions war. She is just one girl. Is she really worth more than everyone else's lives?"

All eyes settled on me. Not a sound happened other than Bastian's ragged breath, and for a moment I was afraid the new shifters here were contemplating giving me up. I didn't want to be the cause of anyone else's death, but the thought of walking away with this man right now sickened me. Walking towards Calvin, Patrick, and a life I wasn't meant to lead just about did me in. I didn't mean to threaten war with Dennis. I was just trying to avoid it, but look where that got me. I looked at my feet in shame. A good leader would give herself up for her people, yet here I was acting like a coward who's too afraid to go.

I shut down my bonds, pulling my shame and despair away from those I loved most, and Bastian turned to face me. I could feel his eyes searching mine, feel his wolf trying to understand, but I wouldn't look at him. I couldn't stand to see the disappointment in his eyes for not offering myself to save our family. My wolf snarled within me desperate to be let go, but I held her in. Even if we killed Calvin like my wolf wanted to, Dennis would still come for us. For my pack and children. *I should go. I should step in front and save everyone...* But I just couldn't move my feet.

Bastian roared viciously, startling us all. My eyes widened when he shifted into his dark wolf. Calvin flung backwards, landing his butt on the gravel drive as Bastian stalked towards him.

Bastian's fangs were exposed and his ears back. His eyes were blood red and saliva dripped off his jaw as he snapped his teeth at the wicked man. Calvin paled, draining his face from any tiny bit of color.

To my surprise, Cade shifted next, and then Elijah. Caleb followed suit, and then Noah. They stood in a line with Bastian, snarling at Calvin. A line in front of me.

The newcomers stepped off the porch and shifted as well. Calvin scurried to his feet as the lions roared, and the panthers stalked towards him, hissing as they went. The anaconda sisters slithered around our group, making their way slowly to his car.

I stood in awe behind a wall of shifters. There was no way Calvin could come close to me. Not without losing a limb *or his life* in the process.

Suddenly, Khalan dove between my legs and hauled me into the air on his shoulders. My heart dropped into my stomach when he gripped my legs and shifted into his large African Elephant. I barely caught my balance as he blew his trunk, stomping in place with his large tusks swinging in the air.

The anaconda sisters slithered back towards us and up his legs, wrapping themselves around his tusks. My eyes widened as I looked to everyone. *They were choosing me...* They were choosing the threat of war *for me.* My heart melted just a little.

"We are done, Calvin!" Cain shouted, standing in front of Khalan and I. "We have lived in peace with humans since the wars, but what you're asking is unacceptable and disgusting! You are no longer allowed on my lands, and if you or your son so much as looks in Shanely's direction, then we *will* go to war. NOW GET OFF MY LAND!"

Bastian and the other wolves howled in the air as a single tear slid down my cheek. *I didn't deserve these people.*

Calvin glared back at us before scrambling to his door. "You just made the worst mistake of your life."

He slammed his door shut as Bastian lunged and finally drove off pack lands. For the first time since this all started, I felt free. Like a weight was lifted from me, and I could breathe again. We stood our ground, and we won.

CHAPTER 9

I gently scratched behind Khalan's floppy ears, which he seemed to enjoy. Although, I wasn't quite sure as this was the first elephant shifter I had ever been around. Everyone shifted back but Khalan. I leaned over on his head and grinned down at everyone. The anaconda sisters had shifted back too but stayed on Khalan's tusk, leaning back against him in a casual manner.

"Not gonna lie," I said, biting my lower lip, "everyone's silence had me worried a little bit."

"Nah, we like you too much, Baby Girl," Cade said as everyone laughed.

"You gonna come down yet, mate?" Bastian asked, moving his hand to shield his eyes from the setting sun.

"I don't know," I said, grinning. "I kind of like it up here!"

Bastian grinned and shook his head. Khalan started moving, and I shrieked. His large legs shifting awkwardly around the others, and my eyes widened as I let out a belly laugh.

"Aww Khalan, you're such a softie," I said, rubbing behind his ears again. He shook them, making me giggle. This quiet man, who looked angry all the time with his natural scowl and dark features, was really a gentle giant deep down. The girls stayed on his tusks, laughing the entire time Khalan gave us a ride.

"You guys came back," Bastian said, shaking my uncle's hand. Cain sighed before staring down the empty drive.

"I'm sorry we weren't here sooner," Ash replied. Sorrow filled my heart as he dropped his gaze.

"You guys are here now. That's all that matters," Bastian said firmly, clasping Ash's shoulder. The two silently nodded to one another, saying something in that one look they both seemed to understand.

Cain said quietly, "I'm sorry you've been left to deal with this alone."

"We're Alpha now, Cain. At some point, we have to figure this out. I've handled everything the way Ash and..." my mate gave Ash a look before continuing, "Aspen taught us. I've doubled the patrols and secured the lodge, and we've got a small number of wolves here already. The pack is moving to Abe's, and soon more wolves will be here to help too."

"Good," Cain said, patting him on the back. "Have you mentally prepared yourself for war though? This seems unavoidable."

His gaze drifted to me.

My heart sunk as Bastian stood at attention. Much like the way he used to when he was Cain's personal enforcer. "I have. My brothers and I will fight to protect our pack."

My bear snarled within me, and my hand shot in the air.

"As will I!" I shouted. Panic flashed in my mate's eyes, but I glared down at him. My bear chuffed, pleased with our decision to protect our mate and pack. "Bastian, you fight, I fight. Simple as that."

"At some point, Shanie," Elijah interrupted, "you won't be able to fight. The twins will bar you from shifting."

My hand slowly fell. I hadn't thought about that. I had maybe a month left. *What was I to do then?*

"You need a contingency plan in place if that day comes. Shanely may need to go into hiding," Cain said firmly, and I shot him a glare. "Like it or not, my niece, they are right. Get something in motion if this happens when she's far enough in her pregnancy that she can't fight. But figure out a way to be okay with her fighting, boys. She's the White Wolf, and she has the most power between us all."

The four of us looked to one another. No one looked very happy, but there was no getting around this one though. If I could fight, then I would. *But what if I couldn't shift anymore?* My heart swelled with sadness, and my wolf pushed her thoughts to me then. I sighed, feeling some weight lifting off me again. Even if I couldn't shift, I would find a way to keep them safe. *I had to.*

"Now hopefully my contact in the Division will help deter Dennis a bit," Cain said as he made his way to the porch steps.

"What do you know of Dennis?" Elijah asked.

Cain shrugged. "Not much. He's Head over Homeland Security and is a decorated military man. His department extends into the human armies as well as the Shifter Division, but shifters primarily deal with Hank and his department. Dennis is only called in when acts of war have happened, which we have not done. The fact that Dennis wants Calvin to investigate

CHAPTER 9

is concerning."

"I'm sorry, Uncle," I said softly. "I did what I thought was right."

He gave me a soft smile. "Shanely, we've done nothing wrong here. Even if Calvin investigates, what is he going to find? They have no grounds to do anything here."

"Will Hank be able to fix this?" Bastian asked sternly.

"If anyone can help us avoid a fight, it's Hank. Just reaching him can be the issue. He handles International and Internal Affairs, so he goes all over the world. To be on the safe side, we need to keep prepping for a war. I may know Calvin, but Patrick is unpredictable," Cain said firmly. He turned to the enforcers waiting for orders. "I want everyone pulled in close to the lodge and Shanely's cabin. Double the patrols here for now. Our land is too massive to cover everything, and I don't want what forces we do have spread thin. Stay out of town as well. We've got enough to hunker down for a bit."

Everyone departed at that, all with jobs to do. Khalan finally shook his head gently, and the twins hopped off before thanking him. He slowly walked over to Bastian and shifted again. It was abrupt, and I screamed as I fell, my stomach lurching into my throat. Khalan caught me in his arms like I weighed nothing, and Bastian gave him a frustrated look, but once I started laughing uncontrollably, he softened.

Khalan grinned wide as he set me down. "Until next time, Shanely."

"Thank you!" I shouted as he followed the twins into the house. Bastian pulled me to the side, and my smile fell when I saw his face turn all broody again.

"What's with you closing your bonds?" he asked quietly.

"I was ashamed," I whispered truthfully. "I should put my family and pack first as Alpha, but I didn't, and I just feel like a coward. I just…"

I stepped away as that awful guilt came back. It was easy to get distracted riding around on Khalan's elephant, but now that the fun and games were gone, that awful, nagging guilt just ate at me. I turned back to face my mate and sighed.

"I didn't want you to feel that. You and your brothers are made to be

Alpha," I said quietly, "and I didn't want to be the only coward."

Bastian's eyes softened as he reached for me, kissing my cheek and holding me close. My heart warmed at his touch, and I felt his love and reassurance pour into me.

"You are not a coward, love," he said, kissing me gently again. "You do everything for your pack and family, and you are the Alpha they need right now. Not me. My wolf is hot-headed and aggressive, and what the pack needs is peace. They need a leader that will make that happen, which is you. I'm here to protect you, and there was no way I'd allow you to accept his deal, Shanely."

"And neither would we," Cade said through the link. I looked to my left to find both him and Elijah glaring at me through the window of the lodge. I pursed my lips together. *Eavesdroppers.*

"I just feel like I'm putting myself before everyone else," I said, pulling away to look in Bastian's eyes. "What if something happens..."

"Nothing's going to happen, love," he said firmly. "I promise you. So please don't stress over it. We're doing everything we can to keep both you and the pack safe."

Bastian pulled me back in, and I rested my head on his chest. I inhaled deeply, trying to force myself to relax and let go of the guilt. But when my eyes found my Uncle Ash just staring at the long drive, it only worsened.

Ash moved, heading straight back into the woods instead of joining everyone else inside. My Aunt Deidre sighed before taking off after him. I gently pulled away from Bastian to hug my Aunt Cassia. She had tears in her eyes as she watched her brother shift into his wolf and gave me a weak smile before going inside.

I turned to Uncle Cain. "How are you guys? Honestly."

"It was difficult, but we'll make it," he answered before giving his mate a brief look. He sighed when she went straight towards a spare room. He turned to us then. "Alright, somebody fill me in on the rest of what's going on. I want to know every detail!"

The three of us were the last to enter the lodge. Everyone was busy with a job already, and another twinge of guilt hit me as I didn't have anything

CHAPTER 9

to do. *I needed to do more.*

"Elijah and Noah found their mates," Bastian said casually.

"Well congratulations, my boy!" Uncle Cain said, clasping Elijah's hand and smiling at my new sister-in-law, "and to you, my dear. Shall we head into the conference room then?"

"Sure thing," Elijah said, whistling once. Everyone stopped to look at him. "Council members in the conference room. Now!"

I took a step towards the conference room, when I realized the triplets weren't moving. Everyone had filed out of the room except them, and I ground to a stop. My brows rose slightly as I scurried back over to them.

"I already know what you're thinking," Elijah said, crossing his arms, "and I want in."

"Me too," Cade said firmly, and I shot my husband a look. His eyes were glossed over, and I tugged on his arm.

"What's going on?" I asked nervously.

"I want to go tonight," my mate said as he wrapped his arm around my waist. "Will that work for the both of you?"

"Wait, go where?" I demanded.

A group of enforcers came through, and we scooted off to the kitchen to get out of their way. The kitchen was in full swing preparing the evening meal, but the sound of the blender grated on my ever-loving nerves. The boys still weren't answering my questions either, and I tugged on Bastian's arm again.

"Go where?" I asked with a clipped tone.

"Night ops, Baby Girl," Cade said grinning. "We're going to scope out pack lands."

My eyes widened. "Wait, why?"

"Because something isn't right," Bastian answered as my brother Caleb walked over. He handed my mate a large pink smoothie, who promptly pushed it into my hands.

"Here," Bastian said, "you need to drink this. The boys are taking too much again, and you're going to get sick."

"Bastian, I feel fine!" I protested as my stomach growled. I rolled my eyes when a smirk appeared on my mate's face, and I took a small sip. I nearly melted on the spot. *I didn't even know Caleb could make smoothies like this.*

"Thank you, Caleb," I said, earning a wink from him.

"I want to go out late tonight," Bastian said once more. "Caleb is staying with Shanely."

Caleb tossed his arm over my shoulders, grinning wickedly. "Just you and me, *Baby Girl.*"

Cade slugged him as my brother laughed hysterically.

"We'll be ready," Elijah said, rolling his eyes at the two. "Can Emmie stay with them too?"

Bastian nodded as I put my hand up to halt them before they continued on.

"Wait, just one moment now. Why exactly are you *scouting* pack lands?" I asked, placing my hand on my hips. "And why can't I come with? Why do I have to stay with Caleb?"

"Calvin knows things he shouldn't, and I want to know how," Bastian said quietly. "And you are pregnant, and it's still cold out. You need to rest and work on the dinner for Elijah and Noah. I just want to take a quick look around anyways."

"Bastian..."

He kissed my cheek. "Please, love. Just stay here with Caleb and Emmie. We'll all be fine, but I *need* to know. If they have cameras or something on my land..."

We all grew quiet as that sickening thought settled on us. Bastian sighed, rubbing his face as his stress and anxiety coursed through my veins. The fight just died within me then.

"We'll be ready," Cade said, patting his brother on the back. Bastian gave them a grateful nod as they turned to leave.

"I'm staying at the lodge tonight, so I've got the girls whenever you need to leave," Caleb said before chasing after Cade and Elijah.

Bastian watched the three walk towards the conference room solemnly. *He shouldered too much,* I thought before reaching over and kissing his

CHAPTER 9

cheek.

He blinked before the corners of his mouth rose, and he pulled me in close. There was no point trying to sway his mind or convince him to take me with. He was determined to do this, and he was right. We needed to know, and with everything left to do, it was time to trust one another to do what they had to. Bastian would be better at seeing what shouldn't be there on pack lands, and I had about a thousand different things to work on between the dinner and calling Abe for another favor.

"I've missed you, Shanely," Bastian said softly as his lips met mine.

"I've missed you too," I replied, smiling.

"The second I'm recovered, I'm dragging you to our spot," he said softly. My brow rose as he opened the pack fridge and pulled out a water bottle.

"Our spot?" I asked, cocking my head to the side.

"You know..." he said with a wicked smile. "Where those two were conceived."

My cheek's instantly heated as a few ladies snickered quietly in the kitchen. My mouth dropped as he winked at me.

"Bastian!"

"What?" he asked playfully.

I couldn't speak. I just stood there in disbelief at the fact that he actually said that. *In front of people.*

I stomped my foot, turning on my heels and stormed towards the conference room.

"Now we're even, mate!"

Chapter 10

Bastian

"What exactly are we looking for?" Elijah asked as we stepped outside the lodge. The cold air hitting me square in the chest. It was already dark outside, but I didn't mind. *It would make things easier anyways.*

I had made Shanely stay put at the lodge with her brother, and I could still feel her frustration coursing through my veins. *Although, that could be for the comment I made in front of the other ladies in the kitchen.* A sly smile formed on my face. It was only fair after the absolute torture she gave me this morning, but either way I didn't want her out tonight. My animals were on edge ever since Calvin showed up and demanded I hand over *my wife.*

"Whatever doesn't belong," I answered, rolling my shoulders. My wolf was itching to be released. "Calvin knows what's happening on my land, and I want to know how."

"Patrols have never picked up on anything," Cade said, straining his eyes to look into our woods. "Nobody's been out here, Bastian. There's not even a scent to follow."

"But he *knows*," I countered. "Calvin knows, and I need to know how. Let's just go. The faster we do this, the faster I get back to Shanely."

They grumbled but followed me into the woods anyways. I shifted into my wolf, shaking out its fur as my paws dug into the earth. It felt good to be in his skin again, despite my throbbing shoulder. I honestly should have given it another day before shifting, but this was too important to delegate. *I need to see this through myself.*

CHAPTER 10

"Between the three of us," Cade said as his wolf slowly approached, "I'm sure we will figure this out."

"Patrols are out in sets of three like Cain suggested. Two near the lodge and one by your cabin," Elijah said, coming up on my right. I scanned the woods, pulling on Shanely's shared ability to see the pack.

"Good. Everyone is doing good," I said proudly.

"So where do we start?" Cade asked. "Pack territory is large, Bastian."

"Let's just run through where patrols were working before. We'll start further out and work our way in," I answered before taking off towards the west.

My brothers followed closely as we ran towards the outer perimeter.

"How are the new recruits doing?" Elijah asked.

"Fine. The wolves are used to it. You've been to one pack, you've been to them all," I said, leaping over a fallen log. Pain struck my shoulder, and I bit down on my inner cheek to keep from groaning about it.

"And the non-wolves?" Elijah asked. "Emersyn said things have been tricky."

I sighed heavily. "James and Mark have been running with the enforcers along with Scout near the cabin. Lions and leopards don't move the way wolves do, so it's an adjustment. Nathara and Havu have been training with Khalan closer to the lodge, but they're holding their own."

"At least it's not tense," Cade chimed in, silencing our conversation from there. We ran the long way around pack lands, and my eyes strained in the dark, trying to find anything amiss. Anything out of place, but the longer we ran the more frustrated I became. Nothing was different. *It was still the same old woods that I grew up in.* Nothing was here.

But something had to be, I thought. We passed by that haunted spot where I nearly lost my mate to her prick of an ex, when Cade's voice bellowed in my mind.

"Bastian!"

I slid to a stop, turning to find his wolf bouncing in place near a large tree.

"Over here!"

Cade bounded around the tree before putting his front paws on the trunk. I bolted back to him.

"What is it?" I asked.

"Look up," he replied. "I think I found something that doesn't belong."

I shifted back, wincing as my shoulder ached in pain, and craned my neck to look up where my brother pointed. A medium-sized bird was perch in its nest on a branch, and I turned back to my brother. My brow rose as the bird chipped.

"What am I looking at?" I asked as Cade as Elijah bolted back and shifted.

"Thanks for letting me know we stopped by the way," Elijah muttered.

Cade rolled his eyes. "I've passed by this tree like three times already, and I keep hearing that stupid bird. It's driving me crazy."

Elijah gave me a look, and I shrugged.

"So?" I muttered.

"So..." Cade said, gripping my chin and forcing my head to look up again, "that bird right there is a Hermit Thrush. A bird that should have migrated south awhile ago."

I slowly looked to Elijah, who's shoulders shook with silent laughter. Amusement flashed on his face as I tried to hold in a snicker too.

"Okay..." I finally said, and Cade gave me an annoyed look.

"Bastian, look at the bird. Notice anything odd?" he asked, placing his hands on his hips. "Besides the fact that *this* bird shouldn't be here."

I sputtered out a laugh as I looked up again. The bird didn't move. It just sat there on its nest looking out into the forest, and I turned back to Cade.

"Cade, I don't understand..."

"It's beak doesn't move!" he bellowed, shoving my head up again. The bird sounded its call, and my eyes widened when the bird sat frozen on its perch.

"See?!" Cade shouted as Elijah stepped closer.

"Well, I'll be..." Elijah muttered. "I thought you were just crazy, Cade, but I've never actually seen one in real life."

"It's not crazy to have a hobby," Cade muttered. I ignored him and turned to Elijah.

"What is it?" I asked, putting my hands on my hips.

"I saw a demonstration of one on social media years ago. Some ex military dude was walking through a discreet surveillance system and what they use in certain factions of the human military. It's a miniature biomimetic ornithopter," Elijah replied, and I slowly raised my eyebrow. "A camera, Bastian."

My eyes widened. I turned to Cade. "Get it down now."

My brother bolted up the tree as my heart thundered in my chest. *I was right*, I thought as my hands clenched into a tight fist. *Eyes were on us already, and I wanted this off my land. Now!*

"It's like bolted down," Cade said as he tugged on the fake bird.

"How did they managed to get this on our land?" Elijah asked as my anger rose within.

"I don't know," I gritted through my teeth.

"We were only gone for the Summit," my brother suggested, and I swore under my breath. *They came when no one was around. They must have... Or are they somehow getting past my wolves?*

A loud crack sounded, and Cade bellowed, "Bombs away!"

Elijah and I stepped back as he dropped the metal bird on the ground. He was down seconds later.

"Take this to the conference room," I said to Elijah. "Let's see what else there is."

* * *

Shanely

I awoke to the morning light shining directly on my face. I scrunched my nose and rolled over in a huff, pulling the blanket further up to cover my face.

Bastian.

I had stayed awake for hours waiting for him to return and must have fallen asleep in the guest room. I tore the blankets off me and bolted down the stairs, pulling on my mate bond as I ran. To my surprise, Bastian was here at the lodge. *I have expected him to be in the woods still.* I let out the breath I'd be holding and shot into the conference room.

"Whoa," I muttered, grinding to a stop. The room was full of enforcers and the conference table was covered with broken pieces of... *stuff*. Metal stuff and *feathers*. Loads of feathers and fur lay scattered around the room, and my brows furrowed.

I have no idea what's happening.

"Shanely!" Bastian said as he strolled across the room. "I'm glad you're awake."

"What is all this stuff?" I asked. My mate tucked me into his arms and gestured to the table.

"This is what we found on pack lands," my mate answered, and my eyes widened.

"Are you serious?"

"Wish we weren't, Baby Girl," Cade said, chucking something metal aside. "Took us all night, but I think we've got it all."

I slowly walked over towards Elijah, who sat at the table with what looked like a bird. Tools lay scattered around him, and I watched him take its head off its body.

"Thanks to Cade and his weird obsession with birds," my mate said, pulling me from my thoughts as Cade scowled, "we found these bolted down in the trees."

"It's not a weird obsession," Cade muttered. "They have weird and funny names, alright?"

"What is this?" I asked, ignoring Cade and gesturing to the table.

"Cameras, love," Bastian answered. "Everything here is some sort of surveillance. We found those in our cabin."

My heart sunk as Bastian picked up a small circular device with a small wire attached. I looked with wide eyes to my mate. "Calvin?"

"I don't know," Elijah answered. His hands were buried in the belly of the bird now. "But there's a SD card in here. I might be able to figure out who's behind it if I can..."

"We all know who's behind this," Bastian said, rage lacing his tone. "I want patrols out constantly. Anyone who finds anything needs to call me directly. One of us will handle it."

CHAPTER 10

Cade left to hand out orders as I buried my hands in my hair. Utter dread filled my chest as I stared at all this... *stuff*. Everything here was used in some way to harm my family.

"This is getting worse, Bastian," I muttered sadly. Bastian's face softened as he pulled me towards him, and I buried my face in his chest, tears filling my eyes. My heart ached as I held back my emotions.

"Shhh," he whispered, rubbing the back of my head gently. "I know love, but we're getting ahead of this. We're clearing out our land and making this place a fortress just like your uncle said."

"Look at the table, Bastian," I said, pulling away. "How long has this been going on? What's going to happen to our family? Our pack? I mean; why are they doing this? Why do they want *me?!*"

The room grew quiet as tears slowly slid down my face. Pain rippled down the bond, and Bastian looked broken when he felt what I did. Guilt ate at me for that too. *He doesn't deserve this. He had enough on his shoulders than to deal with me too.* But I couldn't stop the tears from falling. I couldn't stop the pain from spreading. My Alpha power slowly trickled out all around me, and I kicked myself for not being able to stop that too.

"This is our home, Bastian," I cried. My lower lip quivered as my eyes drifted around the room. People I loved and trusted were here working tirelessly to protect our family, and somehow it all boiled down to me. My wolf howled within me as my nostrils flared. My eyes flashed red when I turned back to my mate.

"Haven't I suffered enough?!" I bellowed, my power filling the room. "After everything I've gone through; will I lose *everything* I love? Why can't they just leave us alone?!"

Bastian eyes glossed over, and I collapsed in one of the chairs, burying my head in my arms. Footsteps sounded, and soon the door closed. I knew he sent the others away because I hated crying in front of people. Bastian knew how embarrassed I'd get when I got this emotional, and like the loving man he was, he sent them away to give me privacy. Bastian was always in control of his emotions. He wasn't one to lose his control. Not like me at least.

I felt his callous hands gently touch my shoulder as he sat down next to me. His fingers got lost in my long hair, and he gave a gentle tug.

"Look at me."

I slowly twisted my head to the side, finding him with his head on his arm facing me. His soft smile that didn't reach his eyes was comforting, and he gently wiped away a fallen tear with his thumb.

"You are not going to lose anything," he whispered. My lips puckered again, and he cupped the side of my face. "I promise you. I am going to figure this out and handle Patrick and his father. They won't get away with this, and they won't take away your peace. They won't take away our happiness or harm our family."

"But how can you be sure?" I whispered. My eyes pleaded with him to tell me everything was going to be okay. I *needed* him to tell me everything would be fine and that we were going to live a long and happy life together because I couldn't deal with this anymore. Maybe it was the twins, or maybe I just truly was a coward, but I just couldn't handle the stress of it all.

I'm suffocating...

"Because I have faith in you," he answered, pulling me from my thoughts, "in us and our pack. I don't believe for a second that *our* White Wolf would finally make itself known, just to have all this happen at the hands of humans."

I took in a deep breath, feeling Bastian's love pour into me. It soothed me to my core, and I took a steadying breath. We stayed there a moment longer before I forced myself to sit up.

"I'm sorry," I said softly. He leaned over and kissed my cheek.

"Don't be. It's understandable to feel overwhelmed by everything," he said, rubbing my back gently. "We'll get to the bottom of this, but this is real evidence that what Calvin's been doing is illegal. Cain's going to help me send a report to Hank. There's light at the end of the tunnel, Shanely. You just gotta hang on."

I sighed but felt a little better. *Maybe I just need to cry once in awhile?* I thought to myself. One of my foster moms always said it wasn't healthy to force away emotions like that. *Maybe she was right?*

"Hey," Bastian said, tugging on my chin, "don't you have that dinner to plan?"

"It seems so silly to be focusing on that now, especially now that you found all this. Maybe we should just postpone?" I said quietly.

"Nah. This is special, and we can't stop living, baby," he said, taking my hand and pulling me up from the chair. "This is important, and besides it would be good for you to have something positive to focus on. I'd rather you just work at making it special for Elijah and Noah, while I'll deal with all this. Alright?"

We walked to the door together, hand in hand, and Elijah was waiting on the other side. I gave him a small smile before saying, "I should be helping you though. We're supposed to rule together, Bastian, and I don't feel right dumping it all on you."

"You'll help, mate, but it's okay to step back today. You have too much on your plate, and the stress isn't good for you or the baby. Let me deal with things today, and you just focus on planning a good memory for our family," Bastian said, and I sighed again.

"Seriously though, Bastian and I've got this," Elijah chimed in. "We're good here."

Sensing defeat, I gave them a grateful smile. "Thank you, Bastian," I said quietly. "You too, Elijah."

Bastian kissed my forehead. "Always."

He patted my butt as I walked towards the kitchen to take my vitamins. My mate spoke softly but not quiet enough that I didn't hear every word.

"Take pictures of everything, and I want to see what's on that card. We're getting answers today. If I have to find Hank myself, *then I will.*"

Chapter 11

I slowly felt better as the day trickled on. Bastian was right. All I needed was a break and a chance to focus on something positive, and I quickly discovered how fun the panther sisters could be. *Well, I already knew Emmie was fun, but Esme surprised me.* They helped plan out the dinner with me. A small twinge of guilt twisted my stomach that they were helping and wouldn't be surprised for their own celebration, but it quickly went away when Esme rattled off the long list of food allergies she had and her very limited taste buds.

I stopped feeling bad then. I would have probably inadvertently killed her had it just been me.

This was our last real day to just be a pack before chaos ensued. Bastian and Cain were working hard to send that report in and locate where Hank was. I tried not to eavesdrop, but I knew plane tickets had been purchased already for Colorado. My mate was leaving with Cain tonight, and from the secretive way they acted around me, I don't think they were planning on taking me with. So I spent the morning making cakes with the girls and quietly stewing over the rest. I didn't want to fight with the one person I needed to get through this, but my wolf was livid this was getting decided without me.

Bastian and I were sending Aerith with my brother early this afternoon. As badly as I'd miss her, I wanted her to stay with John at his hut deep in the woods at Abraham's. She'd be safer with Abraham and his streak, and after Calvin demanded I go with him, I wasn't taking any chances. Plus, she was with me in my warnings. Maybe hiding her would be a big enough

CHAPTER 11

change to prevent them from coming true.

Bay was already back in their lands helping everyone in my pack get settled, so it was just Abraham who picked her up today. Aerith had no idea. She sported her typical toothy smile with her bouncy red curls. It warmed my heart knowing despite all this crap going on, she was still a happy kid.

"Don't worry, Shanely," Abey said with a grin. "Little One and I are grabbing an ice cream and heading straight to Uncle John's. Right, Sweet Pea?"

"Right!" Aerith cried out from the back. I sighed, smiling despite the heaviness in my heart. Abe closed the door after hopping in, and I stood on the runners to see my little girl.

"Well just be safe, you two," I said as Bastian finished strapping Aerith in her seat. "Have fun and be good for John, okay?"

Bastian planted a big kiss on her cheek as she giggled. "Daddy stop! I will, mama. Can we go?"

Abe chuckled as I hopped off and scurried around to her door. I pushed Bastian aside saying, "Not without my kisses! Daddy gets one then so do I!"

She giggled as I peppered her cheek with kisses. I couldn't contain my grin hearing her deep belly laugh as I tickled her sides. *God, I was going to miss her...*

"Alright, Shanely!" Abe cried out in a playful tone. "We've got ice cream to get!"

I chuckled and let my daughter go. "Fine! But please let me know when you get back to your land. Bye baby!"

"Will do. Bay and I will be back for the dinner later. Now say bye, Aerith," Abe said, and Aerith waved as I shut the door.

"Bye mama!"

Bastian and I waved, shouting goodbye as loud as we could, while the two drove off. My mate wrapped his arms around my waist, and I jutted out my lower lip.

"We're doing the right thing," I said softly. "Right?"

Bastian kissed my cheek. "It's the safest option for her, love. But don't worry. We'll still call and talk to her all the time. I promise."

Sighing, we turned to head back into the lodge.

"So when exactly were you going to talk to me about Colorado?" I asked.

Bastian ran his hands through his hair. "Before the dinner, I swear. Cain figured out where the Division Head Quarters had been moved to, and we figured if we can't get a hold of Hank, then maybe we should just go to him personally."

"And you were going to leave me behind?" I challenged. My brows rose as I crossed my arms. I may have ignored this all morning, but it doesn't mean I was happy with it.

"Shanely," Bastian replied, giving me a pleading look, "I can't risk you."

"I'm Alpha right along with you," I said firmly. "They are my wolves too. You should have talked to me first before you just decided, Bastian."

He frowned. "Do you not remember the conversation with Calvin? He demanded I hand *you* over. Not me. Not one of my brothers or Cain since he was Alpha before. *You.* Do you really think I'm going to toss you in the center of these people just like that? What if he isn't the only one, Shanely?!"

My nostrils flared. "What are you talking about?!"

Bastian stepped towards me, and I stilled. His eyes were red, but he gently reached forward and caressed my cheek.

"What if Calvin isn't the only one who wants the White Wolf?"

I gritted my teeth, shaking my head as that stupid title popped up again. *I didn't even ask to be the White Wolf.* I didn't want to be Head over all the wolves or the power and control... *I just wanted a family.*

"Sometimes, I'm sick of being the White Wolf," I muttered angrily. My wolf snapped her jaws at me and guilt filled my chest. I clenched my hands together as Bastian shouted behind me.

"What?"

"Nothing!" I hollered, when thunder rattled the sky. Rain began to fall as dark, ominous clouds began to float over us. The afternoon sky was quickly becoming dark, and the winds began to pick up in speed.

"Seriously? A storm now?" I asked, turning to Bastian. His eyes glowed

CHAPTER 11

red still as he stared intently at me. I swallowed hard. *Maybe he did hear me...*

"Crap. I didn't expect a storm this time of year," Cade chimed in, pulling me from my thoughts.

"Good thing the dinner's happening inside," Emmie said as Bastian's phone rang. He answered it as we stepped under the safety of the porch.

"Hello?"

His eyes furrowed as a loud voice shot through the receiver. So loud that I already knew who it was from the other side of the porch.

"Wait... slow down, Brody. What's going on?" my mate asked.

I held my breath as I watched my mate lock his jaw. His body was tense, and his eyes slowly drifted to the woods. Elijah and Cade slowed down, sensing a shift in their brother's mood too.

"Okay, I'm on my way," he said firmly. "No. No, you did good. We rather be safe than sorry."

He shut his phone and looked to me. "Brody thinks he found something, but he's afraid to touch it."

"A trap?" Elijah questioned.

Bastian nodded saying, "That's what I'm thinking. I'm heading over, and I'll need you and Ryder."

"Done," Elijah said, his eyes glossing over.

Bastian turned to me then, and I knew the question he wanted to ask. He wanted me to stay put. My stomach was in knots as I debated challenging him to go too, but I felt his anxiety come through the bond. *He was really worried,* I thought to myself. I sighed before crossing the distance and kissing my mate. "You be safe, you hear me? Cade and I will stay here and keep things running."

Bastian's shoulders sagged in relief, and he tucked me into his embrace. "Thank you, baby. I promise I'll keep in touch."

"Call me if you need me," I said, pulling back to give him a firm look. "Promise me, Bastian. Or I come with you to Colorado."

A small smirk appeared on the corner of his mouth. "Deal. I love you."

Bastian leaned down and kissed me deeply. I melted into his touch, feeling his love come through our bond. Smiling, I pulled away saying, "I love you too."

Ryder jogged around the corner, and I waved the three off. The knot in my stomach continuing to twist. *What in the world was Calvin thinking setting a trap like that?* I thought as the rain continued to pour from the sky.

"C'mon, Baby Girl," Cade said, nudging me. "Let's get this dinner going."

Sighing, I followed my Beta inside. Someone had already brought up the folding tables and chairs from the basement, and I grabbed the table clothes sitting on top. Cade helped me unfold them, and soon the entire main room started to look fancy. As we grabbed the last tablecloth something struck me hard.

I stumbled, gasping for air as I fell against the table.

"Shanely?!" Cade said, rushing over. Pain rippled through the bonds as four of my beloved wolves disappeared from sight. My eyes widened.

"Shanely! Answer me!" Cade shouted, bringing the room to a grinding halt, but I couldn't focus on anything but this intense heartache. It consumed me, and my wolf howled within. The floodgates opened as I pulled on the bonds.

Mateo.

Nick.

Jamin.

And Jadin.

They were missing from my pack...

Brody's team.

Cade shook me as I yanked on the bond that connected me to Brody. Bastian roared down the bond as he came to the same realization too. *Please, please, don't...*

Brody's bond disintegrated, and I screamed as he disappeared from sight.

"Shanely!" Cade bellowed.

I ran.

The freezing rain iced my skin, but I couldn't feel the sting as it struck my body. All I could feel was the pain of losing *my wolves*. I ran down the

CHAPTER 11

hill towards the red barn where I had my reception, with Cade hot on my heels.

His wolf shot in front of me, and I slid in the wet grass before I collided into him. Cade shifted, his eyes blood red as he yanked me to my feet.

"What in the world just happened?!" he demanded, gripping my arm tightly. My lip quivered as I scrambled to tell him. Bastian's rage seeped into the bond, when I realized where he was headed.

My eyes widened. "Bastian..."

Cade cocked his head to the side, when suddenly pure *panic* pulsed from my mate bond. I sucked in a breath as the emotion rippled through my skin, rattling my animals inside me. Even Cade's eyes were wide as he gripped his chest. He slowly looked towards the woods before us.

Suddenly, Bastian's voice bellowed in my mind. I gripped the sides of my head as he shouted.

"Shanely!"

"Bastian!" I shouted back. *"I felt it. I felt them die..."*

"Shanely, we were wrong!" he shouted. My heart began to race. *"God, there's blood everywhere. You need..."*

"Bastian!"

My stomach twisted when he didn't answer.

"Bastian!"

Snarls came through the link and fear gripped my heart. *Bastian was fighting someone*, I thought as anxiety rolled in my stomach. He snarled again. *He was fighting for his life...* I had to *move*.

"Brody's gone!" I bellowed. The rain fell harder against my skin, sending goosebumps up my arm.

"Elijah told me," he gritted through his teeth. His eyes glossed over briefly as he said, "I'm calling in the patrols. We need to get you to safety, Shanely!"

"Over my dead body!" I snapped as everyone poured out of the lodge. I turned, pulling on my mate bond as I started to run. Cade yanked me back, and I snarled.

"Let. Me. *Go.*"

"First off, we have no idea what this is," he snapped, his eyes still bright red. "Second, if this is the Division, then they're after you. It is my job to keep you..."

The familiar sounds of gunfire pierced the air, and Cade dove into me. We landed harshly on the ground, jarring my right hip. He covered my body with his as the sound of truck engines approached.

"The pack," I muttered as I watched armored men poured from the treeline.

Pain erupted within me again as I lost more connections to the wolves under my care. *My care.* I couldn't breathe as I watched my wolves fall. I couldn't stomach listening to their screams.

My pack needed me. My family needed me! My wolf howled as I centered myself, focusing solely on my mate. His heart was beating rapidly in my chest, but it was beating *steadily.*

He was alive, and he was coming back to me, I thought as I knew what I needed to do.

I shoved Cade aside shouting, "Emmie needs our help! She's in that, Cade!"

I shifted into my White Wolf and took off towards the lodge, howling as I ran.

"SHANELY!" Cade shouted, but his voice quickly blended into his own wolf as he shifted too. I could feel him right behind me, and I ran faster.

Snarling, I dove into the first Division guard I got to and clamped down hard on his arm. He screamed, dropping his gun as Cade landed on his chest, knocking him down. All it took was one bite from Cade to silence him forever. He dropped him before looking at me. His glare said it all though. *He was pissed.*

The entire front lawn was littered with bodies already. *So much blood and death in a matter of minutes.* I shook myself from my thoughts and dodged a heavyset man rushing towards me. Cade stayed close as we fought the Division together. Rage ignited my blood as I switched to my bear, plowing over the man shooting my pack with massive nets to pin them down. Blood coated my white fur, but for once in my life I didn't care that I was harming

CHAPTER 11

another. All I wanted to do was find Calvin. *Calvin brought this upon us, and when I get my hands on him...*

A wolf's howl suddenly pierced the air, and I turned to find my Uncle Cain barreling into the crowd of wolves. I followed his line of sight, and my eyes widened.

No...

I shifted back to my wolf and took off towards the center just as Uncle Ash was hit in the chest. He dropped as another pain of the disconnect shattered me. *Not my uncle...*

Deirdre roared in pain, but it was too late. She went down too just as Cain ripped apart the man who shot them. I wanted to scream. Scream in absolute agony as my friends and family fought against the Division. *This wasn't fair... We were a peaceful race. We stuck to our own kind! Why...*

Cade dove into me, knocking me to the side, and snapping me out my own head.

"Would you pay attention!" he bellowed angrily. "God, Shanely! Now is not the time to play hero! We need to move."

I snarled and shoved him off. "*I can feel their deaths, Cade. I'm...*"

I lunged, gripping a solider by the throat and shook violently until I heard the snap. Just like the boys taught me. I narrowed my eyes to a surprised Cade.

"*Emmie is out here somewhere,*" I growled. "*We need to find her now!*"

He nodded his head. "*Stay close.*"

We shifted, running towards our bond with Emmie, and Cade tucked me into his arms as the slaughtering continued. My heart pounded in my chest as we leapt over Havu, who slithered on the porch and ran into the lodge.

It was as chaotic in here as it was outside. Noah had shifted and was pinned down under a large net near the fireplace. Barely able to get a claw out to help the panther sisters, who hissed at the armed men before them. One raised his gun, and my feet were moving before my mind could catch up.

I shifted in the air as I dove into the large man trying to kill my sister-in-law. *I will not lose anyone else!* I snarled in my head as I snapped my jaws around the man's neck. I shook violently until he fell limp.

"*Thank God, Shanely!*" Esme shouted through the link. Emmie shook behind her. "*I'll free Noah!*"

Esme bolted towards her mate as the back door flung open. Gunfire rippled through the air, and I dove to my right behind the grand staircase. Emmie's panther shrieked, and panic consumed me when she ran out the door to the carnage outside.

Cade leapt on the Division solider, who just barely missed Emmie, and I took off after her. Barreling outside, I saw her sleek panther running into the woods with two more guards closely behind her.

"*Shanely!*"

I ignored my Beta and ran for my sister-in-law. She wasn't trained to fight. She wasn't ready for this, but I was.

I was the White Wolf, and this was my pack.

I howled, feeling more and more determined to protect her as I bolted through the trees towards my home. My fear melted away as my paws dug into the hard ground. I let my Alpha power release fully, running faster than ever towards Elijah's mate. He had saved me more times than I could count, and this time I was going to return the favor.

A low growl emitted from my throat when I finally found her. Emmie was cornered. She coward in the center of five men with brightly colored Division logos on their armor, all with guns aimed at her.

"*Shanely!*" she bellowed when she saw me.

They all turned just as I bolted forward. The first man's eyes widened briefly before I barreled into him. My teeth sunk into flesh, and I shook my head hard. Fresh blood scented the air when I dropped him, and I moved to the next threat to my family.

Emmie slid on her paws, when a woman with a net aimed her gun on her. I had to give it to my sister-in-law though. She was quick, and the net flung past her.

I ran to catch up, when suddenly *pain* pierced my back and stomach. I didn't even hear the shot when it hit, and I stumbled forward, hitting the ground as the wound burned inside me.

CHAPTER 11

I couldn't breathe as it burned my flesh and fur. The pain was agonizing, but my eyes widened when I looked down to find *nothing*. No blood or wound at all. *My body was fine... I was fine. But if I'm fine... Oh, God.*

It wasn't me, I realized. *Someone shot Bastian. Someone shot my mate!* Our bond flickered, nearly shattering my heart as it faded slightly. *He was hurt somewhere, and I needed to find him. I needed to save him now.*

Emmie suddenly stumbled on her feet. She turned to look at me then.

"Elijah..."

Something sharp pierced my side, and I yipped in pain. My vision instantly blurred, and I shook my head as a heaviness fell on me. *What is going on with me?*

"Shanely!" Emmie shouted. "Behind you!"

My right leg seized as sharp pain struck my thigh, and I collapsed to the ground. Too heavy to even lift my head. I slowly blinked, when I heard a familiar voice.

"Don't shoot her!"

Patrick shot through the trees and tore the mask he wore off. My nose curled as his awful stench wafted over to me, and I slowly barred my teeth as he quickly approached me, ripping the tranquilizer darts from my body and chucking it aside.

"You are lucky you shot her with this," he snapped, glaring at the men behind him. Only two were left standing.

"We know the orders, *sir*," his guard replied in a snide tone, "but I'd rather not lose anymore men to that monster."

A familiar howl pierced the air, and I recognized the wolf. *Cade.* His wolf sounded panicked, having felt both Bastian and Elijah get shot, and now me. My heart seized, and I begged him not to find me. My bond with Bastian flickered again, and my wolf whined inside. *I can't lose them all.*

Patrick looked in the direction it came before turning to Emmie.

"I'll give you a chance to run, shifter," he said firmly. "Go now, and I won't shoot you dead. I only want her."

My eyes widened before they settled on Emmie. My bond wavered with Bastian further. *He was dying. He was dying, and I couldn't save him.* My heart broke as I looked to Elijah's mate. I may not have been able to save anyone today, but I could save *her*.

"Go."

Her eyes widened. *"I can't leave you, Shanely! Cade's on his way."*

"Go, Emmie. That's an order," I said firmly. "I won't lose another family member to these awful men. Go, before it's too late. Please!"

Her panther shook slightly as she struggled to decide. I wish it wasn't like this. I wish she had more time with Elijah, but I don't think I had enough strength to feel her disconnect. To watch her fall...

"Please, Emmie. Go for me. I won't lose you too."

"But Patrick will..."

"It's okay," I interrupted. *"It's okay, Emmie."*

Another howl pierced the air. Cade was getting closer.

"Decide panther!" Patrick bellowed. "Before I decide for you."

He cocked his gun and pointed. Emmie took a step back in terror.

"I'm so sorry, Shanely."

She ran, and I exhaled deeply, feeling absolute relief. *She'd be safe. Cade would find her and get her out of here. They can find Bastian and Elijah and...*

Patrick pulled a silver bracelet out of his pocket, and I froze. The same silver bracelet I saw in all my warnings. *This was really happening*, I thought to myself. All my warnings over the years was finally coming true. I didn't stop any of them. No matter how hard I tried, I ended up right here.

"Don't worry, baby," he said softly as he grabbed my paw. Bastian's bond faded even more, and my heart broke, "we're going to get you out of here."

Patrick snapped it on, and I shifted violently. Gasping for air, I struggled to hold myself up. My wolf was gone. My bear was gone, along with *all* my bonds. My bond with Bastian had nearly faded entirely. *What would happen to him? Would Cade be able to save him too?*

Tears welled in my eyes as Patrick tilted my chin up. He smiled down at me as another wounded howl pierced the air.

"Let's go home," he said. Patrick turned to the guards with him. "That's the last Fenrir. Wait until he comes searching for her and kill him. I've got

CHAPTER 11

confirmation the other two have been eliminated."

My lip puckered as I struggled to contain my emotions. I wanted to yell. To scream and warn Cade, who may very well be the last Fenrir brother left. But I *couldn't*.

My eyes blinked as the heaviness weighed me further. The tranquilizer in my blood was in full effect now that my wolf was gone. I was falling, but this time Bastian wasn't here to catch me before I hit the ground.

Bastian wasn't here to save me.

Patrick caught me as I slumped in darkness.

Chapter 12

My head pulsed as I rolled over to my side. Every limb felt heavy and shaky as I tried to move. A musty smell filled my nose, and the bed creaked as I shifted my body, but when my eyes drifted towards the silver bracelet on my wrist the memories came flooding back to me. *The blood, the death, my mate...*

Deep despair filled my chest as tears welled in my eyes. I covered my mouth, trying to stop the intense sob that I knew was coming. The room was dark, but even without my wolf, I could see I was not at home. I was not in my bed, and I was so very alone. My body was entirely empty again, and I mourned the loss of both my wolf and bear.

I wiped my eyes, forcing every emotion away as I slowly got to my feet. The room swayed, and I blinked furiously until the room stilled. I couldn't afford to break. Not now. Not when I had to focus all my attention on getting out of here.

I decided to try the window first and carefully made my way there. Peeking out, I found armed men standing guard just outside my window. My chest tightened as I saw the emblem on their uniform. The officer turned, winking when he noticed me, and I quickly shut the curtains.

I moved towards the door instead, knowing they'd inform Patrick I was awake. *I didn't have long.* With no way to sneak past the guards outside, I turned the handle to my door ever so quietly, but it wouldn't budge. *Locked.*

I swore, spinning around to inspect the room. It was plain, with a full-size bed in the corner, a dresser on my left by a single chair that looked like it came straight out of a 90's catalog, and a nightstand with a lamp sitting

CHAPTER 12

on it. *Nothing here that I could use as a weapon,* I thought with a sigh. I held my wrist up, glaring at the silver bracelet. *I could be a weapon if I could just get this stupid thing off.* I squared my shoulders, bouncing slightly on my feet as I readied myself for the pain to come. *I had broken this once before, and I could do it again.* Taking a deep breath, I searched within and pulled on the spot where my wolf should be. Pain rippled across my body, and I sucked in a harsh breath. *This was worse than before...*

"I wouldn't try that if I were you."

I jumped, finding Patrick standing in the opened doorway. Grinning like a mad man, he entered the room and kicked the door shut behind him before leaning against the dresser. I glared at him.

"Why would you do this?" I gritted through my teeth. Rage burned me up inside, and I clenched my fists together.

"You mean save you?" Patrick asked, giving me a pointed look. "Would you have rather died with everyone else then?"

My eyes narrowed. "Save me? You did this, Patrick! This is all your fault!"

Patrick scoffed.

"No, it isn't," he replied casually. My blood *boiled.* "I stuck my neck out for you actually. Breaking many laws by the way just to keep you safe, Shanely. The least you could do is be grateful."

"Grateful!?" I snapped, storming over to him. Adrenaline pulsed in my veins, leaving my arms tingly and numb. *God, I wanted to rip that smug smile off his stupid face!*

"Grateful to the prick who ordered my family's death?! I know the truth!" I bellowed, and he shoved off the dresser.

"I didn't order the attack!" he hollered loudly, and I staggered backwards. "Someone high up in Command called for your pack's head to be delivered on a silver platter, Shanely. He called for *your* head. I stuck my neck out for you and your kid the moment we were given orders, so don't go blaming me for the mess you shifters made."

I staggered on my feet. The air sucked from my lungs as his words rattled me. *My kid... No. He can't have her,* I thought as my heart ached. *I sent Aerith* with Abraham. *He picked her up long before the attack, and they should have made it home. Didn't they?*

With trembling lips I asked, "You have Aerith?"

Patrick shrugged before sauntering over to the lounge chair in the corner and collapsing on it. He stretched his arms above his head, getting comfortable before replying, "It really wasn't that hard, Shanie Baby. I just had to run that shifter off the road, and then it was easy to dispose of him and snatch her. My team had it done in a matter of minutes."

"But..." my voice broke as tears filled my eyes. "Bastian and I..."

Patrick scowled as he shot to his feet. He towered over me, pushing me back until my legs hit the bed. He gripped my face, pulling me towards him as he snarled, "I suggest you forget about your so called *mate*. He's dead. He paid the price for his mistakes, and he's never coming back. I have Aerith here with us, and you can still keep her if you get it through your head that you will be *my* wife, and your kids will be *my* kids. I don't ever want to hear Bastian's name again. Otherwise, I'll give the kid to the Division to do God knows what with her, seeing how she's half-human."

My heart pounded in my chest as he let me go. I slumped down to the bed unable to stop my body from shaking. *I was living my warnings,* I thought as my reality came crashing down. *They were all true, and I was so stupid to believe they wouldn't happen. I was so stupid...*

I flinched as Patrick yanked out a pair of scissors from his back pocket, and a quiet sob escaped my lips. *I remember this.* The memory of that warning still so clear in my mind. I bit my lower lip as a single tear fell down my face.

"Now let's take care of a few things, shall we? I think you'd look amazing with shorter hair. Although, I'm not sure why you changed the color," he said as he grabbed a wad of my hair.

Nearly word for word what my warning gave me so long ago. The details were different, I realized, but it was still happening. It was *still* happening, no matter how hard I tried to stop it.

"Why? Just why?" I whispered. The words barely audible as they left my lips, but I had to know. I had to know *why* someone would do something so cruel to another. I couldn't fathom why he do all this to someone he claimed to love.

But he didn't get it.

Patrick gave me a dry look before answering, "Because Bastian loved it long. Now sit still or I'll shave you bald instead."

The scissors snapped shut, and my long white hair fell to my lap. Tears silently fell down my cheek as he chopped off my beloved hair. When he let me go, it rested just above my shoulders *just like how* I saw it in my warning.

"Good," he said proudly as he gathered up the mess. "You're the new and improved, Shanely Jennings!"

My stomach churned inside, and I wanted to puke. Bile rose to the back of my throat as my mouth salivated, and I held my breath to keep from spewing everywhere. I held onto my emotions tight, staring at the floor, and desperately struggling to keep the sobs from bellowing forth. I didn't want to break in front of him. *I couldn't break...*

"I'll let you rest, wife. You are carrying my child after all," he said as he made his way to the door.

My nails dug into the palms of my hands as more tears began to escape down my cheek. I couldn't hold it in anymore. My eyes burned with the amount of unshed tears, when I heard the door open.

"Shanely?" he said softly, but I refused look his way, and he sighed behind me. "Just so you know, those inhibitors are state of the art from the Division. We *know* other shifters are creating knock offs, but they are nothing compared to these. Don't try to shift. Trust me, it will only harm you and our kid."

Patrick finally shut the door, leaving me alone in the room.

I let go of the breath I'd been holding and slowly reached up to touch my freshly cut hair. *It was gone. All of it* nearly gone as it just barely touched the top of my shoulders.

Rage filled my core, and I sought out my wolf within. *I broke Abe's collar, I can break this*, I thought angrily. *I am the freaking White Wolf!*

I pulled on the empty spot where she should be, trying to get my bones to shift into place, but a fierce burning sensation traveled through my veins from the inhibitor. I gasped as the pain intensified when it drew closer to my chest, but I kept searching for my wolf. *She had to be here,* I thought as my anxiety grew. *She had to be!*

The pain grew worse as I found nothing but emptiness and despair. The stench of burnt flesh filled the air, and I clutched my hand and let go. My chest heaved as the pain on my wrist became overwhelming. *God, it hurt so freaking bad.*

My wolf wasn't there.

Looking down, I carefully moved the inhibitor aside, and my eyes widened. A solid red ring wrapped around my entire wrist. The flesh wrinkled and bubbled up with fluid. I winced when I carefully touched it. *It was a burn...* I realized. *The inhibitor burned me.*

I couldn't help but stare at the burn mark on my wrist. I couldn't get to my wolf. I couldn't shift into my bear. I couldn't *do* anything. My lip quivered as the tears fell rapidly down my face. I was useless. Defenseless. And utterly alone.

Collapsing against the bed, I sobbed. I let every emotion out as my grief overwhelmed me, gripping my heart until it shattered into tiny pieces.

In that moment, the person I was before this *died.*

The beloved White Wolf died.

She died right alongside her mate and family.

Chapter 13

Aerith

"AERITH DUCK!"

I screamed, clutching my seat as Uncle Abey swerved his black truck on the curved road. The strong scent of burning tires flooded my nostrils, and they squealed loudly when he served again. My eyes widened as another large black truck turned towards us. They were going to hit us. I covered my head with my hands and screamed louder.

"I want mommy!"

Uncle Abe said a very bad word as the truck hit us, and we slammed into a large tree. The straps of my seat forced me back as we came to an abrupt stop. Glass flew everywhere, and the smoke... There was so much black smoke. My chest burned when I took a breath, and for a moment everything fell silent. I slowly looked over to my uncle.

"Uncle Abey?" I called out, but he didn't move. His head lay on the steering wheel, and his eyes were closed. My door suddenly opened.

"UNCLE ABEY!"

My eyes shot open, and I gasped for air. My heart pounded in my chest as I scurried to my feet. *It was a dream*, I thought. *A horrible, horrible dream.*

I took a deep breath and looked around me, frowning when I realized I wasn't at Uncle Abey's or back home. *It wasn't a dream*, I realized. *Uncle Abey really did crash his truck.* I was in the back of a van by myself, and Uncle Abey was nowhere to be found. I stole a peek out the back window, not recognizing the long gravel drive or the woods either. I blinked, trying to figure out what happened, when the side door opened abruptly, and I jumped hard.

A tall man hopped in and dropped his hood as I scurried to the far corner. Water fell from his brow as he grinned at me. I frowned again. *I knew him... Somehow.*

"Well hello, baby doll!" he said cheerfully. "You feel alright? That accident seemed to have given you a few bruises."

The strange man walked over and moved my chin around to look at my face. I pulled away, glaring.

"I want my mom and dad," I said firmly, pulling my knees to my chest. Tears filled my eyes at the man cocked his head to the side.

"Your mom's just inside resting," he said softly. His smile faded as he continued, "She had a difficult day, so we will see her when she wakes up."

None of this made any sense, and I frowned again. "Then can you take me to my dad. Please? I want my dad!"

The stranger scowled, staring at me intensely, and I shrunk further back. He seemed almost angry, but his face softened by the time I blinked.

"Your dad isn't coming around anymore, Aerith," he said firmly. "But I'm here. I'm going to take care of you, your brothers, and your mother."

My lips puckered as he watched me. *My Daddy always comes though for me,* I thought. *He promised he'd always come get me if I was ever hurt or in trouble. He promised he would never leave me.*

"Now!" the man said loudly, causing me to jump again as he clapped his hands together. "Let's get the stuff I bought for you and go find your new room. I think you're going to like it here, Aerith. Oh! And I nearly forgot..."

The man dug in his pocket and pulled out a small glass tube filled with what looked like water. He held it out to me.

"Here. Drink this," he commanded, but I didn't move.

My eyes furrowed as I looked from him to the vial. I didn't know this man, and I didn't know what that was. *I just want to go home,* I thought anxiously.

The familiar stranger sighed before scooting closer. He sat cross-legged before me, and I pulled my legs as close as I could to me.

"Aerith," he said softly, and I slowly looked into his eyes, "my name

CHAPTER 13

is Patrick. I'm a police officer, and I'm not here to hurt you. This is just medicine to help you feel better since you were in an accident. I know all this must be confusing, but I need you to know that I love your mom, and I can love you too if you just give me the chance. I know we could be friends."

'Be careful, Aerith. Not everyone is our friend...'

Daddy's voice sounded in my mind. As crystal clear as if he were sitting in the van with me now. His stern warning warmed my chest, but Patrick was a police officer. *Doesn't that mean he's safe?*

"Please?" Patrick said, gently rubbing the side of my cheek. "We can check on mommy if you take it. I even have a bunch of presents waiting inside just for you."

My eyes widened. *I wanted mom.* She'd know what's going on and where Daddy went, and if all I had to do was take medicine to see her, then I'd do it. I gave him a small nod, and Patrick smiled.

"Great! Drink up then," he said, handing me the vial.

With shaky hands, I slowly drank the sickly sweet liquid, and my insides felt fuzzy almost. That warmth fell away as I handed it back, blinking as a great heaviness fell upon me.

Patrick opened the door, stretching out his hand for me to follow. I felt sluggish as I stood and walked over to him. He picked me up and set me on my feet just outside the van, and my eyes squinted as they adjusted to the blinding sun that was just starting to set. When I could finally see again, I saw a large white house before me with large rounded steps to the grand front door that had a red rose made of pretty glass on it. I didn't recognize the place. In fact, as I looked around the woods where we stood, I didn't recognize anything. I shivered as a cold wind passed by and instinctively tucked myself against Patrick as three large men approached.

Patrick smiled, placing his arm on my back before turning to the men. My eyes widened when I saw their guns, and my shoulders fell when I recognized the black vehicle behind them.

The same one that hit Uncle Abey...

"Send Iron Squad back to base and tell them to wait for my father to report back to Dennis," Patrick said firmly. "Keep your Squad here as security for now. You did good, Scott."

"Thank you, sir."

"What about the child?" another tall man wearing a mask asked. I shuddered as the group looked down at me.

"Above your pay grade," Scott replied with a clipped tone.

"While the issues with the McCoy pack was common knowledge," Patrick said firmly, "this mission is not. Understand?"

"Yes sir," Scott answered for him. "My entire team understands this was not a mission for the books."

Patrick gave him a grateful nod before Scott twirled his finger in the air. He turned on his heels shouting, "Move out!"

Everyone moved past us to the large black vans and began loading up. My heart raced out of control as I recognized some of the men here. I clung to Patrick's hand as my brows furrowed. *I didn't understand. These men... They are the ones who hurt Uncle Abey.* Their dark uniforms had no words or police logos either. I frowned. *Who were they? And why did they have to hurt Uncle Abe?*

"Let's go, baby doll," Patrick said, tugging me along, and I scurried to get my feet to catch up. After unlocking the front door, he pushed it opened saying, "Welcome home."

I chewed my bottom lip as we stepped inside. *This wasn't my home,* I thought to myself. My toys weren't here, and neither was Uncle Cade's large gray blankie that was always on the couch for me to use. Uncle Elijah wasn't here to read me a story, and Uncle Cade wasn't here to play hide and seek. And worst of all, Daddy wasn't here to hold me or tell me everything was going to be okay. This *wasn't* home, and my lips puckered slightly.

Patrick rambled on as he pulled me towards the left and down a hallway. I didn't hear much of what he was saying, but he stopped in front of a white door and unlocked it. Hair stood on the back of my neck as Patrick swiftly picked me up, putting his finger to his lips. He opened the door, and my eyes widened.

Mommy.

She was sleeping on the bed inside. Her chest rising and falling normally, and I let out the breath I had been holding. I leaned to go to her, but Patrick only held me tighter and closed the door quickly. I blinked in surprise as he walked further from the door.

From my mom.

"Can't go waking mommy now!" he teased playfully.

My mouth dropped, and my eyes glistened with tears as he carried me up a flight of stairs. I couldn't stop them from falling down my face. *I wanted my mom! Why can't I go back to her?*

Suddenly, Patrick gave me a sour look, and when he wiped my cheek, his face fell even more. He seemed cross with me for some reason, and I stilled as he set me down in front of him.

"Now Aerith," he said sternly, "there is nothing to be sad about. You will see your mother soon but not until she gets some rest. No more tears, alright?"

I slowly nodded my head, and he took my hand and pulled me to another white door. He unlocked this one as well and gently pushed me forward. Inside, toys and books were scattered about, and a small bed lay to the right with shopping bags on it. Everything was a bright pink, with either a princess or unicorn on it. *Was this for me?*

My heart started to race as he pushed me further into the room and closed the door.

"I couldn't remember your sizes, but I think I got pretty close," he said, pulling clothes out of the bag.

A bright pink shirt that said *Daddy's little Girl* on the front and a yellow polka dot dress sat on his lap as he dug in the bag for the rest. I didn't move as he pulled everything out and set it down on the bed. I was just confused though. I didn't understand why mom and I were here and not heading home like we should be. *Did something happen at home? Is that why I'm here?*

"Don't you like them?" he asked, and I slowly looked to him. My lip quivered as another tear slid down my cheek, and I couldn't stop the next one either. *I didn't want new clothes*, I thought. I just wanted my mom and dad, and I wanted to go home.

Patrick looked angry with me again. He tossed the clothes aside as he asked, "Aerith, what did I say about crying?"

My face became sticky with tears as I sobbed, wrapping my arms around my waist and clinging to myself. I sobbed so hard, I couldn't catch my breath. All while Patrick just glared at me.

It angered him greatly seeing me cry, and he abruptly shoved past me. My whole body trembled as I rushed to follow him, but he held up his hand, grinding me to a halt.

"I think you need some time to appreciate what I've done for you, Aerith. The clothes better be put away before I come back," he demanded before slamming the door shut. The lock clicked over, and I rushed to the door, trying to turn the handle, but it wouldn't budge. The handle wouldn't move, and I stood there with my mouth wide open. *He locked me in. I had never been locked in a room before. Did I do something bad?*

The tears fell down even harder, and I shouted, "Please, let me out! I want my mom!"

I shouted again and again, until my voice was hoarse from yelling. Patrick didn't come back, and I didn't know what I did wrong. Daddy always picked me up and held me when I cried. As did everyone in my family, but Patrick seemed to hate it.

I slumped to the ground and looked around the room, wishing more than anything I was back home with my family.

My *whole* family.

Everything was just wrong now. Absolutely wrong.

Chapter 14

Shanely

A loud crash woke me from my sleep.

What in the world was that?! I thought as my heart began to race.

Shouting ensued as gunfire rattled the walls, and I shot to my feet. A familiar howl sounded from the halls, and my heart leapt for joy. I knew that howl! I thought excitedly as I ran to the door. It wasn't locked, and when I threw it open, standing in the door frame was Bastian.

My Bastian.

He smirked, giving me the same devilish grin I had seen for years. "I told you I'd always find you."

"Bastian!"

I ran to him as tears of joy fell down my cheek. Suddenly, the sound of a gunshot rippled through the air, and Bastian's face twisted in pain. He stumbled forward, blood trickling from his mouth and down his chin as red cover his shirt. Another shot sounded, and Bastian collapsed at my feet in a bloody heap.

I screamed as Patrick grinned wickedly behind him. His shotgun still aiming at my fallen mate.

I dropped to my knees, trying to block Bastian from Patrick's view. I covered his body with mine as I searched for any sign of life, but his eyes were closed, and his blood... God, his blood was everywhere.

"You monster!" I screamed.

Patrick scowled as he stomped over to me. He raised his gun and slammed it against my head.

I let go of my mate.

I shot up out of my bed, gasping for air. My lungs wouldn't fill with air fast enough, and I sat clutching my head with my hands as I struggled to slow my rapid heart.

The room was entirely dark with only a small sliver of moonlight sneaking just past the curtains in Patrick's house. My whole body shook slightly as I pulled my knees to my chest and wrapped my arms around them. *A dream,* I thought to myself. *It was just a...*

"Bad dream?"

I screamed.

Patrick laughed as he turned on the lamp. *I hadn't even noticed him before,* I thought as my heart thudded loudly again. He leaned forward in the chair, grinning wickedly at me.

"What are you doing, Patrick!?" I snapped. "How long have you even been in here?"

He shrugged casually. "Not long. I came in to check on my beautiful girl, but you were sleeping so peacefully that I didn't want to wake you. But I also didn't want to leave you."

"I'm not your girl, Patrick. I want to go home," I demanded, glaring at him.

His eyes darkened, and I held my breath. The gears were turning in his mind, and he tapped the armrest of his chair in frustration. I wasn't sure how to handle him. He had always given me the creeps, and I was afraid of him to a certain extent because of my warnings. But the way he studied me now sent goosebumps up and down my arm. *Something was off with him,* I thought. *More than I ever realized.*

To what extent, I didn't know. But I didn't plan on sticking around to find out.

"Oh baby," he finally said in a low tone, "this is your home."

I scoffed. "You're crazy..."

He lunged.

My eyes widened when Patrick grabbed me by my throat and got in my face. Fear stole any confidence I had as he tightened his grip around my neck.

CHAPTER 14

"I wouldn't make the mistake of calling me names, Shanely. You belong to me now. There is no other way around it. According to the report, Shanely Fenrir *died* along with the Fenrir pricks and the rest of the McCoy pack. The only way you and Aerith stay alive is with me. The *only way* you stay alive is if you stay secret from the rest of everybody. I suggest you get on board before you do something you'll regret."

Patrick glared down at me, gripping my neck so tightly I thought he was going to knock me unconscious. My vision blurred but to my absolute horror, he leaned down and kissed my forehead before letting me go. My heart <u>shattered</u>.

Bastian always kissed me like that... This was just wrong.

"Lay down, Shanely. I am staying with you tonight," he said as I gasped for air, clutching my neck.

My eyes widened further as he crawled into bed. I bolted to my feet but he gripped my wrist tightly and yanked me towards him. Patrick's jaw clenched as he said, "Lay down."

"No," I snapped angrily.

His eyes narrowed. "Lay down or you will never see Aerith again."

My face fell. All the fight I clung to left me, and all I could think was how scared Aerith must be right now. She was all alone too, and that broke my heart. With absolute agony, I relented and laid down on the bed next to Patrick. I rolled to my side far away from him, and he simply settled in behind me. I stifled back another sob as he rolled towards me, the bed sinking as his body lined mine.

His warm breath coated my skin as he whispered, "You so much as move an inch from where I put you, and Aerith doesn't eat for a week."

I sucked in a breath, my anger flaring, but I forced it down again. *There's nothing I could do*, I realized. Not without hurting Aerith, and I won't risk her.

I lay rigid as a board as he got comfortable once more, wrapping his arm around my waist and burying his nose in the crook of my neck. No one made a sound then. We lay perfectly still on the bed, and my future in this house flashed before me. *This was how my life would go*, I thought to myself.

He would use Aerith against me every step of the way, and what could I do to stop him? I wasn't the White Wolf here. Not with this inhibitor on, but I had to figure a way out of here. I *had* to get us out.

My back ached as I waited for him to fall asleep, but I didn't dare move a muscle. Not even when my leg fell asleep, and I had to bite down on my hand as that horrendous tingle shot to my knee, did I move. I was not going to risk starting this whole process over by waking him because my eyes had drifted over to the door. The door that was left opened ever so slightly.

Soon, Patrick's breathing evened out, and his arm fell slack against me. I exhaled slowly. *He's asleep,* I thought to myself. *Thank the lord, he's asleep.*

As carefully as I could, I shimmied out of his arms and off the bed. He snored away, and I sagged in relief the moment my feet touched the floor.

I quietly left Patrick sleeping on the bed and crept down the hallway. Everything was so dark. Not a single light was left on, and I softly drug my fingers along the wall as I made my way down the hallways to the grand foyer.

The whole house smelled musty like it hadn't been cleaned in decades, but at least I didn't see anyone standing guard in the windows anymore. *This place was massive,* I thought as I looked at the grand staircase directly to my left. More doors and another hall lay beyond, but I turned to my right instead. My heavy eyes drifted to the beautiful stained-glass front doors. It was pretty to look at, with a striking red rose in the center that let in plenty of moonlight. I tip-toed over to the door and stole a peek outside. The woods were dark and ominous, and I didn't recognize anything. *We were a long way from home,* I thought. Stepping back, I noticed a small white box with a red light sitting next to the frame.

Great... An alarm. Now I needed to figure out the code before I could leave this place. I pursed my lips together and left it alone for now. I still had to find Aerith before I could leave and guessing was not an option.

Turning away from the front door, I had two options to choose from. *I could go up the grand staircase, and then either left or right to the many closed doors up there, or I could follow along the right side of the stairs that led to a kitchen, maybe?*

CHAPTER 14

I made my way to the right and indeed found a rather large kitchen and dining room in the back of the house. The kitchen seemed dated somewhat, with its simple brown cabinets and checkered tile floor, but it was clean at least. *I'll give the pricks that.*

The clock *tick-tocked, tick-tocked* above the counter near the sliding glass doors. *It was three in the morning,* I thought. *No wonder my eyes felt heavy.* Daylight was a long way to go, but I had yet to find Aerith. There was no point inspecting this door either. A flashing red light on the small white box told me I couldn't leave through here either. Not without a code.

Other than a pantry on the other side of the room there was nothing of consequence in here. Sighing, I walked out towards the foyer again, passing a large steel door with another alarm box next to it. *It must be the garage,* I thought and left it alone. *Patrick's been planning this for awhile,* I thought, gritting my teeth together. *The whole* I saved you *crap he tried to spin was such a lie.*

As I made my way to the stairs, I noticed a wooden door on the left. It was the only door on this side other than the garage. *Might at well start somewhere.* I quietly turned the knob, and it opened freely. A small office appeared with grand windows along the wall in front of me, and a large wooden desk sat on the right. Tall bookshelves stood behind the desk, and as I stepped further inside, I saw something unexpected. An elevator was on the left wall facing the desk. You couldn't see it unless you stepped fully inside the room. It was just tucked away in here, which was so puzzling to me. *Why have an elevator here of all places? And where did it go?* I wondered. Curiously, I walked towards it. My hand extending to push the button...

"What do you think you are doing?"

I jumped, yanking my hand back, and turning to face him. Patrick glared at me with his arms folded across his chest, leaning against the door frame. His hair was messy from sleep, and he looked pissed to be awake.

"I... uh..." I said, my voice slipping as I scrambled to answer him. "I was just looking for a bathroom. That's all."

"In my father's study?" he asked, his eyes narrowing.

"Well, I didn't know what was behind here. I've never left my room before now, have I?" I countered, placing my hands on my hips. He rolled his eyes at my sarcasm and gestured to his right.

"Well, let me take you then."

With nothing to do but obey, I slowly left the room and the curious elevator. Patrick locked the door behind me and motioned me forward saying, "Let me make this clear though. You need to stay out of this room."

"Why?" I asked, more curious than anything. "What's in there?"

"It's my father's private office, and before you ask, I don't know where the elevator goes, alright? It's normally locked anyways, but that's a big rule in this house. Even I don't go in there," he answered. The gears turned in my mind.

What in the world was Calvin hiding in there? To kick Patrick out...

Patrick dragged me along to one of the doors I passed earlier and opened it to reveal a small bathroom.

"Don't you think it's a little odd that your dad doesn't even trust you to know what's going on in there?" I asked, raising an eyebrow. "I mean aren't you two partners in crime after all?"

Patrick merely rolled his eyes saying, "Stop being dramatic. He's entitled to his privacy like everyone else. Now, you said you needed to go so..."

Sighing, I stepped inside, but his hand jutted out and stopped the door from closing. Then he stepped in with me.

My eyes widened. "Patrick, get out. I'm not going in front of you!"

He shook his head replying, "No. See, now I don't trust you. You were snooping in my house in the middle of the night, so prove it to me. Prove you were truly looking for the bathroom and go."

I glared at him. "I can't pee in front of you."

"Too bad," he said, shrugging his shoulders. "Now, let's go. I'm exhausted."

"Patrick, I'm serious alright," I said, shifting nervously on my feet. "Please, turn around or something."

He rolled his eyes and turned around to face the door. "God, you're such a needy little thing."

I sagged in relief and quickly used the restroom. My stomach churned as

CHAPTER 14

I anxiously watched him, trying to hurry myself along. He turned around as the toilet flushed and proceed to stare at me while I washed my hands.

"You know at some point," he said with irritation, "you're going to have to get use to me seeing you. I mean *all* of you."

I snorted saying, "Yeah, that's not happening."

Patrick stepped closer, and the hair on the back of my neck rose. "I guess we'll just see about that, won't we? But for now, I'm tired, and I really just want to sleep next to my beautiful girl. Shall we?"

I quickly left the bathroom with Patrick hot on my heels. He made sure I went back to my cell, and he put me right back where I was before with his arms and leg thrown over me. I was trapped. Utterly stuck to this wretched man. With a lump in my throat, I tried to wait until I heard his soft snores before untucking myself from him.

But I fell asleep before I could.

Chapter 15

Aerith

Patrick wouldn't ever let me leave the room, and I had rummaged through all the books and toys in here. Half the time, I'd lay on my bed and look at my ceiling, fiddling with my fingers as I listened closely for any signs of people. Some days, it was so quiet that I felt alone in the house. Like everyone forgot me somehow, and I grew afraid they wouldn't come back to get me. Those were the days I'd toss the blanket over my head and sit with my knees to my chest. I didn't like being alone.

And every night it was the same. I'd call for my mom, but she didn't come to get me. I started calling for Patrick too, and one time he *did* come for me. But he got very cross I was still awake and took the nightlight from my room as punishment.

I don't call for anyone now.

My eyes drooped a little as I stared at one of the books Patrick gave me. It was about a small duckling searching for his lost family. It just made me sad, so I set the book down.

Yawning, I grabbed a packet of fruit snacks Patrick had given me earlier this morning, popping a red one in my mouth. He brought me a bag of snacks and a drink every morning before leaving again. I don't know why I wasn't allowed to see my mother. I don't know why daddy never came to find me either, and I don't know where anyone else is. Patrick scowled whenever I asked too many questions though. Being quiet was better.

I yawned again before slowly looking to my bed. Leaving the books and snacks on the floor, I made my way to bed. I was tired. So very tired from

CHAPTER 15

not sleeping well at night. But there were monsters in the dark, and I couldn't sleep without them haunting my dreams. Quickly, I ran over to the window and opened the curtains. Bright light filled the room, erasing the scary shadows in even the tiniest nooks and crannies.

I smiled softly before climbing on the bed and going to sleep.

Chapter 16

Shanely

The headaches started on day two, and by day four, I was dealing with insane nausea again. I wasn't eating enough, and I hadn't had my vitamins since Patrick took us. The boys were taking too much from me again, and my body was sure paying for it.

A week had passed with no signs of rescue or leaving this ridiculous room. Patrick still wouldn't let me see Aerith, and the door remained locked all day everyday. I tried the window, which unknowingly also had an alarm on it, and I got the scare of a lifetime when the alarm rattled the house. Patrick was pissed with me that day, and I didn't get to eat dinner. Fear gripped my heart that neither did Aerith because of my mistake.

Someone knocked on my door while I laid in bed one morning. I didn't bother rolling over to watch Patrick come in with oatmeal or cereal. Whatever quick meal he could make. I was too weak to move anyways. The mornings were always my worst time.

"Good morning, Shanely. How are you feeling?"

My eyes widened, and I forced myself to sit up. Calvin stood in the doorway with a tray of food and a black bag. This was the first I had seen the man since he offered up a trade. *One I should have taken...*

"You're looking a little peaked today," he said, closing the door. "Has my son been taking good care of you?"

Calvin set the tray of food down on the dresser before dragging that hideous chair over to me.

He didn't seem bothered by the fact I wasn't answering. He merely

CHAPTER 16

opened the small bag with him, pulling out medical supplies of all things. Calvin pulled out a needle, some gauze, and these small tubes before leaning back in his seat. My eyes narrowed.

"I need you healthy, Shanely. So if Patrick isn't..."

"What do you want?" I asked, pulling my knees to my chest. His smile didn't reach his eyes, and for a moment the two of us just watched each other. It was unnerving to say the least.

"You know, you and I have a common enemy," Calvin said finally. He grabbed the rubber tourniquet from the bag, and I scooted further away from him, my hands shaking slightly. I didn't like where this was going.

"Shanely," he warned, "don't make this more difficult than it needs to be, alright?"

I scoffed. *Like I'd do anything to make* their *life easier.*

Calvin sighed. Anger flashing on his face as he chided, "I've spent my entire life trying to accomplish something, so I can finally avenge my wife, and I will not let the attitude of a spoiled brat get in my way."

My face turned beat red as I squinted my eyes to him. *A spoiled brat!?* I thought, clenching my fists together. My wrist burned under the inhibitor as my anger flared. He simply ignored me.

"I was going absolutely nowhere until you came to town actually. Once I figured out who you were, and just how special you were, *everything changed*," he said, slapping his knee. "Now, let's get a move on, Shanely. I don't have all day."

I didn't move. *If there was ever a time I could puke on demand, let it be now,* I thought to myself. His eyes narrowed at my defiance.

"I will be moving forward with my work, Shanely," he snapped, "but you are not the only one here who is important. I can always draw blood from Aerith, seeing how she is *half-human*."

My mouth dropped. *No, he wouldn't. She's just a child! A small, defenseless child!* But to my horror, Calvin tossed the tourniquet back into the bag.

"You know that's probably a better idea for my project anyways," he said, cleaning everything up and standing then. "I'll just go see her instead."

"No!" I shouted. I gritted my teeth before rolling my sleeve up, exposing the veins in my arms. I reluctantly scooted closer to the edge and could smell that awful cologne he always wore as he sat back down.

It was the same one Patrick wore.

He grinned wide. "Why thank you for cooperating, Shanely."

Calvin took vial after vial before he finally putting it all back in his bag. He placed a Band-aid over the spot and patted my leg like he was proud of me. I swayed slightly on the bed as he stood and walked to the door. The room spun, and it was all I could do not to vomit all over the floor. But curiosity got the better of me.

"What happened to your wife?" I asked.

He merely tsked at me in answer. "All in good time, but for now I just want to thank you again. I think you will be the key to completing my wife's work."

The door swung open, but Calvin hesitated. He turned to me, that sour expression returning to his face, as he said, "I'm not ready to inform my son about my little project, Shanely. So, if you want me to stay away from Aerith, then I suggest we keep this between us. Sound good?"

I nodded slowly, feeling utterly sick at the thought of him doing this to my child, and he shut the door to go do God knows what with my blood. The lock clicked back in place, and I laid back on the bed as the room spun even more. My mind was reeling, trying to come up with all the possibilities as to why Calvin wanted me here too. *He and Patrick clearly orchestrated this whole thing, but what was Calvin's motive?* Because it sure as heck wasn't to keep his son happy. *He wanted my blood, but for what?* Calvin mentioned avenging his wife and completing her work, but I had no idea he even had a wife. She was never once mentioned in all my time spent in Diablo. *And why would Aerith be better because she's half-human?*

All these questions only made my headache worse. We were all wrong, and I had never felt more stupid in my life than I did right now. Here I thought Patrick was undermining his father with Calvin struggling to pick up the pieces, but they each had their own agenda, it seemed.

Figuring out what that was would take time. Time that I did not want to give.

CHAPTER 16

I debated telling Patrick what his father was doing, just to stir the pot, but I quickly put that out of my mind. Patrick wasn't someone I could rely on or trust, and I wouldn't risk Aerith going through whatever Calvin had in store. Until I could figure out what was going on, and use it to *my* advantage, I was keeping my mouth shut.

I rolled over on my side and looked to the tray of food. As much as I wanted to defy the Jennings family and refuse to eat anything, I needed my strength to get out of here, and for the love, I needed to stop feeling so nauseous all the time.

Forcing myself to my feet, I made my way to the food. I drank the orange juice until it was gone and gobbled up the sandwich. I didn't even realize how hungry I was until I took my first bite. After I ate, I laid back on the bed thinking of my mate and my daughter. Somewhere in the midst of all my thoughts, I fell asleep again.

Chapter 17

Aerith

Heavy footsteps sounded just outside my door, and soon I heard keys jingling. Patrick opened the door, smiling as he walked in. He brought more bags with him too.

"Hey, Baby Doll," he said with a smile. He held up the bags, shaking them slightly, and I could hear the items inside rattling. "I bring presents!"

I watched him carefully as he kicked the door closed and made his way across the room. He plopped down on the bed next to me, and I bounced with the heavy movement. I pulled my feet towards me, wrapping my arms around them, and leaning my head down as I watched. I didn't say a word. He seemed angry whenever I spoke or asked questions, so I waited for him to tell me what to do.

I didn't want to cause trouble again.

Patrick sighed heavily. "Look Aerith, I know I've been grumpy this last week, and I'm sorry. I was just tired, and dealing with stuff, but I am really happy you are here. And I brought you a bunch of stuff to keep you occupied on the days I'm working. I'm sure the toys here are starting to get boring. Here, look!"

Patrick pulled out a large Barbie doll house from the massive bag. He set it down in front of me and opened it up. The bright pink toy lit up and sparkled as Patrick dug in the bag again. I had seen this toy at the store before. Mommy told me we'd ask Daddy about it the next time we came, but we never made it back. A frown slowly appeared as I stared at the doll house.

CHAPTER 17

"Here," Patrick said as he handed me a Barbie doll. It was a mommy doll, and her belly was large. The belly moved slightly, revealing a baby tucked inside. My nose scrunched at the sight.

"This is mommy and..." he said as he pulled out another doll with red hair just like mine, "this is you."

I held the two dolls in my hand, not sure what to do or say. Mommy always told me to say thank you when I got gifts, but I wasn't sure if Patrick really wanted me to say anything. Then he pulled out another doll from the bag. A police officer... *Just like him.*

"And here is me," he said with a large smile. "Our family. Pretty cool, huh?"

Our family? I thought as sadness washed over me. *But my family wasn't here.* I had many people in my family, and Patrick was not my dad.

He waited for me to take the doll, but I didn't know what to do. I didn't want this. I didn't want the dolls. I just wanted to go home. But I didn't want to upset him either.

"Go on, Baby doll," he said softly. When I still didn't move to take it, he placed it in my hand. "It's okay. Daddy wants you to have this."

My eyes watered as I wrapped my hand around the doll. He wasn't my dad. He wasn't *my* dad.

Patrick bounced to his feet happily while I sat on the bed, trying not to cry. He made his way to the door again before twirling back to me.

"Oh, I nearly forgot your medicine again," he said, handing me another vial. My shoulders fell. My tummy was just now starting to feel better, and I didn't want to take it again.

"I feel better though," I said softly as I slowly looked at him beneath my lashes. I held my breath, waiting for him to scold me again, but exhaled when he smiled.

"Then that means it's doing its job. Grandpa says you need this because you don't have a wolf. But that's okay because it just makes you more like me. Right?"

He forced the vial into my hand, and I stared blankly at it.

"Aerith," he said more firmly. "Drink it."

Hands shaking, I downed the medicine. He gave me a wide toothy grin as he pocketed the empty vial.

"Well..." he said in a cheerful voice again, "Daddy has to check on mommy and see how she's feeling before going to work. Have fun today!"

Patrick kissed my head before leaving the room. I heard the familiar click of the lock as I sat on my bed and waited. I didn't even bother asking if I could go with him. I already knew the answer. His heavy footsteps grew quiet, and I stared at the police doll in my hand. The stupid doll with a bright shiny badge and pale eyes like Patrick's.

My hands clutched it tightly before launching that stupid doll across the room. It clattered against the wall, falling to the floor and breaking. Its arm lay next to the rest of its body.

I pulled the blanket back up and laid back down.

I didn't want to play anyways.

Chapter 18

Shanely

Yet again, no food or water was anywhere to be found this morning, and I groaned as I sat up. The lack of *everything* was draining me too fast, and my stomach twisted violently. I put my hand to my mouth.

I am *not* throwing up in here.

I ran to the locked door and started banging on it. "Let me out! Please!"

My mouth watered, and I swallowed hard. *Please, please, don't throw up right now!* I gagged, but quickly stuffed the feeling down, and hit the door harder.

"Patrick!"

The door swung open abruptly, and Patrick snarled, "What in God's name are you..."

I shoved passed him, running as fast as I could to the bathroom. He was seconds behind me and about to get a front row view of this embarrassment. I slammed the door open and barely made it to the toilet. I could feel his eyes watching me as I emptied my stomach. *God, this was awful.* My vision blurred, and I couldn't stop heaving, even when I had nothing left to give. I sagged to my knees when it finally passed. He didn't move to help me. Didn't say a word as I dragged myself to my feet and rinsed out my mouth in the sink. When I turned, Patrick looked confused almost. I snorted.

"What? Never been around a pregnant girl before?" I asked, drying my hands.

His eyes flashed with anger. "I'd check your tone, Shanely."

"Or what?" I snapped. "Are you going to threaten me again? Keep me locked in my room again or take away my dinner?"

"I'm doing the best I can," he snapped, stepping closer, "and if I could trust you, I'd let you out of your room!"

I rolled my eyes, knowing that was a lie. "Patrick, you know nothing about shifters. You don't get it, and you never will because you're human. The fact you think you can just step into Bastian's role..."

He grabbed my throat squeezing hard. He moved so fast, I didn't even register his reaction. Air was cut off, and I dug my nails into his hands, desperate to get him off me. Anything to get him to let go.

"Did I not warn you about saying his name?" he gritted through his teeth. "He's dead, Shanely. He was weak from when I shot him in Canada, and my men gunned him down on pack lands! He's not coming for you! So try not to piss off the one man *trying* to take care of you."

He tossed me backwards, and I hit the sink, gasping for air. I rubbed my neck, trying to slow my rapid breath. *He wasn't advancing at least,* I thought to myself as I watched him carefully. Patrick was just studying me somewhat lost in thought. I missed my wolf. *I wish I had her back so I could get a better read on him.*

"So, if it's so different from a human pregnancy," he said quietly, "then what do I need to know?"

"What?" I asked. My heart raced so loudly in my chest, it was hard to hear anything but that.

"You said I don't know anything, so tell me," he said, leaning against the door frame. "This is my child now, and I want it and you to be healthy."

I stilled, slowly looking into his eyes. *He was serious,* I thought. *Dead serious right now.* Heat rose to my cheeks as my lips curled in disgust. *How dare he...*

I was ready to kill him. I wanted nothing more than to kill him with my bare hands, and I tried hard to summon my wolf or my bear again, just like I did at Abraham's. *I broke his collar. Why can't I break this inhibitor too?* Fire surged through my veins down to the bracelet. Next came heat, and I sucked in a breath as my skin burned again.

"Shanely?"

CHAPTER 18

I gritted my teeth and kept searching for my wolf, but all that came through was pain. Pure pain as I searched for something that was no longer there. Finally, the pain struck my chest, and I gasped. I shut my eyes tight, feeling sick all over again as I let go. Patrick chuckled as he grabbed my wrist to inspect the inhibitor. He clicked his tongue when he saw the burn.

"Fighting the inhibitor, are we?"

I turned to hide my face from him. I was an utter fool to try again, that's what I was. I crossed my arms, glaring at the silver bracelet.

"I want my daughter, Patrick."

He sighed, and his hands slowly rubbed my shoulders. My body tensed at his touch, but I didn't make a sound. I didn't shove him off because I knew deep down this was a fight I would not win.

"I'll make you a deal," he said softly. "Tell me what you need to feel better, and I'll bring Aerith here tonight. Alright?"

I turned to face him. I knew I looked desperate right now, but I couldn't bring myself to stop searching his eyes for the truth. He seemed genuine in this moment, but I didn't know if this was just some trick to get me to cooperate. *I'm going to have to trust him though,* I thought. There was no other way, and this was an opportunity I wouldn't pass up because I haven't seen my daughter once since coming here. I needed to make sure she was okay.

"It's not just one baby, Patrick," I said quietly, "it's two. I'm carrying twins, and they take everything from me. It makes me violently ill and dizzy when I don't get the nutrients I need to support myself. I had these special vitamins and a powder supplement back in my cabin that I would take to help. Between not eating regularly and not taking those, I'm getting ill."

Patrick nodded then. "Okay, I'll swing by your place after work and pick them up."

He took me by the arm and pulled me back to my room. I sighed heavily when he opened the door to let me in, but to my surprise, his face softened.

"Anything else you want from your old place?" Patrick asked, and I narrowed my eyes. *Was this some game to him? A game to get me to trust him somehow?* I wondered. I didn't know how to respond, and the awkward silence filled the space between us. He shrugged, shifting uncomfortably on his feet. *It seems he doesn't like the silence either,* I thought.

"Now's your chance," he said, pulling me from my thoughts. "I won't be returning there again so if you want something *reasonable*, I'll grab it while I'm there."

My eyes widened. This was not something I expected, but I slowly sat down on my chair to think. There were too many memories, and I highly doubted he'd bring me any photos. Even then, they might be hard to look at.

"Today, Shanely."

Suddenly, I knew what I wanted. "There's a jewelry box on my vanity. Inside is a necklace with a wolf and bear pendant on it. I took it off when we got home, so it's in there. I want that."

Patrick smirked. "Done. See? I'm not such a bad guy after all."

He slammed the door, locking it behind him. Then he was gone for the day.

I slumped back feeling sick for a whole new reason. Asking him to grab my necklace just felt like I accepted Bastian's and my family's death. Like I just accepted what my life was now, and that couldn't be further from the truth. My lips trembled as the tears flowed freely down my face. *I don't know why I did that,* I thought as my temper flared. I don't know why I just asked *him* of all people to grab something so special.

Hours felt like minutes, and soon the sun had set, and Patrick's heavy footsteps sounded outside my door again. I didn't know where the time had gone. I was just lost... Lost in the despair of what I'd done.

Patrick opened the door, smiling wide as he chucked my necklace on my lap.

"Found it right where you said it was," Patrick said still grinning. "I also got those vitamins too, so now that I'm home, I'll make you something to eat and bring everything to you. I worked it out with dad as well, so I can be home for awhile until you're back on your feet and doing good. So from now on, it will just be the three of us here at home."

CHAPTER 18

Patrick bounded out of the room excitedly, all while I stared at the necklace in my hands. I saw what happened to my pack. I felt what happened to Bastian and Elijah. But seeing this... *It broke me.*

I screamed and threw the necklace across the room. The veins on the side of my head popped as I screamed even louder, picking up the lamp next to me and hurling it at the wall. The base shattered.

I grabbed the stupid picture of a flower off the wall and threw it too. Anything to stop this unbearable pain inside my chest. It was ripping me in two.

My screams turned into unflattering sobs, as I pushed the dresser over. My chest heaved as I tried to lift the bed, but it was too heavy. I swore in anger over the fact that I couldn't break it too.

They were gone. They were gone, and they never coming back.

I collapsed on the ground and sobbed.

Chapter 19

My eyes fluttered open as I took in my new surroundings. I was lying on a new bed in a new room. This room was larger than the other with a massive king size bed loaded with fur blankets that I was currently tangled up in. A tray of spaghetti and garlic bread sat on the bench at the end of the bed. The food was steaming hot, but I didn't move towards it. My eyes roamed around the room further. A door was right in front of me with an opened closet next to that. *Where was I?*

I slowly sat forward and saw the rest of the room. A desk sat off to the left beside an old radiator fastened to the floor. A large window was above that, and by the looks of the trees outside, I was on the second floor. Lastly, a comfortable lounge chair sat in the far corner next to the window.

"This is my room," a voice said.

I turned to find Patrick leaning in the door frame. He pointed to a tray of food at the foot of the bed.

"Eat."

"Why am I here?" I asked.

"Because you destroyed the room you were in," he snapped, his eyes flashing. I dropped my head, and he sighed. "Besides this was always where I always planned to bring you. I was just waiting until you got more accepting to the idea of being mine. Now eat."

I rolled over and refused to move. Maybe I was being stupid, refusing to eat like this, but after asking for the necklace earlier, it just felt like another way I'd show him I accepted this. *I just couldn't do it.* He sighed again before coming to the other side of the bed. I glared at him as he knelt down.

"Shanely, you need to eat," Patrick protested, "and I went all that way to a house I never wanted to see again, just to get you the stuff you needed. Now sit up and eat! Or you'll miss your time with Aerith."

Aerith.

I slowly sat up in defeat, and his eyes glimmered with triumph as he grabbed the tray. The vitamins lay on the side, so I took those first before starting to eat. Tears came to my eyes as I thought of Cade, and the first time he made spaghetti for me. *He hadn't even found his mate, and now he was gone because of me.* He was seconds behind when I got hit. *They probably shot him then,* I thought. The food turned to ash in my mouth, but I continued to eat.

Patrick watched me until I ate most of my plate. It was churning my stomach to keep going, and the last thing I needed was to throw up spaghetti.

"I can't anymore," I said, pushing the tray away. He nodded his head as he patted my leg. I *pleased* him.

"Hang tight," he muttered before taking the tray and leaving me. *Where else could I go?* I thought to myself. Another little piece of me died then. I wasn't getting out, and even if I did, home would never be the same.

Patrick was only gone for a few minutes before the door flew opened again and in ran Aerith. I sagged in relief as I tossed the blankets back and scooped her up.

"Mommy!" she cried.

I clung to her and nearly broke right there when she started to cry. I rubbed the back of her head as she stayed wrapped in my arms.

"Oh, Aerith," I said softly. I inhaled her scent, and it settled something inside me. The heavy despair lifted some, and I just wanted to help her. With a calm voice, I pulled back and asked, "Are you alright?"

"I'm fine," she answered, and my brows furrowed. I did *not* like the look that spread across her face just now. "Where are we?"

"You're home baby doll," Patrick replied, and I glared at him.

"I can answer for myself," I snapped, and he rolled his eyes.

"Yeah," he replied, "but you'd feed her some lie, I'm sure."

"Can I please just be with my daughter alone? Don't I deserve that?"

He studied me a moment before sighing. "Fine. I'll be back later to fetch her."

"Why can't she stay with me?!" I bellowed. My voice sounding more shrill than angry.

"Because you haven't been a very good girl, Shanely. Beside this is where mommy and daddy sleeps. Aerith's room is just a few doors down."

I opened my mouth to protest, but he was already slamming the door behind him. I gritted my teeth and took a deep breath. Forcing myself to smile, I looked down to my daughter.

"I have missed you, love," I said, kissing her forehead. Her bottom lip jutted out as tears welled in her eyes. *She is breaking my heart with that look.*

"Uncle Abey..." she whispered before she bawled. Her little arms wrapped around my neck, while she soaked my shirt. My heart broke in ways I didn't think it could. The horrors she must have seen when they took her. I gently tried to shush her, rubbing her hair with my hand, while I let her release all the pent up anguish she had been holding onto.

"What happened, baby?"

"He was yelling, mommy," she said, trying to breathe between the sobs. "Someone was chasing us, and Uncle Abey looked scared. The big van hit us, and we hit a tree. Uncle Abey was laying on the steering wheel when the men in dark clothes took me away. He didn't get up, mommy. He didn't get up!"

I held her tight as she sobbed again, and I didn't know what to even say. Silent tears slid down my cheek. *My brother...*

"Mommy, where's daddy?" she cried out as she pushed back. Her silver gray eyes looking for answers. Answers I couldn't give her. "I want daddy! I wanna go home!"

I quickly wiped my face, trying to look brave and strong for her. *God, this was too hard. I don't know how I'm going to help her,* I thought.

"I know, honey. I want to go home too, but..."

I didn't want to even say it. Aerith wiped her wet nose, looking at me for answers, but the only ones I had to give would hurt her more. But she *needed* the truth. With a shaky voice, I said, "I don't think daddy's going to save us. Not this time, sweetie."

Her lip quivered, and another piece of my heart shattered. "But daddy *always* saves us. He promised! He said he'd always find us."

She started to cry uncontrollably, and I couldn't even find the words to make it better. Nothing I said would. This wretched feeling twisted my stomach watching my daughter fall apart like this. I wrapped my arms around her and pulled her close.

"I'm sorry," I whispered. "I'm so sorry."

"Can't you just talk to him now?" she protested. "In here."

Aerith tapped my forehead, and I pursed my lips together. *God, she was too smart. She remembered everything.*

"I can't, baby. See this," I said, pointing to the bracelet. She nodded as I continued, "This keeps my wolf and bear away. I can't hear daddy right now. I'm so sorry, honey. But I promise you, Aerith, I will find a way to get us out of here. Trust me."

She nodded before leaning her head back on my chest. I pulled the heavy blanket over her, and we stayed quiet for awhile. It wasn't long before I heard her soft snores, and only then did I allow myself to break again. I struggled to keep my breaths even. I didn't want to wake her, but God this pain hurt. It hurt so freaking bad in my chest, I honestly thought I was going to die. But my promise kept me grounded. It was keeping the determination to save the both of us alive. So I let myself fall apart while no one was around to watch. I had work to do, but not tonight. After soaking the pillow beneath me, I finally passed out too.

* * *

A cold breeze caused me to shiver, and Aerith's body shifted off me. My eyes shot open, and I found Patrick pulling her from our cozy spot on the bed. I clung to her body and yanked her towards me again.

"Don't touch her!" I snapped as Aerith's eyes fluttered opened. Patrick glared down at me.

"Let her go, Shanely," he said crossly.

"No. Do not touch her, Patrick!" I shouted back.

His jaw clenched as he reached for her again. "I said let her go!"

Patrick yanked her up into his arms as I scurried from the bed.

"Let her go! Don't you take her from me!" I bellowed louder. Aerith began to cry, and she lunged for me. Patrick swore, stumbling on his feet before promptly readjusting her.

"Knock it off you two!" he yelled as he took a step to the door, but I got in his way. My heart pounded in my chest, but I refused to move. His eyes narrowed. "Move, Shanely."

"Put her down," I demanded.

Patrick backhanded me across the face, dropping me to the floor. Without a word, he stepped over me and left the room.

I bolted to my feet, trying to turn the handle before he locked it again. My face throbbed, but I didn't care. I screamed when the handle wouldn't move, banging harder on the door as I begged for him to bring her back. I could hear her soft cries from down the hall, and my heart broke even more.

"Patrick! Please! Bring her..."

The door slammed open, and I fell on my butt. I couldn't move fast enough to get away. He lunged, gripping me by my throat before yanking me to my feet.

"What makes you think you have any control of this situation? When I say your time is up, then I mean your time is up! Don't you ever challenge me in front of her again. Do you understand?" he shouted in my face.

Rage coursed through my veins like a burning fire. A guttural scream erupted from my chest before I swung, hitting him hard across the face. I put all my weight behind that one strike, and he dropped me. I couldn't stop. It was as if the rage and blood lust took over, and all I could see was his death. I needed to watch the life leave his eyes for all he's done. I swung again. And again. Screaming every name in the book as he fought for control of my hands.

CHAPTER 19

His face bled by the time he finally caught them, and he shoved me against the wall. My head rebounded off the wall hard enough I thought he might have given me a concussion, but nothing prepared me for the blow that was about to come. His fist connected with my jaw, and my whole body went limp. My vision blurred as pain exploded in my head.

Patrick swore harshly. I rapidly blinked as I fought to stay awake. He was gently touching his own face, inspecting the minor wounds I have given him.

"For the love, Shanely..."

I couldn't move. My head spun where I lay, but to my dismay, he threw me over his shoulder and carried me out of the room. My body swayed with every step as we made our way down the hall. Aerith's sobs coming from one of these rooms, but I couldn't tell which one. We moved so quickly down the stairs and towards the garage.

The temperature dropped significantly as we stepped inside. Metal sounds rustling from behind, and the next thing I knew, I was being tossed like a rag doll inside a large dog crate. The metal rods cutting into my skin as I slowly forced myself to rise.

"You asked for it, Shanely. I've tried to show you I'm not such a bad guy, but then you go and do something like this?" he said, pointing to his face. "That's not how a wife should treat her husband, so now I have to punish you."

My eyes widened when I realized he was really going to leave me out here. He was just going to leave me in this crate in the cold. My head throbbed harder and vomit sat in the back of my throat as he grabbed a lock and attached it to the door.

"You can't leave me, Patrick," I said quietly. Every word excruciating. "I'll freeze to death."

He stood up away from me then, his eyes still so dark. "Nah, you won't freeze. I never did."

My mouth dropped, but he shrugged me off.

"Who do you think that cage was for, Shanely? I never had a dog," he replied nonchalantly.

He left me utterly alone in the freezing cold with no light or anything. Nothing to give me comfort.

I clutched my head as the room spun more. I needed a doctor, but that was never going to happen. I wish more than anything I knew how to pick locks. I had never been inside this room before and wondered if it had any answers to how I could escape the wretched place.

Shifting from leg to leg as the cold concrete ground and metal wires pushed into my skin, I was left with nothing to do but think. It was killing me to sit like this, but there was nowhere to go for any relief.

Exhaustion set in as the hours passed. The temperature dropping more and more as the night went by. I know I had dozed off more than once, only to wake up in such pain that I had to shift sides again. The easiest way to keep the warmth in was if I stayed curled up in the corner, but the stupid bars just made it hard to sit still.

This was his punishment?! His cage! I thought as I waited for him to let me out. *Did Calvin shove him in here as a small child?* It was sickening to know his dad put him in here at *any* point of his life. *How could someone do this to a child?!* Just the idea made me want to puke, but then I froze. *Would Patrick try to punish Aerith like this?*

Rage coursed through my veins at the thought of that man trying to do something like this to my daughter.

Over my dead body.

My temper flared as I spent the rest of the night thinking of all the ways I'd kill him for even trying. Surprisingly, it helped me deal with the pain of sleeping in a metal cage, but still I shivered. To the point I was sure my teeth would break from the constant chattering.

Patrick never came for me though, and I began to wonder how many days would he keep me here before he decided I had been punished enough.

The outside world was slowly waking up, and I prayed the sun would warm the garage at least a little. By this point my fingers were numb, and I know my lips had probably started to turn blue already.

If Bastian were alive, he'd burst through those doors to save me. That thought brought a small smile to my lips. I imagined seeing that look of

CHAPTER 19

relief in his eyes right before they turned feral. Just like they did when he found Cade and I in Dead Man's Hallow. *He'd fix this if he knew,* I thought to myself. *He'd destroy them all just for tossing me in here. For taking Aerith and I in the first place.*

I was stuck in my fantasy when the door opened. I blinked, when I realized the sun was now shining on my face. *I had stayed awake the entire night,* I realized.

My eyes began to droop as heavy boots walked towards the cage, and then two calloused hands hauled me up and out. A familiar awful scent filled my nose, but those hands were warm to the touch. The body I laid against was warm, and I craved the heat. I leaned further in, and they tucked in me closer.

It reminded me of the many times Bastian carried me. Whether I was hurt or sick, he picked me up like I was nothing and took me wherever I needed to go. *I missed that... I missed him.*

My eyes grew too heavy, and I let them close, relaxing into the warmth once more. Soft fur covered my body, and I didn't stay awake after that.

Chapter 20

Aerith

My chest heaved as I heard more shouting from mama.

"Stay put, Aerith," Patrick snarled. My eyes widened when he said, "Or else."

He locked the door and stomped back down the hall. My breathing quickened as he yelled again, and I could hear loud banging come from the other room.

I ran to the door.

"MOMMY!" I shouted as I pounded against the door. "MOMMY!"

Footsteps sounded again, and I froze. I saw the shadow of Patrick's steps pass by my room, and I exhaled when he didn't stop. My stomach started to hurt as I thought about mama. *She was all by herself and... And I was too afraid to help her.*

My hands tightened into fists. *Daddy was never afraid of anything,* I thought as I glared at the door. *And neither should I.*

Tears fell down my cheek as I hit the door harshly. It rattled on its hinges, and I hit it again. Over and over until a sharp pain shot through my wrist, and I yipped loudly. My wrist throbbed, and I cradled it, falling against the door in a heap.

"Don't hurt mommy..." I begged softly, but silence filled the halls, and I had no idea what was happening.

I sniffed loudly when suddenly an idea came to mind. *I had never done it before, but maybe I could?* I thought anxiously. *Mama always said I was a shifter too.* I tried to use the link. I searched inside just like Daddy always

CHAPTER 20

told me to do, searching for my wolf. I couldn't feel anything though, so I tried to push out a thought like they do.

"Daddy?" No answer.

"Daddy!" I shouted. *"Please, come help us! Mommy's hurt."*

Silence still, and I leaned my head back against the door. My lip quivered, and I tried my hardest to make it stop, but I was angry. So angry that I couldn't stop the tears from falling.

"You promised. You promised you'd come!" I bellowed through the link, but it didn't matter what I shouted because no one was listening.

Tears fell faster down my cheek as I sat alone in my room. No one was coming, and I didn't know how to help mommy.

Chapter 21

Shanely

I groaned, shoving off the tremendous amount of blankets currently burying me alive. My head pounded in my skull, and my body felt sticky with sweat. I already knew where I was without having to open my eyes, and I regretted it the moment I did. That annoyingly bright light coming from the windows only made my head feel worse.

"Did we learn our lesson?" a snide voice asked from my left.

I turned to find Patrick sitting in his chair watching me sleep. *Again.* I couldn't keep the smirk from my lips when I saw those bloody scratch marks had crusted over on his face. One looked surprisingly deep.

"Don't you ever do that to me again, Patrick," I snarled before leaving the bed altogether. He was on his feet before I could even get my balance.

"Why can't you just accept this? I have done *everything* to save you from the slaughterhouse," he said, arms raised. "I'm taking care of you, the twins, and Aerith. On top of working all day for dad. It would be nice if you could find a way to make this work. You know, be here to take care of *me* when I come home from a long day at work. Rub my feet, make our dinner, raise our kids, put out when I need! You might actually come to find that you can be happy here with me."

My eyes widened in rage. I stormed towards him yelling, "I'm not your wife, Patrick, and my kids are not your children! You're delusional if you think we're just going to become one big happy family after what you've done!"

"This is your life now, Shanely," he cried out, "and it can actually be a

CHAPTER 21

good one if you'd just be a little nicer and started treating me the way I deserve!"

I scoffed. "The way you deserve?! What about what *I* deserve?! Do I *deserve* to be physically abused every time I say something you don't like? Do I *deserve* to have my child taken from me as punishment for simply not obeying your every whim? Did I *freaking deserve* to have my mate slaughtered with the rest of my pack and family just because you wanted me, and I said no?! I didn't deserve anything you and your father did to me, and I lost *everything* because of you!"

His nostrils flared as he took another step closer. He continued to advance until my back hit the wall with nowhere left to go. Patrick towered over me, and I lost my confidence just a tad.

"It wasn't my fault!" he shouted so loud it rattled the walls. "Look, I've made mistakes in the past. I'll admit that. I lost my temper in Canada and took that shot, but that stupid prick survived! Bastian *survived* my mistake, but he didn't survive the Division. That one wasn't on me, Shanely! You're lucky the team assigned to me owed me a few favors. I saved you!"

I shook my head in disbelief. *He truly believed every word he spoke, but I knew the truth.* If Patrick was willing to shoot my mate because he lost his temper then he is more than capable of lying.

"Calvin told us everything," I said, glaring at him. "From the deal he tried to make because *you* wanted me to stacking the deck against us with the Division. *Everything*, Patrick. Why couldn't you just leave us be? Why... Why did you have to kill the man I loved? Just why?!"

Silent tears fell down my face as I stared at him. I was so angry, so heartbroken over everything, and the only reason I haven't withered away in my grief was because of my kids. They needed me to save them because there is no one else coming. *There was no one else left.*

Patrick's eyes darkened, and I braced myself for the strike, but he didn't swing. His arms raised above my head, pinning me against the wall and caging me in.

"I stuck my neck out for you, Shanely. I saved you and your kids," he snapped. "The least you could do is try to make this work."

Patrick lips slammed down on mine, and my heart stopped. My hands flattened on his chest, and I shoved, but he only pushed back harder, tightening his grip on me. I could barely breath as panic took over *every* part of my body. *This was wrong!* I shouted in my head. *This was so wrong.*

His hands tangled themselves in my hair, and I tried to pull my face to the side, but Patrick wasn't having that. He gripped my jaw harshly, holding me still as he continued to kiss me. Tears rapidly fell down my face and bile rose to the back of my throat. *I'm so sorry, Bastian. I'm so very sorry.*

Patrick finally let me go, and I stood there shakily. My ragged breaths the only sound in the room until he sighed heavily. His hand gently rubbed my cheek as my stomach twisted in knots.

"Think about it, Shanely," he said quietly. "What are your other options anyways?"

He left, slamming the door behind him, and I slid down the wall in a sob. Pulling my knees to my chest, I let go of everything. My hands gripped my hair as I wallowed in my misery.

What did I do to deserve this? I thought, tightening the grip on my hair. It was like living with Peter all over again except this time it was worse. It wasn't just me like last time. Now I had three littles that needed help too, but the task just felt impossible with the grief weighing down on me. I wiped my nose on my sleeve, trying to slow my tears.

I was dealing with a psychopath. He seems to genuinely think he *saved* me from the people he worked for. I gritted my teeth, thinking back to that awful day. *They were all wretched,* I thought, *and deserved a slow agonizing death.* I didn't need my wolf or bear to amplify the hatred in my heart for those men. I had enough all on my own.

This has to come to an end, I thought. *The only way out of here is killing them. Then we could run. We could run and finally be free. They would get what they deserved, and my family would be safe.* All the reasons I should just kill Patrick began to make sense. I wouldn't need an alarm code or anything to leave this place if they were dead. It would be the only way we could live without worry or constantly checking over our shoulder to see if we were being hunted. If everyone else believed we were dead, then we

CHAPTER 21

could simply disappear.

Light flashed across the room as I slowly lifted my head. Revenge was the only course of action I could take to give my family a safe life. *But how could I kill him?* I thought as I slumped against the wall again. *I am so much weaker than he is.* I looked down at the silver inhibitor, wishing more than anything I had my wolf. My eyes widened then. *If I couldn't use my shifter abilities, than maybe I just needed to use the good old fashioned* human *way of killing someone.*

And a police officer should have plenty of options.

The light flickered again as I shot to my feet and ran to Patrick's closet. I searched his whole room for his guns, knowing he had to have quite a few just lying around here somewhere. Peter always did, and it made sense that Patrick would too. The old Shanely would have thought this was a bad idea, but the new and angry Shanely was ready for it. *I was going to shoot that prick like he shot my mate.*

I found nothing in his room and made my way to the door. For the first time in a long time, he left the door *unlocked.* I carefully stole a peek into the hall. At the far end, Patrick was coming out of a room I had yet to explore. He moved about in a huff, still probably angry with me, but he didn't notice me watching him and was down the grand staircase in a matter of minutes.

This was it, I thought.

I moved, staying along the edge to avoid the creaks in the hardwood I had yet to memorize. It didn't take long to reach the room, and I quickly shut the door behind me.

My mouth dropped at what I saw. All over the wall on my right were pictures of *me*. So many pictures of me taken when I had no idea. Like a freaking shrine, Patrick had hundreds of pictures on the wall. Even notes written down about my favorite things or the stuff I disliked. I wanted to puke.

I had to look away. I had to look far away because I couldn't even begin to process that. Adrenaline was already coursing through my veins and making my hands shake. If I kept staring, I would surely puke. Ignoring the massive creepiness on the back wall, I turned to the rest of the room.

Several computers sat on his desk, showing the many cameras they had around the outside of the house, and a couple filing cabinets sat next to that, just on my left. But I smiled when I found what I was looking for. In the back corner was a large gun rack just sitting behind a cage. *Yeah... That'll work.*

My feet moved anxiously across the room. I had never actually shot a weapon before. I held Peter's handgun many times when he was too lazy to put them away, but loading one and actually shooting it... That was a different story.

Patrick's keys hung next to the cage, and on the fourth key, the lock popped open. I stared at the many weapons on the rack. They were all long and way different than the handguns Peter usually kept around. Multiple black cases sat at the bottom with boxes of ammo next to them. *Which one do I choose?*

I chose one that looked aggressive and nearly dropped the stupid thing. *Good lord, it was heavy!* I thought to myself. *How does he even use this thing?* It had two barrels, so it looked simple yet powerful. I turned the gun sideways. *There had to be a way to load this.*

After fiddling with it for a few minutes, I sagged in relief when the gun finally split in two. Fumbling to find the right size bullet, I loaded the gun and pushed it back together again. The corners of my mouth rose in triumph.

"I did it," I whispered.

The door suddenly opened, and I jumped. My heart stopped as Patrick came into view. He ground to a stop with a cup of coffee in his hands. My breath started to quicken, and I tried to slow my racing heart. *I could do this...* I told myself as my arms began to shake. *I could...*

Patrick's face darkened, and I could see the rage spread across his face as he looked at the gun in my hands. I swallowed hard and held it up. I aimed it at his chest, unable to control my breathing. Unable to control the shaking.

"What do you think you're doing, Shanely?" Patrick asked, with his hands slightly raised.

CHAPTER 21

"You killed my mate," I growled, "and I plan on making it even, can't you tell?"

Patrick carefully took a step forward. I shifted the gun, and he halted. His eyes widened just a tad, and he kept his hands raised. "Now, now, let's think about this, baby girl. You don't want to do anything you might regret."

Hearing Cade's nickname come out of *his* mouth pushed me over the limit.

"I am *not* your Baby Girl," I cried out as I pulled the trigger.

The gun went off loudly, knocking me back against the cage. I nearly dropped the gun as my hip slammed into the metal harshly.

Patrick hollered in pain, clutching his arm that now dripped red.

I missed... I thought in disbelief.

I scrambled to raise the gun again when he charged. He shoved the gun towards the ceiling as I pulled the trigger. Dry wall rained down on our heads, and I began to panic as that was my last shot.

He yanked the gun away from me and tossed it to the side. Clenching his fist, Patrick swung, and I fell into darkness.

Chapter 22

Aerith

Patrick left me in my room the following day. I knew he punished mama for fighting him, and I worried for her. All I wanted to do was go see her, but the door was locked, and I was alone. I hated being alone, and I hated being here.

With nothing to do, I played with the mommy Barbie, and the one that looked like me, leaving the Police Officer across the room. His arm was still broken, but I didn't care.

I walked the mommy Barbie up the stairs in my doll house when I heard shouting. I jolted to my bed, dropping the dolls. Someone was arguing, and I covered my ears as Patrick's voice rattled the walls. But then there was another voice. A kinder voice... *Mommy! It was mommy's voice!*

I took off to the door to listen in. I needed to make sure mama was okay.

The door slammed down the hall, causing me to jump, but I didn't run back to bed this time. My chest hurt to the point it burned, but I stayed still as a mouse as Patrick's heavy footsteps passed by my door. I slowly crept down to peek under the door. *He wasn't coming here.* Soon his feet passed by again, and he made his way downstairs.

The house grew quiet again, and I stayed watching through the crack of my door. I sighed loudly as I sat back on my knees. This was no different than the other times. I had no idea what happened to mama, and unless Patrick let me out of here, I wasn't going to find out.

Suddenly, I heard footsteps. I dove to look back under the doorway and saw a set of smaller footsteps pass by.

CHAPTER 22

"Mommy!" I whispered, but she kept moving. My heart sunk. *She didn't come for me*, I thought to myself. *Maybe she didn't hear me?* I dug my fingers under the door and whispered again, "Mommy!!"

I slowly sat up when she didn't come back for me. *But Mommy wouldn't leave me, would she?* I wondered as my lips puckered. *But Daddy left us*, I thought as my chest burned again. A single tear fell down my face as I leaned against the door. *I just wanted to go home. I wanted things the way they were, and I wish Daddy were here. He'd find a way to make things better. He always did.*

Suddenly a loud sound rattled the walls, and I jumped hard. I had *never* heard a sound like this before, and I buried my face in my lap and covered my ears as it sounded again. I scurried away from the door and emptied my bladder. I couldn't catch my breath as I stared at the door, plugging my ears in case the sound happened again.

But it didn't.

I started to cry as I looked down to my mess. *Patrick would be so angry when he saw,* I thought to myself, but I didn't dare move. My body shook, and I wrapped my arms around myself and squeezed tightly. My silent cries turned into wailing sobs, and I couldn't stop. I knew Patrick hated when I cried, and I was going to get in serious trouble again, but the tears continued to fall.

My door suddenly opened, and Patrick stood in the doorway, taking one look at me and frowning.

"I... I didn't mean too," I sobbed. "I'm sorry."

I stood there waiting. Waiting for him to scold me, but Patrick come over and knelt down next to me.

"It's okay," he said quietly. I sniffed hard and used my sleeve to wipe my cheek, and he just gave a half smile. "I used to have accidents a lot when I was younger too."

Patrick raised his arm and winced, tucking it back to his side again before wiping my cheek with his other hand.

"Let's just get you cleaned up before grandpa gets home," he said as he made his way to my dresser. He grabbed me fresh clothes from the drawer before turning back to me. "My dad always thought kids should learn to take care of themselves as young as possible. He said a firm hand was a good one, and that if he wasn't stern with me when I was young then I wouldn't have grown up to be the man I should be. My dad was a smart man, so I'm going to show you how to clean yourself up if you have another accident in the future."

"That sounds lonely..." I said softly, and he stilled.

"Yeah..." he muttered softly. "Yeah I guess I was, but I'm not alone now. I've got you and your mother and grandpa. How about I help you get cleaned up, and then you and I can make dinner together?"

I blinked. *He wasn't mad at me for having an accident like I thought. He wasn't mad at me at all.*

Patrick extend out his hand as he smiled softly. Relieved, I slowly reached up and took his hand. He guided me to the hall bathroom and set my stuff inside, grabbing a towel and running a bath, while I waited by the door. He put everything I'd need on the side of the tub then, moving ever so slowly as he did. My eyes narrowed when I realized he wasn't using his left arm.

"Can I see mama?" I asked quietly. Patrick didn't answer. He went on checking the temperature and promptly shut it off halfway.

He turned to me then. "I'm going to clean up your room, so why don't you take your bath and get dressed. Let's be quick though, okay Aerith?"

I gave him a nod, and he smiled softly. "Good girl. I'll be back in 20 minutes."

Patrick shut the door behind him, and I quickly locked it. I stared at the bath for a moment before slowly taking off my soiled clothes and stepping in. The water was wonderfully warm, and I fumbled getting the soap open. A giant glob fell out onto my hand, and I did my best to get cleaned as fast as I could. *Something bad happened tonight,* I thought to myself, and I didn't want to upset Patrick more.

I got out and dried myself off before getting dressed. My hair was still dripping wet, and I dumped my soiled clothes into the basket before trying to figure out how to make the water go away. I had pulled the plug but nothing happened. I frowned. *Would he be mad I didn't clean up my mess*

CHAPTER 22

when he came back?

The door suddenly rattled, and I jumped again.

"Bout done in there?" Patrick asked through the door.

I opened the door to let him in and turned to the tub. "I don't know how to drain it."

He smiled at me, flicking a switch on the side. The water gurgled then before slowly going down the pipes.

"That's okay, Baby Doll," he said. "Took me awhile to figure that out too."

He had a new shirt on with a white bandage sticking out of the sleeve of his left arm. *What happened?*

"Are you ready to make dinner now?" he asked.

I nodded softly. "Can mama come too?"

He frowned then, and I held my breath. *What did I say wrong now?*

"Not tonight," he answered before taking my hand.

I stayed quiet as he pulled me to the kitchen. Once there, he picked me up and set me on the stool. His eyes drifted away from me for a moment, darkening when they settled on something outside. I tried to look past, but he knelt down to me saying, "You stay right here. Do not move from this spot."

I nodded obediently, and Patrick went outside through the sliding glass door. My eyes followed him as he walked in the heavy snow to...

Mommy.

Mommy was outside in a cage. *Why was mommy out there?!* I wondered as my heart began to race. I started to move off the stool, when I suddenly froze, remembering what Patrick told me. He would be *very* angry if I moved. *But mommy needed help...*

My lip puckered slightly as I watched them outside. My chest heaved as I held back my tears, but I forced myself not to cry again. Patrick always hated when I cried, and I had already done enough wrong tonight. I quickly looked to the counter before me. I couldn't watch mama anymore, and I hated myself for it. *Daddy wouldn't be afraid,* I scolded myself. *He would have run to save mommy, but I... I can't.*

The door slammed shut, and I jumped again, finding Patrick walking in with a sour expression. He kicked the heavy snow off his boots, when our eyes met.

"Mommy did something very bad today, and she's getting punished for it," Patrick said firmly. He slowly pointed towards her. "I may be trying to do things different than how I was raised, but some punishments I can't stop. *That* is what happens when you do very bad things, Aerith. Do you want to spend time in the cage?"

My eyes widened, and I quickly shook my head no. I stole a glance to mama before gluing them to the man in front of me again.

"Good," Patrick answered, his face softening. He walked the few steps over to me and gently rubbed my cheek. I refused to let my tears fall. I refused to let him see me cry again, and he smiled. "You're a good girl, Aerith. I knew I wouldn't have to worry about you."

He kissed my cheek before making his way to the stove. My heart pounded in my chest as I watched my mother outside. She was hunched over in the corner with her head on her knees. *Please, open your eyes. Please!*

"Where is that freaking pan?" Patrick snapped as he grumbled about the kitchen. I sat still on my chair. So very still as he searched the cabinets. I couldn't take my eyes off my mother, and my chest burned fiercely.

Daddy would never treat mommy like this, I thought as anger slowly trickled in and masked my fear. *Even if he was angry. He would never...*

"There!" he cried out, setting the large metal pan on the stove loudly. "I'm going to make stir fry tonight, Baby Doll. You like stir fry?"

I nodded, even though I hated onions. He smiled again, and I watched him clatter on in the kitchen. My eyes drifted back to the sliding door and my mother who lay just beyond. Something pulled inside my chest. It wanted me to help mommy. To *save* her. It burned inside, and I held my breath as it grew more and more painful. *I can be brave,* I told myself. *I can be just like daddy.*

Patrick continued to cook on the stove, while I sat there trying to think. *How could I help mama? What in the world could I do to stop this?*

A plate of food was suddenly placed in front of me, and I didn't realize how

CHAPTER 22

long I'd been thinking for. Rice was buried under a mountain of peppers, onions, and grilled chicken.

Patrick sat down next to me, taking a huge bite off his plate. I shoved the fear aside, listening to the tiny voice inside my head telling me I could do this. My chest burned again, and I took a deep breath.

"Thank you," I said quietly, and Patrick smiled at me.

"You're welcome," he said, taking another bite. Silence filled the space between us again, and Patrick began to eat his food.

"Eat, Baby Doll," he said, nudging me. "If you hurry, we can get a movie in before bed."

I carefully looked to my mom, and I swallowed hard. Light flickered against her body, causing her to shift in the cage. *Would she be stuck out there for that too?* I wondered.

"Eat," he commanded again, and I quickly picked up my fork. I ate a bite of chicken, earning a smile from him.

I took another bit. Then another, and Patrick seemed happier with each one. *Maybe this is all I needed to do? Make him happy enough to let mama come inside?* I just needed to ask, and I quickly ate as much of my plate as possible. Even some of the onions.

"When can mommy come back inside?" I asked quietly. Patrick's face fell slightly.

"When I say," Patrick answered coldly.

I frowned, scooting the food around on my plate. Despite my belly feeling full, I still had quite a bit on my plate. I bit my lower lip, when an idea came to me.

"I don't like onions," I blurted out.

He raised an eyebrow to me before chuckling. "You don't say?"

"I don't," I said with a soft voice, "but I was wondering..."

I took a deep breath, noticing Patrick had lowered his fork and was watching me intently. I quickly just spat out the rest.

"I was wondering if I ate all my onions, could mommy come back inside?"

A heavy door clattered across the room, and we both turned to see someone else walk in. He wore a police outfit too.

"You're a good kid, you know that?" Patrick said quietly, and I found him looking at me again. "You eat your whole plate, and I'll bring your mom back in."

I couldn't contain my grin then and promptly picked up my fork.

Patrick smirked, watching me scarf my plate down before turning to the other man. "You're home early, Dad."

I scrunched my nose as I took another bite. My belly was beginning to ache from being too full, but Patrick's dad just watched me. I didn't like the way he looked at me, so I looked back to my plate.

"Dennis had finally relented some and plans changed," he finally said. "Where's her mother?"

"Shanely messed up today," Patrick replied, pulling his sleeve further up his arm to show the bandage, "so I tossed her in the cage outside."

The man's eyes widened, and I stopped mid-bite.

"You did *what?*" he snapped angrily.

"Oh c'mon," Patrick said, rubbing the back of his head. "She really messed up today, but I'm watching."

"I don't care what she's done," his father shouted. "You don't throw her in the cage for it!"

Patrick narrowed his eyes. "It was your preferred choice of punishment for me growing up, and I turned out just fine. Like I said, I'm watching."

"I never tossed you outside in the middle of winter!" the man hollered back, and Patrick scoffed.

"Yes, you did," he countered, crossing his arms, "or do you honestly not remember when I got locked outside for hours after a punishment when I was nine, and you didn't come out of your office until nearly bedtime."

Patrick's father glared at him. "Where is she, Patrick?"

"There," Patrick said, pointing to the glass door. "But like I said, she's fine."

The man grew very angry and stomped towards the door. "You're going to kill her doing this, Patrick! She can't stay... My God. What else did you do to her?!"

The two stomped outside, and I slowly exhaled the breath I had been

CHAPTER 22

holding. I looked down at my plate. I was only a couple bites away from finishing, but I quickly pushed what was left onto his plate.

Patrick unlocked the door to the cage and grab my mother. She fell limp against him. Then they stormed back inside.

"You're messing up with her, Patrick," his dad snarled. "Control her, but try not to kill the girl in the process. Are we clear?"

"She wasn't out there long," Patrick said firmly. I watched Patrick carry my mother upstairs then, and I sat there unsure what to do. He didn't tell me to follow.

"Best get to your room, child," Patrick's father said, and I looked to him.

My heart pounded in my chest as he studied me carefully, but then he walked towards me and something burned in my chest to run. It screamed for me to run far away from this man, and I hopped off my stool. He was right behind me as I turned around, and I held my breath.

"Let your new dad deal with your mother," he said as he gently patted the top of my head. I winced when he plucked a hair out and examined it.

"I... I..." I tried to say, but my voice was stuck in my throat. "I want to see her."

"Like I said," he muttered lost in thought, "best get to your room."

His eyes focused on me, and a shiver shot through me. My chest burned again, and this time I listened.

Obeying his command, I shot towards my room. I wanted to keep going to check on mama, but I already knew I wouldn't be allowed in there. So I dove under the covers on my bed and buried myself in a mountain of blankets.

Please be okay, mommy. Please just be okay.

Chapter 23

Shanely

"I can't keep being the only one who puts in any effort, Shanely."

Shivering as the snow soaked my clothes, I slowly looked up to Patrick. His glare said enough. He was pissed, and this may finally be the moment where he kills me.

I freaking missed.

"You and I are going to change some things," he said, pulling me from my thoughts. "Starting tomorrow things will be different, but you have to stop fighting me. You nearly killed me tonight!"

I said nothing as he paced back and forth in front of the cage that held me in. The snow had soaked my pants already, and I shivered as a brutally cold wind passed by.

"No more stunts," he snapped. "I mean it, Shanely. You will be punished if you do crap like this again."

I slumped against the metal cage as he stormed back to the house. My heart hurt when I found Aerith sitting on the stool watching us.

I'm sorry, baby.

I am so sorry.

A light fluttered across the cage as I laid my head on my knees.

Steaming hot water shot up my nose as I plunged under the water abruptly. My eyes shot open, and I flung myself forward, gasping for air. Pain rippled through my body as it was forcefully brought back to a normal temperature, and my heart began to pound in my chest. Two hands yanked me to the surface as I sucked in more water.

CHAPTER 23

Those hands pounded on my back as I sputtered over the side of the tub, coughing up bath water. Soaked to the bone in the clothes I froze in earlier, I pushed my hair out of my face, glaring up at Patrick.

"What is wrong with you?" I stuttered. I wanted to sound more aggressive, but I couldn't stop my body from shaking. I sounded more pitiful than anything. My eye was still swollen from where he struck me, and my head pounded out of my skull. *All because I missed.*

"What?" Patrick asked, raising an eyebrow. "Dad said you were getting too cold, so I figured you'd like a nice hot bath. Feel better?"

"I could have died, Patrick!" I snapped, and he shrugged. Anger burned in my veins as I tried to stand. *I just wanted out of this tub.*

"Yeah well, I nearly died today too. Call it even," he snapped back before forcing me to sit again. "Just give yourself a minute to warm up."

If I had the strength to roll my eyes, I would. *I'm only in this mess because of you,* I thought as I lowered my head to the side of the tub. A heaviness filled my chest as I just laid there, too weak to move. *I missed. I had freaking missed, and we were still stuck in this mess.*

A single tear slid down my wet cheek.

"I meant every word, Shanely," Patrick muttered quietly. "I don't like being harsh with you, but you can't do stuff like this again. Maybe if you just try being nice to me, I can show you I'm not such a bad guy."

"Good guys don't threaten to kill everyone when they don't get their way," I mumbled, feeling utterly exhausted. "Good guys respect when a girl says no."

Silence filled the room then. *Maybe I did have a death wish,* I thought as I waited for Patrick to snap again. Losing Bastian destroyed my will to live. *If the kids weren't stuck with me...*

I couldn't finish that thought.

"I'm not perfect," he said softly, "but I didn't threaten to kill everyone just to have you, Shanely. The Division made the call."

I scoffed. "Ask your father then. Go ahead and ask, Patrick because you are sorely mistaken over how things went down."

More silence.

"I trust my father," he finally said.

"I wouldn't," I mocked, slumping further into the water. My eyes were heavy and hard to keep open. The water was beginning to cool off and goosebumps traveled up my arm.

Patrick's hand gripped my chin, and he pulled me up to look at him. I wasn't sure what I expected to see but sadness was not one of them.

"I know I'm not your first choice," he said before snorting. "I know I was never a choice at all, but I risked *everything* to make sure you didn't die that day. Bastian was going to die regardless. Even if I never stupidly took that shot in Canada, Dennis would have demanded his head on a platter the moment those reports got to him. He wanted you *both*. Dad showed me the order, and I'm surprised the raid didn't happen sooner. But besides the point, I am here. I am trying to be someone to you, so please stop fighting me every step of the way."

The two of us stared at one another then. I had no idea what to even say, but it was strange to see the turmoil in his eyes. And suddenly, I had to know.

"Do you regret shooting Bastian in Canada?" I asked, my voice so quiet I barely heard myself.

He sighed. "It nearly got you killed so yes. I shouldn't have taken the shot that day."

Patrick let my face go, and I stared at the water again. I didn't know what to think. I didn't know how to feel. All I've known since losing my mate was hate and anger. It's all I saw, all I felt. Even the rare moments Patrick behaved kindly towards me, it still wasn't enough to erase all he'd done. I don't understand the blind faith he has for his dad, especially since Calvin lies and clearly abuses him, but the two are equally to blame here. No apologizing or admitting you made a mistake was going to wipe the slate clean.

"Do you need help getting out of the tub" he asked, startling me.

I rolled my head to the side to look at him. I didn't even have it in me to fight him on this. I slowly nodded my head, and he walked over.

"Wrap your arms around me," he said, and I obeyed.

CHAPTER 23

Water went everywhere as he hauled me out of the tub, and I groaned when he set me on the bathroom counter. He quickly wrapped a towel around me before grabbing another to help dry me faster. My vision swayed, and all I wanted to do was close my eyes and sleep.

"Hang tight," he muttered as he left the room.

Something's seriously wrong, I thought as I leaned against the wall. I sneezed and immediately regretted doing that. Clutching my head, I shut my eyes, hoping Patrick would hurry up.

It felt like an eternity, but Patrick finally came back and dropped a pile of clothes on the floor. He picked up the towel again and began to wring out my hair. He frowned then.

"Gonna have to buy you a blow dryer, it seems. I don't own one."

I kept the scowl from my face as he continued to help me dry off. My teeth began to chatter and worry flashed on Patrick's face.

"We need to get you out of these clothes," he said, and my eyes widened.

"I can get dressed myself, Patrick."

I gripped my shirt as I pushed myself off the wall then, as if to prove it to him that I could do it, but he gave me a stern look in return. He picked up the clothes and set it next to me.

"Shanely, you're about to fall over," he said, motioning for me to move my hands. "Now, just let me help you so we can get you in the warm bed. Or would you rather continue freezing in here?"

Patrick grabbed the bottom of my shirt and ripped it over my head before I could stop him. His eyes went straight to my belly though, and I looked down. The twins had already begun to show. My heart twisted again.

"They're really in there, aren't they?" he whispered. His callous hands gently touched my skin, and I grabbed the black shirt, nearly toppling over just to reach it.

"Did you think I was lying, Patrick?" I asked as my cheeks heated. I struggled to pull the shirt over my head as the room spun slightly. He sighed loudly, and I felt him pull the shirt down for me.

"No," he muttered, placing both hands on either side of me, "it's just this is the first time I've really seen you show with the twins. Will you slow down already?"

I was already reaching for the shorts he brought when I realized how big they were. *This was not my stuff*, I thought as my face turned a darker shade of red. *I didn't realize I was putting on his stuff. I am wearing another male's clothes.*

I slowly closed my eyes, taking a deep breath to keep the emotions at bay.

"What's the problem now, Shanely?" Patrick asked.

I hesitated before answering him. Tears welled in my eyes, and I tried not to think about Bastian. I wanted nothing more than to rip these clothes off and demand new ones, but I didn't want to go back to the cage either. What I was doing wasn't working, so with a heavy heart I shook my head.

"Nothing," I muttered as I grabbed the shorts. I swayed as the room spun even harder.

Patrick really did have to help me then, and soon my wet pants were in the hamper. He helped me put my feet through the shorts and motioned for me to slide off the counter. As soon as my feet touched the ground, my legs gave way. Patrick caught me before I hit the floor.

"C'mon you," he said chuckling softly. He wrapped his arm around me as he pulled up the shorts.

My eyes blinked rapidly as I tried to focus on something. Anything to get the world to stop moving. I hadn't felt this weak since the Summit, but this time I didn't have Bastian here to save me. I didn't have our bond to strengthen me, and I genuinely didn't know if I was going to make it.

Before we even left the bathroom, I had passed out in his arms.

Chapter 24

Aerith

For two days, I was stuck in my room with nothing to do. Every morning I had a sack lunch waiting on the table by the door for me, with a note telling me to *Be Good*. Patrick never did come back for me after bringing mommy inside, and I worried if she was okay. I missed my mom, but I waited in my room like I was told to do.

I was sick of playing with the dolls here, and I had read all the books already. Half the time I lay upside down on my bed thinking. Mostly, I just worried about mama.

And I missed my dad.

But I was proud that I made a difference that night. If Patrick's dad hadn't demanded she be brought in then I would have been the reason she got help. *Just like daddy,* I thought with a smile. I helped her just like he would have, and that made me feel good.

I was hanging upside down, munching on some fruit snacks, when I heard Patrick's familiar heavy steps approached. I sat up as he opened the door.

"Let's go, Aerith," Patrick said, and I scurried to my feet.

I frowned as I followed him out the door. He didn't seem very happy as we made our way down the stairs, and I made sure not to fall too far behind. I didn't want to upset him further.

We walked into the kitchen where two sandwiches sat on the counter with chips. He motioned me towards the stools where weird metal boxes sat.

"Go ahead and take a seat," Patrick said, grabbing the food. "I thought we could eat lunch together today."

I slowly made my way to the other side and climbed up on the stool next to him. He popped a couple of pills, guzzling them down with water before picking up his own sandwich.

"Eat, Baby Doll," he said quietly, so I picked up my own sandwich. Patrick smiled as he watched me eat, and the two of us stayed quiet next to one another. His left arm was still wrapped in a bandage like the ones Aunt Cassia always used at the clinic when I'd help her work, and he definitely favored the other arm. My cheeks flushed when he caught me watching.

"What?" he asked.

I slowly pointed to his arm. "Does that hurt?"

Patrick's eyes darkened as he looked at the bandage. "A bit."

"What happened?" I asked. His eyes slowly drifted to mine.

"Just an accident," he answered, pulling his sleeve down and hiding the bandage from view. No one spoke after that.

Patrick began to unscrew a plate on a bottom of the metal box in front of him. I leaned a little to steal a peek inside, but it wasn't anything interesting to look at. *Just a bunch of wires.* I took another bite as I looked to the rest on the island. There was something here that looked just like the toy Uncle Cade had one time. He called it a model plane, but this looked different. Instead of the cheap plastic that Uncle Cade said his toy was made of, this plane was made of sleek, black metal. It wasn't bigger than the length of my arm, and it had wings like a plane with a giant bulb on the bottom.

This was pretty cool.

"It's called a drone," he said, and my eyes went to him. I swallowed hard. I didn't know he saw me watching.

"You like it?" he asked, and I shrugged, not really knowing what to say, but it did look interesting.

He smirked at me. "It's a camera, Aerith. Let's me see stuff very far away and way up in the sky if I want. I fly it with this."

Patrick held up a small black box that he had taken apart, and I cocked my head to the side. He frowned then, and I straightened in my seat.

CHAPTER 24

"You act more like a wolf than I realized," he muttered before going to the fridge. "When was the last time I gave you your meds?"

I didn't say a word as he dug around in the fridge, pulling a vial out of a white box. He set it in front of me.

"Drink."

I obeyed, feeling that awful fuzzy feeling in my stomach once more. I hated this stuff, but it kept my chest from burning and made him happy.

"Anyways," he said, eating a chip, "this is one of the special toys I get to play with at work. We have a lot of different stuff though. One even looks just like a real bird, so whoever you're spying on will never know they're being watched, but the drones are my favorite. It's like driving an RC car."

He chuckled to himself. "You're probably too young to know what those are," he said, pushing his plate away and grabbing the drone. "Do you want to see?"

Curiosity got the better of me, and I nodded my head. As bored as I was, I'd say yes to anything to avoid going back in my room, but I was honestly curious about the drones. I didn't bother correcting Patrick that I knew how to drive RC cars. He doesn't like hearing anything about my dad or uncles, so I kept my mouth shut.

He smiled again and shoved the last of his sandwich in his mouth.

"Grab your sandwich," he said taking the drone in hand. "You can come hang out with me today."

I grabbed what was left of my lunch and followed Patrick back up the stairs. My steps stopped at the top of the stairs as I turned to look down the hall towards mama's room. I bit my lower lip as I debated asking Patrick to see her again.

"Your mom's fine," he said, and I turned to find him at another door on my left. "She got a little sick and is just sleeping it off. I gave her some meds to help, so don't worry. If you're good today, I'll let you see her afterwards."

My heart leapt for joy, and I couldn't contain the smile that spread across my face. I bounded over to him, and he chuckled softly.

"I like seeing you smile, kiddo," he replied. "We need more of that around here. Now I need you to stay right here, okay? I just got to grab a drone that's charged and not broken."

I nodded as Patrick slipped inside the room, barely catching a glimpse of computers along the back wall, with papers scattered about. He shut the door to the messy room, and I waited for him to return while I finished my sandwich. I couldn't help but turn to watch mama's door. I wished more than anything that she'd open it and come join us.

But she didn't.

Patrick walked out with another drone and motioned to the stairs again.

"C'mon! Before it gets dark," he said, and I scurried after him. The drone he brought looked old and scuffed up somewhat. Not as shiny as that black one he was fixing, but I didn't mention that to him.

I set my plate on the counter next to his before scurrying to catch up with him. He tossed me an oversized coat as we got to the doors in the kitchen. "Can't have you catching a cold either."

He fitted the large coat over me and put one on himself. His hand stilled at the door, and I frowned when he didn't open it. *Had he changed his mind?*

"Listen carefully to me, Aerith," he said, kneeling down. I held my breath as he gave me a firm look. "The woods outside are not safe. Very dangerous equipment go around the whole house to keep us safe from very bad people. Do. Not. Run. Do not go anywhere without me or you *will* die. Do you understand me?"

My eyes widened as I nodded my head. *I wouldn't run*, I thought as my stomach began to hurt. *I would never run without mama.* My eyes drifted to the woods outside, and suddenly everything just looked dark and scary.

Patrick seemed satisfied with my answer and opened the door. The cold air hit my cheeks, and I shivered as he drug me along. We stopped just outside the double doors, and he set down the drone.

"Alright, Baby Doll," he said, grinning with his arms stretched out wide. "Welcome to Division training! As you already know, this is a drone. It's sole function is to go out and collect intel, which just means we used it to spy on stuff. Every drone is equipped with night vision and thermal technology, which is a fancy way to say they can pick up anything warm

CHAPTER 24

blooded even if it's dark."

I scrunched my nose as he motioned me forward and pointed to the bulb at the bottom. All of this just sounded confusing, but I tried to pay attention closely. He seemed really excited, and I wanted to keep it that way.

"This is the camera," he said before pointing to the antenna, "and this is the receiver. It's what lets me communicate with my remote here."

Patrick knelt behind me and put the box in my hand. I felt his warm breath on my neck as he turned the box on.

"Alright, let's teach you how to use it," he said, grinning wide. "This is what turns on the propellers here. It's what makes it fly."

He pushed a button on the console, and the drone turned on. It's propellers firing up loudly as a small smile crept on my face. Then Patrick pushed the small nozzle on the remote, and the drone began to lift off the ground slowly.

"And this is what moves it forwards and backwards," he said, pushing my fingers on the console. My eyes widened as it moved where we told it to.

"And this turns on the camera," he said, pushing another button. The box in my hand lit up, and I saw myself on the screen with Patrick right behind me. My eyes went from the screen to the drone. *This was cool.*

"My, my," he said grinning, "that's a good picture."

He pushed another button, and I heard the device flutter.

"I never realized how much I'd enjoy being a father," he said softly. "But I'm very glad you and your mother have become my family."

Patrick kissed my cheek, and my smile fell away. I missed my dad. *My real dad*, I thought to myself, but was I really part of *his* family now?

Would I never see mine again?

"Alright, let's take her up and scan the house, shall we?" he said excitedly. With a flick of a button, the drone shot in the air making me jump. He laughed and pointed to the screen. "Just watch, Baby Doll."

We roamed over the empty woods, Patrick guiding my fingers on the console as the tiny metal drone disappeared from sight. The white snow blurred on by, and soon the drone lifted in the sky again just before a broken building. Patrick slowed it down some, so I could get a better view.

It was abandoned and clearly falling apart. The large windows revealed a bunch of stuff that Grandpa Danny used to have at work, but other than that, there was nothing but trash and boxes. My heart sunk. *I sort of hoped someone would be there,* I thought to myself. *Not like it would help any.*

I bit my lower lip again as the drone shot towards the roof and to the streets behind. The street was empty, minus a large black truck, and soon Patrick was zooming the drone away from the small town and towards the driveway again.

"See?" he said quietly. "Fun, isn't it?"

I gave him a small smile in return, watching the woods go by on the screen. *I liked playing with the drones,* I realized. Patrick was nice when he was in a good mood.

"You try," he said, removing his hands from the remote. My eyes widened as Patrick stepped back giving me another toothy grin. I nervously stepped towards him. *I didn't want to break it,* I thought anxiously. *He'd be so mad if I broke this.* But he held his hands up refusing to take it back.

"You can do this, Aerith," he said firmly, "I know you can."

I held the small black console in my hand, staring at the drone hoovering before us. A blinding light pierced my face, and I stepped back in Patrick's shadow.

"Don't be afraid, Baby Doll," he said, pushing me forward again. "If you break it, Daddy will just fix it. I can even teach you how to fix it too."

I bit my bottom lip as I debated what to do. I shifted on my feet, and very carefully, pushed the knob on the console. The drone moved away, and I slowly drove it through the trees.

"There you go!" Patrick said excitedly, placing his hand on my shoulder. "You've got it!"

My heart raced as I pushed the drone faster and faster through the trees and around towards the building once more.

"You are a natural, Aerith!"

The smile on my face grew, and I watched the screen closely. I wanted to do a good job. It felt good to do something right this time.

CHAPTER 24

"Patrick!"

"Yeah, Dad?" Patrick shouted, turning slightly as I moved the drone up the building again.

"I need you!" his dad shouted louder, and Patrick sighed.

"Hang tight," he said as he opened the sliding door and stepped inside.

Ignoring the two, I focused on the screen. The drone slowly moved up the building, peeking into every window. I didn't let it get too close. More afraid to crash it and make Patrick very angry and ruin the day we were having. I took my time scanning everything. The place was very dirty, with nothing more than boxes scattered about and a small table sat to the side with a bag on top. A large gray blanket lay near the window with a dingy sneaker near the bottom, and I pushed the drone closer to get a better look.

Suddenly, Patrick placed his hand on my shoulder, and I jumped hard. I looked to the screen, grateful I didn't crash into anything.

"Sorry, kiddo," he said with a smile. "We got to bring her back in. Can you do that?"

I gave him a nod and moved the drone away from the building and towards us once more. When the drone got close, Patrick took over and shut the toy off. He gathered all our stuff before heading back inside. My steps slowed when I saw Calvin watching the two of us closely. *He scared me more than Patrick.*

"Any issues today?" Patrick's dad asked, his eyes narrowing on me.

"Nope," Patrick replied. "Shanely's responding well to the meds and is still asleep."

His dad grunted and pointed to me. "Why is she out?"

I shrunk further away from him. My heart pounded in my chest as I slowly reached up and took Patrick's hand. His whole face lit up then, and he squeezed my hand tightly.

"I wanted to teach her some stuff," he said grinning at me, "and have some daddy-daughter time before we checked on Shanely. I'll make sure to finish up those reports for you by tomorrow though. After that, I should be all caught up. Promise."

Patrick's father gave him a long look before walking out of the room, and

I exhaled deeply. He didn't respond and shut himself in his office.

"Don't worry about Grandpa," he said, patting my back. I slowly looked up to him. "He's always just a tad grumpy, but let's go see how mama's doing. Shall we?"

My smile widened, and he chuckled again.

"Lead the way then!"

And that's just what I did.

Chapter 25

Shanely

Sweat clung to my body as I rolled to my side, shoving off the mountains of blankets on me. I just felt sticky *everywhere.* Even my hair seemed permanently stuck to my forehead as I lay in Patrick's bed. My head hurt as bad as my throat did, and when I tried to sit up, I barely made it halfway before I collapsed back down again. *God, this sucked...*

"You're finally awake," Patrick said quietly. I turned my head to find him walking out of the bathroom, buttoning his shirt.

"I feel like death," I muttered, and he snorted out a laugh.

"That's what happens when you get sick. You've been out of it for the last week," he said, handing me a drink. I took it from him and gulped it down, but it still wasn't enough to help my throat.

I blinked. *Wait... Did he say a week? I've been out for a week?!* My heart thundered as I thought of my little girl. *God, Aerith...* I pushed myself to sit up, trying to find the strength to stand. *I had to check on her. God knows what happened while I was out.*

"Whoa, you better go easy now. I don't think you're ready to move yet," he said, pushing me back down.

"No, I need to see Aerith. I've been out way too long. I need to see her!" I begged. I couldn't imagine what she must be feeling or what she must be thinking. Memories of her and Patrick eating dinner together while I sat in that cage resurfaced, and I pushed against him harder.

"She's fine, alright? I can go get her, just chill out. Good lord, you are a handful," he muttered, and I sagged in relief.

Patrick left the room, and it didn't take long before I could hear her little feet running down the hall. The door slammed open.

"Mommy!" she cried out, jumping on my lap.

I held her close to my chest replying, "Hey, there's my baby girl. How are you? I've missed you!"

"Are you feeling better? Patrick said you were sick," she said quietly, and I glanced at Patrick in the doorway.

"I'm better now, sweetie. Mommy just got way too cold one day, and it made me really sick."

"Careful," he warned me, and I glared back at him.

I ignored him though. Pushing my luck, I looked back to Aerith and asked, "Want to spend the day with me today? Patrick said he's going to the store for your favorite dinner tonight, so it's just going to be you and me for awhile."

Patrick snorted, leaning against the door frame as he asked, "Is that so?"

"Yes, it is," I replied. I held his stare saying, "Don't you remember?"

His eyes narrowed, but when he looked to Aerith, he softened. My eyes narrowed when he said, "What do you want, Aerith?"

She leaned against me, thinking for a moment. Then a smile appeared as she asked, "Can we get pizza?"

I looked from him to her, frowning as I watched the two interact. *I didn't think he'd let me get away with this,* I thought as I watched them. *But maybe it's not me...*

He gave her another smile. "Alrighty then. I'll be back in an hour. Shanely, you know the rules. Don't move from this room. Not like you could leave the bed anyways, but I thought I'd remind you just in case."

I rolled my eyes as he left us and took a deep breath when he was finally gone. Finally feeling a little at peace, I pulled Aerith in close and snuggled with her. She immediately started talking about what she did while I was asleep and recovering. Going on and on over getting to fly the drone through the woods, but my mind was stuck on the fact that he *willingly* took her outside. I knew nothing about those sort of electronics, but it was nice to see her so excited over something. The only time I had ever seen a

CHAPTER 25

drone was when Bastian and his brothers found a bunch on our land. *The day before...*

"I miss daddy," she whispered, pulling me from my own wretched thoughts. My heart ached as I pulled her closer to me.

Kissing her forehead, I whispered, "Me too, baby. Me too."

We let the comfortable silence fill the empty space between us. Just enjoying our time with one another together. Patrick had kept the two of us apart for so long, I barely get to spend any time with her now. It was then I realized, we had been here for well over a month. That thought sickened me. *I wasn't protecting her like I should... I was only making things worse,* I thought as I started coughing uncontrollably. My chest ached as I settled back down and stared at the ceiling. Everything suddenly just felt overwhelming, and I had to get out of here. I didn't care how weak I was. I was *sick* of being in Patrick's room.

Kicking the blankets off us, I forced myself to sit up. "C'mon, let's find something to do together."

Aerith's eyes lit up as I struggled to find my footing. I would give this girl a moment of happiness, even if it was just for twenty minutes. Patrick wouldn't be too much longer.

I hobbled to the door, thankful it was left unlocked, and pulled her down the empty halls. The floors creaked with every step, and I tried every door until one finally opened.

A movie room.

"Wow," Aerith said excitedly as she barreled into the room. "This is so cool!"

I smiled, stepping inside with her. *I have to agree,* I thought as I looked around. A large projector screen hung along the furthest wall with a massive L-shaped couch before it. A huge cabinet loaded with DVDs and VHS tapes sat to the right of the projector, and a small table with two chairs sat directly to my left. Patrick had so many board games on the shelf. I had no idea he even liked to play games. *This had been here the whole time?!* I thought to myself.

"Can we watch something?" Aerith asked, bouncing on her feet.

It pulled on my emotions seeing her so happy. *Watching a movie shouldn't be a luxury like this,* I thought as I nodded. She bounded to the cabinet. *This shouldn't be the life she has.*

"Find something you like?" I asked, leaning against the wall. I struggled to contain my cough as she sorted through the movies.

"He has Balto!" she said excitedly, holding up the DVD with the dark wolf pictured on it.

"Hey!" I said excitedly. "One of your favorites."

She looked at the cover again, her face falling as she studied the wolf. Her brows furrowed before she frown and slowly put the movie down. My heart *broke,* and I shoved off the wall. Terrified she'd change her mind and not want to watch anything at all, I knelt down and gently took Balto from her. I set it aside and took her hands in mine.

"How about we play a game?" I suggested. "This is how your mother watched movies back in the day."

I smiled wide and grabbed a handful of VHS tapes. I was desperate to get that smile back, so I quickly shuffled the movies behind my back before shoving a tape into the player.

"What did you pick?" she asked quietly.

I shrugged, grinning again. "No idea. One of the foster moms I stayed with used to do this when none of us kids could decide on a movie. She'd make us choose one without looking and shove it into the player as a surprise. It was called mystery movie!"

She giggled softly, and I pulled her towards the couch, burying us under a blanket.

"I like that idea, Mama," she said quietly. Aerith leaned her head against my chest, and I sighed, not knowing how to help her with this. Because seeing that silly cartoon wolf pulled at my heart strings too. I missed Bastian.

"C'mon, baby! You can do it!" a woman's voice cried out as the movie kicked on, and I froze as I realized my very *grave error.*

"Look at him go, Lorelei!"

I'd recognize that voice anywhere. I sat frozen on the couch as a beautiful

CHAPTER 25

young woman in a white lab coat held her arms out to a small child just trying to walk.

"Here set the camera down," Lorelei said with a smile. *Patrick's smile.* "Help him."

The camera jostled around before settling on the counter. Calvin suddenly appeared, and he looked so young. His hair was dark and thick, and his shoulders were broad and looked so much more capable than the man I knew today. My heart began to race. *We shouldn't be watching this...*

They looked to be in some sort of research lab, and my mind drifted back to what Calvin told me. *"I've spent my entire life trying to accomplish something, so I can finally avenge my wife..."*

What happened to her?

"Go on, Patrick. Go to mom," Calvin said as he helped Patrick stumble his way forward.

I should turn this off, I thought as my anxiety rose. *I should put the movie back where I found it before Patrick got home.* But for some strange reason, I couldn't look away.

Patrick stumbled and fell, giggling hysterically before reaching for his mother. This baby, who looked so happy and carefree, turned into such a monster. My stomach twisted as the home video continued to play.

Lorelei laughed. "I guess he's not quite ready, love."

Calvin scooped Patrick up in his arms and kissed his wife's forehead. "He'll get there. We just got to..."

The screen grew fuzzy as it suddenly changed to Lorelei sitting in front of her computer with Patrick on her lap. I was at a loss for words. Patrick seemed so happy as a baby. They all did really. It was striking to see such a strong resemblance Patrick had with his mother. He took after her in every way it seems. Every way but the most important.

Lorelei opened her mouth to speak, when the video suddenly stopped.

I turned to find Patrick standing there holding a pizza and the remote. His eyes glued to the screen. I scurried to my feet, feeling the room spin as I tucked Aerith behind me.

"I'm sorry," I stammered. "We just wanted to do something together, and I didn't realize..."

"It's fine," he said, setting down the pizza. He walked over and kicked out the VHS. "I used to watch them all the time. They just sit here now."

My brows knitted in confusion. *He nearly choked the life out of me for saying Bastian's name. Why doesn't he care about this?* I wondered, shifting nervously on my feet as Patrick put in another movie. I gently pushed Aerith towards the door and wobbled on my feet. Patrick was suddenly there to steady me, and my eyes widened when he caught me.

"I told you not to move," he said quietly. "You aren't well enough to be on your feet."

There was nothing I could do as he guided me back to the couch and helped me to sit again. He tossed a blanket over me like he wanted *me* to be comfortable, and I gave him an odd look. I slowly looked back to the VHS tape now sitting on the top shelf. Something happened to Lorelei, and it ruined Patrick because of it. I would *not* let that happen to Aerith too. Patrick seemed off though, and I pursed my lips together in a tight line.

I had to be careful.

"Aerith needed something to do, so I brought her here," I blurted. He turned to look at me then, and I scrambled to get the rest out under his intense gaze. "If you don't want us in here, that's fine, but I've been away from her a lot lately. A child needs their mother, Patrick. And I *need* her."

Patrick frowned. His gaze drifting from me to the stack of videos. He stared a long time at that tape just sitting there before finally glancing back to Aerith. I narrowed my eyes as I watched him closely.

"You're right," he finally said, and I blinked in surprise. *Did he just agree with me?*

Patrick walked around the couch and grabbed the box of pizza. Setting it on the ottoman, he opened it to reveal a delicious looking pizza full of meat. It was loaded to the max, and my stomach rumbled at the sight.

But all I could think of was Cade.

"Make sure you take your vitamins too, Shanely," he said, pulling my attention back to him. He dug in his pocket and pulled out the bottle. "You've been missing them since being sick, and I want you to get better."

CHAPTER 25

My stomach churned as I saw the sincerity in his eyes. He took my hand, dumping the pills inside. He grabbed a slice of pizza for Aerith and then me, before grabbing one for himself, while I sat in stunned silence. When my eyes drifted to my daughter, I was surprised to find her watching the two of us instead of the movie. She cocked her head to the side. *Just like Bastian always did.*

The two began to eat, but I couldn't stop thinking about the movie I stumbled upon. They used to be a happy family. *What happened to them?* I wondered. *What happened that was so bad that it turned the men in this family into monsters?*

And where was Lorelei now?

Aerith chuckled quietly, and I turned to her. *This wasn't the life she was supposed to have,* I thought. She was supposed to have everything I didn't. A happy home. A wonderful family with two parents there to remind her how much she was loved. Instead she was here in a worse fate than I had ever been. But it had been a *long* time since I heard her laugh.

Unable to bring myself to fight him anymore tonight, I simply replied, "Okay, Patrick."

Chapter 26

The door burst open, and I jumped hard, clutching my chest.

"What in the world is wrong with you?" I asked as my heart pounded. I was currently curled up on the chair in Patrick's room, watching a light flicker off in the distance of the setting sun, when he stormed in here. My hand drifted down to my swollen belly. The weeks had flown by with me getting no further in escaping. *Which was impossible to accomplish when you never left your room.*

Patrick kicked off his muddy boots, looking utterly stressed and annoyed. He shimmed off the police vest before stepping into the closet. I held my breath as he clattered around putting his gear away, wondering how tonight was going to go. He left before dawn this morning for work, which was surprising. Lately, he'd been locking me and Aerith in the room together during the days, but I woke up stuck in this room with no signs of my daughter. He sauntered back into the room.

"Just a crap day at work," Patrick replied with a sigh as he leaned down to kiss me. I turned my cheek abruptly, and his lips touched my ear.

"Shanely..." he said in a warning tone, "c'mon now. I'm getting pretty sick of this. I've had a crap day at work, and I've missed my girl. Can't you just be happy to see me?"

My anxiety grew in my chest as I tried to stand, but he placed both arms on either side of me, pinning me to the chair.

"Patrick, please..."

"I've been patient, Shanely," he said firmly, "*more* than patient with you. I've done nothing but work and take care of you and Aerith. It's been

CHAPTER 26

months, and I deserve..."

My anger flared the moment those two little words spewed from his mouth. My chest burned in agony as I shoved him back and got to my feet.

"Don't start with that whole *what you deserve* speech again," I snarled. "After what you did to my mate..."

"God, it's the same argument with you," he growled, tossing his hands in the air. "I told you *the Division* made the call to slaughter the pack!"

Patrick began to pace before, me with his hands in his hair. Suddenly, he stormed towards me, and my body tensed as he jabbed a finger in my face.

"I stuck my neck out to save you and your kid! They ordered your death too, Shanely. The least you could do is try to make this work!"

"You didn't save us!" I bellowed loudly. "What happened to my pack and family is all your fault! We're not even friends, Patrick, and I know you and your father maneuvered everything to get what you want. Don't you get it? I will never be anything but a prisoner to you!"

Patrick lunged, gripping my neck so hard and so abruptly that I couldn't stop him. His eyes turned to a wild rage, and I clung to his hands, struggling to breathe as he pushed me against the wall. My heart pounded in my chest as my feet left the ground until we were eye-level with him.

"Let me try this again," he gritted through his teeth. "Either get on board with the idea of being mine or I will toss you to the wolves at the Division. Dennis wanted you *dead*, and my father helped me fake your death to save you and Aerith. No one orchestrated anything. You are only alive because of us, and I am done waiting for you to figure that out."

Patrick dropped me, and I gasped for air. I collapsed on the floor as his clunky boots walked across the room. He opened the door before turning to me.

"Think about it, Shanely. You can learn to love me or your kids can die right alongside you when the Division finds out Aerith is a half-blood. I'd think long and hard before making *another* rash decision."

He slammed the door shut as a sob burst from my lips. I couldn't breathe. My chest hurt so bad as I sobbed uncontrollably. *He's not Bastian... Oh God, how can I love a man who murdered my soulmate? How am I supposed to do this?* My stomach churned as my fingers gripped my hair tightly.

My eyes slowly drifted down to my belly. *If I didn't, they'd die. Aerith would die.* The last connection to my mate was safely growing inside me, completely unaware of the mess we were in. My daughter down the hall, experiencing all the horrors of this place right along with me. *They counted on me to protect them.*

The door suddenly opened again, and I quickly wiped my eyes as Aerith came running into the room.

"Mommy!" she squealed as she dove into my arms.

"I thought you'd need some help deciding," Patrick growled as he glared at me. His icy glare said it all. *He fully expected me to change my behavior tonight or else.* My stomach twisted as he slammed the door behind him.

I clung to my daughter as the weight on my chest grew heavier. *She was just perfect,* I thought to myself as my hands gently rubbed the back of her head. *She doesn't deserve this, but what can I...*

The door.

My eyes widened when I realized I never heard him lock it. I had heard that stupid lock click over a thousand times already but... *He didn't lock us in.*

"C'mon baby," I whispered, pulling her along. My hand twisted the handle, and I nearly shook with relief when it opened. I blinked rapidly as I stood at the opened door. *We're free,* I thought anxiously. *We can run.* Shaking myself from my thoughts, I knelt down to Aerith.

"Do not speak a word. Okay, Aerith? I need you to stay as quiet as a mouse," I said softly, and she nodded her head.

Gripping her hand in mine, we left the room. The hall was silent as we tip-toed down the wooden floors. Patrick's office was shut, and I didn't bother checking to see if *that* door was unlocked. I wasn't trying that again.

We hugged the railing as we went down the stairs. I could hear clattering somewhere in the house, and my heart pounded further in my chest. *I had to move faster.*

As we approached the kitchen, I ground to a halt. The garage door was cracked open, and my eyes widened. *It couldn't be this easy,* I thought to

CHAPTER 26

myself as I slowly crept towards the door. Stealing a car would be a whole lot easier than moving on foot, but as I extended my hand to push the door open, I froze when Patrick walked past. He didn't see us as he chucked tools and other crap about the room. He was stewing, doing God knows what out there, but I couldn't let him see me.

I couldn't get caught.

I shrunk away, drifting back into the shadows of the kitchen and out of his sight. In the corner of the room, I gripped my hair, scrambling to figure out what I was going to do now, when my head suddenly perked up, and I turned to the alarm box next to the sliding glass doors. *It was off. Patrick turned off the alarm to go into the garage...*

I grabbed Aerith and hauled her into my arms. *A car was a luxury, not a necessity. I can navigate the woods once we're gone,* I thought. Walking on my tip-toes, I made my way across the room, my heart pounding with every step. I held my breath and carefully slid the door open.

Silence.

It was the best sound in the world.

I ran.

I shot through the snow and around the trees. I slid slightly in my socks but managed to keep us upright, and I kept running. This would be a whole lot easier with shoes, but the frozen ground didn't stop me. It didn't keep my legs from burning as I ran even faster. The icy cold air pierced my lungs, but I hardly noticed the sting. *We were free... We were free, and as long as I kept running, we would never see those men again.*

I'd make sure of it.

The snow crunched loudly nearby, and I cocked my head to listen. I gritted my teeth, wishing more than anything I had my wolf. I could hear footsteps just barely as a flock of wild birds shot to the skies before us. My eyes narrowed, and I changed directions. *Something spooked them,* I thought as my heart pounded even louder. I was *not* taking anymore chances.

"Mommy, wait," Aerith said, tugging on my shirt.

I faintly heard my name being called off in the distance, and I swore, forcing my feet to move even faster, but I was winded already and *pissed* over it.

I had to disappear, I thought as my eyes filled with tears. *He can't find us... He can't!*

"Just hold on, baby."

"No, mommy!" she shouted loudly.

"Aerith, just..."

"Mommy, STOP!"

A roar of an engine sounded behind us, and I nearly dropped her when she shoved away from me. Patrick flew in front of me on his quad, and I slid to a stop, landing hard on my butt. My teeth clattered from the impact, and Aerith scurried to the side, standing tall as she waited.

She's waiting for Patrick, I thought in disbelief. My vision blurred from unshed tears as Patrick swung his leg over the ATV and hopped off.

"What in the world do you think you're doing out here?" he bellowed angrily. "Did you really think you could just run off like that!?"

He took two long steps and hauled Aerith into his arms. *She's not fighting him...*

Panic rose when he shoved me back with his boot, placing the soles on my chest. I tried pushing his boot off, feeling more and more anxious as he pressed harder.

"Please..."

"After everything, Shanely," he growled, "you were just going to leave me?!"

A sob escaped my lips as he glared down at me, but it was Aerith's calm expression that killed me. *She just watched. No expression or emotion on her face.* I sobbed even harder.

"What am I going to have to do to get it through your head where you belong?!" he bellowed, pushing me further in the snow.

My lips quivered as the cold soaked my clothes. The discomfort was nothing compared to the pain in my chest. *God, I was so stupid. Every time I've tried to run or end this misery, he was there. Patrick was always there. He knew my every move, was always one step ahead of me, and there was no*

CHAPTER 26

escaping him. I didn't answer. I don't even know how he found us, but it didn't matter. Nothing mattered now. *He would punish me for this...* I just prayed he wouldn't take it out on her.

"I tried to warn her," she said softly, and my eyes widened. Patrick slowly turned to her as she whispered, "I tried to stop her."

My heart broke. *She wanted to stay?* I thought as more tears slid down my face. They had spent far more time together than I realized. A bond seemed to be forming between the two, and I wanted to scream. I wanted to scream until my voice gave out because he was not her father! *He wasn't Bastian.*

Patrick *softened* with her, gently reaching up and rubbing her cheek, and she *let* him. I tore my eyes away. Unable to bear looking at them anymore. *Oh my baby...*

To my surprise, Patrick removed his boot and let me stand. Soaking wet and body aching, I rolled to my side and got to my feet. I quickly wiped my face, waiting for the blow. For the punishment.

"Look, Shanely," Patrick said firmly, "I want this to work. Like actually work between us, and I think it can given some time. Today was my fault. I should have been more patient earlier, and I shouldn't have lost my temper, but you have to genuinely try to work with me here. You *can't* keep doing this."

"I can't give you what you want," I snapped as another tear fell down my face. I wiped it away saying, "I can't do the things you expect. Love doesn't work that way, and I just..."

Patrick cocked his head to the side, his thoughts spinning as we stood in the snow facing one another. A cold wind passed by, smelling faintly of earth and smoke, and my shoulders fell when Aerith shivered. I didn't even think to grab her a coat before trying this. I had nothing to give her either as I wore nothing but my shirt and pants to keep me warm.

He finally looked over to Aerith, rubbing the side of her cheek, which was now bright red from the cold. To my surprise, he set her down and pulled off his sweat shirt. She let him toss it over her head, and she stuck her arms through the sleeves. She dwarfed in it, and my stomach churned when he picked her back up.

"Alright, here's what's going to happen," he said, giving me a look. "You need to understand that while I have made mistakes in our past, I did *not* make the call to wipe out the pack. I followed orders, and I risked everything to bring you and Aerith here safely, so stop blaming me for that. I have been in love with you since I first saw you in that bar all those years ago, and I *can* make you happy. I can be the man you deserve, because like it or not Shanely, there is nowhere else to go. You leave this house, and the Division will kill you."

Patrick glared at me as my heart broke even further. *Was there really nowhere else for us to go?* My stomach twisted violently as his words settled on my chest. I had no money, no home, and no family. Just three children desperately needing me to keep them alive and safe, and an entirely faction of the government wanting to kill me. *Maybe there was no way to hide in the shadows,* I thought to myself. *I couldn't even run away from him. How could I run from the government?*

"But you are right," he said, pulling me from my thoughts. "Love doesn't work this way. Not this fast. I don't know what else to do to get you to try with me, so I'll make you a deal, alright? I promise to give you more time to adjust to the idea of us if you promise not to run away from me again. I *cannot* have that. But certain choices have certain consequences, Shanely. If you try running away, or attempt to shoot me again, it's the cage. If you..."

"You can't keep threatening me," I cut in, and his eyes narrowed. "Not even an hour ago, you threatened to toss me to the Division because I wasn't *behaving* the way you wanted. Now you want me to not run away *because* the Division will kill me? It's maddening..."

"Well what am I supposed to do?" he demanded loudly. "When you misbehave, you get punished. That's the way it works! That's the way it's *always* worked! Am I going to have to..."

His voice trailed off as his gaze drifted to Aerith. When his eyes hardened to steel, my stomach dropped.

"If punishing you won't work then maybe you'll figure it out with her,"

CHAPTER 26

he said firmly. Aerith's eyes widened.

"Don't you..."

"Quiet," he snapped, and I clamped my mouth shut. "You have been nothing but a handful since saving you. My father is pissed off over the stuff you've done already, but no more. When you screw up and pull another stunt like this again, then Aerith will take your punishment. Understand?"

My jaw dropped. *He wouldn't,* I thought as my heart raced again. *He wouldn't be so cruel to do that to her, would he?* But my mind drifted back to the cage and the demented way he was raised. Bile rose to the back of my throat, and my shoulders sunk.

"I will be patient and give you time to adjust because I want a *real* relationship," he went on as I stared at the snow in defeat, "but you cannot behave this way anymore. Do we have an understanding, Shanely? Are you going to come home with me or are we going to do this the hard way?"

I could feel Patrick's eyes boring into my soul as he waited for my answer. Everything inside me just wanted to crumble. To fall apart in the snow and completely give up. I slowly looked to my daughter. The idea of her being in that cage killed me. It broke me further that she didn't try to come to me at all. Not even when she heard what he would do to her, she just let him wrap her up in his hoodie and hold her while we talked. The last shred of who I used to be died right then. *She doesn't want me...*

"Fine," I said in a defeated voice, "I'll go back with you."

"You'll go back with me where?" he asked, giving me a pointed look.

"I'll go home with you," I said quietly. "Can I have my daughter now?"

"Our daughter," he replied gruffly before handing her over. "And just so you know, you are so lucky I caught you when I did. My dad has these woods booby-trapped around our perimeter. It's specifically designed for shifters, and if you had gone another 10 feet, you would have been dead."

His words were a punch to the gut, and I scrambled to keep up with his long legs as he drug me to the quad. *I almost killed my children just now. All because I went without a plan again. I made another rash decision, and Patrick of all people ended up saving me.* That reality felt like a knife to the heart.

"How did you even find us?" I asked quietly.

Patrick studied me closely before sighing, "I had never planned on telling you, but I guess it would be better that you knew. I put a tracker under your skin, so I could keep an eye on you. Proved beneficial today."

My eyes widened. *He chipped me? Like an animal?!* I gritted my teeth as we walked, dragging my feet with every step. That heavy weight settled further in my chest, and I slumped my shoulders as Patrick sat down.

Patrick pointed just passed the ATV to the woods beyond saying, "I've explained this to Aerith already. I didn't think I needed to bother with you right now, but there is a plate sensitive floor hidden just underground over there. It goes around the entire house, Shanely. Anyone who walks on it gets electrocuted, so don't get any ideas of pulling this stunt again. Dad has motion cameras and infrared around the house too, and it's covered in the Division's scent blocker. No shifter will be able to find the house, and anyone who stumbles upon it will die instantly."

I covered my mouth as another sob threatened to escape my lips. *God, the thought of some innocent person hitting those plates. The thought of one of my wolves...*

Rage suddenly filled my veins when I pictured a wolf finding the plates. They would have no idea, and then their life would be over in an instant. I turned to him and snarled. "That's absolutely horrid, Patrick. What if a shifter is merely passing through? What have we done that was so bad to deserve this?!"

He shrugged casually. "It's happened before, but I don't call the shots. My dad just disposes of them, and we move on."

Every time he opens his mouth, and I'm left in utter shock, I think there's no way he could ever say anything else to top that. Yet, he does. He in evidently does.

Patrick pulled me towards the ATV, and I reluctantly swung my leg over and sat down. He wrapped his arms around Aerith and I and drove back to the house. My body felt numb as the afternoon events replayed in my head. *I nearly killed my daughter just now. I nearly killed my boys before they were even got a chance at life.* Patrick actually *saved* our lives, and that just felt so wrong.

CHAPTER 26

He pulled us around the front of the house and into their large garage. A variety of vehicles were parked inside with spare fuel sitting along the right wall. That dreaded cage was back in its spot again.

I dragged my feet but followed him inside on my own accord into the house again. Warmth from the house coated my skin, and all I wanted was to change clothes and get Aerith warmed up. I didn't have the energy for much else.

Calvin was just leaving his office when we all walked in, and Patrick swore softly under his breath. Calvin took one look at the three of us before glaring at his son.

"Having issues controlling your girl, son?"

I bristled but said nothing. *What was the point?*

Patrick gritted his teeth. "Nope, we just had a little misunderstanding. Didn't we, Shanely? Everything's been cleared up though, and I'm going to take them upstairs for a game night."

"A game night?" his dad asked.

Patrick nodded. "Yup. Shanely brought up a good point earlier that I've been thinking about. We don't know each other very well, and I intend to remedy that. No more only watching movies, where no one speaks to one another. We're going to have actual date right here at the house."

Calvin narrowed his eyes before saying, "I need you to work at the station in the morning."

"Wait, why?" Patrick complained. "I've been solely with the Division stuff the last few months. Why am I going back now?"

"Because I told you so. Now go enjoy your games," he replied before heading up the stairs to his room.

Patrick frowned and took my hand in his. He pulled me along, and after getting dry clothes for Aerith and I, we went back to the movie room. The idea of talking and playing games with Patrick just sucked, but I didn't have any fight left in me today. His threat against my daughter rattled around in my head, so I set Aerith down. Patrick motioned her to the movies again.

"Go on, Baby Doll. Go pick a movie," he said. "Just not the VHS tapes, okay?"

I watched her pick some cartoon movie, and Patrick set it up for her. He then grabbed a card game called Phase 10 and pulled out a chair for me.

Aerith was already snuggled on the couch watching the movie when I went to double check. She didn't once look my direction or even needed me to hold or comfort her after today. She just watched the movie, and that bothered me. *She may not need me, but I needed her.*

"Shanely?"

I let her be and turned back to Patrick. He motioned me to sit, so I did.

"Let's just pretend today never happened, okay?" he said with a grin. "I like the idea of us becoming better friends, and I think this will be fun. I've never played this game before though, so take it easy on me if you have."

"You've never played Phase 10?" I asked, refusing to look over to the couch anymore.

He shrugged. "Need two people to play so no. It was one of my mom's games."

My eyes widened, and I chewed on my upper lip. He didn't seem to notice the pity that flashed across my face and dealt out the cards. I pursed my lips together. *I shouldn't feel pity. I shouldn't care what happened to him...* But all I could think of was Aerith being in his shoes. *No child should ever go through something like this.*

"Your father never played with you?" I asked, taking the hand he dealt me.

"Not really," Patrick said as he studied his hand. "Dad worked all the time growing up. If I wasn't in school, I usually kept myself entertained."

I frowned. "Even when you were little? I mean weren't you lonely?"

Patrick shrugged again. "I guess, but as a single Dad, he just was busy. It's alright though. I always had a bag of snacks waiting for me and plenty of toys to play with. As I grew up, I had homework and then a part-time job. I spent way more time with Dad once I joined the force."

I blinked in surprise. *Calvin was an awful parent.* Although, that shouldn't surprise me in the slightest. *He's a terrible human being to everyone. Can't imagine him being a good dad too.*

Patrick continued to mumble on about his childhood, and how his dad

CHAPTER 26

taught him valuable lessons over the years. I bit my lip to keep myself from asking what lesson the cage taught. I was exhausted already and didn't want to go back there tonight.

It didn't take long before I stopped listening to him altogether. I couldn't help but let my mind wander. The guilt ate away at me, becoming all consuming. *Every chance I've had to escape, I've squandered. Every time I've been so close, I've ruined it.*

"Shanely?"

I jolted. Shaking my head, I asked, "What?"

"I said it's your turn," Patrick replied. "You're distracted tonight."

"Sorry," I mumbled and played my card. I was still stuck on the third round, and Patrick was nearing the end.

"It's okay," he said, laying down his hand and winning the round again. "I'm just checking on you."

"I'm just tired," I replied. *Not a lie.*

"Well, you better start using your head. I am destroying you in this game!"

I stilled, my eyes slowly looking to him as it suddenly clicked. He was smiling, reshuffling the deck, and completely lost in his own happy bubble, but Patrick was right. *I wasn't using my head,* I thought. *I wasn't being smart.*

The hand was dealt as my mind drifted again. I had *squandered* every chance I had because I was letting my emotions get the better of me. I wasn't even taking a moment to think my plan through before I rushed off. Bastian, Cade, and Elijah *always* used their head. That enforcer training shaped them into the courageous shifters they were, and they got things done. *I needed to be smarter next time. I needed to be like my mate.*

I started listing all the things I knew needed to do before I could leave. All while Patrick played that stupid game.

First; I needed to figure out where that tracker was on me. I needed to cut the thing out, so I could escape with my family.

Second; I needed to learn everything I could about the traps outside and how to get around them.

And lastly; I needed to do it all before I gave birth to the twins.

I was not going to ruin another chance to get myself and my kids out. Patrick was on borrowed time and was none the wiser as he played the game smiling. I gave him a soft smile in return.

I'll play this game with him, I thought.

If this is what he wants then I'll play the loving wife. I'll let him think I've changed. That I'm finally accepting my life and him.

He'll drop his guard. He'll think there's nothing to worry about. That I'm happy where I am. All while I escape this wretched place.

And kill him before I do.

Chapter 27

Aerith

Mama had tried to run. She tried to run away, and the look on her face when I yelled stop...

I had hurt her feelings.

I sat at the end of the couch, watching a cartoon movie, while Mama played games with Patrick. He'd laugh. She'd smile. I narrowed my eyes as I watched them. *She just tried to run away, but now they played games like they were old friends,* I thought to myself. I didn't understand it.

I blinked, trying to keep my eyes open, so I could watch them. I needed to watch Mama because she shouldn't be nice to bad people. She shouldn't be friends with him because Patrick had done very bad things.

But Patrick wasn't always mean. It was fun flying the drones with him, and I liked when he was goofy, but when he got cross, he was very scary.

Not like Daddy at all.

Sadness welled up inside me, and I bit my bottom lip. It made it easier to stop crying when I did. Patrick didn't like it when I was sad, and he didn't like me talking about Daddy either. That made him really mad. I slowly looked over to my mother, but she was too busy playing.

Daddy and Mommy never liked Patrick before. I remembered. They were always upset when he came by, but now she seemed happy with him. I frowned slightly.

I didn't know what to do.

But Daddy would watch over Mama. That's what he would do. He would protect her from anything, and since my dad isn't here to do his job, then I guess I will. I will protect her and my little brothers just like my dad. There were strong Alphas inside mama's belly. Alphas who needed watched over too.

I could feel them somehow. It would come and go, and some days it was stronger than others, but I could feel them like they were standing in the room with me. One wolf and a grizzly. One was as strong as Mama, and the other would be like Uncle Cade. One with the power to protect and lead, and the other with the chance at mending like Aunt Cassia. But when I really concentrated, I could feel something was wrong. I wasn't sure what is was or with who, but something was wrong with one of the twins.

"Would my girls like some ice cream?" Patrick asked, and I bit my upper lip. I didn't like ice cream anymore. I never wanted to eat it again after what happened last time with Uncle Abe, but Patrick waited for me to answer. *He'd be cross if I said no.*

"Do you want some, Aerith?" Mom asked quietly.

I frowned, not sure what to say really. I really didn't want it, but I was afraid to upset Patrick.

"You are looking a little sleepy though," Mama said, pursing her lips together. "Maybe we should get you to bed early tonight?"

Patrick frowned. "But we're having fun. Why send her to bed now?"

I sucked in a breath, knowing I needed to speak up. He would be cross with her again, but she simply smiled and walked over to me.

"Aerith might be entering a growth spurt, Patrick. Her little eyes are droopy, and she needs the extra rest," Mama said softly. "Why don't I tuck her in, and we can eat ice cream instead. Maybe play another round?"

Patrick's eyes softened soft, and I exhaled the breath I held. He nodded his head then.

"Okay," he said softly.

I scurried over to my mother, gripping her hand hard as she opened the door to the hall, and we stepped out.

"Hold up," Patrick called out, and I froze. *Is he changing his mind?* I wondered.

Mama stepped in front of me as he joined us in the hall.

CHAPTER 27

"I'm coming too," he said, and mama nodded her head. She gently squeezed my hand, and the three of us made our way down the hall.

I sighed as Patrick unlocked the door to my room. *I hated this room. I hated the dark, and I hated sleeping alone.* It was completely dark when he opened the door, and my heart slowly began to race.

"It's going to be okay, Aerith," Mama said softly, and I looked up to her. I hurt her feelings earlier yet she looked down at me with such kindness in her eyes. I swallowed hard, feeling that lump in my throat again. I didn't want to cry, and she seemed to understand.

She picked me up and carried me in the room. She grabbed the pink pajama set Patrick bought, and I frowned again. I hated pink. Everything in this room was pink, and I wanted nothing more than to stomp my foot and refuse, but I got changed anyways.

"Can you leave the light on?" I whispered, my voice shaking ever so slightly. *Daddy wasn't afraid of the dark,* I scolded myself as I twisted the blanket between my fingers.

Mama gently rubbed the side of my face saying, "Of course, baby."

She kissed me goodnight as Patrick ruffled my hair.

"Goodnight, Baby Doll," he said with a grin. His arm wrapped around mama, and I frowned slightly.

"Sleep well, my Baby Girl," Mama said as her and Patrick walked to the door. With one last smile, she shut the door behind them, leaving the lights on.

My eyes glistened with tears as I thought about Uncle Cade and my dad. I missed them more than anything. Rolling to my side, I let the tears fall.

Patrick wasn't around to notice anyways.

Chapter 28

Shanely

The next morning, Calvin woke me bright and early. His incessant knocking pulled me from the best dream I had had in a long time. I could still feel Bastian's lips on mine when I sat forward on the bed. The weight of everything settled right back on my chest as I turned to glare at Calvin.

"What do you want?" I asked in a huff.

"Get dressed, Shanely. We need to talk," he muttered.

I swung my legs over the side of the bed, blinking rapidly as the morning nausea hit me.

"I've got nothing to say to you," I answered, standing up to walk in the bathroom.

"It's your blood or Aerith's," he said, and I ground to a halt. He shrugged casually then. "I've been using your blood solely, Shanely. Do you want me to start comparing yours against hers? Or would you like to have a calm discussion this morning."

My face twisted into a scowl. "Give me a minute to change," I snapped. I grabbed new clothes and ducked inside the bathroom.

After a moment, I met him in the halls, and he motioned me to follow him. My brows furrowed when he stopped just in front of his office door.

"You know, Shanely," he said, unlocking the door, "I think it's time I told you a story."

Calvin guided me inside and locked the door behind us. Curiosity got the better of me as I looked around. *Any information was good,* I told myself.

"What story?" I asked, watching him approach the elevator.

CHAPTER 28

He gave me a weak smile saying, "My own."

My eyes widened. *Why was he finally telling me about his late wife?* I had to admit, I was dying to learn her story. Whatever happened to her ruined the two of them, and Calvin was so secretive when he was here at the house. This room, the elevator... None of it made any sense.

The elevator opened, and Calvin pressed B2 once we were inside. As it began our descent, he continued, "Did you know my wife was a brilliant scientist? She worked for the Division in one of their labs. I bet you didn't know that about the Division, huh? It's diverse and not just a security force for shifters. It's not just military."

The doors chimed as they opened, and my brows knitted as I looked around the room. A long white hallway with vinyl flooring and glass windows made the room looked almost like a hospital wing. Everything was pristine and clean, albeit a little dated. Lights slowly clicked on one at a time as we walked down the hall, and I peered into each room as I followed Calvin.

This is a laboratory, I thought to myself. Test tubes and microscopes were scattered about in every room. Some had scary looking machine like contraptions, but I had no idea what they were for. Biohazard signs hung in various spots on the wall, and my eyes widened when I looked back to Calvin. *Is this where he's been taking my blood?*

A sickening feeling hit the pit of my stomach as he shoved open the heavy door to one of the lab rooms. A machine whirled in the back corner, but other than that everything was quiet. *What was Calvin up to, and how long has he been working on it?*

"It's where I met my wife actually," he said, pulling me from my thoughts. "I was in training while she was climbing the ladder in Research and Development. Different sections, mind you. Soon, she was Head Scientist for the Division and was placed in charge of seeing if she could somehow transcend Shifter Abilities to humans. So I built her all this, so she could work from home if she ever wanted or needed to."

My eyes went wide as Patrick's words rattled me to my core. *"Dennis wanted you for some reason and was livid when the report came in that you* died." It made my stomach churn just thinking about it. No shifter would ever comply with the Division... *So how many did they forcefully take?*

Is this why they wanted me so badly? I wondered. *They can't do anything without having shifters to test this on, and Patrick said Dennis wanted me delivered to him personally.* My stomach twisted again. *Is this the real reason he wanted me? Were they trying to steal the White Wolf's abilities?*

Glass clattering pulled me from my thoughts, and I watched as Calvin shoved aside empty beakers to check the back machine. He nodded his head, pursing his lips together before grabbing the tourniquet and that black bag.

"My wife always hoped she'd be able to help people," he said as he dragged me to the opposite stool. Yanking up my sleeve, he smiled saying, "Give sight to the blind, the ability to walk to those lame or deformed, and so on and so forth. All because your bodies heal yourselves at an incredibly fast rate. Lorelei figured it out too, and that's when things went south."

He drew vial after vial of blood then. "It was brought to her attention that certain Heads didn't care about saving people but rather wanted the Alpha Power instead. They wanted the ability to transfer that grand and mighty power to humans or more specifically to themselves. Then they could control anyone with nothing but their voice."

My mouth dropped. Bile rose to the back of my throat. *God... that sort of power in the hands of humans?* I couldn't begin to imagine the atrocities that would happen at the hands of the wicked.

Calvin smirked as he applied the bandage. "That was her reaction too. She said that it was wrong. That *shifters* had learned responsibility over a power like that. Strong Alpha power wasn't given to every shifter, but those granted with it at birth knew how to use it properly. The balance and control they had was unprecedented and that humans were too selfish and hateful to have it. Oh, she let him have it that day. I was so proud of her as I stood in the back, waiting for her to get through the meeting. She was just a little thing, who was afraid of nothing, much less her boss."

His face hardened as he cleaned up the mess. I didn't move a muscle for fear he'd clam up and stop talking. This was something I needed to know.

CHAPTER 28

The damage done to my kind...

"They didn't take too kindly to being told no. She was fired and told to leave at once. I should have just taken her right then and there, but she convinced me to grab our baby boy instead and meet her back home. Little did I know what was going on or what she was up to. Lorelei wiped the files on her lab computer at work and fled home. She destroyed her life's work, so the Division couldn't replicate it with a new scientist. She made it home before we did but..." his voice trailed off, and I watched the man visibly shake with fury. His eyes glossed over, and I knew that haunted look. *I had worn it too many times.* Calvin was lost in the memory, and there was no way I'd pull him out of it.

Finally, he straightened his shoulders and opened a drawer. "The Division followed. They slaughtered my wife right here in her lab, but they were too late. She had erased everything and burned what needed to be destroyed. They destroyed my house looking for anything more on her work, but only I knew her secret hiding spots. It's where I found these."

He tossed a worn folder my way, and I stilled. He gave me a nod of approval, and I slowly opened it. I couldn't make heads or tails of anything in here. It was all over my head, full of formulas and little scribbled notes down the side. The equations alone would be enough to scare me away, and I briefly looked back at him.

"I know, it was confusing to me too," he said, his lips tightened in a thin smile, "but I learned. I studied and learned, so I could carry on her work."

Carry on her work... My heart pounded in my chest as I watched him.

"How do you even know it was the Division?"

The first question I dared to ask.

"Ah," he said, walking over to the computer, "because my wife was brilliant. She had cameras hidden everywhere, and I found this."

He clicked a few buttons before turning the screen. A black and white video played on screen, showing a small woman running frantically around the room. Nausea struck as my eyes drifted to the far corner of the room briefly. The very same machine that was currently running was in the video. My eyes drifted to the other side, realizing Calvin hadn't changed a single thing of hers. *It was this room,* I thought to myself. *Oh God, she died right here, didn't she?*

Lorelei moved quickly from computer to computer, typing furiously away at each one. There was no sound, and for that I was grateful. I definitely didn't want to hear anything. *I didn't want to watch this.*

She jumped hard as glass flew across the room, and I held my breath. Armed men came into the room in perfect formation and fired. They fired multiple times, even though she had fallen with the first shot, and my hand shot to my mouth. *This was horrible. Absolutely horrible.*

Once they confirmed she was gone, they tore the room apart. I recognized the uniform. The men I faced looked a little different, but so much of it was the same. Seeing them on screen was like adding salt to a wound, and my hands slowly covered my mouth.

My stomach churned just watching, but I realized Calvin simply stared at the screen. Lost in it almost, and my heart began to pound inside my chest. *How many times has he watched this?*

The screen went black, but he didn't make a move to turn it off. He just stared blankly like he couldn't tear himself away. I didn't dare breathe. Calvin clearly wasn't as stable as I thought. *He wasn't just a wicked man,* I thought. Her death broke him, and the man sitting across from me was nothing more than a broken shell.

Much like me...

I shoved that thought away. *Calvin and I were not the same,* I thought as my temper flared.

"Why still work for them then?" I asked, needing to know the answer. If I were him, I could never work for them again. *Pretending alone would be impossible,* I thought to myself. My question was enough to pull him out of his thoughts, and he gathered the files back up, putting them in the drawer once more.

"I told you, Shanely. I'm finishing my wife's work," he said flatly, "just with a new purpose."

Calvin took my arm, pulling me from my seat towards the door. My feet scurried to catch up.

CHAPTER 28

"Wait, what? I don't understand," I said, shaking my head. "I thought your wife didn't want that power to fall into the Division's hands? Why would you do this?!"

"Because I want the Alpha power," he said coldly. My eyes widened.

"Your wife was against that!" I bellowed. "She did everything to keep this from happening, and you're just going to do it anyways?!"

"I'm not going to waste it like those cowards were planning too," he snapped as he shoved open the door. "I'm going to avenge my wife with the very thing they killed her for."

I stilled. My jaw hung as I stared at him wide-eyed. *Oh my God... Everything made sense now. Calvin was going to destroy the Division entirely. He was going to kill them all.*

"This can happen one of two ways, and frankly I have no issue either way. Either I'm able to control shifters, and I force them to slaughter everyone, or I can force humans to submit to my Alpha power. Then I'll make them kill each other," he said firmly.

I wanted to vomit. Saliva filled my mouth as my stomach twisted and churned, sending bile to the back of my throat. *This is why he wanted my blood... He was trying to take the Alpha power that ran through me. Oh God... Was this the real reason why he attacked my pack?! Why he offered that deal?*

Calvin stopped in front of a large door with a sign that said *Experimental Room 1* on it. My mind reeled, going in a thousand different directions at once. Every thought leading me to the same conclusion. *He has to be stopped. Calvin cannot possess my Alpha power.* As much as I hated the Division, I couldn't stand by and watch innocent lives be slaughtered like this. My heart thundered in my chest as I thought of all the people who would be caught in the cross-fire.

What am I going to do?

"I've been testing my theories on one shifter for quite some time. A very strong Alpha, but I've hit a roadblock. Unable to transfer her power, I was ready to tear what little hair I had left out until my son actually proved to be useful. He got himself attached to a pretty girl who just moved to town.

A girl who happened to look *a lot* like the one in here," he said, shoving the door open.

I stumbled forward, breathless at who stood before me. Her strawberry red hair with matching widow's peak. Her hooded, hazel eyes that widened when they saw me. She was very thin and very short just like me. Like looking at my reflection in a mirror, I knew who she was.

"Shanely," Calvin said, as I struggled to find my breath, "meet your mother."

The mother I had been dreaming about since I learned to walk was here. *She was here... My God, she's been here the whole time?!*

My body shook slightly as she ran to the glass wall that separated the two of us. She shouted something but not a sound reached me. My hands slowly clenched into fists. *Calvin stole my mother. All these years of not knowing what happened to her or where she was...* My blood boiled to the point it burned.

"You took my mother?" I gritted through my teeth. My fingernails dug further into my palm. Anything to keep myself from lunging at him. She was now a factor in my escape plan, and I couldn't lose my temper before he told me *everything*.

Calvin snorted at the question.

"Who do you think gave her father the inhibitor?" he asked condescendingly, and my eyes shot to his. "As soon as I realized what a golden opportunity had fallen in my lap when she mated that bear, all it took was one conversation with her father to get what I needed. Just one."

He held up a single finger, and my body shook with fury. *I'm glad Dad shredded Jack. That prick...*

My mother banged on the glass angrily, and I turned back to her. She shouted again, but I could only watch her in agony. Her screams quickly turned to sobs, and there was nothing I could do for her.

"Little did I know she was pregnant with you though. Mercedes was quick too. I lost her for a little while after I gave that Alpha the inhibitor, but then one day she just emerged from out of nowhere," he said, sitting on top of the only table in the room. His soft smile crept up his face. "Without

CHAPTER 28

her wolf, she was easy to take, but I never knew about you until you came into town yourself. I mean after decades of getting only so far with this one, her long lost daughter just strolls into town? What luck!"

Calvin chuckled to himself like he just told a joke. *A very sick joke...*

"My idiot son came barreling into work one afternoon, so angry that this cute girl he had his heart set on was suddenly engaged to Bastian Fenrir," he went on, grinning wide. "That got me curious, and when I saw you, I just *knew*. I knew you belonged to this woman, and I just had to have you too. If she was this strong, I could only imagine what you'd be, and with progress coming to a grinding halt, I had to look outside the box."

Calvin got to his feet, pacing the floor between the two of us. Warm blood trickled from the palm of my hands as he said, "I can obtain the Alpha power from Mercedes, but not for more than a few minutes. I cannot hold it for long, and my plan won't work unless I can obtain it, and *keep* it, like you all do, which is where you come in. You're not just a powerful Alpha like I thought. You're the shifter's prophetic White Wolf."

My eyes widened slightly, and he grinned again. "I do my research, Shanely. Being the White Wolf, your genetics should be pure. Therefore in theory, your Alpha power should be easier to adapt to."

My brows furrowed as I glared at him. *All this time,* I thought angrily. *All these years just taken from me. All because of this man.*

"Is this the real reason you slaughtered my pack?" I snarled, causing him to sigh.

"You have been a difficult shifter to kidnap, Shanely," he replied, placing his hands behind his back. "I had to do something because you were never alone. You were never an easy shifter to take, and when you bonded with the Fenrir brothers, it only complicated things further. Cain wasn't the same man as Jack, and you already know what happened when I offered the same deal to Bastian that I did your grandfather."

I struggled to keep the tears at bay. White hot rage traveled through my veins, staining my cheeks blood red. I wanted to rip him to shreds. To kill him for all he put me and my family through.

"I had an opportunity land in my lap awhile ago," he said, and my eyes widened. "Did you know that?"

He smirked, clicking his tongue as he straightened. "Imagine my surprise when Patrick comes home one day, telling me all about the fact that Bastian wasn't your kid's real father. That he met the real dad at the bar, and that you ran off and kept your child a secret from the guy for years. That man had no idea he even had a kid until he showed up in town to take you home one day. My son was nervous because you now had a half-breed that we were supposed to report. He didn't want too, and frankly neither did I."

My shoulders tensed as I remembered the fair that year. *He and Patrick were together,* I thought as I scrambled to figure everything out. *Was Calvin involved with Peter trying to take me too?*

Calvin chuckled again saying, "He made a joke about the guy being a little off his rocker, and hoped maybe he's just snap and kill Bastian for him, so I gave him a little push. I told Patrick to give that guy all the information he needed because he was the true father and *deserved* to know his kid. It was easy to guilt my son into helping him, and all I had to do was sit back and watch the pieces fall apart, but then the fool went and disappeared one day, and I was back to square one."

That's how Peter knew where to go, I thought as my chest seized. My eyes slowly drifted to Calvin. *He has no idea Peter didn't just disappear one day.*

My mother knocked on the glass, and I turned to her. I could see her mouth muttering *I sorry* over and over again, and those two little words tightened around my heart. I didn't know how to even process that she was alive and standing no more than five feet in front of me. *Let alone how I was going to get her out.*

"I had compiled almost enough evidence to call in a raid, when you nearly ruined my entire plan by calling Dennis early," he said, his eyes narrowing. "You know he was the one who wanted the power in the first place. He is the loud mouth my wife argued with the day I lost her."

Calvin glared at me, and I dropped my gaze as my stomach twisted. *I had no idea who I was calling back then. The problems I caused...*

"But it was that phone call that got him interested with the McCoy pack," he said, tapping the glass in front of my mother. She barred her teeth. "And

CHAPTER 28

because you started to merge all the shifter kinds back together, I was able to spin enough doubt to call in the raid. That phone call actually helped me out, and here we are."

"Why are you telling me all this?" I asked snarling.

"Because my son nearly lost you," he said, his smile falling, "and I wanted to make sure you don't ever do something stupid like that again. You're too important, Shanely. Far too important."

My eyes widened as he stormed towards me. My back hit the wall, and he was inches from my face.

"You breathe a word of this to my son," he snarled, "and I'll make sure your daughter and mother pay. Trust me when I say my son *learned* his cruelty from me."

I held my breath, knowing full well he'd follow through on that threat. I had to be smarter than him. I couldn't afford another mistake. Not only would Patrick take his anger out on Aerith, but so would Calvin.

He suddenly grabbed my arm, yanking the door open and shoving me through. I tried to turn, tried to reach my mother, but Calvin was stronger than he looked and only pushed me harder. I stumbled on my feet as the door close. The red light flashing twice above the door as the lock clicked in place.

"The whole act of helping Patrick get the girl of his dreams was just a lie. He's not really in charge of me," I said snidely, "is he?"

Calvin snorted as we walked back down the hall. "No, I could care less about that. You keeping Patrick happy and out of my hair while I work is a win-win for me, but you're a real handful unlike your mother. I thought you needed an extra incentive to be good from here on out."

I gritted my teeth, wishing more than anything I had my wolf. "Patrick really believes he saved me from the Division. I always thought he was lying, but he believes it's the truth, and it was just you manipulating everything the whole time. What do you think he's going to do when he finds out the truth?"

He rolled his eyes, dragging me back into the elevator. Smacking the button on the console, it slowly rose as he said, "And who's going to tell him? Me? You? He's not smart enough to figure anything out for himself, and you won't because of what I'll do to the last of your family."

"But he's your son," I said in disbelief, "the last piece of your wife... Why do you despise him so much?"

"Because!" he bellowed loudly, and I flinched waiting for the blow that surprisingly did not come. I slowly opened my eyes as he shouted, "If I hadn't had to grab him that day then I would have been able to save my wife! She's gone because I was stuck picking him up from daycare. He's been nothing but a difficult child anyways. Constantly screwing up everything he does, and his whiny self *continues* to get in my way. I will finish my wife's work!"

My eyes widened just as the door opened. There was no point saying anything more, I realized. Calvin stormed through the house, dragging me along with him. My hand covered my mouth as a wave of nausea rolled in my stomach. *He took too much from me,* I thought to myself. *I needed my vitamins.*

"Remember what I said," Calvin snarled as he opened Patrick's door. I glared, walking inside and slumping on the bed. The lock clicked over once more, and I laid back, staring at the ceiling.

My dad wasn't wrong... My mother was alive.

I covered my face with my hands, taking a deep breath. *My escape plan just got a whole lot harder,* I thought to myself. *How could I leave knowing she was trapped here too?* I had to get her out, but how was the question. I was still figuring out how to get out myself.

I slowly rose to my feet and walked over to the window. It had become my favorite spot in this awful place, and I curled up on the window sill to clear my head. It looked beautiful outside, all bright and sunny. Spring was right around the corner with all the melting snow. Only a few massive piles were left. Everything else had turned to mud. My lips fell into a frown as I stared at the empty woods. Rain slowly started trickling down, and soon it became a down pour.

All these years without my mother, I thought, feeling sorry for myself. *All the abuse I suffered in the foster system, and all the missed time we could have*

CHAPTER 28

spent together. The wondering where she was or if she ever loved me. Now, I know. All this time gone *because* of Calvin.

The trees swayed in the wind as the rain poured from the sky. The forest looked gloomy as could be today. *Fitting really*, I thought as I followed a rain drop sliding down the window. A small smile curved on my lips, thinking back to the memory of when I was a kid riding the school bus while it rained. I began rooting for the rain drop to win the race to the bottom. It slid faster, stopping briefly when it crashed into another drop before gaining speed again. It soon hit the bottom.

Sighing, I laid my head back. This heavy weight in my chest made pretending near impossible, but I had to get it together. Patrick would be home soon, and what I was about to do would be hard enough as it was. I took a deep breath before continuing to stuff my feelings inside the mental box again. A stupid tactic I used to do growing up.

"The pain was never this bad though," I mumbled.

Every day it was getting harder and harder to bury this pain. I could barely think about my family or my mate without crumbling in agony. So I shoved it aside. One day we'd be free, and I'd mourn my family then. I shut my eyes again. *Time to channel my inner Bastian*, I thought to myself, remembering the time when Cade said that.

I smiled, opening my eyes, and started to plan. I needed to free my daughter *and* my mother from this prison all before I give birth to my boys. I couldn't fail again.

I needed two keys now. One to get into Calvin's office and then a key card to let my mother out. I needed to find and remove the tracker buried somewhere on my body, and I needed the code to turn off the alarm.

Those things needed to get done just to actually leave this place. Leaving was a whole different thing all on its own. I couldn't go anywhere unless I figured out where those plates were and how to cross them safely. Patrick and Calvin come and go from this place all the time, so there must be a way through.

All these things I needed to figure out quickly, and that meant a lot more snooping around the mansion. In order to do that, I needed out of this room.

My jaw locked. I knew the only chance I had was to get Patrick to relent some. He had to start trusting me, and that was only going to happen if he believed I loved him.

I watched the woods awhile longer, hearing Patrick's truck pull into the drive. Guilt twisted my stomach as I shoved more inside the box. *It was time,* I thought to myself. *It was time to start lying.*

I let go of the breath I had been holding, taking one last look at the woods below. I wanted so badly to run through the trees. To feel the soft earth beneath my paws, and the wind whipping past my fur. To hear Bastian howl as he chased after me...

I shoved that thought away, straightening my shoulder as I stood, when something flashed off in the distance. I blinked.

Squinting my eyes, I searched for the source. Light shimmered again, and I wondered what lay behind the woods here. Endless trees stood for miles, but something shimmered back there. My lips pursed together as Patrick opened the door.

"Hey, baby."

Chapter 29

Patrick took off his police vest and tossed it on the bed. His forehead lined with worry, and I couldn't help but wonder if it was because of Calvin.

"Why was the door locked?" he asked. "I thought I left it open for you today."

My eyes narrowed. "Uh... It was locked when I woke up. I just thought you wanted me here like normal."

Patrick scratched the back of his head saying, "Huh. Well, sorry about that. I must have locked it out of habit, but I was going to let you spend the day with Aerith because I wasn't working too far from the house."

He kicked off his boots, and I frowned. "But you've never really let me out of the room by myself before."

Patrick slowed his steps, leaning against the bathroom door. "Call it an experiment, Shanely. I told you I want this to work, and I meant it. I thought we'd start here."

"So I can have free run of the house then?" I asked, perking up.

Patrick sighed before walking over and sitting on the arm rest before me.

"Last night got me thinking," he said softly. "Neither one of us trusts the other, and if this is truly going to work between us, then things have to change. I don't need to be so strict, and I don't want to punish Aerith like that either. You now know what dangers lie outside and what would happen if you left, but I think it would be okay if you had access to the rest of the house."

My eyes widened in surprise. *And here I thought I'd have to convince him*, I thought as a small smile crept up my face. He grinned back at me.

"There are still rules I need you to follow though, Shanely. Otherwise I won't be able to trust you, and we'll go back to the way things are now."

"You can trust me," I lied, grinning wide. This was the first real smile I've had since coming here, but after everything I learned today, I was ready to get on with the rest of my plan. I just couldn't believe he offered this in the first place.

He smirked, crossing his arms and giving me a pointed look. "Is that so?"

I nodded my head. "Like you said yesterday, I have nowhere else to go, and I don't want *this* to be our life forever."

A half-truth, but Octavia always said the best way to hide a lie is in the truth. My heart twisted, and I shoved the memory aside.

Patrick studied me closely. "So start with friends?"

He held out his hand and waited. I refused to let my smile fall and slowly shook his hand.

"Friends," I finally replied.

Suddenly, my heart seized in pain as I stared down at our connected hands. Guilt plagued me once more over what I was doing. *It's just a lie,* I told myself. *A necessary lie to save the people you love.*

Yet no matter how many times I repeated those words, it didn't make me feel any better.

"Can I help you with dinner?" I asked, pulling my hand back and tucking it at my side.

"I'd like that," he said, grinning wide.

I followed him out the room and down the hall, my stomach churning the whole way. *This was wrong, but it was working.*

"C'mon, Baby Doll!" he cried out as he opened Aerith's door. "Your mama and I are making supper!"

She came running towards us, reaching for my hand as she looked to Patrick. I gave her hand a small squeeze, pulling her attention back to me. She didn't return my smile, and I pursed my lips together. *What was I going to do to help her too?*

We entered the kitchen together, and in one swift motion Patrick plucked

CHAPTER 29

Aerith up and set her on the stool by the island. He then turned on the TV in the corner for her to watch before opening the fridge.

"Okay, so we have stuff for pizzas, pasta, chili," he said, sorting through everything in their massive two door fridge. "What exactly are you in the mood for?"

I walked over to the fridge and peeked around his arm. I felt his gaze settle on me, and I shifted on my feet as he stepped a little closer. I quickly grabbed a few vegetables from the drawer and stepped back.

"Maybe Vegetable soup?" I stammered. "The twins are taking a lot from me so adding all these different veggies would be healthier. Do you mind?"

He grinned again. "Not at all! Gotta make sure the boys are doing good too!"

Patrick grabbed every vegetable he had between the fridge and pantry and then a large stock pot and cutting board. I wasn't sure how I would turn this hodge-podge into a decent meal, but I wasn't about to object. He was happy, and I needed it to stay that way.

He unlocked the drawer in the corner, pulling out a small kitchen knife, and my brows rose. *He locked the knives away?* I thought to myself and nearly rolled my eyes before remembering the incident. *Yeah... That makes sense.*

Patrick extended his hand to me, when he suddenly hesitated. His pale eyes slowly rose to mine, and his mouth turned down into a frown. *He was nervous.*

"I won't hurt you, Patrick," I said softly, lifting my hand until it wrapped around his and the knife. "I promise."

He stilled but let go of the knife, and I started chopping the onions and garlic. I paid him no mind as I got to work prepping dinner. *I was not about to do that again. Not in front of Aerith. The more I behaved kindly, the more he would relax,* I told myself. Eventually, he grabbed another knife and board to help out.

We kept the conversation light as I struggled to figure out a way to push it towards the questions I needed answered. My poor baby seemed bored as she watched the cartoon in silence. Not a single giggle came from her, and it broke my heart to see. *This was one of her favorite shows too,* I thought. *Her and Elijah always watched this one together. They both rose so early, and I often found them curled up on the couch together with a bowl of cereal in hand, laughing as they enjoyed that cartoon sponge.* That memory gripped my heart so fiercely, I had to look away. I quickly blinked, trying to keep my emotions at bay.

The garage door sounded, and soon Calvin walked in the kitchen. His brows rose when he spotted me chopping a bell pepper.

"Well, what do we have here?" Calvin asked, giving me a curious look. I glared right back.

"We're making soup. Are you sticking around tonight?" Patrick asked.

His father grunted. "No, I have to work late tonight. Just wasn't expecting this, is all."

Patrick turned to look at me then and smiled. *He expected me to answer.*

"Yeah well..." I stammered as I tried to think of the best way to say this, "I guess someone finally talked some sense into me. I realized I might as well make the best of it since the only family I have left is here."

Patrick tucked me into his side, grinning proudly, and I let him. I didn't shove him away like I wanted to. I merely held Calvin's stare, hoping he understood my point. *I needed him off my back too.*

Calvin's eyes never left mine as he watched the two of us together. Anger coursed through my veins, and I bit my inner cheek to keep from barring my teeth. *The less I behaved like a wolf the better.*

"I'm glad to hear your change of heart," Calvin said, breaking the awkward silence. "Enjoy your night, you two!"

I watched him the entire way to his office where he disappeared from sight. *The wretched prick,* I thought as I turned to grab the large stock pot. I knew he would be down there all night screwing around with my blood until he got the formula right, and what a horrific day that would be if I couldn't stop him in time. I wished more than anything I'd have the opportunity to snoop through his bedroom, but I didn't see Patrick letting us out of his sight tonight. He was in a good mood, so I let the idea go and focused on dinner. I grabbed the olive oil on the island when I noticed Aerith. She still

CHAPTER 29

watched Calvin's office door, and I cocked my head to the side. *She had been watching Calvin too.*

"I'm really glad you're giving this a chance," Patrick said behind me, and I jumped having him so close. He chuckled, bopping me on the nose before he tossed in the pile of onions and garlic we had chopped. *I didn't even hear him sneak up on me,* I thought as my heart raced inside my chest. I slowly gave him another fake smile and got back to work.

He's never questioned my intentions once, I thought as I watched him from the corner of my eye. Patrick was just so happy, tossing in the bell peppers and celery and whistling some tune I didn't recognize. *Calvin ruined him.*

"So what do we want to talk about?" he asked, pulling me from my thoughts. I grabbed the salt.

"How about you?" I offered quietly. "I hardly know anything about you. Why not start there?"

Patrick grinned. "Sure. What do you wanna know?"

Now's my chance.

"Have you lived here your whole life?" I asked, my hands scrambling to do something other than just standing here like an idiot.

He dumped the entire container of chicken stock in the pot as he answered, "Yup! It's just been dad and I in this house for as long as I can remember."

"So you never knew your mother?" I asked, and his face fell.

"No," he answered quietly. "I don't have any memories of her other than what I've seen from the home movies. Someone broke into the house and took that chance away from me."

Patrick grew quiet after that, and I wasn't sure if I just ruined my chances to keep him talking. *Mom was a touchy subject,* I thought as my lips pursed together.

"What about you?" he asked, and I looked over to him. "Did you spend your whole life in Indiana?"

I shrugged. "I was born here," I answered honestly. "I ended up in the foster system and was transferred to a family in Indiana who wanted to adopt me. It fell through, and I bounced from foster family to foster family."

His brows knitted in confusion, and he quickly snapped his fingers towards me. "But that bear shifter... What was his name? Daniel!"

My heart seized hearing my father's name.

"Yeah, Daniel," he went on. "He's your dad right? Why didn't you go live with him if your mom didn't want you?"

My jaw clenched so harshly, I had to turn around. I couldn't let Patrick see the rage in my eyes. I opened the fridge, grabbing a stick of butter for some sort of an excuse.

"He didn't know I existed until I came to Diablo," I finally answered. I grabbed the knife, squeezing it tightly in my hand and chopping the butter into smaller pieces. "My mother wanted me but something bad happened to her when I was a baby, and since my father didn't know he had a daughter, I went into the system."

Silence filled the kitchen.

"That's something we have in common," Patrick said quietly, and I stilled. *God, he's not wrong,* I thought. And that just pissed me off for some reason.

"Did you always want to be a cop?" I asked with a clipped tone. I inhaled deeply, trying to stuff my feelings aside again. But good God, we needed off the topic of my parents. I tossed in the butter and began to stir.

Patrick leaned back on the counter as he answered, "It was what my dad and grandfather both were, so I wanted to follow in their steps."

"That's pretty cool," I lied. "Was your Grandfather apart of the Division too?"

"He was," he answered, nodding his head. "They both worked for the Sheriff's office and the Division. He sent my father to the same training facility that I went to a few years back. Dad felt I was ready to learn about shifters earlier than most. He said I was further ahead than any recruit he had ever met, so he put in his recommendation for me to start training. Now I do mostly stuff for the Division."

I could hear the pride in his voice, and my stomach knotted. *God, it was just false praise yet Patrick was eating it up. He craved his father's approval and affection.* As much as I hated this man, I pitied him growing up with a father like Calvin.

"When did your dad add all the security measures here? I'm sure they weren't here when you were little," I asked as nonchalantly as I could. I continued to stir the pot, wishing it would heat up already. Bile rose to the back of my throat as my stomach rumbled. *God, I was starving.*

"He did that while I was at the academy. I came home to a whole new way to enter the house. It took awhile to memorize."

"Memorize? Is it that intricate?" I asked, forcing a chuckle. He shrugged again, grinning wide at me.

"It's not bad, but there's no room for error," he answered, turning to grab us bowls. "The pack was changing, so he made sure the house stayed undetected."

My eyes widened.

"So this place is close to town?"

Patrick narrowed his eyes, giving me a questioning look. "It's better if you don't know, Shanely."

Goosebumps trailed my arm as Patrick studied me closely. The silence in the room was unbearable as I turned off the burner.

"I didn't mean anything by it," I said quietly, hoping he believed me. He didn't answer though, and suddenly doubt crept in. *What if this was a bad idea?* I thought to myself as I walked over to Aerith. Elijah always teased that they could always see everything clear as day on my face. *What if I ruined my last chance because I couldn't keep my face stoic?*

"Can we watch a movie after dinner?" Aerith asked, startling me. She hadn't said one word this whole evening, and I slowly turned to Patrick for an answer.

"Come get your bowl," Patrick said quietly. He stepped aside to let us go first and crossed his arms. I blinked in surprise. "And that's fine, Aerith. Whatever you want."

I quickly moved to get Aerith her bowl. "Thanks for dinner, Patrick."

The corners of his mouth rose as he watched me fill three bowls. My hands shook slightly, but I managed not to spill a single drop, and Patrick sat down next to Aerith at the island. *I was not cut out for undercover work*, I thought as I took my seat. *Not one bit.*

I took a bite, surprised that it was actually not half bad and quickly took another. No one said a word for a little bit. Not one sound until Patrick pushed his chair back abruptly.

I narrowed my eyes, unsure what he was doing, when he opened the fridge again and pulled out the vitamins for me to take. *I had forgotten them entirely*, I thought surprised. He brought me the bottle and a glass of water before grabbing Aerith a juice box. *How different of a person you could have been had your father not raised you.*

"So, what's so secret about your dad's office?" I asked casually before taking the pills. They went down hard, and I chugged the water.

He shrugged answering, "Not really secret, just private. I really don't ever go in there."

"Aren't you curious where that elevator goes?"

"All I know is it belonged to my mother," he replied, "and I'm not allowed to go down there."

I let him be then, already feeling like I had pushed too much too soon. Nothing but the sound of spoons clattering against the bowls kept us company, but I felt way better once my belly was full.

"I can wash your bowl," I offered, holding out my hand to take it. *It's what you wanted, right?*

Patrick flashed me a grateful smile as I extended my hand to take his bowl. He let me, and I took our dirty dishes to the sink.

"So how was your day, Aerith?" he asked. *At least he was perking back up.*

"It was fine," she answered. My body tensed when she straightened and asked, "When can we play with the drones again?"

He chuckled again, his eyes lighting up in a way I had never seen as he said, "I'm glad you had so much fun. Might be easier to practice during the day though, but maybe if grandpa doesn't mind me working from home again, I can take you out this week. Sound good?"

She gave him a soft nod and turned back to the TV. Every cell in my body screamed as he tossed his arm on the back of her chair to watch with her, and *she didn't move.* She didn't do anything but let him cuddle with her as they continued to talk like father and daughter. She seemed comfortable with him almost, and it was all my fault. *She was bonding with this man, and it was all my fault.*

My stomach churned as I washed the bowl in hand. The dinner I ate threatened to come back up as it sat in the back of my throat. *What if she accepts him as her dad?* I thought as my anxiety rose. *What if she forgets Bastian?*

My heart thundered in my chest, and I struggled to catch my breath. I hunched over in the sink, avoiding the two altogether as tears filled my eyes. I couldn't quiet the fears inside my head. I couldn't stuff these feelings in the box. No matter how many times I repeated the facts. *Aerith has no idea... She has no idea, and she just wants to feel safe and loved. She...*

The bowl shattered, and I gasped loudly. The water turning red as my blood spilled out from the gash in my hand.

"Oh Geez, Shanely," Patrick said as he jumped up and rushed to me. "What happened?"

"I'm sorry," I stammered. "I didn't mean to break the bowl."

Patrick carefully wiped my hand off then. "Don't worry about the dish. Are you alright?"

A tear rolled down my cheek, and I was suddenly grateful to the stupid gash on my hand. Patrick had no idea how I felt, and this gave me the chance to hide. He gently reached up to wipe the tear away.

"Let's just get you cleaned up," he said softly. "I'll take care of the mess later."

He guided me over to the stool before grabbing the first aid kit. I wiped my nose as Aerith leaned over to check on me.

"I'm okay," I whispered.

"Let me see your hand," Patrick said, and I obeyed. He cleaned and wrapped the wound, and it was all I could do to be quiet. To not snap when he kissed the bandage, blushing slightly when he pulled back. *God, Bastian... I need you.*

"Leave the rest," he said. "Let's start that movie."

I didn't object. My body felt heavy as we followed him back upstairs. I didn't want to watch the movie. I didn't want to spend another second with him. Exhaustion had taken over, and all I wanted to do was sleep. To let the dark and empty take over and feel some semblance of peace. I was spent, but I slowly looked down to Aerith. *If I bailed now, they would stay up together.*

So I squared my shoulders and stepped into the movie room.

Patrick put on a comedy movie this time, and Aerith promptly plopped down at the end, with one of the plush blankets wrapped around her. I sat next to her, and Patrick sat on my other side. That vile cologne hit my nose, and it took everything in me not to gag.

You can do this Shanely, I thought to myself. *You can do this.*

My mind was elsewhere though as the movie played. I couldn't get my mate out of my mind. How much I was betraying him by sitting here snuggled up to another man. *One who tore our family apart.* My heart ached inside.

I was drowning in my own thoughts when the movie suddenly shut off, and I blinked finding Patrick putting everything away.

"It's over?" I asked.

"Yeah," he replied as he studied me. "You seemed pretty distracted tonight."

"I'm sorry," I replied. "My hand hurts, and I guess I'm just tired."

Patrick gave a slow nod then before patting my leg. "Why don't you go soak in the tub? Take your mind off everything and just relax. I'll put Aerith to bed."

"Oh no, Patrick. I can..."

"I want Patrick to put me to bed," Aerith said, and I blinked in surprise. He grinned wide.

She wanted him?

"See?" he said. "We'll be fine! Just go and take a minute. I think the boys are just wearing you out."

My heart shattered. Pure pain surged forward, and I quickly got to my feet. "Well, if you insist."

CHAPTER 29

Aerith gave me a smile before wrapping her arms around my waist. "Goodnight, mama."

My lips puckered as I knelt down, and I took a deep breath, struggling to keep my emotions at bay. "I love you, Aerith. More than anything."

Her tiny lips kissed my cheek. "I love you too."

And then she pulled away and took Patrick's hand. I couldn't breathe as I watched the two of them make their way down the hall towards her room.

"So, what book shall we read tonight?" Patrick asked as they disappeared inside, and I bolted.

I practically ran down the hall towards Patrick's room and locked the door behind me once I was safe inside the bathroom. My hand covered my mouth as a sob burst forth. I couldn't stop the tears that fell down my face. *She wanted him. She wanted Patrick!* I continued to sob as I fell to my knees.

Agony. I was in pure agony as the man who helped murder my mate and family read my daughter to sleep.

Chapter 30

Aerith

My eyes began to droop, and it was all I could do to keep them open, but I had too. Mama was here, and so was Patrick. We had been in this movie room every night this week, either playing games or watching movies. While it was nice to be out of my room, I was worried about mama. She was being really nice to Patrick now. I wasn't sure why because she does not like that man, but I wanted to watch out for her. I helped her when she cut her hand, and I wanted to be there to see if she'd needed anything else.

Patrick chuckled at the cartoon animals fighting on the screen, and I chewed on my lower lip to stay away.

"So are there any other rooms that are off limits for Aerith and I?" Mama asked.

Patrick's brow rose. "Why?"

"No reason," she said softly. "It's such a big house, and I just want to make it more comfortable for us both. I don't want to impose."

Mama wanted to stay. My brows furrowed as I listened closely.

"I like the idea of you guys making this place more like home," he said as his hand brushed against her cheek. "There are only three rooms in the house you need to stay out of. The one at the end of the hall, that's dad's bedroom, his office, and my office. You know, the one you stumbled into that day."

He gave mama a stern look, and she dropped her head. I frowned. *I don't like the look on her face.*

"I'll make sure we stay out of those rooms then," she said, looking back

CHAPTER 30

at the movie, "but you will have to decide where you want to put the twins."

He ruffled her hair saying, "Good girl, and that's true. They'll need their own space."

What was Mama doing? I watched her closely, but when our eyes met she merely winked at me. *Were we staying here forever?*

My eyes blinked again as exhaustion swept over me. They felt so heavy, and I sat up in my seat. I couldn't contain my yawn though. I tried to smother it in my blanket, but when I felt Patrick gently rub my cheek, I knew I'd been caught.

"Aww, Baby Doll," Patrick said softly, "are you getting sleepy?"

Mama smiled at me and opened up her arms. I scurried over to her, laying my head on her chest. Her heart beat softly against my ear, and soon my eyes began to droop.

"Why don't I tuck you in?" she offered, pushing a stray hair aside. My mouth rose slightly. As confusing as mama was acting, she was still my safe spot. My chest warmed as she gave me an extra squeeze.

"Let's do it together," Patrick suggested as he stood. "I'll carry her for you."

"Sure," Mama replied.

Patrick lifted me from my mother's arms and carried me from the room. Mama's smile fell slightly, but when our eyes met, she beamed back at me. I leaned my head against Patrick's shoulder, struggling to keep my eyes open.

Mama lifted her hand to her mouth and blew me a kiss. My lips puckered ever so slightly. *I wanted mama.*

Patrick set me down on my bed and pulled back the covers. I slowly tucked my legs in, and he covered me with the massive pink comforter.

"You sleep well, Baby Doll," Patrick said with a smile. I gave him a nod as he rustled my hair softly.

Mama knelt down as he stepped towards the door. She kissed my cheek, wrapping her arms around me tightly. I clung to her, inhaling her honey scent, and wishing more than anything she could have her wolf back. I missed cuddling with her as her fur was so soft and warm. I missed being with the pack, and I missed my dad. I just missed home.

"I'm sorry," she whispered.

I blinked as Mama stood and followed Patrick out the door. He shut the light off and closed the door behind them. I sucked in a breath as my eyes tried to adjust. The room was in complete darkness now, and my heart started to pound in my chest. I gripped the blanket tighter as my eyes roamed around the room, catching every shadow on the wall.

No...

I scurried to the switch on the wall and flipped it up. The room lit up, and I took a deep breath as my heart continued to race. Slowly, very slowly, I made my way back to bed.

Rolling to my side, I fell asleep.

Chapter 31

Shanely

The door rattled loudly.

I shot out of bed, my heart racing. *What in the world?!* Calvin stood in the door frame glaring.

"Get up, Shanely," he snarled. "Now."

The door slammed shut, and I jolted again. I groaned, rubbing my eyes as I struggled to settle my heart. I looked at the clock annoyed. *I thought I was going to have the day to snoop.* Patrick was at the station again today, and I didn't know how many days I had left before he was assigned to work from home again.

Calvin pounded on the door, shouting for me to hurry along. Rolling my eyes, I got out of bed and got dressed. I took my time picking out what I wanted to wear and spent a good ten minutes just brushing my hair. It was a silly thing, but it felt like a win. He looked pissed by the time I stepped out of the room.

"What?" I asked, smirking.

"Let's just go," he snapped as he grabbed my arm. "I don't have all day."

"You know," I said, pulling my arm from his grasp, "I actually have things to do today, so this really isn't going to work out for me."

Dark circles lay beneath his eyes as he glared. "This isn't funny. Now move."

"No."

We stared at one another for a moment, and I realized Calvin looked thin. He swam in his shirt, and I wondered when the last time he actually ate anything or slept for that matter. *He must be working himself to death*, I thought. *It's the only explanation unless he wore one of Patrick's shirts by mistake?*

The wheels were turning in his mind, but he said nothing, and the corners of my mouth rose in triumph. I had no desire to participate in any of his research. *This may the silliest way to slow him down but if it gets results*, I thought to myself.

Calvin finally grunted, pursing his lips together as he glared at me. "You have three seconds to start moving or I do this with Aerith instead."

"Don't you dare!" I snarled, my hands clenching into a tight fist.

"One," he said, holding up a finger. "Two..."

I bolted down the hall, grumbling as I passed him.

"Prick," I muttered. *And this is why they took Aerith*, I snarled in my head. *But at least she's safe.*

Already knowing where he wanted me to go, I walked to his office. He didn't say a word as we made our way down into the lab again and back to the same room as before. I sat down on the stool and rolled up my sleeve, but to my surprise he didn't try to take anymore blood.

Calvin merely moved about the room, ignoring me as he grabbed things left and right and tossed them into his bag. He stopped at the machine in the corner then, and my eyes narrowed. *What is he doing?* I wondered.

He opened the lid and pulled out a strange looking vial. The contents were yellow, and I watched him remove all six vials before placing them in a small protective container. He tossed it in the bag after that.

Calvin motioned me to get up. "Let's go."

We walked out, and not surprisingly, we went to my mother's cell. Anxiety rolled in my stomach as I stepped inside. I hadn't seen her since that first time, and it was still hard to wrap my head around the fact she was here.

She looked worn out but stood promptly when she saw the two of us. Her eyes widened when I was pushed to a chair next to an old machine.

"Geez, will you stop pushing me?" I asked sarcastically, but he ignored me, and my butt hit the seat harshly.

CHAPTER 31

Suddenly, my mother rushed to the glass and started to smack against it. Her utter panic had the hairs on my neck standing straight, and slowly my own anxiety began to rise. *My mother knew what was happening,* I thought as I looked around me. *She knew, and it scared her.*

Calvin flipped over the bands I didn't even notice on the chair, locking my wrist in place. I tried yanking my arms away, but the bands wouldn't budge. Panic rose further in my chest.

"Let me go!" I hollered as I tugged again.

"I have a good feeling about today, Shanely," he said, sitting opposite me. He grabbed one set of wires and attached the sticky ends to his forehead. "You see, I've isolated the shifter gene in your blood, and I'm going to inject myself with the gene. These wires will help monitor my results and record how I am able to effect you. It should only take a minute for it to kick in."

My eyes widened. *He's already figured it out?* I thought as I scrambled to figure a way out of this. I jerked my head away as Calvin brought the other set of wires to me. His eyes flashed, and he gripped my face tightly. My teeth clattered together as he placed the wires where he wanted.

The machine whirled when he started it up and got comfortable. The needle sketching marks as it printed a long sheet of continuous paper.

"Calvin," I stammered nervously, "you need to stop and think about this. This is wrong, and you know it! Your wife knew it!"

Calvin flicked the syringe that was now filled with the yellow contents from the vial. "Nah, my wife made it work. I can too."

He jammed it into his leg, making me wince. The contents emptied into his system as he gave me a feral grin. Mother screamed in her cell as I watched the horrors unfold.

Calvin twisted in his chair, grunting as the serum traveled through his system. The incessant beeping from the machine sounded as the needle flung across the paper. I scurried as far back into the chair as I could and pulled my legs up when he paled, doubling over like he was about to vomit.

My heart pounded in my chest when Calvin convulsed again, and I nearly let out a scream as he slammed back in his chair, shutting his eyes tight.

Suddenly, his blood-red eyes shot open, and I paled. *Just like an Alphas should be.* Gone were the dark circles under his eyes and the pale skin. *Oh God, he had figured it out... He had actually transferred the Alpha power to himself.* I was stuck across from a violent, unstable Alpha.

I had to get out of here.

I jerked my arms harshly, trying to loosen the locks that kept them down. My wrists screamed in protest, but I pulled harder. *I had to move. I had to get away,* I thought as my chest heaved.

"Don't move," he spat out painfully.

Fear took over as I felt a charge in the air, and I froze. It was different than what I was used to feeling when stepping across an Alpha. I slowly looked down to the inhibitor around my wrist. *Being the White Wolf, most Alpha powers didn't work on me.* I was always stronger than the others, but I didn't know what to expect with the inhibitor. *Would it work because my wolf was locked away? Oh God... What would Calvin force me to do if it did?*

Calvin smiled viciously at me. His low laugh filled the room, and I waited for the command. *It was coming,* I thought, and I prayed that he wouldn't command me to hurt someone.

He leaned forward and released my wrists from the band. I tucked my arms in, scooting further in my seat as I waited. My eyes shifted to the door behind him. *If I could just get passed him...*

"I want you to stand, Shanely," he commanded, the charge in the air growing thicker. I waited for my body to move without consent but nothing happened. I rubbed my wrists and stared at Calvin. There was no force pushing me to stand. My body felt no pain, and I cocked my head to the side as Calvin frowned.

"I said stand!" he bellowed, and I jumped in my seat.

"No."

Calvin roared, launching the bag he brought across the room. He knocked his chair backwards as he got to his feet, pulling the wires from his head. My eyes widened when he suddenly grabbed his chair and threw it against the wall. It shattered on impact.

"It worked! I can feel the power within me! Why isn't it working on you!?" he shouted angrily.

My heart thundered in my chest as he paced the room. Slowly, ever so slowly, I got to my feet. My back hit the wall, and I carefully took a step to my left. *The door was right there,* I thought as I took another step. I had to leave. I had to get out of this room. Somehow the Alpha power healed him, and I wasn't about to stick around and see what other strengths it gave him.

But once I got out, where would I go? I shook myself from those thoughts and took another step. I'd figure it out once I got out of the room safely.

"Unless..." he muttered quietly, and I ground to a halt.

Calvin scurried across the room to a panel on the wall. He smack one of the buttons then.

"Can you hear me, Mercedes?" he said gruffly. My eyes widened as I looked to my mom.

"Yes, Calvin," her small voice said.

My mother's voice. I had always wanted to know what she sounded like, but I never thought it would be like this. I blinked as tears started to well in my eyes. *I couldn't break now,* I thought and took another step. *There had to be something I could do to stop him.*

"Good. Now sit down," he growled out. That charge filled the room again, and her eyes went wide as her body was suddenly pulled to the ground. My heart ached. *It works... His Alpha power actually works.* Calvin started laughing uncontrollably.

"Yes! I have done it!" he bellowed. "I've figured it out, my love!!"

Calvin celebrated across the room, beaming from ear to ear, and I frowned. He blocked the door to the labs.

"Mercedes," he shouted, "stand now!"

My mother quickly stood as if an invisible hand lifted her up off the ground. My stomach twisted at the sight. *I can't watch this...*

"Calvin, stop it! This is wrong!" I shouted. He grinned excitedly, ignoring me as he gave another command.

"Jump!" he shouted.

My mother began jumping in place, and he roared in excitement. I stood watching in disbelief. *I thought I had more time, but now that he has an Alpha power, he is even more dangerous than before.* I didn't know how to stop him either. *Not without my wolf.*

Mom began panting, her face turning bright red as she continued to jump.

"Hit yourself," he commanded, and my hand covered my mouth as my mother struck her own face.

"Again!" he bellowed. "Don't stop until I say!"

Mother's face turned a horrible shade of red as she continued to harm herself. *He's going to kill her,* I thought as fear gripped my heart.

"You let her go!" I shouted, rushing over and shoving him. Calvin gave me a feral grin and smacked another button on the panel. The door to my mother's cell suddenly opened.

"Mercedes, protect me," Calvin said, and my eyes widened.

My mother moved so quickly, rushing towards me like a battering ram and shoving me across the room. I landed on my back with a hard thud and groaned as I slowly rolled to my side. My mother took a fighting stance in front of Calvin, ready to attack me should I come any closer. Her fists were clenched tightly but fear was in her eyes.

"Shanely! I'm so sorry! I can't stop it!" my mother shouted as I scrambled to get to my feet.

I could already feel the bruise forming and took a deep breath. *There had to be a way out of this,* I thought as Calvin blocked the exit once more. But a sickening feeling hit the pit of my stomach that I wasn't leaving this room alive.

"It seems your own power does not work on you, but it works just fine with your mother," Calvin said, pulling me from my thoughts. "I knew you were a stronger shifter than she was. You are the key, Shanely."

I scowled, taking another step away from the two of them. *Think Shanely... C'mon, use your head!* But no matter how hard I tried, I wasn't coming up with a plan. I wasn't coming up with a way out.

Calvin clapped his hands excitedly. "Now let's see what fun we can have today, shall we? Mercedes, I want you to..."

CHAPTER 31

Suddenly, Calvin clutched his stomach, groaning as he dropped to the ground. I held my breath as my mother relaxed her stance.

She rushed towards me, pulling me into her arms, while I stared at Calvin. I couldn't take my eyes off him as he roared in pain on the ground. The room grew quiet then. The only sounds were him breathing hard as he laid hunched over on himself.

"It's alright," mother whispered. "You're alright."

Calvin roared in anger, screaming from the top of his lungs. He shoved off the ground and rushed to the machine. The dark circles under his eyes had returned, and his skin was pale once more.

His hand slowly rose to his forehead where the wires once were. *It never recorded,* I thought as I sagged in relief. *He doesn't know what went wrong.*

Calvin screamed again, throwing the machine across the room, startling us both. He drew his gun, aiming it at my mother's head.

"Don't hurt her!" I shouted, but she pulled me back.

"Move," he demanded, "or I'll turn the gun on her."

"Calvin, don't!" mom shouted, raising her hands. "I'm moving alright. Just leave her be."

Mom let me go.

"Back in your cell," he snapped at her, and she took another step away.

"Mom! Don't listen to him!" I hollered as tears filled my eyes. I stormed towards her, but Calvin grabbed the back of my hair and yanked me towards him.

"She knows her place! It's time you figured out yours! You have three liabilities, Shanely, and I will kill every single one of them to get what I want. I will not fail!"

I barred my teeth, glaring as rage filled my chest. But he held all the cards here, and he *knew* it.

Calvin dragged me over to the console and hit the third button. Mom's cell door shut again and the locks clicked over.

"Let's go," he said.

I quickly glanced her way, my heart aching, as we left my mother alone in that room. Calvin shoved me forward, and down the hall we went. The familiar feeling of cold steel on my back. We were at Patrick's door in moments, and it didn't surprise me when the lock clicked over, and I was left on my own.

I slumped back on the bed, covering my face with my arm. My body hurt but nothing compared to weight on my heart. My hand slowly inspected the bruise on my hip. I groaned, covering the mark up again. I wasn't going to do anything to hide it either.

My mother attacked me, I thought solemnly. *She attacked me today because a wicked man commanded her to.* What atrocities would she commit the next time he tried this? *Would she be the one to kill the Division Heads?*

I shook myself from those thoughts and stared at the ceiling. My world felt bleak, and it was hard to find hope again. Hope that we'd actually make it out of this. It was just hard to see anything but what we were dealing with right now, and thing's weren't looking good.

We had to get out, I thought to myself.

I had to find those keys.

Chapter 32

Aerith

I laid upside down on my bed just waiting for someone to open the door. Mama usually came to see me by now, but she wasn't here. I had heard footsteps early this morning, but no one came to get me, so I stayed locked inside the room.

I was utterly bored.

I had read every book in here. Colored every page in my coloring book, and I had even popped the head off the police doll already.

There was nothing to do here.

Suddenly, I heard a faint wailing sound.

I slowly sat forward. *What was that?*

I looked around the room as the sound happened again. *It... It sounded like someone was screaming,* I thought as my brows furrowed. It sounds so faint though. Like I could just barely hear it coming from somewhere far away. My chest burned again, becoming an oddly comforting feeling now a days. I concentrated on the sound, focusing really hard like Uncle Aspen always told me when I took classes with him. My nose scrunched as I strained to hear the sound again.

And suddenly, I could hear it! It was louder now, and I was right. Someone was screaming out in anger. *A male's voice,* I thought before scooting further back on the bed.

I shrunk down and brought my knees to my chest, rocking on the bed as the wail sounded again, and then it was quiet. Not a sound until footsteps appeared nearby.

I waited for anything to happen. For someone to let me out of this room, and this house. I waited for hours all alone.

And no one came for me.

Chapter 33

Shanely

Guilt ate me up inside.

Watching my mother yesterday reminded me of when I used my power to command Cade and Elijah. *I commanded them for selfish reasons,* I thought as I wallowed on the chair in Patrick's room. I hated my actions after watching it happen to her. The idea that Calvin and I were similar in *anyway* broke me. I never wanted to use my Alpha power against another again. *I wanted nothing more to do with it.*

Calvin never left his bedroom for the rest of the evening. Another easy lie to convince Patrick that *he* was the one who locked me in, but it was comical how quickly he believed me. I had started to hope Patrick would begin to figure things out for himself, but I quickly pushed that thought aside. The sad truth was that he'd probably side with his dad if he knew. Calvin could do no wrong in his eyes.

I looked at the clock on the nightstand, and it was nearly four in the afternoon. Patrick would be home any minute, and with Aerith napping in her room, I had nothing to do. I slowly looked back to the ceiling, my mind reeling. *What was I going to do to stop Calvin?*

Suddenly, I heard a loud creak coming from somewhere in the house. I slowly got to my feet. A door shut, and I scurried to follow the sound. *It came from the other side of the house,* I thought as I cracked open my door.

The top of Calvin's head appeared as he strolled down the stairs to the foyer, and I tip-toed after him. *This was the first he's left his room since that test he ran on mom,* I thought as I stepped in the shadows of the grandfather clock. Calvin left through the front door.

My feet scurried down the stairs after him. I watched through the window as he stepped up into his blue pickup truck and placed a small black box on the dash. He slowly turned the truck around and pulled down the drive. Only slowing for a moment before driving on and disappearing from sight.

He left.

My heart thundered in my chest as I looked at the grandfather clock. *This was a major risk,* I thought as I shifted on my feet. *But one I may not get again.*

I bolted back up the stairs, feeling more winded than I liked, and went right towards Calvin's bedroom door. I jiggled the handle, finding it locked and groaned. *Of freaking course...*

I yanked a bobby pin from my hair and jammed it in the lock. I had never done this before, but it looked easy in the movies.

I scowled as I moved the bobby pin around frantically. *Usually Nancy Drew breaks in by now,* I thought, huffing in frustration. I groaned, yanking the pin out and glaring in defeat. *There had to be a way in...*

Suddenly, an idea came to me, and I grinned. *Growing up in the foster system was about to pay off,* I thought. I bolted back towards Patrick's room, feeling the familiar strain from pregnancy. God, all I wanted to do was lay down again, but I gritted my teeth and shoved open the door. I went straight to the desk, digging around until I finally found what I was looking for.

An old gift card.

Rushing back to Calvin's door, I slid the card through the crack as I turned the handle. The door gave way, and I couldn't contain my wicked grin.

I quickly shut the door behind me and took a look around. My heart thundered in my chest as I carefully searched his room. *I have to be quick.* It was a simple bedroom really. Nothing more than a bed and desk, but it made my job that much easier. I went to the desk first, putting everything back exactly the way I found it, and came up short. Frowning, I struggled to get to my knees to check under the bed. Still nothing. I went through his drawers and the closet as my anxiety grew. *It has to be somewhere!*

CHAPTER 33

I opened the last closed door and nearly gagged when the smell struck me. My eyes watered as the smell of vomit and other unmentionables hit my nose. The bathroom was a wreck, and my stomach churned as I stared at his soiled clothes and trash. I promptly shut that door, refusing to search *anything* else in there.

I jumped when the sound of cuckoo bird chimed. The clock on his nightstand said a quarter past four, and I shook my head angrily. *I would have to try another time. It Patrick found me in here there would be no way to lie my way out of this one.*

Stomping my way to the door, I spotted something on the upper shelf. I had missed it coming in, but a small crystal bowl sat on top and sitting inside was a pile of keys. A squeal left my lips as I shook the bowl. Every key was labeled. Everything was so neatly marked that I wanted to scream for joy. Because buried at the bottom was a set labeled, *Office Key*. I shoved the key in my pocket and put the bowl back where it belonged. *I did it*, I thought as I locked his bedroom behind me. *I actually did it. Maybe I can hack it as a Spy?*

I chuckled as I made my way across the landing. Suddenly I heard the garage door.

Patrick.

I ran towards Patrick's room, scrambling to think of a place to hide it. I could *not* keep it with me. If they found it on me, I wouldn't be able to lie my way out of it. Aerith getting stuck in that cage flashed in my mind's eye, and I moved faster.

There must be some place I can hide this key, I thought to myself as my heart thundered again. *Maybe I can find a spot behind the desk?* I wondered as I rushed over. I had to try something.

As I approached the desk, a floor board creaked loudly. I slowed my steps. *I've heard this board creak a thousand times... Maybe I can move it?*

I dropped to the ground, landing roughly on my knees, and dug my fingers into the crack between the boards.

"Ouch!" I cried out, when the board stuck under my nail. Blood dripped from my finger nail, and I shook my hand before trying again. I pulled again, hearing it crack before finally coming free. I toppled over, swearing as I pulled myself back up to look inside. There was about half a foot of space under the flooring in here. *This will do,* I thought grinning. I dropped the key inside and covered it back up. Everything looked just the same, and I sagged in relief.

Footsteps sounded in the hall, and I rolled to my side and shot to my feet. My eyes widened when I saw blood speckled next to me. I rushed my foot over the mess, wiping the floor clean before moving to the window sill. My butt had barely sat down, when Patrick opened the door.

"There's my girl! Ready to make some dinner?" he exclaimed in a cheery tone, kicking off his boots. He was on cloud nine as the corners of his mouth curved into a smile.

"Sure," I said between breaths. I forced myself to return his smile as he sat down and removed his vest. Bright red blood seeped from my nail, and I pushed on my finger to stop the bleed.

"I talked to dad today. Just a couple more days at the station, and I should be back home then," Patrick said. My stomach twisted. Only a few more days without him hovering constantly. *Great...*

I gave him a small nod and left the window. I didn't trust my voice not to shake at the moment. Once he dumped all his stuff, he grabbed my injured hand and pulled me down the hall towards Aerith's room.

Aerith came running towards us the second he opened her door, and I quickly pulled my hand from his to scoop her up.

Patrick frowned. He held up his hand, and my eye widened. A small drop of blood lay on his palm, and I froze. He wiped it off, inspecting his other hand then.

"Are you bleeding?" he asked as I wiped my finger off on the inside of Aerith's shirt.

"No," I answered quietly and forced myself to move towards the stairs. *God, my nerves.* Patrick thankfully didn't question me further, and I led the way to the kitchen.

Aerith simply snuggled against me, and my heart ached for her. This wasn't the life I thought I'd give her. *This wasn't what she deserved,* I thought

CHAPTER 33

to myself. Somehow, her life ended up worse than mine, and that reality sickened me.

Another thing to stuff inside the box.

As I set her down on the stool, I realized that this had been her first birthday without her dad or family. No one to say how big she's grown or measure her against the door frame in my cabin. To throw her in the air for every year she turned older or *anything* like that. I had even missed it because of Patrick.

She didn't even mention it...

Leaning in, I kissed her forehead and whispered, "I love you, my beautiful big girl."

She gave me a grin before reaching for the TV button. I helped her put on cartoons before turning to the fridge.

Patrick rattled on behind me about wanting tacos to eat tonight while I pushed more and more inside the mental box. My body was worn out from keeping it inside all the time, and the mental box was just getting bigger and bigger by the day. Fear crept in as I tossed a pound of ground beef on the stove. *If I can't find a way out of here soon then I was gonna snap and be unable to put it all back together again.*

It was just exhausting not getting a chance to mourn.

We made dinner like normal, but tonight I noticed Patrick found *every* excuse to touch me in some way. I felt numb as I puttered about the kitchen, trying to avoid him without him catching on. I was barely able to stomach treating him like a friend. Becoming anything more, even just pretend, was more than I could handle. I just kept moving, kept working, anything to keep the aching pain in my chest at bay.

Tacos tasted bland, but I ate two anyways. Aerith seemed to enjoy them though, and I watched her eat her dinner in silence. It was the only joy I felt today.

Back in the movie room, Patrick gently nudged Aerith.

"Want to play games with mom and I?" he asked, but she just shook her head.

"Can I watch a movie instead?"

My lips pursed together. Patrick gave her a nod saying, "Go ahead. Let me know if you change your mind."

He put on another movie for Aerith, who snuggled in her spot on the couch again. I turned to look at the stack of games in the cabinet, feeling defeated tonight. We had played nearly every game here already, and I was still no closer to learning the truth about the plates or where the tracker was hidden on me. I was running out of time…

Patrick cleared his throat, gesturing to the chair across from him, and I quickly took a seat. He laid out some card games.

"Pick one," he said as I looked through the stack. "You seem off tonight. Are you doing okay?"

My smile didn't reach my eyes as I grabbed Uno. "Sorry, I'm just tired."

He slowly nodded as I shuffled the cards. "Must be because of the twins. You're getting close, aren't you?"

I had less than a month if the boys were on time, I thought as I glance to Aerith. *She was early…* I shook myself from those thoughts and nodded my head.

"Yeah, I'm…"

Suddenly, the door slammed open, and I jumped hard. Calvin glared at me, storming over as my heart began to race.

"Where are they?!" Calvin snapped angrily.

Aerith dove under her blanket as Calvin bellowed. My jaw dropped. I didn't know what to say. *How did he even know?* I wondered as my face turned beat red. *Those keys were barely gone a day, and yet he already knew?* I scrambled to come up with an answer as he yelled again.

"I said where are they?!" he shouted again. My mind raced as I shook my head. *Did I forget to close a drawer? Did I leave his room different than when I entered? Where did I screw up?!*

"Whoa dad, what is going on?" Patrick asked, leaning back in his chair. I snapped my mouth shut and waited.

"She took something that belongs to me," Calvin growled, jabbing his finger in my face, "and I want it back now!"

Patrick gave me a curious look. "Shanely, what is he talking about?"

CHAPTER 33

I shrugged my shoulders, trying to find my voice, but the words seemed stuck in my throat. I drug my fingers through my hair, trying to do anything but give away that I was guilty. That I stole the keys to his office. Pure panic gripped my heart. *God, this was all coming apart before it even got started.*

"I don't know..." I managed to say before Calvin gripped my arm harshly. I sucked in a breath, wincing as he yanked me to my feet.

"Yes, you do!" Calvin shouted again. His eyes flashed red momentarily before his pale eyes returned. *Did he keep some of the power?*

"Dad!" Patrick shouted as he put himself between the two of us. Calvin let go, glaring at his son. I stole a peek around Patrick, noticing his eyes were on the tiny bundle hiding under the blanket on the couch. He frowned before settling back on his dad. "Calm down, and tell me what in the world do you think she took?"

"My keys," Calvin snapped. "My office keys are missing from my room, and she has them! I know she does!"

"Seriously, Dad? You lose your keys all the time. You still have your spare set, right?" Patrick asked.

Calvin dragged his eyes to him and glared.

"That's not the point, my boy, and you know it. I want to search her!" Calvin demanded as my eyes went wide.

Patrick rolled his eyes. "You're not serious. I can just make you another set after work tomorrow."

"I want to check her now!" Calvin hollered again.

Patrick finally sighed and stepped aside. My eyes widened, but he just shook his head. "It's just easier, Shanely."

A scowl appeared as I reluctantly stepped forward and lifted my arms. Calvin forcefully dug into each pocket, searching everywhere only to be utterly disappointed. I let go of the breath I had been holding as relief washed over me. *I finally did something right*, I thought. *If I hadn't, everything would be ruined.*

"See, Dad?" Patrick said. "Shanely didn't take them."

"I want to check your room," Calvin gritted through his teeth, and my eyes widened slightly. *He doesn't know about the loose floor board, does he?*

Without warning, Calvin grabbed my arm and stormed towards Patrick's room. Patrick was hot on our heels as Calvin threw open the door and stepped inside. He tossed me to the side and began to tear the room apart. Patrick came to me first, inspecting me quickly before glaring at his father. Veins bulged on the side of Patrick's head, but he said nothing as his dad went through the whole room.

Calvin tore the place apart, while Patrick simply waited by the door. I couldn't help but stare. Stare utterly amazed that he said nothing to his dad right now. Patrick was a grown man, *allowing* his father to treat him this way. I turned away from the spineless wonder, placing my hands behind my back, and tried not to look anywhere near the desk.

Calvin finally stopped trashing the room, huffing where he stood as the gears turned in his mind. A small smirk appeared upon my lips. He never once found the loose board. He never once questioned the sound when he stepped over it, and I couldn't quite believe my luck. Here I thought I was about to get caught, but Calvin was genuinely confused as to where the keys went. I stayed quietly at Patrick's side, while Calvin worked it out on his own. A weight lifted off my chest when Calvin walked towards us.

"Sorry," he muttered as he stormed out.

Patrick sighed, watching his dad leave and go to his own room. Calvin's bedroom door slammed shut, shaking the house, and just like that I had won. I had won this small victory, but to me it was *everything*. It was just one step closer to getting us out and getting the revenge Bastian deserved.

"I'm sorry about that, Shanely. Sometimes Dad gets stressed out and freaks out over the littlest things," Patrick said, rubbing the back of his head. "It happened a lot growing up too."

I blinked in stunned silence. There were a thousand different questions I wanted to ask, but none of them mattered. Patrick was a victim of abuse but so was I, and I would have *never* done the things he had.

Playing the long game, I replied, "It's alright."

We quietly began to put the room back together when I turned, finding Aerith in the door frame. *I didn't even hear her walk up,* I thought feeling that awful feeling in the pit of my stomach again. I had hoped she'd stay in

CHAPTER 33

the movie room away from all this, but her eyes were wide, and her white knuckles clung to the frame. *She was terrified.*

"Why don't you get her ready for bed? It's late anyways, and I can finish cleaning all this up," Patrick offered, chucking the clothes back in the drawer.

"Really?" I asked, cocking my head to the side as I wrapped my arm around my daughter. "You don't mind?"

"Yeah," he replied as he approached the two of us. "I feel bad about dad's temper so go ahead."

"Thank you, Patrick," I said quietly.

Patrick knelt down and kissed Aerith's cheek. "Sorry grandpa scared you tonight. I'll talk to him about it tomorrow, okay?"

She nodded quietly, earning a smile from him. My brows knitted as anger surged forward again. *I really didn't like how close they were becoming.*

Suddenly, I felt his lips on my cheek, and I pulled back surprised. Patrick gave me a sheepish smile saying, "I'll meet you in the movie room when you're done."

My heart thundered in my chest. Forcing a smile to my lips, I quickly pushed Aerith out the door and down the hall.

It's just pretend. It's not real. It's not real.

Once Aerith and I were safe inside her room, I wiped my cheek off. It may be stupid and silly, but I wanted it off me. I *hated* that he kissed me. I hated being nice to him, and I hated what this was doing to Aerith. It hadn't escaped my notice that she was becoming more and more quiet as the weeks went by. More comfortable with Patrick especially. *I was losing my sweet girl, and I hated it.*

Aerith didn't bother grabbing pj's as she climbed into bed, and I just let her stay in her comfy sweats. It really didn't matter what she wore as we never left the house, but I wanted her to have the choice with what to wear. Anything to give her some sliver of happiness and control over her life.

I walked over, trying to muster what I could to look happy as I pulled the comforter down to see her sweet little face. She fiddled with her fingers, and I had a feeling what she was going to ask me.

"Mommy," she said softly, "are we going to stay here forever?"

My eyes shut as I took a deep breath. *What do I even say?* I wanted more than anything to tell her the truth. That I was planning on getting us out safely, but there were so many risks to consider. *What if she accidentally tells Patrick? What if he's listening outside the door right now?* As much as it killed me to lie to her, I couldn't risk telling her just yet. *I'll give her the truth the moment it's safe, but until then, she needs to stay in the dark.*

"We're staying here, Aerith. This is our home now, and we need to just make the best of it," I said softly. Every word was like a dagger to my heart, and I watched her little face fall apart.

"Daddy broke his promise," she said as tears filled her eyes. "He said he would always find us. That he would always be here, but he's not here, mama. He just left us…"

My heart shattered as a sob burst from her lips. I shut my eyes, inhaling her scent as she just broke. *This wasn't Bastian's fault. This wasn't anyone's fault except Calvin and Patrick.*

"I want Daddy," she begged. Tears fell down my face, and I couldn't stop them.

"I know baby," I replied, my voice shaking slightly. "Mommy wishes more than anything that I could bring him to you right now, but you always have me. We're a team, Aerith, and a good one at that. Daddy taught us both what to do now, and I know without a shadow of a doubt that he would be proud of you, Little One. He'd be so proud of how you're handling everything. We can do this, Aerith. Besides, we've got two new littles to raise. You're going to help me, right?"

She wiped her nose on her sleeve as she nodded her head. The tears had finally stopped, and I gave her the biggest smile I could muster.

"Good. They're going to need their big sister to protect them," I said, giving her a squeeze. I gently lifted her chin to look her in the eye. "Promise me, Aerith. You will never forget *anything* you learned from your dad though. You may need it someday, okay?"

Aerith leaned into my arms, and I rubbed her head. I heard her soft whisper then.

CHAPTER 33

"Okay, mommy."

I stayed and rubbed her back until she finally fell asleep. Silent tears fell down my cheek as the two of us stayed like that for awhile longer. I quickly took a deep breath before shimming out from under her. Patrick would come looking, and I didn't want him to find me like this. I wiped my face, taking deep breath after deep breath. When I finally felt calm enough to leave, I kissed Aerith goodnight.

Shoving more into my mental box, I schooled my face to look better than I felt and strolled from her room, leaving the light on.

Chapter 34

Aerith

"Aerith..."

My eyes furiously blinked as someone shook me gently. I groaned, rolling over to my side and shutting my eyes again. I was too tired to move.

"Aerith," the voice said firmly.

My chest suddenly burned as I jumped up, my eyes widening when I saw someone standing above me. Patrick smiled, holding his hands up defensively, and I exhaled deeply.

"Settle," he said softly. "Mommy's still sleeping, but I thought we'd spend some time together before she gets up. Grandpa just called and told me to work from home today. Isn't that great?"

I narrowed my eyes as he pulled the blanket off me. *I liked when Patrick worked at the station,* I thought to myself. *It was just easier, but I didn't tell him that.* I would *never* tell him that.

"C'mon," he said, nudging me awake, "you want to play with the drones again, don't you?"

A small grin formed on my face as I scrambled off the bed. *If Patrick was going to be home at least he's letting me play with them again.*

I slowly took his hand and let him guide me out of the room. I frowned when we turned right instead of going to the kitchen. *I thought we'd go outside.* But *we* went towards the room on the end. The one I'm not supposed to be in.

He unlocked the door and plopped down on his large office chair. I looked around the room, seeing a massive cage full of guns behind him. Along

CHAPTER 34

the back wall that lay bare, I noticed tons of little marks. I stepped over as Patrick dug around in a drawer, placing my finger on the spot. *It was a tiny hole,* I realized, and I looked up. There were hundreds of tiny holes on this wall, and I wondered what they were from, and why they were here. My fingers grazed over a piece of tape, and I frowned again. A small corner of paper lay underneath, and my brows furrowed as I tried to figure out what it was.

"Aerith," Patrick said, making me jump. He held out his hand then. "You need to drink your medicine."

I obeyed, drinking the sickly, sweet drink without question and feeling fuzzy and quiet all over again. He tussled my hair once I was done before turning on the computer.

"Alright, so Grandpa asked me to run a quick check, and then you and I can fly the drones," he said with a smile. "You ready to learn?"

I nodded my head as I stood on my tip-toes to see his computer screen. He chuckled, picking me up and setting me on his lap before moving the mouse around. The computer lit up, showing a small white box on the screen that said *Password.* I watched as he pushed keys on the keyboard.

J-E-N-N-I-N-G-1-7-8-9

I stayed quiet as he pushed the *Enter* key, and the computer unlocked, showing the main screen. I cocked my head to the side. It was a picture of mommy laughing.

"Welcome to the next lesson in Division training, Aerith," he said as he clicked with the mouse, and mommy's picture disappeared. "This is the entire mainframe for the house. Every security measure Grandpa has in place shows up right here. Pretty cool, huh?"

Patrick scrolled through a page full of numbers and letters that made no sense before clicking another button on the screen. Multiple cameras appeared, and Patrick began pointing to the screen.

"Here's the front door," he said. He quickly moved to the next square, "and the back."

I saw the tree where Mommy sat in the cage. The snow was gone already, and my shoulders fell slightly. *I never even got to play in it this year.* He clicked to another part of the woods then.

"Here," he said, handing me the mouse, "why don't you try?"

I slowly clicked screen after screen, going through the house and woods where cameras lay hidden. *There were so many different views though*, I wondered.

"Why are there so many?" I asked.

"Well to keep you and Mommy safe," he said with a smile. "I can see everything right from this computer or my phone, Baby Doll. Nothing can get to us without me knowing. I will keep my family safe."

I frowned slightly when he said family. *He wasn't my dad.* But I knew if I said that, he'd be very cross with me. *He'd hurt Mommy then.*

"So why did you have to check this today?" I asked, pulling Patrick from his thoughts. He rubbed the back of his head.

"Grandpa's mentioned some of the plates in the back have been triggered off and on for the last few months. I just need to double check," he replied.

"Double check what?" I asked, looking closer. "Are they broken?"

"Oh, no. While they require a lot of maintenance to keep'em running smoothly, those plates are high-end technology. They won't even shut down if the house lost power," he said, grinning wide. His smile fell though, and he rubbed his face. "Still wish Dad hadn't made me divert power from some of the smaller surveillance to the house though."

"Why did he do that?" I asked, looking back at him.

He shrugged. "Don't know. Grandpa has his reasons though, and it's just the little stuff. I think we need cameras right on the line and the infrared throughout the woods, but with the pack gone, he isn't too worried. He needed the extra power for something."

I narrowed my eyes as I turned to look back at the computer. So many trees scattered on the screen. It tugged at my heart. *I missed home.*

Patrick sighed before giving me a small smile. "Nothing for you to worry about, Aerith. Grandpa has plenty of working cameras around the house, so you and your mama are safe here. I promise."

He took the mouse back and scrolled through another program than the video feed. All while I thought about what he said. *We were trapped here*, I thought to myself. *With nowhere to go without getting caught. But there was always another way... What would Daddy do if he were here?*

A blue sketch of the house suddenly appeared, and I scrunched my nose. The downstairs was laid out with a bright circle steadily blinking around it.

"What's that?" I asked, pointing to it.

"That's those plates I was telling you about the other day," he answered, and I noticed how his smile was gone. His brows furrowed as he explained, "This allows me to control the settings. I can turn it higher, which means more power will get sent to the plates, or I can turn it down."

"Can you turn it off?" I asked quietly. I held my breath, hoping he'd tell me how to do it. *Maybe this is how I help my mom?*

Patrick didn't answer, and my stomach twisted in knots. He finally set me down on the floor and pushed me aside.

"All you need to know is that they're on," he said firmly, "and don't ever try to leave. Bad things will happen, Aerith. Very bad things. Understand?"

I dropped my head, looking at my feet. *He was mad at me,* I thought. I pushed too far this time.

"Aerith," Patrick said firmly.

I snapped my attention to him, finding him glaring at me.

"I think you better go back to your room until your mother wakes up," he said, motioning to the door. "We'll fly the drones another time."

The drones were the last thing on my mind as I scurried to the door before he scolded me more. *Don't ask direct questions... Don't ask about the plates.*

"And Aerith?"

My feet slid to a stop as I turned around, finding a sour look on his face.

"We don't tell mommy any of this," he commanded firmly. "Not one word or you will be punished. Understand?"

My eyes widened as I nodded my head. I knew he meant the cage. I would sit in the cage until he finally let me out if I said a word to my mother. My heart began to pound in my chest when he finally motioned me out, and I rushed back to my room and shut the door. I buried myself under my many blankets and waited. Waited for Patrick to change his mind and scold me for asking questions. I waited to be forced inside that cage, but he never came.

He never came, and soon I had fallen back asleep.

Chapter 35

Shanely

Calvin watched me like a hawk after the whole key debacle. He even pulled Patrick back home for a couple of days, with some stupid excuse of issues concerning their security system, but I know it was just to keep me out of trouble or catch me in the act of snooping so he could punish me further. The two bickered incessantly over the faulty security. It was giving me a headache listening to them go at it all the time.

It took a week for Calvin to calm down after stealing his office keys. He seemed to have forgotten they went missing or he was feeling crappy enough that he stopped caring, but either way it worked in my favor. I knew he was working day and night with the serum he had left. He'd run out eventually and demand more blood or finally figure it out and go on a rampage, but the obsessive behavior was going to kill him if he wasn't careful. It wasn't healthy, and every time I saw him, Calvin just looked like crap. Not like I cared about that one bit, but I was worried he'd figure out why his body wasn't accepting the Alpha power one day very soon. *God help us then.*

Today was going to be different though. I had waited patiently, biding my time until the two finally stopped looking at me. All for *this* chance. They both left early to work at the station, leaving me with an empty house, free time, and an unlocked door. And I was going to make it count.

Their typical work day ended at four so plenty of time to snoop, I thought as I stood at the railing overlooking the foyer. I had waited and watched them drive down their long drive to make sure they left, but for some reason I had a hard time leaving the railing. A small part of me wanted to do something else with my time. I should search Calvin's room again or see if I could get into Patrick's office again. Although I highly doubted that would happen as Patrick added another lock to the door recently. All these things I *should* do, but my hands gripped the railing. My gut pushed me in a different direction. To something more important.

My mom.

One foot after the other, I made my way down the hall. My anxiety grew with every step, twisting my stomach into tight knots. *I am going to meet my mother. I am actually going to have a chance to talk to her, just us. No interruptions. No Calvin or Patrick. Just her and I.*

And that scared me half to death.

I had gone over the story Calvin told me a thousand times in my head, but there were so many questions left unanswered. Questions I was afraid to ask. I knew he took my mom, but I couldn't get past this nagging feeling that she wouldn't like me for some reason. That maybe she had made the choice to give me away all on her own. I wasn't sure I could handle a rejection like that. Not now. Maybe if I had Bastian here with me I'd find a way to accept it, but I was all alone and without my wolf. My mental box was already ready to burst at the seams. *If my mother really didn't want me, I don't know how I'd handle that.*

Sighing, I shoved those thoughts away. There was no way to know unless I tried. *I needed to just rip the Band-aid off and meet her,* I thought to myself. I was already starting to have false labor pains. I was nearly out of time.

I quietly opened Aerith's door to check on her before I went down to the lab. It was fairly early, so I didn't expect her to be awake yet. A small smirk formed on my lips when I found her sleeping soundly with her mouth wide open just like Cade. I quietly closed the door behind me and buried another memory deep inside. I missed my Beta too.

I snuck downstairs and stopped at Calvin's door to his office. I took a deep breath. It was now or never.

Putting the key in, I turned the handle and opened the door. *Everything looked the same,* I thought. *Not a paper out of place.* My legs wobbled as

CHAPTER 35

I made my way towards the elevator. The doors opened, and I stepped inside. My stomach rolled when it began its descent, and I slowly took a deep breath. *You can do this Shanely,* I told myself. *You've dealt with far worse. You can meet your mom.*

The elevator chimed as the doors opened, and my heart began to race. Slowly, I stepped off and looked around. *Calvin was gone. He wasn't home, and no one was going to catch me,* I thought as I took the next step. The lights fluttered on as I made my way down, stealing peeks inside each lab. With Calvin it was always a rush, but I wanted to take my time today. If there was anything I could use to help me and my family down here, I was going to find it.

The first lab was mostly empty tables so I moved on from there. I stilled when I approached the next room though. The sign on the glass read, **DO NOT ENTER. Trial Room 1.** Beds lined the back wall and a massive first-aid box hung in between each one. A few cabinets full of blankets and other medical supplies sat next to everything. *Human trials,* I thought as my stomach twisted. *Is this is where Lorelei tested her serum on people?*

"Leave it," I muttered to myself. "Just do what needs done, Shanely."

I made my way to the end of the hall, when my whole body froze. My jaw dropped as I stared at an old looking camera in the far corner of the hall. *What have I done?*

I spun on my heels as my heart thundered in my chest. My eyes widened, when they settled on another camera tucked in the shadows above the elevator. *Had it been there the whole time?!* I thought anxiously. *God, I was so royally screwed. Calvin was going to kill me this time...*

I slumped against the wall, leaning my head back in defeat. *There was no way out of this,* I thought as the weight of everything crushed me. I turned to face the camera, giving Calvin a rude gesture for him to watch later. *I was dead already. Might as well let him know how I feel.*

Suddenly, something caught my eye. I realized the little red light wasn't there. Frowning, I shoved off the wall and moved to look at its other side. There was nothing there too.

It can't be that easy, can it? I thought to myself. *Would Calvin really be that careless to not have the cameras online anymore? With all the other security measures he has outside; why would he have nothing down here?*

I scurried back to the last lab and carefully stole a peek around the corner. It didn't have a red light either.

"Good lord," I muttered angrily, resting my hand on my chest. *My heart would never heal after all this, I swear.*

I stormed inside the lab, knowing full well there was no point trying mom's door without a key. *There had to be an extra one around here somewhere,* I thought as began looking through the drawers. There was nothing here of any importance really, but I kept looking just in case. My lips pursed together when I came up empty handed. I place my hands on my hips.

"Calvin lost his keys constantly," I muttered as I laid out the facts, "but this was not a key you could replace at the store. So what would I need if I had to replace it?"

My eyes drifted around the room before finally settling on the computer. I cocked my head to the side. *It would make sense he'd use a program to make a key,* I thought, remembering Elijah and his never ending rants on software and technology. *Maybe I can make my own?*

I hurried over and turned on the dinosaur of a computer. It whirred to life, and my brow rose, wondering if it would actually do what I needed it too. *This was nothing like Elijah's stuff,* I thought. The main screen finally appeared, and I whistled. Calvin had a tremendous amount of files covering all over the main screen. You couldn't even see the picture behind it anymore, and I frowned. *This was going to suck.* Elijah's computer was always clean and organized, with everything having a place. *This was just chaotic,* I thought. *No organization whatsoever.*

I decided to just start somewhere and clicked a random file. My heart sunk at what I saw. There was so much data on my mother. So many trials and their test results. I cringed as I scrolled through it all. Thankfully there were no videos, but it was still hard to read. *She's been through so much,* I thought.

Suddenly, I narrowed my eyes. *Why didn't he have any videos or pictures?*

CHAPTER 35

Scientists usually recorded everything they did so they can improve. *Lorelei made videos,* I thought, remembering back to the ones upstairs. *Wouldn't he want that too?* Pursing my lips together, my eyes slowly drifted over to the dead camera in the corner. *He recorded nothing down here,* I realized. Not a single minute.

Curiously, I left my mother's file and started scrolling through Calvin's financial records instead. My eyes widened. He made less than I would have thought as a Division Head Officer, which I guess was his official title, but things just weren't making sense. This house was massive and beautiful. I couldn't even begin to imagine the utility bill on a place like this. I'm sure Patrick helped out with the bills, but still I would have expected Calvin to earn more.

I scrolled further, finding a receipt had been scanned in. It was for all the outside security features. *Calvin added a lot to his house,* I thought. *More than what Patrick even told me. He wasn't messing around with this place.* My eyes widened when I saw who signed the check.

Whoa...

The Division paid for everything. Every single thing Calvin requested, they paid for and installed. *It was not cheap either.* I leaned back in my chair.

Everything makes sense now, I though as I looked back at the camera. The Division owned Calvin's entire network. They had access to everything here at the house because they paid for it. I couldn't stop myself from snorting. *I bet that's why the cameras are all off down here. He doesn't want them to know this lab is even functional, let alone being used everyday.*

Shaking my head, I scrolled further, but there was nothing more of interest. Just loads and loads of receipts or bank statements, which was incredibly boring and useless to me.

Back on the main screen, I clicked on a file labeled *Personal*. Inside were the typical documents I'd expect to see like Patrick's birth certificate and Calvin's marriage certificate. I looked further along and found Lorelei's death certificate. Next to that was a letter from the Division themselves.

My eyes widened as I quickly read the letter. It was odd, stating how very sorry they were to hear about the break in. That Lorelei would be missed amongst her peers, and she would be honored throughout the entire Division. Every line I read made me frown more. *It was all nonsense,* I thought. All I noticed was how many times they used the word *accident*. Like they were trying to prove to Calvin they weren't involved in this. Dennis Hemingway signed it personally, and my stomach twisted.

Why would he save this? I thought in disgust. *How could he pretend to be chummy with these people after seeing that video and knowing they were directly responsible!? Why not turn it over to someone who could go after them?* My lip curled as I closed that file and clicked the next one. I was sick of trying to understand these people. I was sick of feeling pity to people who didn't deserve it. My stomach twisted again. *What Calvin and I were doing to right our wrong weren't that far apart from one another...*

I shoved those thoughts away and selected a whole new file this time. My brows knitted when it loaded on the screen. It was full of videos, I realized. Each one dated years ago, and my eyes widened. *Lorelei...* I quickly clicked the first one, and Lorelei sat with Patrick smiling at the camera. I slowly pushed play.

"Shifters have this unique connection to one another," Lorelei spoke as Patrick played with a toy. "It's amazing to watch. Their deep primal connection to their animals connects them all together. In a way humans fail to connect period. Even different packs seem to have a responsibility to one another simply because they have a wolf, according to Dr. Marcos's study of shifters after the grand war."

Patrick made a gurgling baby sound, playing contently on his mother's lap. *That sweet little baby... How did he end up like this?*

"The heightened ability to heal themselves is remarkable," she went on. "Diseases like Cancer, Alzheimer's, Sickle Cell or even just something more common like asthma *rarely* happen in the shifter community if at all. There's not one documented case of Alzheimer's that I know of."

Lorelei's face fell slightly. "I had cancer when I was a baby."

I frowned as she sighed on screen.

"I managed to beat it, and thankfully it has never come back, but ever since joining the Division and learning about this *amazing* race of shifters,

CHAPTER 35

I've wanted to help people like me. I wanted to figure out a way to share their healing abilities with humans," she continued, staring hard at the camera.

Suddenly, I just felt so guilty. I had a healing ability unlike most shifters, and I never once thought about the gift I really had. It was just there and useful when I needed it, but then I'd move on and not think twice about it. Millions of people suffered everyday with only the hope that medicine could cure them. Now it's gone along with my animals, and I may never have it back again. *I would want to share my gift,* I thought as a heavy weight laid on my chest. *I would have helped you, Lorelei.*

"The Alpha power they posses..." she said, startling me. Her voice trailed off as she sighed, "while useful to keep the animal side in check, I fear it poses a far new set of issues for humans."

She sighed heavily, picking up the toy and dangling it in front of Patrick's face. His eyes lit up excitedly as he tried to grab it, and Lorelei smiled softly.

"I'm afraid of the problems that seem to be coming from my research."

My eyes widened. *This is what Calvin was talking about,* I thought as my anxiety rose. I eyed the clock, knowing I was running out of time, but I couldn't help but continue watching. I needed to see this through.

"I have been honest with my employer on how I *do not* agree on controlling shifters the way we do. I believe shifters and humans were meant to coexist together," Lorelei continued on. "Shifters can find their mates amongst their entire kind. They can even find mates amongst humans. It's perfectly natural and forcing a separation will only weaken the race as a whole. But maybe that is the whole purpose of the Division. To weaken those who are potentially stronger than the rest of us."

Lorelei rubbed her face, sighing as Patrick continued to play blissfully unaware of his mother's stress and worry. Finally, she looked back at the camera saying, "We are meant to blend together, but we can't do that with the control we have over them. The control is just a facade though, and one day shifters will figure that out."

My word... My hand covered my mouth as I stared at the screen in disbelief. *I think she was the only one at the Division who thought this way. No wonder...*

I couldn't even finish that thought, and I shook my head. My mind reeled as Lorelei went on.

"It is my belief that we could benefit from one another," she said, playing with Patrick again. "I have painstakingly researched shifters and their abilities, and it is my firm belief that I could use a component in what shifters refer to as the *Alpha power* to heal humankind. The blind could see. The lame would walk. Cancer would be a thing of the past. All shifters have this power too, some just more than others, but even the ones deemed submissive still have this power to a certain degree. It's in *all shifters.* It's why they heal the way they do. Why their senses are greater, and why some can do things no one else can…"

Lorelei seemed lost in thought for a moment. She sighed finally, kissing Patrick's cheek. "I begin trials next week on a formula I've been working on for the last year. It is my hope that we shall see a positive response to the serum I have created. Maybe then we can finally do some good in the world."

The screen went black, and I immediately chose the next video. *I had to know. I had know what happened next.* Calvin wasn't lying about this, and my heart began to beat wildly. The next video loaded, and this time Lorelei was alone with a worried look on her face.

"The trails were a success," she whispered, barely looking at the camera. "We were able to heal test subject 2 from a degenerative disease he's had since birth."

My eyes widened. *Calvin said she had done it, and she really did. My God…* I noticed the time stamp at the bottom. According to the death certificate, this was a week before she died.

She snorted then. "God, I hate being right all the time. I hate when humanity proves how awful they can really be."

Lorelei finally looked at the camera and sat back in her seat. "It has been informed to me and my colleges that we are to move on to phase two of my employer's plan. As I suspected, no one really cares about helping others in need or making a difference in the world. No… Only power and money are what matter in this world."

CHAPTER 35

Disgust flashed on her face, while my stomach twisted.

"It seems no one is interested in the serum I have created from the Alpha power. No one is interested in the fact that something like cancer could essentially be eradicated from history, and why would they? Not when cancer is profitable. Those in charge of the Division of Shifters just want the power themselves, but I'm not playing their game."

My eyes widened as a determined look swept across her face.

"I've called a meeting this Friday to explain my case to another on the board, who will hopefully take my side. If not, then I will take dramatic steps to erase my work so no one will have it," she said firmly. "Shifters have the balance within themselves to control the Alpha power, and they use it in the correct way, but humans continue to dominate one another. They do not possess the morals or integrity that is require to have such power. It is not a weapon but a gift!"

Guilt lay heavy on my heart. *I commanded Cade and Elijah... I took away their free will because I was upset.* My mind drifted then to all the corrupted shifters I have met over the years. *There was wrong on both sides*, I realized. *There had to be a way to bring about peace. For everyone.*

Lorelei stood from her seat, pulling me from my thoughts.

"This may be my last video report," she said to the camera. "I've gone above and beyond for this company, for this government, but I will not stand idly by while my life's work gets turned into the next weapon that will only bring about mass genocide. I became a scientist to do good in this world. Not destroy it further. For whatever reason, shifters were given the chance to be something more. They were chosen, not us. The Alpha power belongs to them, and *only* them. And maybe... Maybe my using it to make the world a better place was wrong too."

The screen went black again, and I slumped on the stool, burying my head in my hands. *How could someone with morals and kindness marry a man as wretched as Calvin?* I thought as my mind spun. *Didn't he see this video?! He should realize how much of a betrayal this is to the woman he claims to love.*

Suddenly, the video started up again, and my head shot up as it played. *This was not the same lab as before*, I thought as Lorelei rushed across the room, stopping at one computer to another. It was an entirely different place, and everything was a mess behind Lorelei. The whole lab was destroyed, and my eyes widened further. *This was the Division lab at their Headquarters. It just had to be.*

Lorelei looked flushed when she finally stopped in front of the camera and hunched over her desk. Her eyes were wild. Filled with fierce determination and rage. I swallowed hard, seeing the resemblance on my own face before.

"No one would stand by me," she said in anger. "Every one of those overweight, stuffy, arrogant men *voted* with Dennis. They fired me when I refused to continue my research, and now they demand I give up my entire life's work! I'm supposed to hand *everything* over, just like that..."

She gritted her teeth, pulling out a phone as she said, "But I won't have innocent blood on my hands. Because I know that is what *will* happen if I hand it over."

She turned slightly away from the camera then as my stomach twisted. "Cal? Oh, thank God. No. No, they didn't listen to me, but it doesn't matter. I am going to fix this. No. No, Calvin, just listen to me! Don't come here for me. Grab Patrick from daycare instead."

I covered my mouth with my hand as I listened to the moment that ruined Calvin and Patrick's lives forever. My heart hurt as I watched desperation fill her eyes as she argued with Calvin.

"Please, Cal! I need you to get him and bring him home. Grab the emergency bags stashed in the closet and..."

Lorelei stayed silent on the screen for a moment, and it was so hard not to break for her. *She tried so hard to do the right thing.*

"I don't trust anyone but you to grab him, Cal," she finally whispered. "Please. You are his father, and he needs you more than I do. I'm leaving now, and I will meet you at home. I love you."

Lorelei pocketed her phone and looked back to the screen. "Dennis, since I know you'll be watching this later," she said, leaning close to the camera, "*screw you.*"

The screen went black. A single tear rolled down my cheek, hitting the keyboard. *Everything made sense. Everything.*

CHAPTER 35

The shifter war had never ended.

It merely grew quiet.

I wondered if this was the true reason for the war in the first place. I gritted my teeth in anger. *Either way, it was going to end.*

Rage filled my chest as now I was more than ever determined to see this through. I was getting my family out of this house and away from these wretched people, and once they were safe, then I would finish the whole White Wolf business.

It's why it's me, I thought as I shoved off the stool. I was two prophecies in one, and my people needed rescuing. The White Wolf and the White Bear had finally made its appearance, and I wasn't going to let anyone down. Lorelei died trying to right the wrong, and I going to see this through.

I am going to destroy the entire *Division.*

As I was about to shut the computer off, something caught my eye.

A program for key cards.

Chapter 36

Calvin made the key cards right here in the lab, I thought, eyes widening. *Which meant now I could too.* Scrambling to open the program, I quickly scanned the instructions to figure out how this worked. Lorelei had three rooms down here listed as trial rooms.

Only one was lit up red.

I selected my mother's room and all the other access point just in case and clicked continue. Suddenly, the computer beeped. The screen began flashing *Insert Key Card* across the screen, and I groaned.

"Always freaking something," I muttered.

Hopping off the stool, I started rummaging through the cabinets I hadn't touched yet. *There had to be extras around here somewhere,* I thought to myself. I opened one of the tall cabinets in the back of the room and started searching. *Calvin stored all sorts of items in here,* I thought as I dug further in. This shelf was clear so I went to the next. Floppy disk, CD's, and spare wires that went to something was spread out haphazardly.

"I didn't even know this was a still a thing," I muttered to myself as I tossed a floppy disk back onto the pile. Suddenly, my eyes widened.

My hand shot towards the back of the upper shelf, and I snatched a box of spare cards. I grinned wide.

I took a card out before setting the box back where it was and rushed back to the computer. Placing the blank card in the slot, I clicked continue and held my breath. It took just a few minutes as the machine did its job before it finally beeped, popping out the brand-new, *usable*, card.

Maybe I could be a spy? I chuckled to myself.

CHAPTER 36

I sauntered out the lab, feeling rather good about myself until I saw the door. I stopped dead in my tracks just staring at that white door. I swallowed hard.

"Like a Band-aid," I muttered, swiping the card before I could chicken out. It beeped once and then clicked open.

My heart fluttered as I slowly placed my shaky hand and pushed it open all the way. My knees felt wobbly as I took that first step. *All that was left to do right now was to go in and properly meet my mother,* I thought to myself. *No Calvin, no threats, just me and her.* Sighing, I walked into her room.

A scowl was on my mother's face, but when she saw me standing in the doorway, her face soften. Her shoulders collapsed in relief, and she bolted to the locked door, tapping the glass and pointing.

Right.

I scurried over to the console. I had no idea which one would work, but the tried and true method of pushing them all at once seemed to do the trick. The door to her cell opened, and she stepped out.

"Shanely..."

My mother rushed me, hugging me tight in her arms before I had a chance to process anything. I froze, standing there rigid and unable to comprehend that *this* was my mother. She was *my* mother. Alive, and in the flesh, and currently hugging me so tight I couldn't breathe.

I shook my head, snapping out of my daze, and hugged her back. I felt my warm tears landing on my shoulders as I cried. We stayed like that for a few moments before she finally pulled back. She had tears in her eyes too.

"Oh, look at you baby. You're all grown up and with white hair?!" she said softly, placing her hands on my curls before touching my cheek. She smiled wide, easing every fear I had before.

"Yeah," I replied, chuckling as I wiped my eyes, "it happened when I became the White Wolf."

Her eyes widened. "You're the White Wolf?"

"And the White Bear actually. You and dad each gave me an animal," I said softly. "I have both, Mom."

She covered her mouth as a sob escaped her lips. Her face was distraught, and I wondered if I said the wrong thing, but she yanked me towards her, wrapping her arms around me tightly. I held onto her until she could catch her breath.

After a moment, she slowly pulled away and wiped her face. Mom turned to sit on the only table in the room, and I shifted on my feet. I wasn't sure if I should follow, so I waited patiently as she stared off into space.

"You've met your father?" she asked quietly. Her eyes slowly drifted back to me. "You met Daniel?"

I nodded my head, feeling jittery once more. "I did. I found him when I first moved to Diablo."

"How?" she asked, shaking her head in disbelief. "How did you find him?"

"Grandma Willow," I said, forcing a grin to my lips. "She left me her cabin in her will, and the lawyers managed to find me somehow. I moved in, and everything spiraled from there. If it wasn't..."

"Wait," she interrupted. Mom's brows furrowed as she leaned forward on her knees. "Her will? She left you her cabin in her will?"

My face fell. *Oh God, I was so stupid!* My mother knew nothing of our family. That inhibitor would have barred her from any connections or loss, and I just blurted out her mother died so carelessly.

"I'm sorry," I said, dropping my head. "I shouldn't have said it like that. I should have been kinder, but she is the reason I was able to find my way back to my family. It was all because of her."

Tears welled in her eyes, and she buried her face in her hands. I slowly made my way over and sat next to her, waiting for her to gain her composure again. *I knew her pain,* I thought to myself. *I knew her pain all too well.*

"I guess I should have figured," she said quietly as she straightened, wiping her eyes. "My mother was growing weak when I left with you. I just... I don't know. I always hoped I'd see her again. Tell her how much I appreciated what she did for me."

"If she hadn't left me her cabin, I would have never found my family," I said, reaching out to take her hand in mine. I gave it a squeeze as I said, "I would have never found my dad, brothers, or my mate. I can't tell you how

CHAPTER 36

grateful I am to her, even though I never got to meet her."

Her lips pursed together and another tear slid down her cheek. "You have a mate?"

"I had a mate," I replied, my heart cracking once more. "He died a couple months ago."

"Oh, my child..."

Mama pulled me in close, breaking the dam I had tried so hard to hold onto. I couldn't take it anymore and let go of the emotions weighing me down. She soothed me just as I always imagined a mother would. Her hand running through my hair as she clung to me, letting me set the pace on what I needed in this moment. It was how I comforted my daughter, and how I'd comfort my boys too.

"Oh honey," she said softly, and I forced myself to sit up. "I am so sorry. I can't imagine how you feel."

"It will only get worse when I can finally removed this stupid thing," I replied, holding up my left wrist. "It's stronger than the collars, so it's keeping most of the aches and pains away. It's keeping the loss of our bond away."

She looked grimly at her own bracelet. Sighing, she asked, "Shanely, why are you here? What does Calvin want with you?"

"The same thing he wants from you," I answered. "He's on a crusade and thinks I can get him the Alpha power. That or Aerith will, and he's nearly done it too."

Mama brushed a fly-away hair away from my cheek. "Who's Aerith, baby?"

"Oh!" I snorted, chuckling to myself. "Gosh, Mom... There is just so much to tell you, but Aerith is my daughter. You're a grandma."

"So, this little one isn't your first?" she asked with wide-eyes.

I shook my head smiling. "No, I have a five year old. She's sleeping upstairs right now. I'll have to head back upstairs here soon to check on her, and this little one is actually not one but two. I've having twins."

Her eyes bulged from her head. She chuckled softly saying, "My, my, three little ones all five and under! You must be busy, Shanely."

I laughed, feeling another weight lift off me. "I am," I replied, "but I have an amazing family to help me..."

My voice trailed off as my smile fell. I didn't have anyone to help me now. Anger rose within me for forgetting momentarily, and I shoved a little more inside the box.

"Well had," I continued. "I don't even know who's left, Mom. The Division attacked the pack and the clan. Patrick took me, and I felt my mate get shot. Our bond was so weak when Patrick put this bracelet on, and I just..."

The words burned like acid as they left my mouth. I swallowed hard, trying to figure out how to say the rest. I didn't want to. I didn't want to relive what even happened, and my hands tightened into fists.

Mom reached over and took my hand in hers. I looked to her, seeing nothing but sympathy as she squeezed my hand tightly. Relief washed over me then. *I didn't have to explain,* I thought to myself. Mom understood everything I couldn't say, and the two of us leaned on the other.

"Mom," I said quietly. She leaned forward, cocking her head to the side to look me in the eye.

Sighing, I said, "I have a great many things to fill you in on, and so much more I want to ask, but I don't have a lot of time. I *can't* be discovered down here, otherwise they will never let me out of my room again, but I have a plan. A plan to get us out."

"Really?" she asked, straightening in her seat. "What are you working on?"

"All I need to do is figure out the security system above," I answered. "It's intricate, so we can't just walk out of here. Just hang in there, okay? I'll be coming down to grab you one day really soon, so be ready. Actually, do you know if there's another way out of here?"

She shrugged. "I don't know, honey. I'm rarely let out of this room, but let me try to see if I can find out anything. I want to help anyway I can."

I gave her a hug before I stood up to leave. "Thank you. When this is all over, I want to sit down and catch up over everything."

With heavy steps, I made my way to the door.

"Shanely?" Mom said, halting me in my tracks.

I turned, seeing fear in her eyes, and I frowned.

"I have things I need to tell you too," she said with a sigh. "More than just what happened before."

I smiled wide. "Like Abraham?"

Her eyes widened in surprise. "You know about him?!"

"I do," I chuckled. "It's long story, but just so you know, he grew up to be a wonderful man. Someone you would have been proud of."

"Is he..." she choked out, and my heart began to hurt, "is he alive, Shanely?"

I placed my hand on the door and shook my head. "I don't think so, mama, " I replied, hating myself for giving more bad news to her. "I'm so sorry."

She nodded her head as the tears fell again. *There was nothing I could do to make it better. Nothing to ease the pain for either of us.* I hated having to deliver news like this, and there were so many people we've lost that I had yet to tell her about. *I just don't think I have the strength to say much more.*

"I have to go," I said softly as I opened the door. "Be safe, Mama. And make sure you are back inside your cell before 3, just in case. I love you."

"I love you too," she whispered between her quiet cries, and I forced myself to leave.

I left the door ajar for her and made my way back upstairs. My heart ached with every step. *It just feels wrong to leave her there,* I thought to myself. *To not pull her out and make a run for it, but I needed more time.* I needed just a little more time.

I made sure to lock Calvin's office and hid both keys under the floor board before I went into Aerith's room. My heart felt heavy, and the pain was almost worse than when I woke up this morning. I had spent way longer than I thought, and Aerith was already awake and playing. I felt awful that I wasn't here and slumped down on her bed.

"Hi Mama," she said as she climbed up to snuggle with me.

My smile didn't reach my eyes, but I wrapped my arms around my baby girl and held her close. Aerith stayed with me. Not squirming or trying to get away like she used to when we were back home. Fun was always to be had, and she was always on the go. *Just like Cade.* But today she simply stayed, and I was forever grateful she did.

I wish my mate was here, I thought as a single tear rolled down my cheek. I felt the familiar kick from one of my boys, and I bit my lower lip to keep from falling apart again. I needed Bastian more than anything, but he was gone.

And he was *never* coming back.

Chapter 37

Aerith

It was dark when Patrick said goodbye this morning. I had barely opened my eyes, when he started talking to me about our plans later that day. He was working at the station today but promised to take me outside to fly the drones when he got home as long as I was good. He was gone by the time I blinked, and the sun had rose fully, brightening up my room.

Rubbing my eyes, I slowly got off the bed and looked around. It was quiet in the house, and I wondered where mama was. My eyes drifted towards the door then. *Maybe she was still sleeping?* I wondered as I made my way towards the door. The halls were quiet too, and I carefully moved around all the creaky spots on the floor towards mama's room. Her door was cracked, and I carefully stole a peek inside.

"Mama?" I said softly, but the room was empty. My shoulders fell as I looked around. "Mama?"

No one answered, so I closed her door. I wasn't sure what I should do or if I should just go back to my room. I made my way over to the railing and looked down. *Everyone was gone,* I thought to myself. Deciding to just go back to my room and wait, I hopped off the banister and made my way down the hall. Until my eyes settled on the room in the far corner. The one where Patrick kept all the drones.

I bit my lower lip as I debated what to do. *He would be really upset if I went in there,* I thought as I looked back at the boring old toys and coloring books sitting on the floor in my room.

But the drone's were in there.

And I was bored.

I quickly made my way to the door at the end and opened it. My heart thundered in my chest as I shut it behind me, and I waited for someone to yell. To holler and scold me for being in here in the first place. But nothing happened. No one came, and I smiled slowly. I made my way over to the black case where the shiny black drone sat. My fingers gently touched the propellers, spinning them carefully, and grinning wide.

My smile fell when I saw something peeking out of one the drawers of the desk. Yanking it open, my eyes widened. There were hundreds of photos of mama. The entire drawer was filled to the brim of photos of mama. They were all cut and some were jagged on the sides like it tore against the scissors. I dug my hand around, pulling out each and every one.

Mama looked so happy in these, I thought to myself. My finger gently outlined her hair before touching her smile. *Her smile was pretty. I wonder if my smile looks like hers.* I pushed another photo aside and stilled.

It was Daddy. It was Daddy, Uncle Cade, and Uncle Elijah with Mama in front of the lodge. They were laughing at something, and they just looked happy. *Patrick didn't cut this one.*

I pulled the photo from the drawer and folded it in half, tucking it in my pocket where it would be safe. *I wanted this picture more than any toy Patrick could ever buy me, but it had to stay a secret. He would hate me if he found out I stole it.*

I shut the drawer and left the others. My eyes settled on the massive chair then, and I climbed up. The chair spun as I got settled, and a small smile curved on my lips as I spun around a few times. I accidentally bumped the desk, and the computer suddenly came to life. Leaning forward, I studied the screen. *I could see everything with the cameras*, I thought as my smile grew wider. I wanted to see everything again.

I looked down at the keys frowning. My brows furrowed as I tried to remember what he did to open it. *He pushed J first*, I thought, so I pushed the key down. *Then E.*

N.

I.

CHAPTER 37

N.

G.

I sighed. I couldn't remember the numbers very well. I decided to guess. I pushed 1-6-8-9, and then enter.

Incorrect Password flashed across the screen. I narrowed my eyes and tried again, but changed the number to 1-7-8-9.

Incorrect Password.

I slumped in my seat, scratching my head. It didn't make any sense to me. *I know it was his last name... Maybe the number was still wrong?*

I tried again, but this time the screen flashed a new message.

Incorrect Password. Too many attempts have been tried. This account is now locked.

My heart thundered out of my chest. *Patrick would know I was in here,* I thought as my chest began to hurt. *He would know I was messing with things I shouldn't.*

I shot out of the chair and fled the room. I ran to mine and quietly shut the door behind me. I stuffed the photo of my family under my bed before burying myself under the blanket. I couldn't breath as I waited for the trouble to come.

I was in *so much* trouble.

* * *

Mama came to see me later that day. Patrick hadn't come home yet, and I felt sick to my stomach waiting for him to show up. I couldn't eat the snacks he left. I simply fiddled with the doll in my hands. Not really wanting to play with anything, but Mama seemed sad when she sat on the bed. *She needs me.*

I climbed onto the bed next to her saying, "Hey, Mama."

Mama just smiled and pulled me close. She didn't say anything, so I didn't ask why she was sad. I just sat with her, feeling the pain in my chest go away and listening to her soft snores. I slowly looked up to her. She had fallen asleep, and I realized how different she looked. Her beautifully soft, white hair felt rough to the touch, and there were dark circles under her eyes. *Mama needs her wolf,* I thought to myself. *She needs Daddy's wolf too.*

Suddenly, a door clattered shut downstairs. I held my breath as Patrick's heavy footsteps sounded in the foyer.

"Shanely?" he cried out, and my heart thundered inside.

Mama jolted, rubbing her eyes as she stood to go to the door. I clung to her hand as fear crept in, and she paused.

"Don't," I whispered, my eyes begging her to stay here with me. She cocked her head to the side frowning.

"Don't go," I whispered as the door opened.

"There you girls are!" he said with a smile. I let Mama's hand go, stepping away as he greeted her. I felt his hands tussle my hair then as he asked, "You two have a good day?"

"We did, Patrick," Mama answered, taking my hand again, and we followed him out of the room. "Just spent the day playing in her room."

"Sounds like a good day then!" he said excitedly. "Why don't you two head on into the kitchen and get started on dinner. I just got to check on something."

I held my breath, gripping my mother's hand tighter as we stopped in front of the stairs.

"Something wrong?" Mama asked.

Patrick just shrugged. "I got an alert on my phone is all. I just gotta check the computer and see what's wrong, but I won't be long."

Mama smiled and started down the stairs. My eyes wouldn't leave Patrick though. He walked casually down the hall towards his office. *He would know,* I thought as my chest began to burn. *He would know I messed up his computer somehow.*

"Aerith?"

I turned to face Mom. She gently rubbed my cheek as I stood there frozen at the top of the stairs. I had *minutes* before Patrick would come unglued, but I didn't know how to fix this. *Maybe the screen would just go back to normal?* I thought as I bit my lower lip. *Maybe I won't get caught and thrown into the cage like Mama?* My stomach began to ache as all the possible ways

CHAPTER 37

Patrick could punish me went through my mind. Mama tugged on my arm again.

"Everything okay?" she asked as a loud bang sounded in the other room. We both turned to look, hearing Patrick swear loudly from his office. Nausea racked my body, and I bolted down the stairs.

"Everything's fine," I replied, bolting into the kitchen with her right behind me.

"Aerith?" she said again, but I ignored her. I had barely made it to the fridge when she turned me around asking, "Aerith, what's going on?"

My mouth opened, but no words would come out. I stood there shaking as tears slowly filled my eyes. Her brows knitted, but before she could say anything more, Patrick's loud voice bellowed across the room.

"Shanely!"

His heavy footsteps thundered down the steps as I stood there rigid. My lip quivered, and I slowly took a step back, hiding behind the room as he came into the room.

"Didn't I tell you to stay out of that room?!" he bellowed angrily. His eyes flashed, and before I knew it, he was in my mother's face.

"I don't understand what you're talking about," she said, her voice even and calm. "What room?"

"My office!" he bellowed again. "That is the one freaking room that I said to stay out of, and what exactly did you think you were going to accomplish on my computer anyways?"

Mama backed up nervously, but Patrick kept coming towards her. He wouldn't give her any room to breathe, and I slumped to the ground.

"I have no idea what you're talking about!" Mama cried out, placing her hands before her to stop him, when suddenly she turned to me. Her eyes met mine, softening with understanding before she turned back to Patrick.

I should speak up. I shouldn't let Mama take the fall for this, but I couldn't get the words to come out. I slowly wrapped my arms around my knees and squeezed hard, letting the tears fall down my cheek. *I was letting my Dad down,* I thought to myself. *This was my fault. All my fault.*

"I'm sorry," Mama said quietly. "I shouldn't have gone in there but..."

Patrick's fist connected the fridge, denting it, and I jumped hard. Mama never blinked. She simply stood there, glaring at him defiantly. *I always thought Daddy was brave, but Mama wasn't afraid right now,* I thought to myself. *She wasn't afraid of anything.*

"Go upstairs, Aerith," he snarled. "Now."

I hesitated for a moment, but when Patrick turned to face me, I bolted. I ran as fast as I could up the stairs, barreling into my door before the sobs burst from my lips. I couldn't breathe as the sobs wracked my entire body. I dove far under my bed and didn't stop until I hit the back wall.

I covered my ears when the screaming started and waited. I waited well passed the point when the house fell silent again.

But no one came to punish me.

And I felt sick inside.

Chapter 38

Shanely

My eyes furiously blinked as a knock sounded at the door. I slowly rose, my head still pounding from the day before and chose to ignore whoever was at the door.

Patrick was livid last night. I had barely convinced him I was only trying to use the internet to shop for items for the baby. It was a huge stretch, but pointing out we had nothing for the twins made him start to doubt. It was my saving grace, and the shiner was nothing to knowing Aerith was safe from punishment. God, seeing the fear in her eyes scared me half to death. There was no way I'd let the truth come out. Ever. Even if her little stunt just sent me back to the way thing's were, with locked rooms and access to nothing in this house again, it was worth it to know she's safe.

Another knock sounded, but I ignored it. I shuffled my way about the room, struggling to find the energy to get through the day. My mind was stuck on Aerith though. Somehow she had snuck in there and messed with his computer. *Why though?* I wondered. *What could she have possibly wanted in that room?* I didn't sleep at all last night. All the worst case scenarios came to my mind. *What if Patrick's gun safe was unlocked? What if Patrick caught her messing around in there? Would he try to toss her in the cage for it?*

I gritted my teeth together. *Over my dead body...*

The door finally slammed open, and Calvin walked in glaring.

"Did you not hear me knocking?" he snapped.

"Did you not see the door was locked?" I growled, cocking my hip to the side. My back ached when I did, and I straightened.

He rolled his eyes. "Let's go."

I frowned. His pale skin had gained some color since that first test. *I had hoped the serum would have killed him by now,* I thought to myself. He snapped his fingers, bringing me back to the present.

We made our way down to the lab once more. I could walk to the lab blindfolded by this point, but I hated walking here with him. Calvin's hand never left the gun on his hip. As if he expected me to try and take it from him. I didn't though. My belly was big enough to remind me that I wasn't alone. They depended on me not to make a mistake, but he never said a word about me snooping in the lab at least. My secret was safe.

For now.

We strolled down the vinyl hall, and my mind ran amuck. *There had to be another exit somewhere,* I thought. Mom knew there was a safety route in case of a fire, but the labs I explored didn't have any doors. *There were a few locked still, so maybe the exit was somewhere there?*

We strolled into the furthest lab like we always do, and I collapsed on the stool and rolled up my sleeve. He didn't grab the supplies to take my blood though. Multiple vials filled with that yellowish liquid already sat in the case just waiting for Calvin to use, and my face fell. *He was going to run another test,* I thought groaning. *How many times would we be doing this? How many times before he finally achieves his goal and kills everyone?*

Maybe I should just let him? I thought as I slumped in my seat. *I hated everyone he did, and they clearly deserved it.* My stomach twisted at the thought. *Could I really be certain he'd only kill those deserving of it? How many innocent people would die in the crossfire?*

I turned away from the case. I couldn't stand to even look at it as guilt rattled my core. I looked to Calvin. *No matter how angry I was; I couldn't turn into that.* I dropped my head, turning away from the madman and looking at the door instead. My eyes widened. A small map of the lab was posted on the wall to the right of the door. *How had I missed this before?! It showed the whole place...*

There *was* another way out.

"Move it, Shanely," Calvin snapped as he grabbed my arm. I barely

CHAPTER 38

got the chance to glance at the map as we passed by. There were more halls further past Mom's cell. *They must be behind one of the locked doors,* I thought to myself. *Would my key work on the door? Did the escape route go past the plates?*

My mind reeled as we stumbled into Mom's cell room. She shot to her feet the moment we walked in, and I noticed how small she really was. *Her clothes weren't this baggy the other day; were they?* I wondered. Worry lined her brow as she watched Calvin strap me down to the chair and applied the wires once more.

"This time I'll see what's going wrong," he muttered, heading to the wall to grab the remote that worked the console.

"One of these days, your experiments are going to kill you," I said, glaring at him.

"Keep running your mouth, Shanely," he threatened, "and I'll bring Aerith into this faster than you can bat an eye. The results of her initial DNA test were remarkable after all."

My eyes widened before narrowing on the man.

"I have done everything you've asked," I bellowed. "When did you do a freaking test on her?!"

Calvin rolled his eyes and sat down across from me. "I can run tests without her present, Shanely. But her DNA *is* remarkable. If she had a wolf then she'd already be down here, but she doesn't so here we are. Either way, *you* are the White Wolf, which means your power is greater than hers. It's greater than everybody's but keep testing my patience and see how fast I change my mind."

I lunged forward, snarling. Rage burned my skin as I tugged on the straps., but then I looked down to my swollen belly and the silver band on my wrist. This utterly powerless feeling swept over me then, and when that vile smirk crept up his face, I felt like I had lost before I even tried. Defeat weighed me down, and I slumped back against my seat. *What would I even do if these straps weren't here? Patrick was already pissed with me, and anything I tried with Calvin would only result in more harm to my children.* There was nothing I could do, and he knew it.

Calvin grinned, attaching the wires to his own head before reaching for the vials in the bag.

"Now sit still," he said as he injected that yellowish liquid into his left leg.

The machine began to slowly beep, recording everything that happened between the two of us. Pain struck Calvin once more, and he doubled over, clutching the arm rest. *Please, just kill him already*, I begged. He stayed slumped over, and for a moment I thought my prayers had been answered. But then he shot up, his eyes glowing red, and I knew my wish hadn't been granted.

He was an Alpha.

"Mercedes," he commanded. His voice was deeper and far huskier than before, and my eyes drifted to the skin on his arms, waiting for fur to suddenly appear. I had no idea the consequences of his actions nor was I sure if shifters *could* be created through science.

"There's a specific way humans can become shifters," Aunt Cassia warned in my head. *"It's requires a very special kind of bite. One that makes room for a wolf to be present."*

Calvin pushed a button on the remote, and the door swung opened. I held my breath, watching this whole thing unfold once more as Calvin commanded, "Come here."

My mother moved with a swift grace, stopping only when she stood a few feet behind him. Her eyes flashed with fear as Calvin chuckled.

"Good girl," he said. His fiery red eyes gleaming down at me. "See I've adjusted the serum this time. I gave a more concentrated dose of the shifter gene and less fillers. This should last long enough for the permanent change to take place. Now, let's try this again on you, Shanely."

Calvin smiled menacingly at me. Goosebumps ran up and down my arm as I waited for the command to hit me. I shut my eyes tight. *Please don't work...*

"Shanely, stand."

Nothing happened. I opened my eyes and relaxed in the chair as I exhaled the breath I had been holding. *Oh, thank God.*

CHAPTER 38

Calvin frowned and pulled the paper printing from the machine, studying it carefully.

"Why isn't this working?" he asked, but neither of us answered him. *Maybe because this is wrong and unnatural,* I thought to myself.

Calvin studied the paper longer before looking to me.

"Shanely, stand."

Nothing happened, and I raised an eyebrow. A small smirk forming on my lips.

"Maybe you should say please?" I suggested with a smile. He glared.

"Mercedes, sit down."

Mom submitted a low growl, her breathing picking up in speed as she fought the command before finally giving in and sitting on the ground.

Calvin narrowed his eyes to the two of us. "It works on you, but not you. Interesting."

"Not really," I muttered, crossing my arms. "Commands have never worked on me. I could have just told you that without all the theatrics."

Calvin looked at the paperwork once more. "Have you ever commanded humans, Shanely?"

I pursed my lips together. *Like I'd answer that,* I thought although I really wasn't sure how to answer that. *I had never tried.*

Calvin barred his teeth in anger, and I blinked in surprise. *That was very much a wolfy thing to do,* I thought to myself. *Was the serum actually rearranging his DNA?*

"The bite makes room for the wolf..."

Suddenly, Calvin groaned, and my mother stumbled, clutching her head. I scooted further into my seat, smirking as he doubled over in pain. A sickening satisfaction washed over me as I watched his body shake violently.

Mom straightened, giving me a nod as she got control once more, but then her eyes drifted to the gun on his hip. She stepped closer.

The machine beeped loudly. The needle flew across the page as it recorded what happened to him. Mom took another step, and my eyes widened. Calvin screamed again as the machine began to smoke.

My mother reached for the gun.

I struggled to control my breathing as her fingers grazed the gun. Calvin snapped his head to her just as she lifted the gun from the hostler, and he lunged. He gripped her throat hard, the red still lingering in his eyes as he got to his feet. Calvin tore the wires off him as my mother's face turned beat red. She scratched at his hands, and I screamed.

"Let her go!" I begged, pulling against the straps that held me down.

"I command you to never take my gun, Mercedes. In fact, I command you to never touch a weapon for the rest of your life," Calvin snarled. "You are never to go near a weapon at all, and you will never try to shoot me again. Do you understand?!"

"CALVIN!" I screamed louder, feeling that agonizing burn pulse through my veins. "Do not hurt her!"

Calvin snarled in my direction as the red flickered in his eyes. My mother clung to his hand but could not break free of his grip. Her eyes began to roll, and I yanked on the straps harder, barring my teeth at him.

"You won't have that stolen strength much longer, and my mother will get the upper hand," I snarled as my left wrist slipped further from the strap. *Just a little more...* "Even with the inhibitor, my mother is *stronger* than you. You are nothing more than a pathetic human, Calvin. And you will *never* be able to keep the Alpha power like you think you will."

Calvin blinked, but I held his stare. With one harsh tug, I yanked my wrist free from the strap. He shoved her to the ground and grabbed his gun. I froze when he pointed the gun at my head.

"You move an inch, and I pull the trigger," he snarled.

That agonizing pain had reached my chest, making it hard to breathe. My eyes drifted to my mother. Her eyes were wide, but she was breathing. Alive and breathing, so I sat back in the chair slowly.

"Get back in that cell, Mercedes," Calvin demanded, keeping his gun pointing on me.

Mom didn't move. Her body shook slightly as she looked at me, and I gave her a small nod. *Live to fight another day,* I thought, hoping she could understand it too.

CHAPTER 38

"I said…"

"I'm going!" Mom yelled as she stumbled to her feet. I said nothing as I watched her step behind the door, and Calvin locked it behind him.

Calvin tucked the gun back in its holster before going to the machine. It smoked slightly from the back, and I wondered if it was finally broken enough not to work anymore. *Not like it would stop him,* I thought to myself.

My eyes narrowed as I watched him go through the results. It didn't escape my notice that his eyes widened ever so slightly in surprise, and a small smirk formed on my lips. His gaze drifted off as the wheels in his mind turned.

I was right, I thought as that smirk turned into a full grin. *And maybe it would be enough to end this deadly game?*

Calvin grabbed the gun and unhooked my right hand from the chair. He motioned to the door, and I gave my mother one last look before following him out of the room. The sound of our steps being the only thing that echoed the halls as we walked back to Patrick's room. Calvin opened the door for me. His pale gray eyes flickering red.

"Tell my son I will not be around this evening," he muttered, and I stepped inside. He shut the door, the lock clicking into place before I had barely taken a step. I gritted my teeth as I slumped onto the bed.

My body hurt, and the pulsing in my head wouldn't be going away anytime soon. *This was getting dangerous,* I thought to myself. But no matter how I tried to sort it out, nothing would come to mind. No answer. No easy way out. Just nothing.

Too tired to think anymore, I rolled to my side, watching the setting sun just past the trees. *We had been downstairs longer than I realized,* and I sighed. Patrick would be home soon, and I had a long night of groveling to do. I couldn't stay locked in my rooms anymore. I had to find that tracker, and I had to figure out the plates.

I was running out of time.

As if the boys heard my thoughts, they kicked, making my stomach flutter. I smiled softly, placing my hand on my stomach as a light flickered across the room. I watched it flicker a couple more times before drifting off to sleep.

Chapter 39

Aerith

A couple days had passed since I got Mama in trouble. I hated myself for not telling Patrick the truth. That it was me who was in his office messing with his computer. Mama's eye was black and blue already, and I could barely look at her because of it. Patrick brought home two large boxes the very next day for my baby brothers. He said from now on if Mama needed something for me or my brothers to just ask. She thanked him and agreed to his command, giving me a small look before helping Patrick load them into a spare room. I knew that look was a warning. I was not to go in there *again*.

Thankfully, Patrick has gotten out of his wretched mood, but he still seemed off with us both. I felt awful for running before. Next time, I wasn't going to leave Mama. I wasn't going to be afraid.

The door to my room opened, and I turned to find Mama and Patrick waiting for me.

"Ready for dinner, Aerith?" Mama asked as she extended a hand to me. I solemnly walked towards them, noticing Patrick kept a hand around Mama's waist. Patrick wasn't his goofy self, but Mama smiled wide, acting like everything was okay, so I took her hand and followed them out the room.

"How was work today?" Mama asked as we walked down the stairs and into the kitchen. Patrick sighed heavily.

"It was work," he answered, dropping into the chair at the island. I slowly took the one next to him. "The Division reassigned the guys who were on my team this morning. They ship out at the end of the week, so that was great."

"Why did they do that?" Mama asked casually. She pulled out a bag of frozen chicken and placed it on a platter to defrost. Patrick leaned back in his seat, rubbing his face in frustration before tossing an arm around my chair.

"I don't know," he snapped, and I held my breath. "Someone real high up has returned to the States, and he pulled everyone out of this area. Real pain in the butt, if you ask me. I'm actually supposed to let dad know. Have you seen him?"

"Not today," Mama answered. "He said he wouldn't be around, but that was a couple of days ago. I'm not sure where he went."

Patrick frowned again but said nothing. Mama started chopping onions and carrots, tossing them into a frying pan while the two of us watched. Every so often, she'd place her hand on her lower back, and I wondered if the babies were heavy in her belly. I cocked my head to the side, watching her make dinner.

"So," Mama said, breaking the silence, "do you know who it was that recalled your team?"

Patrick stood abruptly and grabbed a beer from the fridge. "I don't know. One of the Heads I haven't met yet. I think his name is Hank. Hank something or another. He wants to meet with dad."

Mama stumbled, dropping the knife in her hands. It clattered on the floor loudly.

Patrick narrowed his eyes as Mama scrambled to pick it up and put it in the sink. She dropped the veggies in the pan before tossing in the butter. I frowned watching her.

What's wrong with Mama?

"Ah. Well, I'll do my best to remind you to talk to your father," she said, and I heard her heart start to race. Her voice wasn't steady, and I wondered why.

Patrick's gaze never left my mother as he set his beer and stalked over to her. I gripped the edge of my seat as panic began to creep in.

CHAPTER 39

"Do you know him, Shanely?" Patrick asked as he stood behind my mother.

My mother didn't respond. She didn't say anything at all, but I knew she was scared. Her heart pounded fast in her chest.

Patrick turned her around abruptly. "I asked you a question!"

I covered my ears as his voice boomed throughout the room. It sounded so loud that it hurt my ears, and I just wanted to run away. I wanted to run back to my room and hide, but I was too afraid to move. Too afraid to do anything but watch. Patrick gripped her wrists tightly. *It was happening again.*

Mama stammered, "No! I don't know him, all right! Why are you shouting at me?!"

"Because I know you, Shanely. You're already on thin ice with the computer issue this week," he snapped. "What did you do?! Did you cause me problems with this Hank guy?"

Mama's eyes widened as she tried to step back away from him. Her back hit the stove as she stammered, "I didn't do anything! You're being ridiculous!"

"Then why is one of *the top bosses*, whom I have never met before, coming down to investigate Diablo? He has never once taken an interest in our area before! Why has he taken my team..."

"I don't know!" my mother shouted back as I cowered on the chair. My chest burned as pushed back. "I didn't even unlock the computer, so how would I have contacted him?!"

Patrick narrowed his eyes as I scrambled to figure out what to do. *Daddy would protect Mama. He'd do whatever he had to save her, and it was my fault Patrick was so suspicious right now. It's my fault, and I...*

Suddenly, I knew what to do.

"Daddy?!" I cried out loudly.

Mama and Patrick stilled, snapping their attention to me. Mama's jaw dropped, but Patrick *softened*. He looked at me in shock, stepping away from Mama and towards me instead. I held my breath as a slow smile appeared on his face.

He knelt down, gently rubbing the side of my cheek as he asked, "Did you just call me daddy?"

I nervously nodded my head yes. "Is that okay?"

Patrick grinned even wider. "Of course it is! What did you need, Baby Doll?"

"Can we play a game tonight? Instead of a movie," I asked, tugging at the end of my shirt. "Please?"

"I would love to play a game with you," he said as he scooped me up and hugged me tightly.

I didn't look at mama. I couldn't look at her and see her so upset with me, but my chest burned. It burned in such a way that it felt *right*. Like something inside was proud of me, and I let myself take a deep breath. *I did what Daddy would do,* I thought to myself. *What my real Daddy would do.*

Patrick carried me towards the stairs before turning to my mother. I laid my head on his shoulder and shut my eyes, wishing this night was just over.

"I'm sorry I raised my voice, Shanely. I've just been stressed this week with work, but I shouldn't have taken it out on you. I shouldn't have lost my temper these last few days. I guess I'm just a little bit jumpy after everything, and I don't want anything to happen to you both. The idea of something bad happening to you two *scares* me."

Daddy would be proud, I told myself. *And Mommy will understand.* A burning smell filled the room as I heard my mother's soft voice.

"It's okay, Patrick," she said softly.

"Aerith and I are going to grab one of the board games to play," he replied. "Let me know when dinner is done, and I'll help you bring food up."

My mother said nothing as Patrick carried me out of the room. It was then I opened my eyes to look at Mama. Her shoulders shook softly as she hunched over the stove, her back to me. Tears filled my eyes, but I quickly wiped them away. I kept my sadness tucked deep inside because Patrick gets mad when I cry, and I can't have him be angry anymore.

This had worked.

And now I knew how I could help her.

Chapter 40

Shanely

Hearing Aerith call Patrick *daddy* just about broke me. I couldn't even eat dinner that night. The second he took her upstairs, I vomited in the sink. This was too much. *Everything* was too much, and I had to get her out.

Before she got even more attached to him.

Calvin came upstairs late that night. I didn't even realize he had been in the lab this whole time, but Calvin wobbled straight to his room, ignoring us all. Patrick explained later that he had came down with a flu apparently. His dad was running a high fever and was vomiting constantly, so Patrick wanted Aerith and I to stay far away from that side of the house just in case. Calvin and I both knew the truth though. These experiments were killing him, but it had been a little while since our last test. *Did he try again without me?* I wondered, hoping my mother was alright.

With Calvin sick at home, Patrick was stuck running the station *and* taking over his father's role as Division Head Officer. His schedule was all over the place, and I'd never know when he'd show up. Sneaking past the two had become rather difficult, but I had to figure out getting past the plates. Patrick always drove down the driveway with no issues, and he bounced between vehicles constantly, so it ruled out one specific vehicle being the key.

But I wasn't sure what to do.

The added stress of handling everything by himself just made Patrick more demanding of me. He'd come home in a huff and collapse in his chair, while I made dinner or cleaned things up. Patrick wanted to be more than friends, but he was curbing his temper around the two of us lately. Rubbing his shoulders or hands was grating on my nerves though, but I played the role I needed to get him to trust me again. Aerith had become a buffer of sorts between us. Patrick had a soft spot for her, and she'd beg to play a game or fly the drones whenever he got grumpy. The two went outside constantly, and she called him Dad all the time. And he just ate it up.

It just made me sick.

I had two weeks until my due date if the twins were on time. I was no closer to figuring out the plates, and with Patrick and Calvin constantly hanging around the house, I couldn't visit my mom in the lab or explore anymore down there. My nerves were shot, and everything on my body ached. I didn't remember feeling this miserable with Aerith, but then again I had Bastian with me before. I wasn't so utterly alone or scared of my mind. I was happy then.

And it made a difference.

Calvin finally graced us with his presence after his so called flu one morning. I was at the stove, making Patrick's favorite breakfast, while he and Aerith sat at the island.

"How ya feeling, Dad?" Patrick said, sipping his coffee. I placed my hand on my lower back as I stirred the pot of grits. *God, I was so sore.*

Calvin grunted, pouring himself a cup. I kept an eye on him as he moved around me for the sugar. "Fine. Been sick of lying in bed all day. I'm anxious to get back to the station, and see how messed up it's gotten."

Patrick sighed, and I stilled. *Calvin just has to stir the pot,* I thought as I slowly glanced towards Aerith, who kept her attention on her cereal. She knew what to do when Calvin was around. She knew *exactly* how to behave around him.

"I've actually done a fairly decent job this week, Dad," Patrick answered, and I exhaled slowly. "You'd be surprised how smooth everything's gone. I've handled it exactly like you would have. Payrolls gone out on time, I reassigned the roster that's easier on the guys on the station, and I've been dealing with that Hank person all week. Easy peasy."

Calvin's eyes widened as he slowly turned to his son. "You what?"

Patrick crossed his arms, cocking his head to the side as he studied his father.

"I told you about this already," he replied.

"I don't remember you saying anything about Hank!" Calvin hollered. Patrick leaned forward, blocking Aerith from view.

"You've had a raging fever for about four days, so maybe you don't remember, but I did tell you. Hank Cartwright has taken a special interest in our area. He's evaluating the districts, I guess. But he pulled my team about a week ago and has been going over everything from the last five years."

"You gave him access to everything?!" Calvin bellowed as he shot across the room to grab his coat.

"What was I supposed to do?!" Patrick snapped back. "He's one of the four Generals! Besides, it's just an audit, and everyone's..."

Calvin slammed the garage door shut, ignoring his son altogether. Aerith and I watched in stunned silence.

Patrick gripped his mug angrily. "God! For once, can he just trust that I did a decent job? Can he *just once* not assume I've screwed everything up!"

He launched his mug across the room, shattering it on the wall. Aerith and I both jumped, and she scurried towards me. I promptly shoved her behind me, watching him closely. He buried his head in his hands as silence filled the room.

After a few moments, Patrick slowly sat back in his seat, softening as he looked to us. His eyes went from us to the shattered mug and spilled coffee on the floor. He sighed again, standing from his seat to grab the broom from the closet.

"I'm sorry," he said softly. "I didn't mean to scare you two."

I didn't move as he swept the mess up and tossed the glass in the trash. *I half expected him to ask me to clean that,* I thought as I watched him closely. He never made a move towards us though, and my head slowly cocked to the side. *Patrick just seemed defeated almost.*

"You shouldn't let him speak to you that way," I said softly. "You don't deserve to be treated like that, especially by your father."

The look he gave me was hard to stomach. He just looked so broken, and for a brief moment, I saw Lorelei. Her thin lips and soft eyes. *She did all this to protect everyone only to lose her son to the monster they created.*

Patrick snapped out of his trance and grabbed his coat. He opened the door and hesitated.

"I work late tonight," he muttered quietly, "but how about I bring us back a pizza for dinner? We can have a movie night just the three of us and get back to how things used to be. Sound good?"

I gave him a nod, and he seemed satisfied with my answer. His eyes glistened as he said, "I love you guys."

And then he was gone. I exhaled the breath I had been holding, rubbing my face before turning to Aerith.

"Are you okay?" I asked, and she nodded her head. My shoulders fell as I grabbed the pot of burnt grits and tossed it in the sink. *She was just used to their behavior,* I thought. She was reliving Patrick's childhood, and that killed me.

"C'mon," I said, pulling her along with me. "Let's spend the day just you and me together."

I knew I should try to break into Patrick's office, but Aerith looked so sad as she followed me up the stairs. *I had until 4 to snoop,* I told myself. *She needed me.*

I led her to the movie room, and we snuggled under the blankets once I popped in a movie. We stayed quiet for awhile just letting the movie play, sitting together in peace. We needed a moment just the two of us, and as if on cue, one of the twins kicked. *We could never forget you two,* I thought to myself as I chuckled. After some time had passed, I decided it was time to talk. I gently rubbed Aerith's cheek, smiling when she looked up at me.

"I promise, *one day* this will all be better," I said softly. "One day, you won't have to live like this. I just need you to hang on a little."

Her eyes widened. "Are we leaving?"

I pursed my lips together. She looked at me with hope for the first time in months. *Keeping her in the dark wasn't helping any,* I thought. *I couldn't say everything, but I had to give her some truth.* "One day very soon, I will get you out of here. I need you to be strong, baby. And I need you to keep this a secret. Can you do that for Mama?"

I watched her eyes fill with tears, but she held them back so fiercely. I just wish she'd let them go. Just let herself feel and release this awful feeling. *It was just us*, I thought to myself, but when she blinked they were gone.

"If we can go," she said, pulling me from my thoughts, "why don't we just go now?"

I sighed. "I wish we could, but there's more to it. It's not that simple, Aerith."

"Why not?"

I grinned softly, seeing Bastian pull through as her brows furrowed. *She was his shadow.* She had always been his shadow, but seeing it now was comforting. I gave her a hug saying, "Because there's someone else here that needs saving too."

Her right brow rose, and I nearly snorted. *And there's Cade*, I thought, chuckling.

"Who else is here?" she asked.

I grinned. "Someone I'm excited for you to meet, but for now let's just keep that between us. Now, why don't you tell me why you were in Patrick's office the other day?"

Aerith dropped her head, and I gently tucked a curl behind her ear.

"Hey," I said softly, "look at me, baby."

She slowly looked up to me.

"You can tell me..."

A door slammed, echoing throughout the house. My heart thundered in my chest as heavy footsteps sounded. I gripped Aerith's hand tightly.

"Shanely!"

God not now, I thought as I got to my feet. I looked to the clock on the wall, my heart sinking when I saw the time. *He was home early way too early.*

"Shanely!" he shouted again, his voice louder and closer than before. *I couldn't go through that test again*, I thought as my anxiety rose. The door rebounded off the wall, and Calvin glared.

"Calvin please..."

"Move it now!" he snarled as he grabbed my wrist. To my horror, he grabbed Aerith too.

Rage burst forward as I slammed my fist into his chest. It caught him off guard, and he stumbled backwards, letting her go.

"Don't touch her!" I bellowed. I pushed her further behind me, my chest heaving as Calvin straightened.

His nostrils flared as he raised his arm and struck me across the face. Aerith screamed as I hit the floor.

My head spun, but I stilled when I heard the familiar click of his gun.

"I said move," he snarled again. I slowly looked up to him, finding the barrel inches from my face. Aerith was curled into a ball at his feet.

"You promised," I said softly between breaths. "I have done everything you asked."

"That was before I ran out of time," he replied. He knelt down, keeping the barrel in my face and grabbed Aerith's arm. "You can either come with or let her go by herself. Your choice."

I barred my teeth as I slowly got to my feet. An aching pain shot through my back as I straightened, and I sucked in a breath as Calvin jabbed his handgun in my back and pushed me towards the door.

"You take one step in a direction I don't want," he whispered in my ear, "and I'll shoot. In fact don't even open your mouth. I am getting results *today*. Understand, Shanely? Today."

I held my tongue as he shoved me forward. *There must be something I can do*, I thought, racking my brain for any idea that could work. Pain pulsed down my legs as he forced us to the lab. Aerith's soft cries were the only sound as we walked the long white hallway to my mother's room.

Calvin unlocked the door to mom's cell, and I waited for her to come out. *Maybe between the two of us, we could get the upper hand here?* Suddenly, I was shoved forward into the cell, falling at my mother's feet.

"Shanely!" she shouted, kneeling down to me.

No, no, no! I scrambled to my feet and rushed to the door, but it was too late. *I* was too late. The door slammed shut, and I was locked in with mom.

CHAPTER 40

I was locked in, I thought, my eyes widening. *And Aerith was out there.*

Rage burned in my chest as I pounded on the door, screaming at Calvin to let me out. My wrist throbbed as I hit the door wrong, and I screamed again. My daughter's eyes stayed firmly on me, begging me to help her, but there was nothing I could do. The door wouldn't budge, and she was alone with a monster.

Calvin dragged my daughter across the room and locked her in the seat he always put me. All while she cried.

"What is happening?!" my mother bellowed. "Who is that?!"

"My daughter," I replied in a defeated tone. Her eyes widened.

Aerith suddenly screamed, and I turned to find her arm wrenched to the side. Calvin drew vial after vial of her blood, while she sobbed uncontrollably. Her back arched and fear gripped my heart. I clenched my fists together as my chest burned again. The pain traveled to my inhibitor, burning my skin around the band, but my wolf never showed. I snarled, hitting the glass again as my back seized again.

"I'll kill you!" I screamed as loud as I could. To my surprise, Calvin slowly turned his head to me. *He could hear me...* I bellowed again. "I'll kill you for this Calvin! Do you hear me?! I *will* kill you!"

He narrowed his eyes before grabbing the blood he stole. Then he walked out, leaving us entirely alone. *I have to get out. I have to get us out of here.*

My eyes drifted back to my daughter. Aerith shook in her seat, sobbing hard. The tears wouldn't stop, and her breathing become more and more erratic. I rushed to the other side of the room and hit the glass again.

"Hang on baby!" I shouted. "I'm coming. I promise!"

She wouldn't look at me. Aerith stared at the floor bawling. Her chest heaved, and I dug my hands in my hair. *She's having a panic attack,* I thought. *She couldn't catch her breath.*

"She can't hear you," mom said softly. All the pain I felt sat heavy on my chest as I looked at my terrified daughter. "I wish so badly she could, but it's sound proof. I'm so sorry, child."

I exhaled slowly, trying to get ahead of my own panic and anxiety. I dropped my head and took a deep breath. *Aerith needs me,* I scolded myself.

She needs me to be strong, so take a breath and move, Shanely. Move.

"Screw this," I muttered as I knocked on the glass again. I knocked louder and louder until she finally dragged her eyes to mine. I forced a smile to my lips. "Breathe, baby."

Pulling my hands up, I took in a massive breath of air before pushing my hands down and exhaling. I did it again. And again. But she just looked at me.

"C'mon, baby," I muttered, repeating the process.

Her chest continued to heave rapidly, so I kept going. Over and over while her brows furrowed. Even my mother copied me.

"You can do this, Aerith," I whispered. "In and out."

Finally, Aerith began to copy us. Relief washed over me as she steadied her breathing and slowly calmed down. Her body settled, and I smiled proudly.

"That's my girl," I said, placing my hand on the glass. Aerith said something, and I wish more than anything I could hear her. My mother placed her hand on my shoulder.

"She's beautiful, Shanely," Mom said, and I smiled wider. "Looks just like you."

"She looks like you too," I chimed in.

The door slammed opened once more, and Aerith froze. We all did. My stomach cramped as Calvin entered the room carrying that black case with him. Panic surged through me as I bolted to the door. *He was going to inject himself once more,* I thought as my heart pounded. *He's going to run a test with her. I have to get out of here!*

Calvin didn't bother with the wires this time. He sat down across from her, and I watched as fear flashed across her face. Anger burned against my skin, and I clutched my hands together tightly. There was nothing I could do but watch as he stabbed that vial into his leg. Calvin doubled over, and I couldn't look away. The three of us stared as he convulsed in agony in the chair before my daughter.

Aerith struggled in her seat. The straps were cutting into her wrists as she pulled to get away, and I was stuck behind this glass with my mother.

CHAPTER 40

Nothing to do but watch the horrors unfold before me. I had no idea what would happen now. *Would Calvin even let me out of here?* I wondered anxiously. *He could lie, and my mother and I would be stuck down here forever. With no one to help my daughter.*

"Let us out!" I screamed again as my emotions began to run away from me. A small sob escaped my lips as I begged, "Please..."

Finally, Calvin sat back and exhaled deeply. His back to us, Calvin's shoulders rose softly up and down, taking breath after breath, while we watched.

"Why isn't he letting us out?" I asked my mother. I shifted on my feet nervously to keep the pain in my legs at bay.

"I don't know."

Suddenly, Calvin tipped his head back and laughed. My stomach rolled as he slowly turned to face us. His eyes were shifter gold. He pressed a button on the remote and static sounded.

"To think, *all this time* I just needed her," he said, laughing again. "You were right, Shanely. I was never going to get what I wanted the way I was going. She's the key. Not you."

My steps faltered. Like the rug was yanked from underneath me, I realized my grave mistake. *I gave him the answer. It was because of me that he figured out the last piece to the puzzle.*

"You leave her alone, Calvin!" my mother shouted. "She's just a child!"

He shot to his feet, hitting the glass wall and cracking it slightly as he glared at us. His eyes shifted from gold to blood red. "I'll bleed her dry if it gets me what I want."

"I'll tell Patrick," I snapped angrily. I squared my shoulders as I found my voice again. "The second I get free, I'll tell him what you've been doing, and what you really think of him. I'll tell him *everything!*"

Calvin chuckled, shaking my confidence ever so slightly. "My son's an idiot. He will never find the two of you down here, and I'll simply command this one not to say a word. He *will not* get in the way this time, and neither will you."

My shoulders fell as he strolled around the room casually. A healthy color returned to his cheeks, and he stood taller than before. His muscles looked bigger, better, and my stomach churned as my back hurt again. *The shifter gene was healing him. It was fixing his frail body, and there was no way I could stop him.* Not without my wolf.

Calvin adjusted the cuff link on his shirt saying, "I'm sorry Shanely, but I don't need you anymore. I don't need either of you. Only her."

He cackled another laugh as I realized what was going to happen now. *He was going to kill me,* kill us, *and get away with it too. Because Patrick never disobeyed his father's orders. He would never look down here.*

"Now let's test this again," he said gleefully. "Shanely, grab your mother by the throat."

My eyes widened as an invisible force grabbed my body. I shook hard as I tried to fight it, but I staggered forward on my feet. My mother took a step away.

"Shanely..." she stammered as her back hit the wall.

"I'm trying, Mom!" I bellowed, but the force pushed me forward again. Like a puppet on a string, my hand rose towards my mother's throat. My chest burned in agony as I dug my heels in. To no avail.

"Shanely!" Calvin shouted louder, and I shook violently. "I command you to grab Mercedes by her throat."

"Hit me, Mom!" I begged as that slimy feeling pushed me harder. A tear fell down my face as I took another step. "Knock me unconscious, please!"

"I won't fight you, Shanely," she said softly, letting my small hand wrap around her throat. "I won't hurt my family."

My lip quivered as my fingers tightened their grip around her. A sob burst from my lips when her face reddened under my grip. I couldn't breathe, and all I could think was how wrong I was for *ever* using my Alpha power like this. How very wrong it is to control someone and take away their free will. Cade and Elijah flashed before my eyes again as the power compelled me to squeeze harder.

Calvin roared with laughter. "Oh, this is too good! I've done it, Lorelei! I've *finally* done it."

"Please stop!" I begged between sobs as Mom's eyes began to roll to the back of her head. Calvin continued to laugh, and my stomach churned. *I was going to kill her. I was going to kill my own mother because of that wretched man.*

"Alright, alright," he finally said, "I've had my fun. Shanely, stop."

My hand fell, dropping my mother to the floor. She gasped for air, clutching her neck, while I sagged to my knees in relief.

I wrapped my arms over her whispering, "I'm so sorry. I'm so, so sorry."

"Mama!" Aerith shouted, and I turned to her. My eyes widened as Calvin unhooked her from the chair and started for the door.

"No!" I shouted as the tears fell faster down my face. "Please, Calvin! You've already won, alright? You have the Alpha power, just leave my family alone!"

Calvin just chuckled again as he opened the door.

"Say goodbye to mommy, Aerith," he said with a smile. "We won't be seeing her anytime soon."

And with that he slammed the door shut. My jaw dropped.

I *failed* her.

I didn't get *her* out in time.

And now I will *never* see her again.

A roar burst from my lips, and I screamed. I screamed and screamed, clutching my chest in agony as my daughter was taken from me.

Chapter 41

Patrick

"I didn't expect to see you in person, sir," I said, staring blankly at one of the Division's bosses before me. "Did Maggie get you everything you requested?"

I had hoped to make amends with Dad and show him I had everything under control before work, but none of that matter when Hank Cartwright sat before me at my father's desk in his office. *By the looks of the place, he had been here awhile.*

"Yes, she did. It's been rather difficult to get your father to actually meet with me, so I decided to come here instead. I've been waiting for him to show up, but it doesn't look like that's happening," Hank said, dropping the file he was reading. Hairs stood on the back of my neck as he motioned to the seat across from him. "Take a seat."

Shutting the door, I took a seat like he commanded. I held my breath as my boss stared me down. I had never met this man before. He was as high up in the Chain of Command as Dennis was, but I've *never* worked with him. I primarily only ever dealt with Dennis since he runs the training program we all go through, but here Hank was, looking ever so sternly with me right now. Nerves rattled my core. *Does he know about Shanely?* I wondered as he studied me closely. I prayed he didn't. I didn't know what he'd do to her and Aerith if he knew they were still alive.

Or *me* for that matter.

"You know, Diablo has been coming up a lot lately," he said, leaning back in my father's chair. "An *awful* lot."

CHAPTER 41

I swallowed hard. "Is that so?"

"I'm afraid it is," he replied. "I've heard the McCoy pack has been... eliminated."

Hank studied me carefully as I slowly nodded my head. *He couldn't possibly know about Shanely, could he? Why else would he be here? And pissed off for that matter.*

"Yes, sir," I replied, clearing my throat. "My father said with the charges laid against them, it was decided to eliminate the problem before it claimed innocent lives."

Hank narrowed his eyes. "Interesting. I always thought the McCoy pack seemed rather peaceful."

I cocked my head to the side. "You've met them?"

This was news to me, I thought to myself. Hank's been out of country for a long time. The new European facility was finally up and running smoothly, but I didn't expect the older man to be in the States so soon. I didn't think the man even dealt with internal affairs anymore. Even though Hank's title said he does, *Dennis* usually handled internal affairs. He took over what happened in our country, despite insisting he only controls the military.

He nodded his head saying, "I had a good friend in that pack actually. I've been trying to reach him with no luck, and then I come home to discover his entire pack was killed. By us."

I shifted in my seat nervously. "You'd have to discuss the details with my father, sir. I only followed orders."

Hank leaned forward on the desk. "Oh, I plan too, Patrick. But right now, I want to talk to you. Did you think the McCoy pack needed dealt with?"

Silence filled the room. I took my time thinking how exactly I should respond. While I hated that prick Bastian and his annoying brothers, the decision to remove the pack from God's green earth wasn't mine. I only capitalized on it to save Shanely, but the last thing I needed was him poking further into all this. *He could not find her.*

"Like I said, I just followed orders," I said, exhaling slowly. "My father said that Lieutenant General Hemingway called the order in because of a national threat and commanded us to eliminate said threat. So we did."

Hank studied me closely again as if he'd catch me in some lie. *It was the truth though.* My father warned me late one night that the team was moving in against the pack and moving in fast. Orders were to kill the entire pack before catastrophe struck because Dennis found a threat against our nation amongst the McCoy pack. War had been called, and they needed us to end it before it started. *Shanely* was that threat, but I knew they were wrong about her. Everyone was wrong about her. Her and Bastian were the targets to be eliminated, and I had to stop it. I *could* stop it for her at least, and that's what I did. The so-called threat had been handled, and Shanely gets to live in secret with me.

"Did Dennis say what the threat was?" Hank asked, pulling me from my thoughts.

"The White Wolf. Anything more was above my pay-grade," I answered, which was technically true. *My Dad trusted me to know, and thank God he did.* I gripped the armrest of my chair tightly, just thinking what could have happened had I not known.

Hank sighed and picked up a file I didn't recognize. "According to *this* file, your orders were to bring in the White Wolf for questioning, *alive*. You were to eliminate all active insurgents, but the orders were clear, Sergeant. The White Wolf and her mate were to be brought in alive. Yet, she did not arrive in Colorado. Explain."

I shifted in my seat, frowning. *That's not right,* I thought to myself.

"Umm..." I stammered, "the mission just went south, sir. They were killed in action."

Hank scoffed, pinching the bridge of his nose as stress spread across his face. "I swear, this is a first."

"Does it matter, sir?" I asked, crossing my arms. "Their deaths were ordered. I saw the paperwork myself, so does it matter when or where they died?"

Hank looked horrified for a moment, and I held my breath. Worry that I just said the wrong thing consumed me, but I was scratching my head trying to figure out the issue here. *Shanely and Bastian weren't supposed to get taken in. They were supposed to die,* I thought to myself. But Hank

CHAPTER 41

continued to stare at me, rattling me to my core. The level of unease I felt made it difficult to think straight, but I had to protect Shanely.

"Bastian Fenrir had grown too powerful," I said, unable to take the silence anymore. "He..."

How close to the truth do I want to go?

I straightened. "Look, I don't know what you were told, but Bastian *had* grown very powerful in the last few years. His wolf had doubled in size, and he was building an army of shifters. The last couple meetings with him didn't go very well either. I assume the Lieutenant General made the call to eliminate them because of that."

I leaned back in my chair, satisfied with my answer. I let that new information sink in and stayed utterly silent while I waited. *Whether that army had anything to do with the shot I took in Canada, I'll never know, but it lead me to rescuing Shanely.* Either way, the shifters have been changing too much, and Shanely and Bastian were at the center of it all. It made sense Dennis wanted to squash the problem before it grew too big to contain. *He just wasn't hurting my girl in the process.*

This whole crazy thing even brought my father and I closer together. The first time my Dad didn't look annoyed when I asked for help was for her. He was so sympathetic and just there for me. Dad gave me my own personal team, all buddies I trained with in the Division program, and then made sure I had what I needed to protect her. He's never been a super affectionate dad, but that moment meant the world to me. He listened, and I got to save my girl.

I got to save Shanely.

"It matters because Dennis didn't order their deaths. We have protocols, Patrick. Strict protocols that we must adhere to," he said firmly. "We don't make mistakes and having the Lieutenant General saying one thing and the task force say another is a huge deal!"

My shoulders fell. *He didn't want Shanely dead? No... That doesn't make any sense. I saw the order myself... I saw...*

Hank sighed heavily before rubbing his face. "Something just isn't adding up here, Sergeant. The only two signatures I've seen on *any* of these documents are Dennis's and your father's. The actual orders are different from the orders given and certain protocols have been skipped over entirely. I've got an entire pack of shifters dead and no idea if any of it was actually necessary. I've gone round and round with everyone *except* your father, and I've thoroughly gone through the report Dennis received. Some of the things that Calvin has listed make zero sense. Somebody's lying, and I think I know who."

"I don't understand," I said, my brows knitting in confusion. "My father didn't recommend this. *Dennis* called the order in. He ordered the White Wolf dead."

The two of us stared at one another. His silence had my mind reeling and slowly doubt began trickling in.

"Didn't he?" I asked quietly. *My father wouldn't lie about something like this? He wouldn't lie to me...*

"Patrick," Hank finally said, and I looked at him, "have you even seen the report your father sent?"

Hank tossed a file before me, and I slowly reached forward and took it. Dad rarely let me see the reports he filed with the Division, but he let me see everything last time. He let me see the order calling for Shanely's death, for Bastian and their pack's death, but as I looked through the paperwork, I realized this was *not* the same file I saw before. My eyes widened when I saw all that was listed. Some of these pictures were taken years ago, not now, and I know this because Shanely's had her gorgeous red hair in some of these. I hadn't heard of the pack doing some of the things Dad listed either. The ones I had seen were greatly embellished. *Why would he do this? Why would he lie about everything?* I wondered as I quickly flipped through the rest of the file, looking for my father's notes. The last page had what I was looking for.

It is my personal recommendation to eliminate the McCoy pack before something catastrophic happens. Shanely Fenrir and her mate Bastian have grown too strong to control as the supposed White Wolf. They have repeatedly threatened my life when questioned over their actions in rallying the wolf shifters in Diablo, and I firmly believe they are gearing up for war against our

CHAPTER 41

nation. They are building an army against you, Lieutenant General. You need to act now before it's too late.

I slumped back in my chair, unable to read anymore. *Dad wanted them gone*, I thought as my mind scrambled to figure out what was going on. *But why not just tell me? Why lie to me and tell me some story about our C.O?* My mind ran in a thousand different directions. None of which gave me *any* answers.

"This is why I wanted access to your father's records. I believe the evidence brought forth was inaccurate, and it cost a lot of lives. Do you have any idea as to why your father would do something like this?" Hank asked, and I slowly looked up to him in disbelief.

I didn't know how to answer him. Memories flooded my brain of the night Dad confided in me. He explained he had nothing to do with it. Dad looked just as surprised as I felt when he told me our orders.

"I think the order is a little harsh, but what Dennis wants, Dennis gets. Nothing we can do about it, son."

I stared hard at the file, my blood chilling.

"Dennis said he made a rash decision for the good of the nation," Hank continued. "He wanted Calvin to bring the White Wolf in and stop a war from happening because of what Calvin said was going on."

Hank slid another paper towards me. My eyes widened as I scanned the report.

I regret to inform you that both Bastian and Shanely Fenrir were killed during the mission... There was a miscommunication with the clean up department... All bodies have been collected and incinerated. My apologies...

No autopsy reports. No bodies reported. No confirmed kills, I thought, gripping the paper tightly. *Dad covered his tracks.*

"Calvin rushed the order," Hank said firmly, and I drug my eyes back to him. "He ignored protocol and rushed the clean up crew before *anyone* could be confirmed or documented. If this White Wolf was truly as dangerous as everyone's saying then her death needed to be confirmed! Her mate's death needed to be confirmed! Otherwise, we'd be opening a whole different issue if we had a shifter with a broken bond."

Sweat coated my brow just thinking of all the possible trouble my dad just brought on us. *Shanely and Aerith were back at my place, expecting me to protect them, but if Dennis wasn't to blame for the pack's fall... Then who was I protecting them from?*

Hair on the back of my neck rose as Hank rattled on. "After everything your father went through losing Lorelei like that, I thought being assigned as a Head in his home town would do him good. For over twenties years, Calvin has never bungled a mission like this. Other than when he exploded on the poor janitor for clearing out Lorelei's office at Headquarters, he's never..."

"Wait, what?" I interrupted. My brows furrowed as I leaned forward in my seat. "What are you talking about?"

Hank gave me a sympathetic look. "It was the only time Calvin has ever been on probation with us. He was floundering at Headquarters and rightfully so. Lorelei's picture was everywhere and watching someone else take her job couldn't have been easy on him."

"What did you just say?" I asked in disbelief. My head began to throb as my mind ran amuck. *Hank had to be wrong. Mom didn't work at the Division. Dad told me...* I couldn't bring myself to finish that thought.

"She was the Head Scientist at the Research and Development Department in the Division back when it was stationed here. Her, Dennis, your father, and a few others, they all worked hand-in-hand together," he went on, "but when she died, your father seemed to struggle long after I got into office. I thought getting him out of Headquarters would do him good, and for years it had! He's been a loyal Head Officer for decades, which is why I don't understand why he'd put the Division in such a spot like this!"

Hank stood up in a huff all, while I sat there reeling. *My father lied. He lied about my mother. He lied about Dennis calling the hit on Shanely. He just lied.*

"We're supposed to investigate more than this, son. We're supposed to have a vote between the four Generals before something this big is decided," Hank muttered as he looked at the map of Diablo hanging on the wall. "I've got Dennis saying one thing, Calvin saying another. Dozens of possibly

CHAPTER 41

innocent people are just dead, and I have no idea why. My friend belonged to that pack, and I know Cain wouldn't do half the things listed here. Dennis is blaming your father for this, and your father hasn't taken a single one of my calls, so you tell me. What am I supposed to think?"

Anger rose within me. My father *yet again* lied to me. He took what little I knew of my mother and twisted it into some story. The longer I sat in silence, the angrier I became. *This is why he was so upset with me this morning. He didn't want anyone to connect the dots with what he's done. He didn't want Hank or myself to find out.* My mind drifted to the night I begged him to help me save Shanely. He listened so intently then, looking at me with pity and understanding, but it was just a lie. *A show.* Every word he said about knowing what it felt like to fall in love. To feel that strong urge to protect someone important to you. That he was just *grateful* I had managed to find someone that meant so much to me like Mom meant to him.

"Just because the pack has been sentenced to death doesn't mean she has to be..."

I clenched my fists at my side. *He didn't care. Dad never really has honestly.* The way he raised me, all the blame he put on me growing up, the inability to do *anything* right in his eyes... It all suddenly became so clear. *He has never loved me, and he never will.* For whatever reason, Calvin had an agenda, and I was going to figure out *what and why*.

Hank watched me with such scrutiny that I forced myself to relax. *He wouldn't stop until he fully understood what happened with the McCoy pack.* I could see that clear as day, and after seeing the file laid out before me, I knew my father did this for a reason. They needed someone to take the blame for everything, and I was *not* going down with him. I may have broken a law about being with a shifter, but I didn't do *this*.

"You're right to be suspicious," I said, crossing my arms and leaning back in my chair, "because all this was kept from us. From the entire task force. My father didn't tell us any of this."

Hank raised an eyebrow. "Tell me what he told you. Now."

"If I tell you," I said firmly, "then I need you to do something for me."

Hank scoffed. "That isn't how things work, Sergeant."

I shrugged. "I want out of Diablo. I want my team back, and I want assigned over another district as Head Officer. I'm more than qualified to run a district, and I'm sick of working for my father anyways. I don't trust him, especially after what you just showed me."

Hank studied me closely, but I held my head high. I didn't drop my gaze even though my own nerves were beginning to get the best of me. The way he looked at me now, so intently as if he could see what was really going on in my head, scared the willies out of me. But I kept my face calm. I inhaled slowly as I went over what I was about to tell him. All the half-truths I was about to give. Every detail perfect, while he contemplated my deal. I figured he'd tell me to stuff it or threatened to have me Court Marshaled along with my father, but to my surprise, he simply nodded once.

"Done. Now tell me what did Calvin say to you?"

And I did just that. I told him *everything* Dad told me about the attack and all the conversations we had prior to it, spinning it in such a way that it made my father out to look unstable. Like you couldn't trust a word he says. I just kept Shanely out of everything.

"Good lord," Hank said, shaking his head slightly. "What a mess."

"My team, sir," I reminded him, and Hank reached into his briefcase and pulled out a sheet of paper. He wrote something down and handed it to me.

"The team you requested are currently here with me in town," he said, and I nearly sagged in relief. *I wouldn't have to wait now.*

"I have to speak with your father today," he went on, "but for now you can make your way to Headquarters in Colorado until this blows over. I'll get you a district after that."

"What's going to happen?" I asked nervously. *Headquarters wasn't exactly where I wanted to take her.*

"Well, your father will be Court Marshaled more than likely. You will be called in as a witness, along with Dennis, and we will get to the bottom of this," he answered, and I stilled. *I didn't want to testify. I just wanted my family and I to be left alone.*

"Go," Hank said, pulling me from my thoughts, "go and head down, and

CHAPTER 41

I'll call in about housing. You can stay on campus while..."

"No," I said, my voice in near panic. Hank narrowed his eyes as I straightened. "I don't want to be anywhere near my father, nor do I want to see anything connected to my mother. I need a district, Hank. Please."

Hank softened some and nodded his head. "I'll make some calls and give you a district tonight, but you will have to come in when this goes to court. You understand I can't change that."

I nodded softly. "I'll fly in, but once it's over I'm leaving. I can't stay there."

Hank sighed and motioned to the door. "Take the team then. I'll call you tonight after I've talked to your father."

I placed my hand on the door, when Hank called after me.

"I know it must be incredibly difficult doing what you just did," he said as he leaned forward in my father's chair. "I just wanted to say I am proud of you, son."

My mind drifted to the only time I had ever heard those words come out of my father's mouth. Carrying Shanely into the house, Calvin looked so happy for me. I blinked furiously before giving Hank a nod and walking out of the office.

I left my boss and made my way further into the station. The fellas I worked with over the years smiled and waved, but I kept on moving. I was pissed. So pissed to find out how much my father lied to me. My jaw ached from how tight it was locked. I shoved open the door and walked outside.

I shouldn't be surprised really. I shouldn't be hurt because Calvin's never been a great dad in the first place. I can see that now. My whole life I followed in his footsteps just to please him. I actually thought since joining the Division that he and I were becoming closer. That he was actually *proud* of me. But it was all a lie. *Everything was a freaking lie!*

Shanely's words came to mind then. She wasn't lying when she it was Dad's fault. She wasn't wrong to lay the blame on us.

Dad allowed me to take Shanely and Aerith. He should have said no. He should have reported it when I asked for help, but he didn't, and that's what's concerning me now.

He pushed me to go for her. My own father wants Shanely for some reason.

Question is; what does he want exactly?

And why did he destroy the pack to get it?

Chapter 42

Aerith

Calvin dragged me further away from mommy. I could hear my mother screaming down the hall, but he wouldn't let go of my arm. *I couldn't help her...*

I pulled hard against him. "Please, let mommy go!"

He ignored me, and I was forced to follow him further down the hall. We went right, through a lab door near the elevator. The moment the heavy door swung open, Calvin tossed me to the floor. I scrambled to get to my feet as Calvin went to the large machine in the middle of the room. I ran towards the door and pulled, but it was too heavy. I couldn't get it to move an inch.

"I wouldn't do that if I were you," he snapped, and I turned to find his red eyes glaring at me. I froze as his Alpha power filled the room. A slimy feeling coated my skin, and my back slammed against the door to get away.

Calvin smirked as he stepped towards me. "I want you to sit down like a good girl until I'm done with my work."

The feeling grew stronger, and my chest burned in agony. I didn't know what to do. He was so angry and mean when Mama didn't listen, but I didn't want to obey him. *I wanted my mom!* I thought as my lip quivered. I was struck again by that invisible force. Fear took over, and I dropped to the ground the moment he took another step towards me. He smiled.

"Good girl," he said, turning back to his work.

My chest heaved in and out like it did earlier. I couldn't catch my breath as I watched him grab a small metal case from the cabinets below, and I shut my eyes tight. Mama suddenly appeared. Her hands slowly rising and falling. Up and down. In and out. I copied her, slowing my rapid breath until I settled down. I slowly opened my eyes, feeling that familiar warm feeling ignite in my chest. *I needed to get Mama out of that cell,* I thought to myself. That fire burst inside as if it *agreed* with me. *She'd know what to do. There had to be a way to help her.*

Calvin yanked the 6 vials from the machine. Each with a glowing gold liquid inside. He placed them inside the case along with a syringe before quickly clasping it shut.

"Let's go girl," he snapped, yanking me up by my arm. He pushed me forward, and we made our way back to the elevator. I forced the tears from my eyes as I heard Mama still screaming from the other room. I frowned as Calvin pushed a button, and the elevator doors closed shut. Leaving Mama behind.

"We're going on a little trip, you and I," Calvin said, adjusting the tie on his police uniform. "You and I will be making our way to Colorado, my dear. So from here on out, you will obey my every word. You will not speak unless I speak to you. Understand?"

His Alpha power touched my skin again, and my eyes widened. It coated every inch of me, and I rubbed my arms furiously, trying to get it to go away. It angered that fire inside, but there was nothing I could do to get it to stop.

"I said, do you understand?!" he snapped again, and I nodded my head. He smiled then. "Good."

Calvin pushed me towards the garage, hitting the button on the wall, and illuminating the whole room. My eyes drifted to the cage near the door. *The same cage Mama...*

I jumped when Calvin set down the case on the work table loudly. He tossed the key card and his office keys next to them, and my eyes widened. *I needed those to get to Mama.*

I wasn't able to get closer before Calvin grabbed his coat and tossed me one of Patrick's oversize jackets. I held it in my hands, wishing he'd come home early. I wished Patrick was here to help me.

CHAPTER 42

He'd help me save Mama...

Calvin's phone suddenly rang loudly. He flipped the phone open saying, "Maggie! Were you able..."

Panic flashed across his face.

"General Cartwright. It's a pleasure to hear from you," Calvin said quietly. He leaned against the table, staring at the back wall, and I took a small step towards the table.

"Hank, this is ridiculous!" Calvin cried out, causing me to jump again. He began pacing in front of the table. "I'm not ignoring you. I've been sick for weeks. Hasn't my son given you the message?"

He tapped his foot before snapping his fingers at me. I quickly put Patrick's jacket on then.

"Well, that was my fault. I shouldn't have given him so much responsibility, sir," he said, and someone grumbled on the other end of the phone call.

"Court Marshaled?! Hank, this is all a massive misunderstanding!" he snapped as he grabbed his truck keys. "Oh, did he? I think I see what's happening now, General Cartwright. I am afraid you've been duped. I didn't say anything like that, and I stupidly allowed my son to give the team orders. I thought he was ready for this weighty assignment, but this isn't the first time Patrick's been insubordinate. I shouldn't have..."

Calvin paced before me as I stepped further into the shadows. His face was becoming as red as his eyes, and my heart pounded in my chest.

"Why don't we call for a meeting now? I'll fly out tonight, and we can get everything out in the open," Calvin said, gripping the phone tighter. "Please, let's just gather the four Generals, and you will see who's really at fault here."

He suddenly stopped pacing, switching the phone to the other ear. "Wait, now? Like right now? But I'd rather meet with everyone at once, sir. Just to clear this whole thing up."

Calvin exhaled heavily as he looked to the ceiling. "No, it's fine. Of course, I'll meet with you first. It just this is all ridiculous, sir. I have been loyal for years, and I've done nothing but follow orders. My son has made a mess of things, and I just want to clear my name."

Calvin began to pace once more, and I carefully took another step. "Okay, sir. I'll fly out tonight."

Suddenly, he froze. Color drained from his face as he slowly turned to face me. "You're already here? In my office..."

The man on the other line continued to speak angrily, but I couldn't understand a word that was said. Calvin gritted his teeth. His eyes turned to a deep red, glaring at me with such rage and hatred, and something deep within me rose to meet it. I sucked in a deep breath, when I felt fur against my skin.

"I understand," Calvin gritted through his teeth as he stomped away. "I'm on my way."

He hung up the call, swearing as he did. I jumped when he threw his phone against the concrete wall, shattering it on impact.

My lips puckered as he took a step towards me. *Don't cry... Don't cry, don't cry, don't cry.* My eyes widened and fear took over as he gripped my arm hard and shoved me into the cage. The lock clicked into place as I rubbed my bloody knee and looked at him. Calvin pocketed the cage key before grabbing the truck keys again.

"Do not breathe a word of this to my son or you will regret it, Aerith. I don't care that you are a child," he snapped, kneeling down to my level, and I scooted further into the cage. His Alpha power hit my chest in full force, and I scrambled to shove air down in my lungs. "Do not tell a soul what has happened today. Don't even open your mouth to speak. You are to sit in this cage until I return, and then you and I are going to Colorado."

Calvin stood as my whole body trembled before him. I hated that I couldn't stop it. I hated that I was scared. A single tear rolled down my cheek. *My Daddy was never scared, and I had been doing my best to be brave and protect Mama.* But I couldn't stop him. Calvin just scared me.

My chest burned as he took one last look before opening the garage door and getting in his truck. I shivered as the cold air hit my cheeks and watched him back out of the space before the door closed again.

A loud sob escaped my lips the moment he was gone. I didn't want to cry.

CHAPTER 42

Crying was bad, but I wanted my mom. *And Calvin was going to kill her.*

I pulled my legs up, shivering slightly from the cool air as I cried. My arm ached, and I ripped the Band-aid off. It had stopped bleeding but still hurt from Calvin jabbing the needle in. I laid my head on my knees. *I needed to help Mama, but how? What would Daddy do?*

I slowly looked to the door of the cage as my chest burned again. *Daddy would break the cage. He'd do everything to reach Mama, and that's just what I was going to do.*

I pushed my back against the wall and kicked the door. It didn't budge. I was too small, but I quickly wiped my eyes and adjusted my body to try again. Everything turned crystal clear with a goldish hue as I kicked the cage again. Barring my teeth like wolves do, I kicked the cage again.

I was going to save mama.

Chapter 43

My leg had grown numb from smacking against the cage door, but I didn't stop. It was bending slightly on the side, and I kept going. *I was doing it. I was breaking out of this cage, and I was going to find Mama.*

Suddenly, I heard the front door slam shut, and I froze. My heart raced inside as I listened to heavy footsteps move through the house. *Please don't be Calvin.*

Patrick shouted his father's name in anger, and I let go of the breath I had been holding. He hollered through the house as fear crept inside. *He sounded angry,* I thought to myself.

"Shanely!"

"DADDY!" I cried out, shoving my sadness away. *My Daddy would never hate me for keeping Mama safe. He wouldn't be mad at me,* I told myself. *He would understand.*

I heard Patrick's steps grow louder.

"Aerith! Where are you!?" Patrick shouted again.

"I'm in here!" I cried back. My shoulders sagged in relief when he opened the door.

"What in the world are you doing in the cage?!" he demanded as he searched for the key on the hook, but Calvin took it. "Where is your mother?"

"Calvin put me in here," I said quietly. Patrick gave me a look of alarm. "Please, let me out!"

Patrick knelt down to face me. "Why did he put you in here?"

My bottom lip quivered, but I reminded myself that Patrick doesn't like

CHAPTER 43

when I cry. I forced myself not to cry because I needed him. He would help us get away from Calvin. He could help me get Mama out.

"Because he didn't want me to run away," I answered truthfully. I extended my arm towards him, showing him the bruise from Calvin. "He took my blood. Ran a test and said we were leaving tonight. He... he..."

Patrick looked alarmed as he gripped the side of the cage. "What did he do?" he demanded. "Where's your mother?!"

"He took her downstairs," I said, a tear falling down my cheek. "She's with my grandma, and Calvin said he doesn't need Mama anymore. That he's going to get rid of her because he has me. He's going to take me away."

I couldn't stop the tears then, and I hated I couldn't control my fear or my emotions. Patrick's look of alarm turned to pure rage, and I scooted further away then. I braced myself for him to scold me for crying, but to my surprise, Patrick merely grabbed a pair of cutters that were hanging on the wall and snapped the locks in place. He chucked the tool aside and yanked open the door.

Patrick extended out his hand to me. "Let's go, Aerith."

Wiping my eyes, I slowly took his hand and stepped out of the cage. He brushed the dirt off me before wiping my wet cheek.

"Show me where Mama is," he demanded, and I pointed to the key card on the counter next to the silver case.

"You're going to need that."

Chapter 44

Shanely

"I've let everyone down, Mama," I said, pulling my knees in as I sat on the floor.

I had no idea where Calvin and Aerith could be by now. Everything had gone quiet, and no one was coming to save us. She was just gone. All because I failed. I wasn't fast enough.

My legs were numb from slumping on the floor like this, but the pain in my back was nearly unbearable when I stood. I just couldn't bring myself to move or frankly even care. *I was never going to see my baby girl again. I deserved the pain I was in.*

"Shanely, that isn't true," my mother said softly. She slumped down next to me.

"It is," I said a little louder, draping my arms over my legs. "It's taken me too long to find a way out of here! We've been here for months, with no chance of escape! Every time I tried, I nearly got us killed, and now... Now, it's too late. Aerith is gone, and Calvin's going to finally get rid of us. She'll be all alone, Mama."

My mother sighed, resting her arm on my shoulder. "You did the best you could, Shanely. That's all a mother can do."

"It wasn't good enough!" I shouted, shoving her arm off me. "What sort of life will she even have? A slave to a monster until he decides to finally kill her too?!"

My mother narrowed her eyes. "Shanely, do you blame me for the life you ended up with?"

CHAPTER 44

My shoulders fell, and I buried my face in my arms. I knew what she was doing, but I didn't want to play along. I just wanted to wallow in this pain because it's what I deserved.

"Answer me, Shanely."

I sighed and sat up. "I don't blame you. Okay?"

"Exactly," she said softly. "Aerith won't blame you for this either. You have done everything you could for her, just like I did what I thought was right when you were little. We will always be able to look in the past and see the mistakes we made. That's the life of a mom, but I'll let you in on a little secret. A good mom will always make sacrifices for her children, but a great mom will go above and beyond to protect them. You, Shanely, are a *great* mother. This isn't the end for us. We just got to put our heads together and think of something."

My mother's word rattled my heart. *It just seemed so hopeless though,* I thought to myself. I shifted to my other hip as my stomach cramped.

"How?" I asked, wiping my nose. "You've been down here for over 20 years, mom. How are we ever going to find our way out of this cell?"

"I don't know," she said softly, "but I do know we will figure it out together."

Suddenly, the familiar sound of screeching metal from the elevator echoed in the room. *Someone was coming,* I thought as we scurried to stand. I clenched my fists together, shifting on my feet as I stared at the door. Waiting for Calvin to open the door to finally kill us. *That was not going to happen.*

"Whatever happens," Mom said, glaring at the door, "stay close."

I nodded once, and after a few moments, the door opened and in walked Patrick.

With Aerith.

My eyes widened. He stared at the two of us with a blank expression as Aerith ran towards me. I rushed to the door as relief washed over me. I had no idea what was going on, but it didn't matter. She was here! She was alive and with me again. *I have a second chance.*

Aerith laid her hands on the glass, smiling wide. Tears fell down my cheek as I smiled back. I turned to Patrick, who just seemed frozen. My brows furrowed as I tapped the glass. He didn't move, and my smile fell. I hit the glass again. *Look at me!* I thought angrily.

Patrick finally looked my way, and I pointed to the wall. He slowly walked to it, but his eyes drifted away from me again.

They were stuck on my mother.

He hit a few buttons on the console before the speaker finally turned on.

"Mama!" Aerith shouted as she smiled up at me. "Mama, I got help!"

She went to him? I thought to myself. I shook myself from those awful thought and gave her a smile before turning to Patrick. "It's the 3rd button, Patrick. Please."

"Who is that?" he asked in a defeated tone.

I turned to my mother then. "She's my real mom. Calvin took her long ago."

Patrick's gaze fell to the floor then. He said nothing, *did nothing*, but stare at the ground with a devastated expression. I nervously looked to my mother. I expected some sort of rage or anger, not *this*.

"It's true, son," Mom said, stepping closer. "Please believe us, and *please* help us. You can still do the right thing, even if your father hasn't."

My stomach churned as Patrick processed everything. I couldn't imagine what he must be thinking. His whole world was crashing down around him. Maybe he would finally do the right thing and let us go. Or maybe he'd still side with his father and not help us at all.

"Why?" he finally asked, motioning all around him. "Why would he do all this? Why would he lie to me?"

"Because I'm the White Wolf," I answered, giving him a pointed look. "He wants our power, Patrick. It's what he's wanted all along."

A scowl appeared on his face. A flicker of red in those pale eyes as he stared furiously at our feet. He was lost in thought, and I began to worry. *Patrick wasn't letting us out. He was thinking, debating on what to do now.* Dread filled my core then as his fists clenched at his side. *Patrick wouldn't help us. He'd chose his father's side yet again, but what else should I expect from him? He's never defended his own self against that man. Why should he*

CHAPTER 44

defend us?

Suddenly, he slammed his hand on the 3rd button, and the door opened. I blinked, staring at the open door.

"Mommy!" Aerith said as she ran into my arms. Relief washed over me as I held her close.

"Oh thank God, you're alright!" I said, stepping through the door. I was never more thrilled to be wrong in my life. I turned and held out my hand saying, "Come, mom. Let's just..."

Patrick pushed past me and shoved my mother back. She collapsed on the ground as he hit the same button and locked her back in.

"Mom!" I shouted, running to unlock the door, but Patrick blocked my path. "Please, Patrick! Let her out!"

"Stop, Shanely," he growled.

I slammed my fists against his chest. I struck him again and again, screaming every obscenity I could think of, but he was quicker than me and grabbed my wrists before I hit him again. With one swift motion, he shoved me backward onto the floor. Pain rattled my spine, and I gasped for air. Excruciating pain from my tail bone started creeping up my back, and for a moment I couldn't move. *God, I feel like it just shattered...*

"I came for you," Patrick said as the walkie on his hip came to life.

"Reporting in, sir," a deep voice said through the static.

Patrick brought the walkie to his lips then and answered, "Good to hear from you, Scott. Are you here?"

I rolled to my side to relieve the pressure, breathing through my mouth as it pulsed again.

"Two minutes out," Scott said. "Where do you want us?"

"I need you inside," Patrick answered, "but have the rest form a perimeter around the house. I don't know when my father is coming home, but I don't want him getting in the way. We're moving out tonight."

"Sounds good," Scott said. "Over and out."

"Please!" I begged as he strolled over to me. Tears fell down my face as I looked to my mother. The desperation in her eyes, the stress in her knitted brow. She looked as scared as I felt. I turned back to Patrick. "Please, don't leave her here. He'll kill her!"

Patrick ignored me. With one arm, he hauled me to my feet and towards the door. I tried to yank my hand free. I dug my feet in but good God, he was so freaking strong. My wrist felt like it was going to snap as he dragged me and Aerith upstairs.

But nothing hurt more than the hole in my chest. My mother was trapped in that room yet again. My heart felt like it ripped in two. Patrick would pull me from this house kicking and screaming, and no one would be here to protect her! My chest burned as the tears continued to fall.

We made it upstairs, and he forced me through the broken door. Aerith ran to the stairs ahead of us, and tall strangers dressed in black passed by the windows outside. Totes were already sitting in the foyer, and the armed Division guards were bringing more in. My whole body shook as my rage consumed me. *He can't take us away from her,* I thought, clenching my hands into tight fist. *I was not losing her again.*

The tight hold I had been keeping on my emotions was gone. I let go, slamming my fist against the side of Patrick's head. His grip on me loosened, and I swung again. Bastian suddenly flashed before my eyes, and I screamed, slamming my fists down on Patrick's chest again. *I was going to kill him...*

Patrick hollered, but all I saw was Cade. Then Elijah, Emmie, Cain and Cassia. I saw my father and all the pain he endured never knowing what happened to my mother. I couldn't take it anymore. I screamed again as my nails dug into his cheek, taking flesh as I struck again and again.

Patrick moved, faster than I've ever seen him before, and grabbed my wrists. He yanked my body forward, snarling the same way shifters did when they lost control, and soon I felt it. His eyes turned red, and his Alpha power coated my skin.

Patrick was an Alpha.

His hand rose, connecting with my face violently, and I dropped like a sack of potatoes. My eyes rolled. The whole room spun as I tried to find my footing. *God, I screwed up... I should have tried another way. I should have convinced him to bring my mother with us the same way I've been getting him*

CHAPTER 44

to relent on everything else. But as my vision cleared, I looked up at the new Alpha of this house. One I could not challenge.

"She is not my fight!" he bellowed as he stood over me. "I stuck my neck out for you! You and Aerith! That's it! I have no idea what my father's doing nor do I care. The three of us are leaving tonight so go upstairs and pack our things."

My stomach cramped harshly, I sucked in a breath as the pain engulfed me. He glared at me when I didn't move, but I physically couldn't. Not with this sort of pain. Patrick took a step towards me as the front door opened, stopping him.

"I said go upstairs and pack, Shanely," he snapped. He shut his eyes for a moment, taking a deep breath, and when he opened them again, they had returned to his normal pale eyes once more.

I slowly got to my feet. My face was already beginning to swell as I made my way to the stairs. *Another mistake,* I thought to myself. *How many more before I finally get myself killed?*

"The men are forming a perimeter, sir," Scott said, glancing my way. I pushed Aerith further up the stairs. "What exactly are we doing?"

"We've been reassigned," Patrick answered firmly. I slowed my steps at her door, taking a glance behind me. Patrick watched me closely, but he soon turned to Scott. "We're moving out tonight, but I need you to understand that you work for me. Not Dennis, Hank, or my father. Not any of the Generals. Just me. I need to move, and the girls need to stay a secret."

Scott gave Patrick a long look. "I told you when we took her that I'd keep your secret. I owed you, Patrick. The team and I are loyal to you and you alone."

"Good," Patrick said as our eyes met once more. I held my breath as he said, "because this whole thing is about to blow sky high, and I'm getting the girls out before it does."

What did you do?

"What do you want us to do when Calvin shows?" Scott asked, and Patrick turned back to him.

"Let him in. Dad and I need to have a conversation before we go," he said as he stepped into the other room with Scott right behind him.

"Mommy?" Aerith said, tugging on my shirt. Her eyes were wide with fear as she asked, "Did I do the right thing?"

My heart broke, and I gently rubbed her cheek. "Aerith, you were very brave today. In fact, you've been so brave since we got here. Your father would be very proud of you."

Voices sounded once more, and I opened the door to her room.

"Go," I whispered. "Get your coat and whatever else you'll need. Okay, baby?"

She nodded when another car door slammed outside, and I stilled. I quickly closed her door when I heard Patrick's walkie.

"Calvin's here."

Patrick stormed into the room with Scott right on his heels, and I quickly stepped back into the shadows. They didn't seem to either notice me or care, but I wanted to hear this.

"Well, there's dear old Dad now!" Patrick yelled as the front door opened. Calvin slowly entered the room. "Glad you're *finally* home!"

Calvin took one look at his son and then his broken office door. "You and I need to talk."

"Yes, we do!" Patrick snapped back. "But me first, okay? I've got some great news I think you're going to love! I'm moving out, Dad. Got promoted today."

Calvin sneered.

The laugh Patrick gave scared me half to death. *He's snapped,* I thought to myself. *He's officially snapped.*

"See normally I'd be standing here, hoping you'd be proud of me," Patrick went on, "but I finally figured out that nothing I do will make you proud. So I'm leaving."

Calvin didn't say a word. The silence that filled the air was awkward to say the least. Thunder clattered off in the distance, while the two glared at one another. I wasn't sure what they were going to do. The wheels in Calvin's mind were turning, and finally his glare shifted to Scott.

CHAPTER 44

"I see you've gotten your team back," Calvin finally said. "Throwing me under the bus has its perks, right?"

My jaw dropped. *That's all he has to say?* I thought as nausea crept in.

Patrick's deep laugh filled the room, and Calvin cocked his head to the side. I've seen Calvin abuse and walk all over his son, and Patrick's never said a word about it. But not today.

"Want to know what I learned today?" Patrick said, putting his hands on his hips. "That Mom worked for the Division and not where you said she did, and the Division only made the choice to go after the McCoy pack based on your recommendations just like Shanely said! You told me Dennis made plans to move against the McCoy pack because they merged with the Bear Clan. Because they were building an army, and because Dennis wanted the White Wolf dead! You freaking lied to everyone. You *lied* to me."

For the first time since meeting him, Calvin looked panicked. His eyes had widened, and he just stared at Patrick. Even I was surprised to hear him say I was right.

"Yeah, I met with Hank today," Patrick snarled, chucking the key card towards him, "and I found this when I let my daughter out of the cage!"

Calvin slowly knelt down to pick up the card. Thunder struck again, getting closer and closer to the house. I swallowed hard as I watched from above.

"Is the woman in the basement really Shanely's mother?" Patrick demanded.

Calvin straightened. "Yes."

"How long have you had her down there?" Patrick gritted through his teeth.

"Long enough, son."

"God, does the Division know about this?" Patrick demanded, rubbing his face. "I'm sure that's breaking all sorts of laws!"

"They do not," Calvin countered, "and if you tell them anything, then you will have to tell them about the little family you've created. Or have you forgotten that it's also illegal to take a shifter wife?"

Patrick snarled. Veins pulsing on the side of his head, and I held my breath.

"So, you knew who Shanely was the whole time? Is that why you were so willing to help me save her?!"

"Once I saw her, I knew exactly who she was," Calvin answered, adjusting the buttons on his shirt, "and what does it matter, Patrick? You get the girl you've been pining after, and I get to continue my tests."

"It matters to me!" he shouted, tossing his hands in the air. "For once in my life, I thought you did something *for me!* But you lied to me about Shanely, and you lied to me about my own mother."

Sadness filled his voice. Like he was finally seeing the truth of his father, but it was too late. *Far too late.*

Patrick rubbed his face again as he said, "You only helped save Shanely for your own selfish reasons, and why do you even need to run tests?"

"You have some nerve calling me selfish, boy. What about you?! You're going to stand here and call out my sins, when you were right there alongside me, stealing that girl and her daughter too!" Calvin shouted angrily.

Patrick's jaw locked. "You told me..."

"You are the one who shot her mate in Canada," Calvin interrupted, "which is the equivalent of a soul-mate, Patrick, and then you stole his wife and child! You really think you can just step into his shoes and carry on like nothing ever happened?! You and I are the same in this. Our reasons may differ, but none of it really matters, son. However, *my work does!*"

Calvin's voice echoed through the room. My stomach twisted into a painful cramp as I watched the two go head-to-head.

"I didn't tell you about this because I didn't *want* you involved! I am so close to finishing your mother's work and avenging my wife. Nothing and no one will stand in my way, and you already got in the way once before. I won't risk you screwing it up again."

Patrick flinched, and for a brief moment, I felt bad for him. *No one should ever be treated like this*, I thought to myself. *I wish Calvin had been the one to die than Lorelei.* Patrick might have had a chance with her. Calvin stormed towards the office then.

CHAPTER 44

"What were you going to do with Shanely and her mother?" Patrick asked, causing his father to halt in his tracks.

"It doesn't concern you," he snapped back.

"Aerith said you were going to get rid of Shanely and her mother. You were just going to kill my girl, and then what? Feed me some other lie about how she died?" Patrick demanded, turning towards his father.

"Keep your whore then," Calvin snarled. "I don't need her anyways, but I am taking the kid."

Patrick glared back as my heart plummeted. *No... He can't take her.*

"Oh no," he said firmly. "You are going to stay away from Shanely and Aerith. You have the freak in the basement. You don't need them too."

Calvin stomped towards his son, his fist clenched tightly, and Scott quickly stepped between them. Scott held the gun on his sling, warning Calvin not to take another step closer, and Calvin scoffed.

"So, you get your team back and think you're so big and bad now. Is that it?"

"Nah," Patrick said firmly, "not big and bad, just better. I'm better than you, Dad. I tested higher than you in the Division's Standardized Test. My time was faster than yours in the Academy, and I am officially the youngest Head Officer in the Division. I've been given this team because they see my potential. They *see* my worth. It's just a shame you don't see it too. But go ahead and keep insulting me. See what happens when *I* get angry."

"Don't you threaten me, son. I've worked for too long and too hard to get to where I am today, and I will see this through. Otherwise, I'll throw you to the wolves, and trust me boy, there are *plenty* out there."

"Seems to me you're not in charge of anything anymore," Patrick said as two of the men on his team carried a couple totes towards the front of the house. A silver case lay on top. "I believe you're getting Court Marshaled."

Calvin's eyes went wide, and he moved towards the case. "That's mine."

"Not anymore," Patrick said as Scott halted Calvin. Patrick quietly strolled over and grabbed the silver case. "The only reason my team even let you in was so I could have this conversation. I am leaving tonight, and I'm letting you take the fall for everything you've done to me. That freak in the basement..." his voice trailed off and a smirk slowly appeared on his lips, "yeah, I'll be calling that in as soon as we leave. You are going to be arrested for this, and Shanely, Aerith, and I will never have to see you again."

My eyes widened. *He was fighting to protect Aerith.* No one protected him as a child, but Patrick stood his ground for her, going against the one person he's never been able to stand against. *It would give me the time I needed to finally escape. A new location without those wretched plates.* My breath quickened as I realized the gift that fell in my lap. *We were getting out.*

Calvin stood there stunned. His shoulders fell as he said, "It was you. You're the one who called Hank in the first place, didn't you?"

Patrick snorted. "Nope. Wasn't me, but I'm taking advantage of it now. Feel free to shut the door on your way out."

His father's mouth dropped, and for a moment I thought Calvin would accept defeat. He seemed so startled that Patrick stood his ground and simply watched Patrick's team start to haul bins out to the trucks. Suddenly, Calvin's face turned beat red. Along with his eyes.

"You think you can bark orders at me, son?!" Calvin bellowed, and the Alpha power flooded the room. Scott twisted uncomfortably along with the rest of the team as I held my breath. "This is my house, and that is my case! Now hand it over!"

Patrick blinked. He didn't buckle or move a muscle. He didn't obey the command, and my heart began to race. Patrick's defiance only angered Calvin more.

Calvin gritted his teeth. "I said..."

"Aerith told me what was in this case," Patrick said as a new power filled the room. "I decided to test this myself. Have to admit, you created something pretty useful."

Calvin staggered backwards in pain. Patrick's Alpha power was far stronger than Calvin's, and I watched in horror from the balcony.

"I want you out of this house," Patrick commanded. "I want you to *walk* back to Hank and turn yourself in. You tell them *everything* except Shanely

CHAPTER 44

and Aerith. You don't say a word about them living with me or where they are. Until my dying breath, I want you out of this house, never to return."

Patrick handed the case to Scott. "Take this to my truck."

Calvin roared in pain, but he still took that step towards the door. I stood in the shadows, watching the Alpha command stick, forcing Calvin to leave. He screamed in agony, "I hate you, Patrick! I wish you had never been born!!!"

Patrick's face revealed nothing as his father screamed every hateful thing he could muster. He screamed so loud, it rattled the walls. Churning my stomach with every word. *How could a parent treat their child like this? How could anyone be so cruel?* I felt sick to my stomach, watching Calvin grip the door. But his feet moved regardless of what he wanted, and soon he was gone. The door closed behind him, and I let go of the breath I'd been holding.

"Start loading everything," Patrick said quietly, and I turned back to him. "I want us on the road in an hour."

Suddenly, a sharp pain shot through my abdomen, and I doubled over. It intensified like a wave crashing against the sea, and I slowed my breath as the pain ebbed and waned. I rubbed my back, when everything suddenly clicked in place. All the cramping these past few weeks. The nausea and back pain. *Oh God...*

I wasn't in labor with Aerith long.

I took a deep breath, trying to steady my nerves as the contraction lessened. *This was bad*, I thought to myself. *Like really, really, bad.*

"I take it you heard everything?"

I straightened, seeing Patrick just staring at me from below. His men were already in motion, trying their best to pretend they weren't listening to us right now. His eyes had returned to normal, but it was scary to know he even had that power. That power that was so sacred to shifters... Patrick owned it. I hated this man with every fiber of my being but... He saved Aerith and I. All I could see was a child who was desperate for help, but no one saw. No one saved him, and that wasn't fair.

He still hurt my family, I thought to myself. *Hurt Bastian.*

"I'm sorry I hit you," he said quietly, pulling me from my thoughts.

Nausea hit me, and I swayed on my feet, biting my inner cheek to keep from puking. Patrick gave me a genuine look of concern, but I couldn't let him know what was going on. He'd put me in his room and never leave my side. I had nearly everything I needed to get my mother and Aerith out. The only thing stopping me was Patrick and his men. *I'd figure out the rest as I went. There was no other option. We had to leave. We had to leave tonight.*

"Shanely?"

I blinked, not realize how lost in thought I was. Patrick had moved to the bottom of the stairs then.

"What?" I asked softly. I swallowed hard as my mouth wouldn't stop watering. It churned my stomach more.

"I asked if we were okay?"

I gave him a small nod, and although it may not be the response he wanted, he seemed to accept it nonetheless. It was all I could give him, because I didn't have it in me to lie anymore. I didn't have it in me to deal with him or any of this mess anymore. I just wanted to get my family somewhere safe.

"I'm going to get us out of this mess. Alright? But I *need* you to pack. There's a storm coming tonight, and I want the trucks loaded up as quick as we can. We're probably going to lose power pretty quick, so make sure Aerith knows so she won't be scared."

He forced a smile to his lips, but I didn't say anything. *Losing power would be a blessing,* I thought as I gripped the railing harder. I just needed to get past these goons to my mother below. Patrick sighed, starting for the door, but stopped. He slowly turned to face me again.

"Oh, and please just stay inside until I come get you," he said softly. "I am *trusting* you, Shanely. Even though we might lose power in the house, those plates run on a whole difference system with a back-up. They'll still fry you, even in the storm."

God, I couldn't catch a freaking break. I gritted my teeth as another contraction hit. My knuckles were white against the rail as I bit back a scream. Hunching over slightly, I exhaled slowly. Trying to breath through

CHAPTER 44

the pain, but it was too much. Everything was just too much.

The wind howled outside as Patrick opened the door. "Shanely?" he said, and I slowly lifted my eyes to look at him. "I won't let my father hurt you or Aerith. I promise."

With that, he left. Other than the men working in the garage, the house was silent. I exhaled loudly, groaning with the last of the contraction. *God, this was worse than with Aerith,* I thought as the pain wouldn't stop. My whole body pulsed with the rise and fall of the contraction, and just standing on my own two feet was difficult enough. My legs were jello, and the second the contraction finally stopped, I got to my feet and made my way to the bedroom room.

Patrick's police vest lay tossed on the floor with his wallet and keys on the dresser. The blankets on the bed were tossed aside haphazardly, and the closet and bathroom door were wide open. *It looked like a bomb went off,* I thought to myself. None of that matter though, and I scurried past the mess and opened the loose floor board. I grabbed the card to free my mother.

It was now or never.

As I stood up to leave the room, Patrick's large frame stood in the open door, and I jumped hard. His icy glare said enough. He was pissed, and I was no longer dealing with a unhinged human.

Patrick's eyes were red.

I just pissed off a very violent Alpha.

"So, you lied to me too?"

Chapter 45

"Patrick..." I muttered.

Goosebumps trailed my arm as I took a step back.

With two long steps, he yanked the card out of my hand and snarled. His jaw locked as he asked, "What exactly were you planning to do with these? Hmm? I'm curious the lie you're going to try to spin now."

I took a step back, shaking as fear gripped my heart. I couldn't think straight as he continued his approach.

"What else have you been lying about, Shanely?" he asked, stepping even closer to me.

I paled, scrambling to put distance between us until my back finally hit the window. He had me pinned.

Patrick grabbed my arm and shook me hard. He struck a nerve, sending excruciating pain into my neck and shoulder, and I couldn't breathe. His nose nearly touching mine as he shouted, "WHAT ELSE HAVE YOU BEEN LYING ABOUT?!"

"EVERYTHING!" I screamed right back.

His eyes widened, returning to their pale gray. Tears filled my eyes as I forcefully yanked my hand from his grasp.

"I've lied every day from the moment I stopped trying to escape. I don't care who's fault it was directly," I snapped angrily, "because I *blame* you. You killed my mate, Patrick. You killed my family, and I am *never* going to stop trying to get away from you."

My words struck home, and I saw more of a reaction from him now than when I made him bleed.

CHAPTER 45

Devastation coated his face as he whispered, "Why does everyone lie to me?"

Patrick's eyes suddenly flashed red with rage as his hand rose. With insane speed, he struck me across the face, and I fell to the ground. Warm blood trickled down my cheek from where my skin split, and I blinked furiously, trying to stay conscious.

I screamed as his rough fingers gripped the back of my hair, yanking me backwards towards the radiator beneath the window. My nails dug into his skin, trying to pry his fingers off me, but his grip was too strong. I was weak without my wolf, and he was a freaking Alpha now.

"Good girls get freedom, and I don't trust you anymore, Shanely," Patrick said firmly. He gripped my chin, forcing me to look him in the eye as he growled, "but I still love you."

Suddenly, he clamped a set of handcuffs around my wrist and yanked my other arm around the leg of the radiator. He snapped the other end down, securing me in place, and I was stuck. Utterly stuck and in labor.

Tears filled my eyes as I begged, "Please."

"I am not like my father," Patrick said as he watched me tug on the cuff. "I won't give up on us like he has with me. One day, you'll see. One day, you will finally accept us, and then we will have a happy life together. But until then, you're staying where I put you."

"Let me go, Patrick!" I shouted, glaring at him. "You want to be different from that wretched man? Then let me go!"

Patrick's cold dead eyes just watched me squirm on the floor. Without another word, he stood tall, chucking the card onto the dresser, and leaving the room.

I screamed as his steps faded down the hall. I screamed until my voice was hoarse. Hot tears poured out of my eyes as I bawled on the floor. *Everything was ruined! I had been careful for so long, and I blow it the night I decide to leave.*

I pulled on the cuffs, trying to snap them somehow, but nothing worked. My wrists began to bleed as my skin tore under the metal cuffs. *They were too tight.*

Another contraction hit. My back arched in pain, and there was nothing I could do to ease it. The pain shot down my legs and air escaped my lungs. It took longer this time before it finally passed, and I slumped over on my side. My chest heaved as I watched my blood roll down my wrist and onto the floor below. *I can't do this anymore,* I thought to myself. Another tear fell as I realized I couldn't do *anything.*

Curling into a ball on the floor, I sobbed hard. My body shook from exhaustion. I had nothing more to give. The weight of losing Bastian was too much to bear. I had kept myself from thinking about him for so long so I could stay alive. So I could keep fighting for our children, but I lost. I lost everything, and there was no getting out of here. Lightening flashed across the sky and was quickly followed by the sound of rain and thunder.

"This isn't fair," I muttered to myself. "I miss you, Bastian. I *need* you."

I let go, and my heart finally shattered. There was no more plan. No more chance of escaping. Everywhere I turned, Patrick was there. He was always there, and I had no more fight left in me.

I sobbed thinking about my mate and how much I missed him. I missed his devilish smile, and the way he growled my name when I was being a brat. I missed the soft kisses in the morning, the opened arms whenever I felt sad or stressed, and the late nights just being together in our favorite spot on the porch swing. His soft skin and perfectly messy hair. God, I missed him.

And I barely got any time with my fated mate.

Another sob burst from my lips as I curled in deeper on myself. *I don't know why I tried to escape in the first place,* I thought. *I wasn't Bastian. Or Cade, or Elijah. I wasn't them, and everything I do just ends in disaster.* I lost. I lost *everything.* I tried to protect my family, but I wasn't any of the incredible shifters in my family. I was just Shanely. Not the White Wolf. Not the White Bear. Just Shanely, and Shanely was pathetic. Lightening flashed across the sky once more as the storm rolled in.

Get up.

I blinked.

Get up, Shanely. Bastian said again.

CHAPTER 45

C'mon, Baby Girl. Don't give up now.

I blinked again, and the Fenrir triplets were suddenly there with me. I could see each of their smiling faces as they knelt before me. All three encouraging me to keep going.

My back ached again, and I twisted in agony. I squeezed my eyes tight as the contraction stole my breath away. Pain rippled everywhere, stealing what little energy I had. I slumped against the floor, when it finally ended.

"I can't," I whispered, feeling the heavy despair weigh me down again. The voice in my head that always tore me apart growing up was louder than they were. Always telling me I wasn't good enough, or wasn't smart enough... It continued to berate me now.

A tear rolled down my cheek, and Bastian leaned forward to cupped my face. I felt his warmth on my skin. His strong hands rubbing my cheek gently. The comfort it gave, only made me cry harder.

Get up, my love. You are stronger than you realize. Get up, and save our family.

Go, Shanie. Elijah smiled.

You are the White Wolf, even with this thing on. Cade said softly as he pointed to the inhibitor. *Your strength doesn't come from the Alpha power or your wolf.*

It's always come from here. Bastian continued, pointing to my heart. *And they can't take that away.*

So go. Elijah said, smiling. *And get this done, Shanie.*

They all smiled once more before fading from my eyes. I closed my own and took a deep breath. I forced that voice to be silent and inhaled deeply. *In and out*, I told myself. *In and out.*

"I am Shanely Fenrir." I gritted through my teeth. The rain fell harder as I wrapped my right hand around the cuff. "I am the White Wolf, and I am the White Bear."

I pulled hard on my left hand, trying to slip it through the cuff. Pain shot through to my elbow as blood seeped out again.

"And I'm not *wasting* my chance!" I bellowed as another contraction hit. I screamed through the pain and pulled even harder. I wouldn't stop. I *couldn't* stop. I pulled harder and harder, bracing my legs against the wall.

The wind howled outside as the storm moved in. Lightening flashed again, and I kept on pulling.

My warm blood soaked my shirt and the cuff itself. Suddenly, my wrist slipped through, freeing me, and I flung backwards. *Who knew blood was an excellent lubricant?* I thought to myself as I slowly got to my feet. I stared at the puddle of blood on the floor for a moment as lightening flashed across the sky.

Move, Shanely. Bastian said again, and I obeyed.

Wobbling across the room, I grabbed the key card. My vision blurred as everything seemed to hurt, but I continued to take that next step. *I've got to find Aerith,* I thought as I reached the door.

I turned the handle to leave the room only it wouldn't turn. I swore, quickly jiggling the handle in hopes of shimming the lock open, but it wouldn't budge. I barred my teeth as a thunderous boom sounded through the house. *The storm was right above us,* I thought, looking around his room for anything I could use to break the handle. *With everything going on, maybe I can sneak past Patrick and his goons?*

Patrick's ugly bed frame stood before me, and my gaze drifted to the hideous decorative tops. *I wonder if they're fastened down...*

I shoved off the door. My wrist burning in agony as I shifted the peg back and forth until it finally came loose.

Feeling a weight lifted off me, I slammed that chunk of wood against the handle. It took a few hits before it finally broke, and the door cracked open. A loud crack of thunder rattled the house just as the lights went out.

I rolled my eyes, shaking my head in frustration. *Of course, they would.* Blinking furiously as my eyes adjusted to the dark, I peered down the hall. Voices came from down the hall, and I carefully watched as Patrick and Scott walked out of his office and down the steps. They carried boxes with them.

"Tell the men to stay where I put them," Patrick said firmly. "My office and those plates are still active. They'll fry you despite the storm."

"Yes, sir. It is still safe to cross, right?" his buddy asked.

CHAPTER 45

"All Divisional vehicles are equipped with the correct transponders to safely cross. I've got others attached to the spare keys in my office if we need to take another vehicle," Patrick said, and my eyes widened. "I don't want to make two trips."

"Wouldn't it make it easier to just shut it off?" Scott asked

Patrick shrugged. "It was my father's request to have it installed. If he somehow gets passed the command I gave, then anything he tries to say about using the plates to keep Shanely locked in the house, I'll just dump on him and that woman. I've already wiped the footage of her and Aerith outside. Those plates need to be left entirely alone."

"I'm surprised your Dad didn't get fry when you sent him packing," Scott chuckled as he opened the front door.

"He's lucky he keeps a transponder on his keys," Patrick muttered quietly. "And he's lucky he didn't lose them again."

The front door shut, and I slowly turned, looking down the hall to the opened door.

Go, my love. Or this is all for nothing.

Bastian's voice pierced my mind again, and I realized he was right. I could get everyone ready with nowhere to go unless I had that transponder. Patrick was outside, but I had minutes to find a safe way to cross before he came back. *This may be my only chance.*

Move it, Baby Girl.

I rushed down the hall quietly and pushed my way inside. Everything was a jumbled mess. Papers were scattered about the floor and two more empty totes sat near the desk. The only lighting in the room came from his computer.

I searched his desk, desperate to find that transponder, but I didn't even know what I was looking for. I had no clue what a transponder looked like. I dumped the drawer. Nothing but paperwork and office supplies.

Rain pelted the house harder as I slumped into Patrick's chair. I was taking too long searching for this. Patrick would be here any minute, and my body was falling apart in pain. *The boys would be here soon*, I thought as I slowly turned to his computer. *Maybe I could shut the plates off in here?*

To my dismay, his computer was locked. I slumped back in the seat as my stomach twisted in agony with another contraction. I bit my lower lip hard, tasting a metallic tang on my tongue. I forced myself to breath through my mouth, praying the boys had a longer labor than Aerith did. Somehow in the back of my mind, I knew I was in trouble. Something didn't feel right. There was so much pain, so much pressure, and the nausea... But I couldn't stop. I had to keep moving.

I didn't want to waste time trying to get into the computer, so I shoved off the desk the moment the pain stopped. *This was a waste of time. I had to move before Patrick found me in here.* I stormed towards the door and stilled. Next to where the creepy shrine of me used to be was an opened box with a rack of keys inside.

And each one had a black key chain on it.

My hands drifted over each and every one before grabbing one at random. I turned the strange key chain over in my hand and found the Division's logo on the back with a small red light above it.

It was blinking...

For the first time in months, I genuinely smiled. *This is it,* I thought to myself. *Looks like Mom and I are stealing a car.* Snatching the Toyota truck key off the hook, I felt a weight lift off my shoulders. I pocketed it just as the front door slammed shut again.

Goosebumps ran up my arm as I bolted to the door.

"I need that cage in the garage loaded into one of the vans," Patrick said, and I could just barely see his dark figure by the stairs. "After that, all that's left is what's in my office. I'll replace the rest once we get settled."

"Do we have orders yet?" Scott asked, and Patrick checked his phone.

"Hank said Colorado. He's pissed Dad never showed today, so he's flying home and sending a team after him. I'm being called in as a witness to my father's crimes, but in the meantime, we're heading to a small town just south of Headquarters. Some place called Castle Rock."

Patrick's phone beeped then. He frowned. "Scott, send Mikey and Kyle around to the west side of the house. One of the sensors is going off."

"It's probably just the storm," Scott said, grabbing his walkie. "The worst just passed over us."

"I rather be safe than sorry," Patrick said, and the two stepped into the garage. I bolted to Aerith's room while I had a chance.

"Mommy!" she cried out as soon as I shut the door.

"Shh, baby," I said, covering her mouth. Pride swelled in my chest when I saw what she had done. Aerith was dressed and ready to go, going the extra mile to make her bed look like she was sleeping under the mountain of stuffed animals and blankets. I gave her a small smile and took her hand in mine. "Don't make a sound, okay? Patrick's still here, but we are getting out of here."

"What about Grandma?" she asked with wide eyes.

I clamped a hand over her mouth as Patrick's keys jiggle down the hall. We froze as his steps faded away, and I knew my time was up. I was about to get caught. His vulgar tongue pierced the silence, and the sound of a door slamming echoed the halls.

"Shanely!?" he bellowed, and I quickly scooped her up and bolted to the closet. *He'd come here next. He'd know I wouldn't leave her.*

Another contraction hit again as I buried us inside, and I doubled over trying not to make a sound. Aerith jerked away from my grasp, putting her finger to her mouth, as if reminding *me* to stay quiet. Her eyes flash gold briefly as Patrick opened the door.

"Shanely?"

But I couldn't tear my eyes away from Aerith. They were gold. *Shifter gold. Had her wolf finally appeared?!*

"Shanely!" Patrick snarled again.

I could just barely see Patrick through the slots in the closet doors, and the two of us didn't dare move. The bed flew across the room, crashing loudly against the wall as Patrick's temper flared again. Glass broke as he threw something in anger, and I bit down on my hand to keep from gasping in pain. He swore again as he checked the window. His radio sounded.

"Scott?" he snapped, pacing the room. My heart pounded so loud in my chest, I thought somehow he'd hear it. *He would hear me and do God knows what to us when he found us.*

"Yeah, boss?"

"Take your men outside and do another sweep," Patrick bellowed. "Shanely's bolted with Aerith, so that sensor must have been them. The plates are still active, so they couldn't have gotten far! Find them!"

The radio made a static noise before Scott's voice came through. "Done. Do you want us to check the house too?"

Patrick went to the door. "No, I'll search in here. Just holler if you see them!"

The door slammed shut, and I slumped to the floor. I was tired. So very tired, and the idea of getting up again killed me. I slowly pulled the truck key out of my pocket. *I had made it this far,* I thought. *Maybe that was enough?*

I looked to my daughter who watched the door so intently. *She was just like Bastian,* I thought. Aerith was just perfect. From her beautiful curls to her warm smile. She was so mature for her age. So smart and cunning just like her dad. *And she had a wolf.* A wolf who would guide her and protect her always. She and my mother would be safe.

Aerith turned to face me, and I looked into her soft gold eyes. My lips puckered. *My little girl.* I couldn't stop the tears that began to fall. *She'll be okay.*

"Are you okay, mama?" she asked.

I snorted out a laugh as I replied, "Shouldn't I be asking you that?"

I sucked in a breath as another contraction hit me. *I was out of time. They were way too close together, and soon I'd have to push.* The boys were coming, and there was nothing I could do to slow it down. I slowly looked to Aerith. Taking a deep breath, I took her hands in mine.

"I need you to listen to me, baby," I said softly. "Mama is going to take you to grandma, and then I'm going to send the both of you away."

Her eyes widened.

"But Mama..."

I shook my head. "No buts. Mama's not going to be able to make it this time, but I promise you I *will* find you again. You deserve to have a happy life Aerith, and Grandma is going to give it to you."

CHAPTER 45

She bit her bottom lip but never once let her tears fall. *God, she was so strong.* Stronger than I was, and I smiled again. *My mini Bastian.*

"Why can't you come with us?" she asked quietly.

"Oh, baby," I said, hugging her tightly. "I want to, but your brothers are just dying to greet the world, and we are out of time. So please, be strong for mama. I'm going to find you again, I promise."

Her eyes flashed gold as more doors slammed through the house. Patrick was losing his temper searching for us, and soon he'd come back to sweep the house again. I took her hand in mine and stood. *All we had to do was make it to the elevator. We could get my mother out, and they can escape through the fire exit.* Satisfied with my new plan, I gave my daughter one last smile before exiting the closet.

Everything was quiet other than the weather outside. I pulled Aerith from the room, carefully stepping around the spots that creaked loudly, and we made it to the stairs. We took two at a time as another contraction began. I leaned on the railing at the bottom, swearing softly as the pain grew worse. My body just wanted to collapse. I was so tired, but I had to keep going. *Just a few more steps,* I told myself. *That was all.* I just had to get to the elevator, and then they'd be safe. But a voice spoke to my left, chilling me to my bones.

"Hello, Shanely," Patrick said.

I *froze.*

Patrick blocked the entrance to his dad's office, glaring at the two of us, and I stumbled away. My heart thundered in my chest as I pulled Aerith behind me. But Patrick was faster with that power and grabbed my throat.

"I see why you're trying to run now," he said with a feral grin. I clung to his fingers, but they wouldn't budge. "Are my kids ready to come into the world?"

Rage burst forward, and I swung. He dropped me, clutching his face as blood seeped between his fingers.

"They are *not* your children," I snarled.

Grabbing Aerith by the hand, we shoved past him. My heart thundered in my chest as we ran.. *Calvin's office was right there. We just had to...*

Patrick's heavy frame slammed into us both, and we tumbled to the ground. He shoved Aerith to the side, gripping me by my hair, and I screamed. His radio suddenly burst to life. Screams and gunfire sounded from the other side, and I heard a roar.

Patrick swore as he yanked me to my feet. My heart thundered as I strained my ears to listen to the radio but static filled the air. I stumbled on my feet as Patrick pulled me away from the office. *Away from my mother.*

"You made a mistake doing that!" he snapped at me. Another contraction hit, and my whole body shook with the pain as the pressure began to build. *I need to push,* I screamed in my head. God, I was out of time... Gunshots rattled the house again, and Patrick's eyes widened.

"Scott?" he hollered on his radio. Silence filled the other end. "Scottie!?"

Patrick swore, digging his nails in my arm, and pulled out his gun. "I've had enough of this. We're leaving for Colorado now."

"Just stop, Patrick!" I begged. I didn't care that I wasn't able to fight my way out, and that I had been reduce to begging to free my family. "Just for once... Do the right thing, and let us go."

Pain flashed in his eyes. They returned to his normal color, and he softened. I clung to the hope filling my heart.

"Please," I whispered.

My heart seized when a viscous roar sounded through the walls, and we both turned to look. Gunfire blasted in the garage, and Patrick swore angrily.

"If we don't leave now," he growled, his eyes becoming red once more, "and find a place to hide you before this whole thing blows sky-high, then the Division will find you and Aerith and kill you both! I'm doing all of this to keep you and Aerith safe. I don't know why you can't just accept that I love you. I love you, Shanely! I can be the man you need, but you are going to learn to love me in return. To be appreciative of what I've done *for you.* If I have to beat it into your thick head, I will! You are mine, Shanely!"

"I don't think so," another voice echoed through the room.

A voice I *never* thought I'd hear again.

Chapter 46

Patrick paled as a lone figure emerged from the garage. Dressed in full tactical gear, carrying some ridiculously large weapon and wearing night vision goggles, the familiar man stood before us. Air had been sucked from my lungs as I watched this masked man step closer.

Shouting continued in the garage, followed by more gunfire, but this man... His gaze was firmly fixed on me. He lifted the goggles and piercing blue eyes stared back at me. I blinked as the room shifted. *It can't be though,* I thought to myself. *I recognized those eyes.* I staggered on my feet as Patrick stepped back towards the front door.

"Let her go," the man said firmly.

That voice...

I knew that voice.

Patrick swallowed hard. "I don't know who you are..."

"Oh, I think you do," the man interrupted, and my shoulders sagged in relief. *I wasn't imagining it. This was real. This was real, and he...*

"Let. Her. Go."

He removed his mask, and there was living, breathing, Bastian.

My Bastian.

"Bastian?" I said, a sob escaping my lips.

"No!" Patrick screamed. He shifted his gun towards my mate yelling, "You freaking died months ago. How do you *keep* coming back?!"

"You murdered my pack, injured my brothers, and stole my wife and child," Bastian snarled, his eyes flashing red, "but you *did not* kill me. Don't think for a second you are leaving this house *alive*."

Patrick stilled. For a heartbeat, nobody moved. Nobody said a word. The two simple stared at one another, and I wished more than anything to have my link back. To hear his voice inside my mind again and feel his heart beating in my chest. *God, he was alive! All this time... All this time I thought he was gone.*

My back arched as another contraction hit, and my knees buckled. I had so much pressure down below, but I couldn't push now. I sucked in a breath as the pain rippled through me. Only then did Bastian's eyes shift to me.

Patrick held me close, and I felt the stolen Alpha power leak into the room again. My heart stopped as Bastian snapped back to him. His brows knitted, but I blinked, and the confusion was gone. The Alpha I loved more than anything stood ready to move in a moments notice. *He was going to save us.*

Cold steel pressed firmly against my temple, and Bastian snarled. Gun fire continued in the garage.

"Not one step!" Patrick bellowed. "You made a mistake coming here. You should have just left..."

And just like that, the room erupted.

The four of us were tossed in the air as fire exploded from the garage. I slammed my head on something hard and fell into darkness.

Chapter 47

I jolted at the sound of more gunfire. Scalding heat licked my skin, and I groaned, lifting my hand to touch the wound on my head. Warm blood coated my fingers and horror flashed across my face as I took in the room.

The foyer had been obliterated, with a massive hole in the wall exposing the garage. Fire was spreading between those still alive, and I searched for my mate. Bastian was on the far side behind a fallen beam, and Elijah was with him. My heart thundered in my chest. He was alive, and Cade was mere feet from me. He clutched a wound on his leg, and my pure joy turned to panic. Blood seeped from a bullet hole in his right thigh, and gunshots continued to rattle the room. When Cade's eyes met mine, his shoulders sagged with relief.

I pushed myself to sit up, and my eyes widened even more. Aerith wasn't far from me either, hiding under a table from the chaos in the room, but as a beautiful wolf pup. *She shifted. My God, she shifted!*

Patrick bellowed as his power struck one of his men. The Division guard moved for me and Aerith, and my heart stopped. *My daughter was closer than I was... He was going to take her.* And when his eyes met mine, I knew I was right.

I shoved off the floor only to tumble in pain. Insane nausea hit me, and I emptied my stomach on the floor. I just wanted to collapse as everything hurt on my body, but my eyes drifted towards my daughter. I couldn't move. *I couldn't reach her*, I realized. *Not in time.* The guard took another shot towards my mate before reaching down and grabbing her by her tail.

"Aerith!" I screamed as she howled.

I jumped as a shot burst my eardrum, and the man holding Aerith dropped in a crumble heap. Aerith ran to me, and I wrapped my arms around her, turning back to find Cade with his gun raised. His red eyes met mine, and he gave me a single nod.

Patrick roared, filling the room with his stolen power, and my grip on Aerith tightened. I glared hard. *None of this had to happen... Absolutely none.*

Suddenly, Bastian and Elijah shot out from behind the beam together. My eyes widened as they aimed their rifles towards Patrick and his guards, taking the shot at the same time. Three shots each. My stomach churned as the bullet hit Patrick twice in the chest, and a final one in his head before he dropped. I couldn't look away. I couldn't do anything but watch as the man who couldn't let me go fall to the ground. The man who didn't deserve the things that happened to him but deserved the death he got...

He was finally gone.

"Shanely!" Bastian yelled as he dropped his gun.

He ran to me, scooping me up into his arms and squeezing me tight. Tears flooded my eyes as his lips found mine, and I bawled. I couldn't stop the uncontrollable sob that burst from my lips. I clung to my mate and soon another set of arms wrapped around me. Then another, and Aerith yipped from joy.

"Shanely..." Bastian said, pulling away to look at me, "I am so sorry. I came as soon as I could."

"I thought you were dead," I replied, wiping my eyes. "I felt the shot..."

"Nah, you can't get rid of us, Baby Girl," Cade said with a feral grin.

"Guys, we can remissness when we're safely back home," Elijah said firmly. The fire was creeping closer towards us, and my eyes widened. "Shanely, where does Calvin or Patrick keep their computers at?"

I pointed to the stairs. "Up and to the left! At the end of the hall is Patrick's office."

He nodded once. "Call it in, Bastian. We will have to flee in the woods."

"We can't go into the forest!" I shouted as I patted my pockets. *The transponder key was gone.* "There are these pressure plates..."

My voice trailed off, when Bastian touched my cheek.

CHAPTER 47

"I know, my love," he said softly. "Why do you think it took me so long to get you?"

My mouth dropped. "You know? Wait, when did you find me?"

"A couple months ago. We can talk more about it later, I promise!" Bastian said as the fire drew closer. "Elijah, can you shut it down from here?"

"Yeah, I just need into their network," he answered as the ceiling collapsed in the kitchen, sending a plum of smoke and debris into the room. The boys covered over Aerith and I, when I suddenly remembered my mother.

"Bastian," I bellowed, gripping his vest hard. "My mother! She's trapped here!"

My vision swayed slightly, and I could not get my heart to slow down. I struggled to calm down and tried to clear my blurred vision, but my eyes just felt so heavy though. All I wanted to do was shut them and fall asleep.

"Wait, what?! Your mother?" Bastian asked nervously.

I nodded my head, trying to shove the nausea away again as I answered, "She's in the lab in the basement. I was trying to rescue her too, but everything's just gone wrong."

Bastian rubbed his face as he looked back towards the kitchen. Worry lined his brows, and it was then I realized the pressure to start pushing had stopped. *Something was wrong. Very, very wrong.*

Cade knelt down and shook my shoulders. "Tell me where."

"No, Cade!" Bastian bellowed. "Your leg is wounded. Take Shanely, and I'll find..."

"Bastian, back off," Cade snapped, his eyes flashing gold. "We just found our girl, and you aren't leaving her again. Besides, I'm the only one without a mate. It has to be me!"

Bastian looked horrified with his brother. His mouth dropped open, but no words came out, and I couldn't help but wonder what was going on. *Something happened between the two of them,* I thought to myself.

Elijah snarled. "Now is not the time, you two!"

Cade turned back to me. "Baby Girl, I need to know now!"

I slowly pulled out the key card, grateful I still had that. I blinked, taking a deep breath as my vision swayed again. "This opens the door to her cell, if it's still locked. That room," I said, pointing towards Calvin's office. Cade followed my line of sight. "There's an elevator inside. Take it down, and at the far end of the hall is her cell. There's another way out down there too, but we never figured out where."

He smiled, taking the key card from me. I gripped his arm as he started to pull away and whispered, "Thank you, Beta."

I kissed his cheek, and he briefly held onto me. Not letting go as his wolf scented me. Cade's familiar woodsy scent permeated my nose too. *It felt like home.*

Cade pulled back saying, "I'll see you soon, Baby Girl."

Without another word, he took off towards the flames and disappeared into Calvin's office. My body shook as I watched him walk away. A bloody footprint with every step.

I turned back to Bastian, who's eyes were glued to the empty doorway. He had this look in his eyes I couldn't place, but I knew something wasn't right between the brothers.

Elijah shook his brother. "I'll hurry upstairs, Bastian. We've got to get out of here!"

Bastian nodded, and Elijah flew up the stairs. As he made it to the top, the wood suddenly groaned, giving way and collapsing into a heap of burnt wood and flame. Smoke and debris flew everywhere across the room, and Bastian dove to cover us.

It was so thick in the air, we couldn't hardly catch our breath. My heart thundered as I pushed Bastian off, searching for Elijah. *Please don't be dead,* I shouted in my head. *Please, Elijah!*

Suddenly, Elijah bolted across the floor towards Patrick's office, and my body shook with relief.

"Bastian, we can't stay here..."

A wave of dizziness struck me, and I struggled to keep my eyes open. Saliva filled my mouth, and I rolled to my side and puked again. A rush of liquid gushed from between my legs, and every time I heaved, more would

CHAPTER 47

pour out.

"Bastian..." I whispered as I slowly turned to him. My body felt weak, and I didn't have the energy to speak any louder. "I think my water broke."

I brushed my hands against my lower half, and when I lifted my hand, I saw red.

Bastian looked horrified. "ELIJAH, LET'S GO!"

I sat there blinking at the sight of blood on my fingers. *Blood. It was blood,* I thought to myself, cocking my head to the side. *Wait, who's blood?* Nothing made any sense, and Bastian pulled me further from the raging fire. My eyes were stuck on the puddle of blood trailing me.

"ELIJAH!" Bastian bellowed louder.

Elijah ran to the railing. I could barely see him through the smoke, but the room spinning didn't help either. My head drooped, laying on Bastian who's rapid breath made it hard to relax. *Everything's so hot in here,* I thought as my eyes began to close. *So hard to breathe. And where's Cade? He should be back by now.*

"It's done! Let me...." Elijah shouted from the second floor railing. He froze when he looked around. *There was nowhere to go,* I realized. The stairs were entirely gone, and the fire was spreading too quickly.

"Shanely's bleeding!" Bastian bellowed. "It's the twins!"

I'm bleeding? I thought. *No, I'm not...*

Elijah swore and launched himself over the railing, landing on the first floor with a hard thud. His face twisted in pain, and he made his way over to us, hobbling with each step.

"Your leg," I whispered.

"I'm fine. Let's get our girls out," he replied, picking up Aerith.

Bastian pulled me in close and made his way to the far side of the house. A relief unlike any other washed over me as we left the crazy heat. I inhaled deeply, filling my nose with Bastian's scent and taking everything in. *He was here. He was alive, and we were finally together,* I thought quietly. I smiled softly. I was finally back in my mate's arms where I belonged. That heavy weight lifted, and I just felt *free*.

"We need an evac now! Make sure Malin and Cassia are there!" Bastian shouted through a walkie attached to his shoulder.

The smoke was thick and heavy in this part of the house, but I still recognized the first room Patrick brought me to. Elijah set Aerith down and grunted as he struggled to open the window.

"This is *TheKing* requesting emergency evac from HomeBase," Bastian shouted in his radio again. "I repeat an *immediate evac* from HomeBase!"

Elijah swore before picking up the small night stand and slamming it into the window. It shattered, and he quickly knocked the side pieces off.

"Here give her to me," Elijah said, and Bastian passed me off. My mate looked out the window to the ground below and then grabbed Aerith.

"Okay baby," he said softly. "I'm going to set you down carefully. Don't run off but back away from the window, alright?"

Her wolf licked his face, and he gave her a small smile before dropping her a few feet to the ground. Bastian then climbed out.

"We're going home," I whispered softly. The corners of my mouth rose, and I let my heavy eyes start to close. It wasn't a necessity for me to hold everything in anymore. My body relaxed against Elijah, and I felt lighter than I had in a long time.

Elijah gently tapped the side of my face, and my eyes fluttered open. "Whoa, Shanely. Stay with me, alright?"

Loud static filled the empty space before a faint voice came through. "This is HomeBase. What's your location?"

Elijah grabbed his mic shouting, "We're inside Target One! It's up in smoke. I'll send a flare once safely outside. Send medic! I repeat. Send. A. Medic."

"Roger that. Is Death Walk down?"

"Yes, Death Walk's down," Elijah stated before passing me out the window to Bastian. The cold rain hit my skin softly, sending goosebumps across my body. Soon, I began to shiver uncontrollably as the rain soaked my clothes, my hair, and well... everything.

Elijah flew out the window, grabbing Aerith again. The worst of the storm had passed, but the wind still froze me to my bones. I tried to find warmth against Bastian, but I was too weak to pull my arms in, and soon

CHAPTER 47

they dropped to my side.

Bastian carried me further away from the house that had been my prison for so long. So long I had dreamed to run away. *To finally be free.* My family had survive against all odds, and we found one another again. *We found each other.*

"You keeping up?!" Bastian shouted as he shifted me in his arms. He lifted a small red gun to the sky and took a shot. Bright red blasted against the dark sky, and soon a second shot burst too.

"I'm fine!" Elijah snapped as a small clearing appeared.

"We see you, *AlphaBeta*," the voice on the radio said. "All assets accounted for?"

"Negative. A new asset was found, and *Tumbleweed* went for her. We have no contact or visual!" Elijah said as Bastian flipped a switch on his mic. My head fell against my mate.

"Cade?" my mate shouted. "Where are you! We have an evac inbound!"

Nothing but static sounded.

Bastian's eyes were glued to the burning house before dropping to mine. *He was torn. He didn't want to leave me.* I could see that, but it was an *easy* choice. *Cade needed help,* I thought quietly. *He and my mother were still in that house. They needed Bastian.*

I slowly lifted my hand and rubbed his cheek. His gaze softened, and he leaned into me before shutting his eyes altogether. I felt his breathing even out, and he inhaled deeply. I smiled wide. *I could still comfort my mate.*

"Go to him," I whispered. Bastian's eyes shot open in alarm, and I smiled again. "Go to him, mate."

His stern gaze held my own for a moment before he kissed my forehead and clicked the button on his radio again.

"Cade! Answer me!"

Static sounded again, and Bastian swore as his eyes flashed gold. His wolf was right on the surface, and I so badly wanted to see him again. To feel his fur and snuggle with him on the porch swing at my cabin again. *I missed his wolf too.*

"His bond points to the house," Bastian said firmly. His grip on me so tight.

"Don't even think about it. I'll go," Elijah said.

"You can't. Your leg's jacked up from that drop!" Bastian snapped back. "One of us has to go find Cade!"

The boys continued to argue around me as my body felt weaker. My gaze drifted to the night sky. It was so beautiful now that the storm had past. It didn't bother me that it continued to spit rain either. I just felt safe and happy. I was with my mate and nothing would ever separate the two of us again. I closed my eyes, listening to the world around me.

For the first time in a long time, I felt at peace.

Chapter 48

Bastian

"One of us has to go find Cade!" I snapped back, clinging to my mate.

I found her.

I *finally* found her, and this night could not have gone any worse than it already had. Getting to my mate was a feat on its own, but now my brother was lost in that God-forsaken inferno, searching for Shanely's long lost mother. *After the things I said to him... I had to find him. I had to make things right.*

My daughter somehow shifted and is too scared to shift back, and worst of all, Shanely started bleeding from her labor and God knows what else that prick did to her. The bruises on her face told me enough.

I could lose everyone right now, and that *terrified* me.

"Bastian, you..." Elijah snarled, when suddenly his eyes went wide. "Oh, God. Shanely, wake up!"

My attention snapped to her, and my mate's eyes were closed. Panic rattled my bones as I gently shook her face.

"Shanely?" I said softly. Fear gripped my heart as I shook a little harder. "C'mon, baby. Wake up please!"

I didn't even notice she went slack in my arms. She wouldn't move, and honestly I couldn't even tell if she was still breathing.

"Baby, you need to open your eyes now!" I shouted louder. I tapped her face, blew on her eyes, anything for some sign of life, but nothing happened. She was just limp in my arms, and my heart seized.

"C'mon, Shanely!" I begged. "Don't do this to me!"

I shook her hard now, but she still wouldn't respond. I looked to Elijah for guidance, but he seem stuck in a trance almost. His face was pale and taut as he stared at my mate. The only one of us who was always calm, always rational, *always freaking prepared*, stared at my mate like he had no idea what to do or how to fix this.

And that *freaked* me out.

I dropped to the ground and laid her on the wet grass. I swore loudly when I checked for a pulse the human way. I couldn't even use our bond to see if she was still alive and rage coursed through my veins. My vision turned red as my wolf wanted out.

I shoved him aside. I couldn't afford to snap and lose control again. I had no idea what I was doing, but sagged in relief when I found a pulse. It was very faint but there. *We were out of time,* I thought as adrenaline rushed through my system. The babies needed to be delivered *now*.

I dug my fingers in my hair, trying to figure out what even to do. I had never delivered a child before, let alone have any healing abilities. I was the one they called in to *eliminate* a target, not save it! I turned to my brother, who still stood frozen in the rain. He was smarter than the two of us. Shanely *needed* him.

"Elijah, think. You're the smartest one here. What happened!?" I bellowed, startling him and my daughter.

Elijah snapped out of his own freak out and dropped to his knees next to us. He shook his head shouting, "I don't know!"

"Well, think!" I snapped back. "Evac's not going to make it. What would make her bleed like this?!"

Elijah scrambled to answer me. I was putting too much pressure on him, I knew that, but I couldn't help it. I had to save my girl.

The panic on my brother's face finally cleared as he took a deep breath, and he quickly leaned over and put his ear to Shanely's belly.

"She could have ruptured her cervix or uterus," he said, switching ears and checking the other side of her belly. "Or maybe it's the placenta, I don't know! Look, Cade's not here, and I can't hear the twins. You have the best ears between the two of us. I need you to check on them!"

CHAPTER 48

I swapped spaces with Elijah, putting my ear to her belly and trying to focus. The rain continued to soak us and felt loud against her skin, but I could vaguely hear a heartbeat. *Just one. Only one when there should be three.*

"I can hear one, I think," I said nervously. My heart sunk as I lifted my head. "Does that mean..."

I couldn't even finish that statement. Elijah grabbed Shanely's leggings, and I shimmed to the side. A sense of calm had wash over him, and I sighed. I wish I had that, but my whole body was struggling to shift as it was. It was all I could do to keep it together.

"Don't go there, man. Evac's out, maybe 5 minutes, but it might too be late for Malin to do anything. Help me take these off," he replied, and I helped him shimmy off Shanely's leggings. The wet fabric stuck to her skin like glue, but we managed to yank them off and tossed them aside. Her soft skin was cold to the touch. *We needed to move faster.*

"Bastian, she might have ruptured her uterus or the placenta tore," Elijah said, and my heart stopped. "I don't have healing abilities, but I think we need to do a C-section regardless of what happened."

"You want to cut her open? Here!" I snapped angrily. My jaw dropped as I looked around. Rain still fell from the sky, and we were in the middle of an open field, and my brother's grand idea was to perform surgery on my mate!

"You got a better idea?! We need to start, and Malin's on the plane. She can finish this, but Shanely's weak. She's DYING!" he bellowed, and my eyes flashed gold.

"We could kill her..."

"She'll die if we don't even try," he snapped back. "Now, I started learning this stuff after Aerith was born. Look, it doesn't really matter. Just help me!"

Elijah yanked Shanely's shirt up and shifted his hand to his paw, revealing his wolf's sharp claw. I roared as he began slicing her lower abdomen. My wolf's fur appeared along my arm as I struggled to hold him back. Blood poured from her abdomen, but Elijah was steady. Steady and calm. I couldn't stop looking at her blood, and my whole body shook against the shift.

Elijah swore. "Her uterus ruptured," he muttered, swearing again. My heart thundered in my chest as I dug my hands in my hair, feeling more helpless than ever before.

Don't die, Shanely. Please, don't die...

"Bastian, I'm at the babies. You're going to need to wrap them," he said, without looking up. His hands were covered in bright red, and I shook violently at the sight.

"With what!?" I growled. *God, we didn't prepare for this!* I thought anxiously to myself. Frank's warning rattled in the back of my mind, but there was nothing I could do to go back and fix it. *I waited too long to save my family.*

"Bastian!" Elijah shouted loudly, pulling me from my thoughts. "Get it together! Just use your shirt. I'll give mine when I can."

I ripped the gear off my chest and undid my shirt. The cold rain hit my skin, but I didn't care. I was grateful for all the gear as it kept most of my shirt dry.

Elijah had two hands inside my wife's stomach, when I heard a loud howl. We both jerked to the left before Elijah snapped back to what he was doing. I barred my teeth, ready to shift in a moment's notice if I had to. With Deathwalk down, and Shanely bleeding like crazy, I didn't know what coming our way. The howl sounded again, and my shoulders slumped in relief.

It was Cade...

A sickening feeling twisted my stomach then. *I had forgotten all about my brother.* I gritted my teeth angrily as Cade howled again. *I should have helped him. I should have been there for him too!*

Suddenly, Elijah pulled out one of the twins and handed him over abruptly. I scrambled to keep him right side up in my arms before Elijah dug back in Shanely's stomach. He jerked her body around harshly. It looked violent, and I had to look away. *I'd shift if I didn't.*

I dropped my attention to my son and wrapped him in my shirt. He cried loudly when I wiped his nose and mouth with the corner of the shirt, and I

CHAPTER 48

sagged in relief. Another howl sounded, and I turned towards my little girl.

Aerith howled as loudly as she could in the direction we heard Cade. She howled over and over again, without even needing me to ask her to. My eyes widened as I watched her react just like a wolf should.

Cade had our bond to rely on, but he'd hear Aerith faster this way. I *needed* to see he was alright. During all these awful months, Cade's been the voice of reason. I needed him more than he realized. *Another thing to fix*, I thought to myself.

Elijah swore again, ripping out a massive blood clot from her insides. It rattled me watching this ordeal shake him like this. He was back inside's Shanely's abdomen, and I felt for the pulse on her arm. My wolf roared inside my head until I finally found it. It was nearly gone. She was *barely* alive, and my heart shattered at the thought of losing her like this. *I couldn't live without her. I barely stayed in control of my wolf without her.* I looked to Aerith and my oldest son then. *They needed her too.*

Cade howled again, this time louder than before, and Aerith howled right back.

I grabbed my radio, utterly pissed off with how long it was taking them. "HomeBase, where are you?!"

"Two minutes out, *King*."

"MOVE FASTER!" I bellowed into the mic.

Cade's wolf burst through the trees, with a small woman running behind him. Her steps were slow compared to my brother's, but my eyes widened as they approached. *My God, she looked just like Shanely.* Shanely may have Daniel's eyes, but she took after her mother entirely.

All this time my mate's mother was alive, I thought as they drew near. *She was alive and living here with that monster.* Cade shifted back as he approached. The wound on his leg still bleeding.

"What in the world happened?!" he asked, his voice shaky. I felt his wolf rise to the surface again as his eyes shifted gold but fear crept through our bond as he looked to his Alpha. The one he was supposed to protect. *His wolf will never let him forgive himself for this.*

"Her uterus ruptured, and we're getting the babies out now! Evac is two minutes out. Now shut up, and give me your shirt!" Elijah hollered as he pulled out the last baby.

My heart seized. *He didn't look like his brother,* I thought as Elijah turned him on his side. His face was bluish-gray, and he didn't move. He didn't cry. Cade removed his gear, taking off his shirt, and I saw the burn on his arm.

"Here hold him!" I said as I passed Cade the infant squirming in my arms. I took my other son and wrapped him in Cade's shirt.

A plane's engine sounded through the air finally, growing increasingly louder by the second, and soon we felt the wind whipping past as Frank turned the small plane around to land in the field next to us.

I focused on my son as Cade watched the plane carefully. I wiped his nose and mouth before starting to rub his chest, hoping he just needed a little help, but nothing would wake him. He lay quiet and still in my arms, and for the first time in a long time, tears had filled my eyes. I couldn't blink them away fast enough and turned to my brother.

"Elijah, what's wrong?" I asked. Fear creeping in my voice as I looked from him to my mate.

"I think he was trying to be born first and had oxygen cut off from him," Elijah answered as he pulled out another massive clot from my mate's stomach. He snarled through his teeth when she bled more. "I can't focus right now, Bastian! You two start CPR or something! Shanely's bleeding like crazy, and I can't answer a thousand questions. I just..."

Elijah pulled clot after clot from her abdomen, blood seeping with each swipe, and I had to look away. I couldn't watch with how rough he seemed with her. Her whole body jolted with every moment from him, but I trusted him to save her, so I turned back to my son.

I started trying to do CPR, but he was so small, I wasn't sure if I was even doing this right. I blew into his mouth and pressed on his chest. I counted to the beat of that awful song, like we had learned all those years ago in school, and I even tried blowing on his little face again. *Anything* to get a response.

Cade swore, but I wasn't going to stop. I refused to give up and let my

CHAPTER 48

son go.

"Plane's landed," Cade said quietly.

"I have to remove her uterus. It's in shreds," Elijah muttered as shouting ensued. I had never been more grateful to have such a massive family.

"Let me through!" Malin screamed as she slid into Elijah. Her hands immediately went to Shanely, and I saw them shimmer white against her skin. Cassia was by my side now, her hands on my son's chest.

"It's his heart, Bastian," she said, her eyes glowing. "Hang on."

A sob nearly escaped my lips as color started to slowly return to his little body and face. The umbilical cord pinched itself, sealing off as the rest fell away from him, and I smiled gratefully to Shanely's aunt. *Cassia never stopped amazing me.*

Suddenly, my boy jerked in my arms and started crying. My hand covered my mouth as pure joy filled my heart. It was the greatest sound I had ever heard, and I let the tears fall, utterly grateful I wouldn't have to bury anyone. *Somehow, we all made it through,* I thought before my smile fell. *Almost everyone.*

Cassia gave me a kiss before turning to my other son. She took care of his umbilical cord like his brother before making her way to my mate.

Abraham had wrapped a large blanket wrapped around Aerith before turning to me asking, "You three okay?"

I nodded as the corners of my mouth rose, giving him a peek at my son squirming in my arms. I wiped my eyes, gaining my composure as my brother-in-law smiled at me. He smacked my back reassuringly before looking at his sister.

"Abraham?"

Abe's head snapped to the woman standing back from everyone. I had completely forgotten about Mercedes. She was so quiet standing behind everyone, but I should have warned him. Abe struggled to breathe as the rest of our group noticed her. I didn't think to warn anyone, and my mind drifted to Daniel back home.

"Oh, my God," Cassia said softly. Her eyes filled with tears, and I gave her a small nod when she looked at me. Abe carefully stood before stepping towards her.

"You..." he said softly. "You look just like Shanely."

Mercedes bawled before slamming into him. Her arms wrapped around his waist and squeezed tight enough to cut him in half. Abe tensed at first, but he quickly hugged her back.

"Abraham, I need this bracelet off her now!" Malin shouted, and he pulled away from his long-lost mother.

He grabbed Shanely's arm and put the key in. How he managed to get a key for these inhibitors, he still hasn't told me, but I was grateful for everything he did for us. Abe was the reason my brothers and I had the plane and gear for tonight. He got us everything, and I will never be able to repay him for it. I owed him the greatest debt.

Shanely's bracelet fell off, and our bond snapped forcefully in place. No delay or wait this time. It just *came* back, knocking the wind out of me, and my left hand shot out to catch myself.

Thump-thump. Thump-thump.

Shanely's heartbeat grew stronger by the second, and a smile spread across my face. For the first time in months, my animals relaxed. They felt as happy as I did, and my mind finally cleared. I felt like my old self, and I slowly looked to my mate. *My strong, brave mate.* Her shifter abilities were returning, and I had never been more grateful she gained swift healing.

Abraham took the bracelet off Mercedes, who about fell over when her wolf returned. I bet Daniel was in a full on freak out back at base. *Cain would have to handle it,* I thought to myself. *I was giving my sole attention to my family and no one else.*

Suddenly, hairs on the back of my neck rose, and my wolf perked up. A strong Alpha was in our presence, and I slowly looked to Mercedes. She was on her knees panting, and I watched her closely. *Was this her? Daniel wasn't lying when he talked about her,* I thought to myself. She didn't come close to my mate, but she definitely would have been stronger than me before bonding to Shanely.

Suddenly, a loud voice boomed through the clearing.

"How dare you?!" Calvin snarled, aiming his gun right at me.

CHAPTER 48

I snarled viciously as everything in my vision turned red. My hand drifted to the holster on my hip, but it was empty. Anger coursed through me as I realized I had none of the weapons I brought. *I must have dropped them in the house, reverting back to my old ways once I found her.*

Calvin took another step forward snarling, "You can't take them! I'm too close, and you are ruining everything!"

My brothers and I snarled again. *This was the last prick left on my list of those to kill.* His knuckles were white against the gun in his hand. He had *no idea* what he had just done though. Calvin willingly walked to his death because nothing was going to stop my wolf this time. *I would kill him even if he shot me in the process.*

Cassia turned to me. "Give me the boys."

Cade and I quickly passed them off and shifted with Abraham. Calvin's eyes went wide as his gun shifted from me to my brothers. But then they turned red, and I stilled. *He had the Alpha power too*, I realized before shaking out my arms. *It didn't matter though. I was going to kill him regardless of the stolen power.*

I stalked towards him, snarling as he pointed the gun back on me. *Go ahead, you dick. And see how fast I rip out your throat.* I had dreamed about this moment since they took Shanely and slaughtered half my pack.

I was going to enjoy this.

"How many do you think will die before you reach me, Bastian?!" he screamed, grinding me to a halt.

"He made a mistake coming back here," Cade said through the link. I barred my teeth.

"Whatever drew him in just saved us a trip," Abraham snarled, snapping his jaws. I took another step.

"He's not leaving here alive," I said to everyone here.

"Calvin Jennings," Elijah snarled as he stepped between Cade and I. "You have committed crimes against the McCoy pack and the nation of Shifters by stealing our White Wolf and murdering members in our pack. You have stolen the Alpha power and have broken the laws we have established between shifters and the Division. Due to the nature of your crimes, *we are* in charge of handling your sentence. As Beta to the Head Alpha, I hereby sentence you to death!"

I howled, agreeing with everything my brother said, and soon the others followed. Calvin held his breath as we glared at one another. Barring my teeth, I took a step towards him.

"You have ruined everything. You and my son," he finally said. His hand shaking as I took another step, and his eyes narrowed on mine. "I should have just killed her when I had the chance."

My eyes widened when he shifted the gun and aimed right at Shanely's head. My feet were moving as Calvin squeezed the trigger. I dove towards my mate, my heart thundering in my chest as the gunshot rippled through the air. My brothers were already racing towards the prick, while I waited for the bullet to strike, but everyone came to a grinding halt when a burst of power shot past everyone.

My brothers skidded to a stop on the muddy ground, and my eyes widened when Mercedes stepped forward with her hands extended out before her. Her eyes were solid white when she glanced my way, sending chills down my spine. Slowly, she looked back to Calvin.

He screamed outside the wall, and my eyes narrowed. I shifted back, taking a look around us. We were stuck inside a white dome. No sound came through the barrier. Not even the rain or wind came through the white wall that Mercedes cast out. I watched Calvin unload his entire clip to no avail. I couldn't believe my eyes. *I had never seen anything like this before in my life.*

"Oh my God," Cassia said in awe. "She's a shield!"

A shield... I had *never* seen a shield in real life before. Not like this. The term has come up with Aerith, but this was entirely different. This was a *rare* ability.

Mercedes took a step forward as Calvin slammed his fists against the shield. Her hair had begun to float around her face, but she held the shield, not wavering once.

Calvin had officially snapped. He tore clumps of hair from his scalp, crying hysterically as he screamed at us. He roared outside, and I had had

CHAPTER 48

enough watching him throw a tantrum. I turned to Cade, who nodded once and moved to stand over my mate before walking towards the man who caused so much damage to my family.

Mercedes raised her arm, blocking me from moving any further. A low growl emitted from deep within as my wolf grew pissy with her getting in our way, but she slowly looked to me unafraid. From the look she gave, I knew the words coming before she ever uttered them.

"He's mine," she said softly.

With that, she snapped her hands shut, killing the shield entirely. Calvin flew forward harshly. He piled it into the mud, but my eyes were on my mother-in-law. Mercedes fell into the shift, and my God, she gave *me* a run for my money. She was massive and solid black just like the rest of her family. Her wolf was so dark, it was actually hard to see her wolf against the night sky.

Calvin's eyes widened as her wolf dug its paws in the dirt and lunged. His screams echoed throughout the woods momentarily before the only sounds were his body being torn to shred. I looked away and left Mercedes to her kill.

It was done. The threat to my family was finally gone.

"Bastian," Malin shouted, and I turned to face her. "I've closed her wound! Let's get them out of here!"

I knelt down to grab Shanely. Cade grabbed one of my boys, while Elijah grabbed the other. Abraham took Aerith, and we made our way to the plane in silence. I was ready to get home. I was ready to finally bring my family home.

But as I watched my brothers carry my children to the plane, guilt ate me up inside. Both Cade and Elijah winced with every step. Elijah was covered in my mate's blood and looked utterly gruesome, while Cade's arms looked blistered and red. *Both were injured. Both nearly died tonight.* I knew I could never repay them for this. I couldn't repay anyone tonight. I was forever in their debt because there was nothing that could ever make up for what they did tonight. My family was finally safe, and it was because of their sacrifice and their love that got them out.

I was so anxious to get them home. To right the wrongs I've done since losing them and give everything I had to erase the heartache and pain from their memories. I knew some of what they went through, and I will never forgive myself for losing them in the first place. Gently moving a stray hair off my mate's face, I turned to find Malin approaching.

"Thank you," I said, kissing her cheek, "for everything."

Malin patted me on the back as she stepped onto the plane. "Anytime, Alpha."

I let my brothers go on first, making sure everyone was accounted for when Cassia hollered for me.

"Bastian!" she shouted. I turned to find her mere feet from Mercedes who was still lost in her kill. My eyes widened at the bloody sight. Cassia slowly turned back to me. "I may need your help."

She's feral, I thought as I slowly made my way back. Her wolf was shredding what was left of Calvin's body. Just utterly destroying him to the point you couldn't even tell *whose* body it was. *Was this how I looked when Cade found me?* I wondered as those memories gnawed at my stomach. I had no desire to get close to that massacre, but I was Alpha here, and this was my responsibility.

"Mercedes..." Cassia said firmly, "it's time to go now."

Mercedes didn't respond. Her wolf continued to tear Calvin apart. My stomach twisted when his arm flung across the field, and Cassie looked to me nervously. *Daniel wasn't here*, I thought nervously as I tried to rack my brain with the options I had at present. I wasn't sure if Mercedes had lost complete control or not, but without her mate, she may not listen to me. *She may not listen to any of us.*

Could my command even stick to a feral wolf? That question rattled my brain. I had never once tried, and Shanely was stronger than I was. Her command would weigh heavier than mine, but she lay unconscious in my arms. My lips pursed together as I looked back to Cassia. Her grim expression said exactly what I was thinking. *If I couldn't pull Mercedes back, we were going to have a feral wolf on our hands, and the town of Rockport surrounded us.*

CHAPTER 48

I sent the link out to Abraham. *"I need you."*

"Mercedes, please!" Cassia begged. "Shift back!"

Her snout was red and dripping with blood as she ignored Cassia. Calvin's guts slid out onto the dirt, churning my stomach when the fowl smell hit my nose, and she clawed his chest again. Cassia gave me another look frowning. *Mercedes had been disconnected from her other half for too long. Lost to being a balanced shifter, and I didn't know if she'd let Mercedes switch back.*

Cassia turned to me saying, "Shanely's unconscious, so it's up to you. It's why you both take the responsibility."

I turned back to the large wolf as the plane's engine roared to life. I sighed heavily. *This was going to suck.*

"Mercedes!" I said with a loud commanding voice. My Alpha power snapped forward, and I directed it right at her. Her own power was strong and worry filled my chest. *Her wolf may only see a challenge or another threat,* I thought as I shifted Shanely in my arms. *Where was Abraham??* I needed to pass my mate off, so I could corral her mother. *She may not be willing to submit to her King.*

Her wolf shuddered, and she dropped the body. Her ears picked up, turning towards me then, and I straightened my stance. She snarled, stepping towards me, but I held my ground. I didn't look away from her, and she barred her teeth at me. I barred mine right back. *Don't do this, Mercedes,* I thought to myself. *Don't force me to hurt you.*

"Bastian..." Cassia said worriedly. She took a step behind me.

"I am your King," I yelled loudly, "and I command you to shift now!"

Her wolf shuddered under the power I sent her way. Her jaws snapped wildly, and I gritted my teeth when she fought my command. *Nothing was ever freaking easy.*

"ABE!"

"I'm coming!" he bellowed.

"Shift now!" I commanded again. I hit her with the full force of my Alpha power this time, and her wolf stumbled. She fought the shift, trying to stay in control, so I hit her again. It forced her to the ground, and my anxiety grew.

"Bastian!" Cassia hollered, her voice shaking. "You're hurting her!"

"If I let her go," I snapped as I continued to send my power out, "she may bolt or worse, charge me with Shanely still in my arms. I can't stop!"

The sloshing sound of heavy steps sounded, and Abraham finally showed up.

"I'm here," he said, opening up his arms. "Give her to me."

I passed my mate to him, hating every second I was forced to let her go. *Now my wolf was pissed,* I thought as I squared up to my mother-in-law.

"Your daughter needs you, Mercedes!" I shouted, praying my words made it to the woman inside. "Your mate is waiting back at base, and he *needs* you. Get control of your wolf and shift back!"

I relented some, hoping she'd get control of her wolf again, but to my dismay, Mercedes snarled.

"Bastian!" Cassia yelled as Mercedes charged.

I shifted to meet her halfway. I clashed with her wolf, snarling and growling in anger. *This was ridiculous. We were shifters. We were family!* I thought as the two of us rolled on the ground.

"What in the world is going on out here?!" Elijah yelled.

"Call Daniel!" Cassia hollered. "We need him!"

I held Mercedes's wolf back, trying hard not to put lasting wounds on her, but God she was strong. Her jaws snapped wildly, dripping blood from her last victim, and I quickly shoved her back. She slid in the mud as I tried the command again.

"Mercedes, shift now!"

Her wolf barred its teeth, shaking violently as it fought the command once more. Mercedes's normal eye color returned, only to flash red again. She was fighting her wolf. She was trying to take back control over her body, but the disconnect had ruined everything.

Suddenly, a tiny howl sounded through the air. My eyes widened when Aerith stood close by, howling towards the moon as loud as she could go. Abraham turned to me with wide eyes as I bolted towards her.

Aerith took a step and howled again. Mercedes stilled. Her wolf's ears

CHAPTER 48

relaxed as she looked to my daughter. Aerith howled again, and Mercedes's red eyes turned human once more. Shock rippled through me as I watched her fight for control. Her wolf whined, shaking violently before slowly dragging her eyes to me. *Such sorrow and pain shown within*, I realized. *She needs more than this.* So I shifted, pulling every ounce of power back to me and took a step towards her. Then another until I was nothing more than a few feet away.

"Bastian..." Elijah growled, but I ignored him.

"You will never be caged again," I said softly, placing my hand on her shoulder. "I promise, you are free."

Her wolf whined before Mercedes finally shifted, dropping to her knees in the mud. Her chest heaved from the pain, and I swore quietly to myself. *This took too much out on her too.*

"Switch me!" Abe cried out, and I took Shanely from his arms. Abraham bent down and carefully picked up his mother.

Suddenly sirens sounded in the distance.

"Let's get out of here!" Elijah bellowed, pushing Cassia towards the plane as Aerith bounded after her. "And next time you challenge another Alpha, will you let me know?! I'm your freaking Beta after all."

A feral grin crept up my face as I raced towards the plane. Cade had both twins in his arms, raising an eyebrow when we stepped inside.

"We're good," I said, collapsing next to him.

Elijah took my second born and settled on my other side. I let out a heavy sigh as the plane hatch closed. *It was over*, I thought, leaning my head back. *It was finally over.*

"All accounted for?" Frank asked through the intercom.

"Roger that," Elijah replied. "Take us home, Frank."

Chapter 49

"I think he peed on me," Cade muttered.

Everyone chuckled softly as Cade lifted my oldest away from him. The smell of urine filled the truck, and I scrunched my nose, grinning wide.

"Yeah, he definitely did," Elijah muttered. I couldn't contain my laughter then, and Cade shot me an annoyed looked. It only made me laugh harder, and soon everyone began to laugh with me. It didn't take long before he was laughing too.

"Just wait, little one," Cade muttered. "The second you're old enough, pay back is coming."

I gave my brother a feral grin as the plane's intercom buzzed to life.

"Hang tight, everyone," Frank said. "We're not far now."

I pulled my mate close, inhaling her scent deeply as I gazed upon everyone. This was the happiest I had seen them in a long time. *Shoot, this was the happiest I felt in a long time.*

We, as a group, had been though a lot, but they never left my side in this whole ordeal. Not once. No matter the foul mood I was in or the discomfort of hiding out in Dead Man's Hallow after the attack, they stayed by my side, making sure I was never too far gone. Handling the things that I could not.

I stole a glance to my brothers too, thinking how far they went to help me. *To help her.* Elijah sacrificed so much even at the cost of his own relationship to help me and my Shanely. If it wasn't for his big brain, my mate would be dead. No one would have gotten out of there alive with that death trap still running, and I hoped one day I could return the favor in a grand way. Maybe fixing things with Emmie would be good start.

CHAPTER 49

I looked to my baby brother then. *I would be lost if it wasn't for Cade.* His quick thinking pulled me from the depths of despair, and he has no idea how much he meant to me. How important he truly is. *Another thing I needed to fix,* I thought. Cade slowly grinned down at my baby boy, reaching out with his bloody hand to gently touch his. *He's really grown into his own.* I can't remember the last time I had to step in to help him honestly. His mouth usually got him in trouble but now... He didn't need me. Not like that, and I doubted if he ever would again.

Elijah chuckled softly as he gently rubbed Aerith's head. My brother's bloodshot eyes showed pure exhaustion, and after all the stress we'd gone through trying to reach my mate in the first place, I truly didn't know if they'd ever return to normal. While Cassia forced me to sleep, Elijah stayed up night after night, trying to get into Calvin's network. He shouldered blame that shouldn't be there. Honestly, we all did. I had heard it all from everybody over these last few months. *I should have done this. I should have done that.* We all carried guilt, and I didn't expect that to change anytime soon.

Shanely twitched in my arms, settling right back down again, and I snorted out a laugh. *Some things never change,* I thought to myself as I kissed her forehead.

Aerith was fast asleep between Elijah and I. Sprawled out with her belly in the air, and I smiled as I watched her sleep. *It was such a deep sleep,* I realized as the plane jostled everyone around. Her little body was worn out from all the trauma, and my smile fell. *No matter what I went through, it was nothing compared to all they endure.*

And that thought broke my heart.

Her wolf was beautiful though, just like her mama. I shoved the bad thoughts aside and got a good look at her coloring. Her wolf was a beautiful chocolate brown with a cream colored chest. Her left paw was cream colored as well, making her about the cutest wolf pup I had ever seen. Aerith had a wolf just like we suspected, but I hated that *this* is what it took to bring her out. *She was more like Shanely that we realized,* I thought as my shoulders fell. The poor thing either doesn't know how to switch back or is too afraid to. Either one kills me.

Aerith rolled to her side, placing her snout on my thigh, and I put one hand along her back. Just in case. *More for my peace of mind than hers*, I thought as she took a deep breath. Pride pulsed through my veins as I looked to my children, to my mate. Both my brothers turned to glance at me, and I knew they felt it too. I couldn't contain my smile as I looked to my family. *They were both so courageous and strong.* I didn't deserve them, but I'd spend the rest of my life making sure they felt safe and loved. That *I* loved them. More than anything else.

I lowered my head and rested it against Shanely's, inhaling her scent constantly. Malin brought over blankets, and I covered both the girls up. The doctor's pale skin was enough to tell me she needed rest too. *Well, we all did.* Exhaustion was slowly creeping in now that the adrenaline had subsided, but there was still so much to do. Daniel would be frantic when we returned home as well as the pack, who are all awake and alert as they waited for us to come home. All I wanted to do was curl up with my family and rest, and that was exactly what I was going to do. The rest could wait a few days. *Our family was back together, and nothing would tear us apart again.*

The plane dipped as Frank landed in the makeshift runway we made all those months ago. It was a bumpy landing, but everyone sighed in relief when we finally stopped, and he killed the engines.

"I've called Cain already," Cassia said, standing up. "The med bay is ready for everyone."

I gave her a grateful nod as the pilot stepped out of the cockpit. I stood to greet him.

"Thank you," I said, pursing my lips together. Maybe it was all the adrenaline leaving my body, but I felt emotional shaking that man's hand. "Thank you for everything."

The surly old man grinned and patted me on the back. His dark eyes took in my kids as they passed by and softened when they fell on Shanely. Frank had become a good friend during all this and was now the only human I would *ever* allow into my pack. *I owed that man everything.*

CHAPTER 49

"You are welcome, Bastian. You have no idea how good it feels to pay off my debt to Abraham in a way like this," he said in his deep voice. "If you don't mind, I'll stick around here for awhile. I'd like a chance to meet your mate."

I gave him a nod. "You are always welcome in my pack, Frank. And I do mean *always*."

I left the grumpy man smiling in the back of the plane before making my way to the med bay. The rain had finally stopped, and I stepped out to find a crowd waiting. What I did not expect was the response.

The second I stepped out with Shanely, the pack howled. I stilled, watching what was left of my pack and family howl loudly into the night. The tigers roared with the wolves and bears before everyone bowed their heads in respect. Pride swelled within me as I heard Cade's voice.

"The King and Queen have returned!" he shouted loudly. My family shook the ground with excitement and joy.

I gave my brother a slow grin as I made my way down the ramp.

"Sounds like something from a kid's movie." I snorted through the link.

"Pretty sure we've seen it with Aerith," he chuckled back as I caught up to them.

The crowd parted as we made our way inside, and I led our group up the stairs and into Abraham's castle. I'm sure we were a sight to see too. Cade and I didn't have shirts on, and everyone could see my brother's limp. Both of their limps as Elijah still struggled with his leg. Aerith was a wolf, and my babies were here. It wasn't what anyone expected when I made the call to go tonight, but nothing compared to the looks Elijah got as we walked in with my youngest. He was *covered* in my mate's blood. It had even splattered on his face, and he looked rough and haggard, even though most of it wasn't his.

"You need a shower," I linked him, and he turned and rolled his eyes at me.

"Duh."

The McCoy pack gasped loudly, and I turned to find Abraham carrying Mercedes inside. My heart softened, and I searched the crowd for Daniel.

They recognized her, and it was a bittersweet arrival. I could see it on their faces, and I understood more than most. Mercedes had been with Calvin for I don't know how long and was a mere hour away from the pack this whole time. All this time lost, and no one had any idea.

Cain's loud voice cleared the crowd inside, and we pushed our way to the med bay. Daniel suddenly appeared in the back, and I had to give it to him as he very gently moved through the crowd. That man had *fantastic* control. I barely kept my head the five months without Shanely. He did it for years, and he was still human as he rushed towards her. *I still had a lot to learn, especially from him.*

"Set her down here," Cassia commanded as she patted one of the empty beds, and I obeyed. I laid Shanely down, and Cassia immediately started an IV on her. Malin copied her with Mercedes across the room, so I turned to Aerith. Someone had set her at the foot of Shanely's bed, so I combed through her fur, making sure there were no injuries I just couldn't see.

Daniel burst through the room, the door clattering against the wall as he ran to his mate. A low growl sounded, and I quickly pulled Abraham back away from her. He glared at me but softened as Daniel approached. We slowly put our hands up and stepped back again. His eyes were gold, and the last thing I wanted was to cause a shift. *Every man has his limits.* Malin brought over a warm blanket, earning another growl.

"Not now," I commanded, and she froze. "Everyone stay back from his mate for the moment."

They obeyed, giving my father-in-law a chance to process this, and I slowly turned to Daniel. "She will need help at some point, Daniel. For now, take the blanket and warm her up."

Daniel didn't blink as he stared at his mate lying in the bed. Malin extended the blanket to me, and I took a small step forward.

"Daniel?" I said softly, and only when I nudged his arm did he look. I held the blanket out and waited. His bear was at the surface, and it took a moment for him to focus on me. He slowly took the blanket from me and laid it over Mercedes. I sighed when he scooped up Mercedes's frail body and climbed in bed with her. Tears welled in his eyes, and I reached for the

CHAPTER 49

curtain to give him privacy. His eyes shot to mine flashing red.

"Bastian? My daughter?" he barely got out.

"She's alive," I answered quietly. "Aerith's good too, and the boys have been delivered safely. Everyone's alive and home."

He nodded in relief and clung to his mate. I closed the curtain, giving them as much privacy as I could right now. *They deserved it.*

The door clattered as Caleb stormed in the room. Johnny held the rest back, giving me a nod as the door shut behind my brother. I couldn't begin to imagine all the laws Caleb just broke driving back from the Wall. He was on watch tonight and was another I owed a debt too. Caleb's eyes went from Shanely to the curtain where his dad and Mercedes were.

"My dad's mate is alive..."

I nodded to Caleb, patting him on the back as I made my way back to my own mate.

"Seems like she's been there since she left both kids," I replied. "I'm hoping we can find out the rest when they both wake up."

"Shanely's really okay?" Caleb asked quietly as he joined me at her bedside.

I leaned over and kissed Shanely softly. "She is. My mate is incredibly strong, just like my daughter."

I ruffled Aerith's fur as she yipped happily. She was wide awake now, wagging her tail and crouching down to play. I couldn't contain my grin.

"You left without me," Caleb said sternly. My smile fell.

"And me," Abe joined in, crossing his arms in frustration. I bite my bottom lip as the brute walked over.

Sighing, I collapsed in the chair next to Shanely, feeling every bruise I earned tonight. I looked to them both solemnly. "I'm sorry," I said quietly. "I saw a window of opportunity, and I took it. There was barely enough time as it was, and with the storm... I didn't want to risk anymore lives."

"He was going to go it alone, but we were already there," Cade said, collapsing in the other chair with me. "And Elijah and I refused to let that happen."

Abe softened his angry stance and snorted. "Yeah, I know. You are *lucky* it worked out the way it did, otherwise I'd have way more to say. Everyone made it out alive, and that's what matters. Saving them was the most important thing."

"Just don't bail on us again. The more numbers, the better, Bastian," Caleb said, giving me a pointed look.

I gave him a nod, and he finally relented some. He smiled down at Aerith who's paws were now on his chest. "Well, look at you, little wolf! I always knew you were a shifter, although I was gunning for you having a bear."

She yipped loudly before leaping off the bed to play with Caleb. I was so relieved she even could at this point. My boys were getting a quick bath to warm up by Malin and Cassia, and Aerith was chasing a grinning Caleb around the room. Shanely was sleeping soundly with her heart beating in my chest. *Everyone was okay*, I thought to myself. My heart swelled at the sight, and I rested my hand on my mate's leg. I could not wait for her to wake up and see those gorgeous green eyes of hers again.

"Did this just happen?" Abe asked, pointing to Aerith.

"When the house exploded, it scared her into her wolf," Cade answered, pulling a clean shirt from the supply closet and tossing it over him. He plopped back down before tossing me one too. I pulled it over my head, glad to have my tattoos hidden again.

"How's the leg?" I asked my brother. He winced as he moved it around to show me. It wasn't closed yet but working that way.

"It's fine. I kept reopening the wound trying to get Mercedes out," he answered, and my shoulders fell.

"You should have never gone in my place, Cade," I said, my wolf pulling through my voice. Cade slowly lifted his gaze to mine.

"Bastian, we both know..."

"No," I snapped, and the room quieted. They all looked to me as I leaned forward, resting my elbows on my knees. "While I will always appreciate everything you do for my family, it does not mean your life is expendable simply because you haven't met your mate yet. You *matter*, Cade."

A soft pink color coated his cheeks as he looked to the floor.

"*Thank you.*"

CHAPTER 49

His low voice came through our link, and I lifted my harsh stare to give him privacy. Cade was loud and goofy on any given day, but lately this serious side had pulled through from him. And while I didn't want to draw unwanted attention to him, it was my harsh words that made him feel like this in the first place. *I needed to fix that. He had to know he mattered even without a mate.*

"Always," I replied through the link.

The door clattered loudly as Emersyn, Esme, and Noah barreled into the room. My brows rose as I glanced to the clock on the wall. With Elijah bailing on his mate like he had, I figured Emmie would be front and center to chew him out when he got off the plane. *Although, I was glad she wasn't,* I thought to myself. *He looked a mess.*

Luke gave a simple nod with Johnny as they stood guard just outside the door. The whole pack was camped just outside, waiting to see their White Wolf and Mercedes again. I gave them my thanks through the link. I needed a moment to recoup before I let everyone in.

"Whoa..." Cain said, putting his hands up to slow my brother's mate. The eye patch over his right eye still took some getting used to, but we all tried to pretend we didn't see it. He lost it during the initial attack and refused to let Cassia heal it. Cain made her heal the pack first, and then it just became what it was today. Part of me thinks he wanted the pain and scar that came with it. A reminder of when we failed. I slowly looked to the scars on my own body. *I didn't blame him.*

He blocked Emersyn's path saying, "Slow down now. Everyone's..."

Emersyn paled as a sob burst from her lips. Her eyes widened, and her hand covered her mouth in shock. Elijah had emerged from the back room still covered in Shanely's blood.

"You dum-dum," I said to my brother. *"You didn't freaking think to put on a new shirt?"*

Elijah slammed to a stop, his eyes widening. He lifted his hands defensively as he stammered, "It's not mine!"

Emmie's legs wobbled, but then she was running. Running like mad to my idiot brother, who didn't think to put on clean shirt. *Or get permission to come with me tonight.*

The two stayed wrapped around the other for quite some time, and it was agony listening to her sob against his chest. I looked to Cade, who's face said it all. *We still had a bone to pick with him.*

But it seemed like Emmie had plans of her own, when she abruptly pulled back and started wailing on him.

"Don't you ever leave me like that again!" she bellowed, and the room wisely found something else to do. Cade and I snickered quietly as we watched.

"Emmie, I'm sorry!" Elijah protested, and Noah snarled. He was pissed too apparently. Cade laughed hard then. *Noah was not someone you wanted for an enemy,* I thought to myself.

"Don't you *Emmie* me!" she yelled back. "I was *terrified* when you just shut down our bond, and then I find a note in our room saying you left for the mission already! What were you thinking?!"

"Go Emmie," Cade muttered, earning a glare from our brother.

I grinned again. I didn't blame her one bit for being pissed. He left with us, leaving only a note behind, which was a crappy thing to do. I didn't realize until we were in the air to make the drop, otherwise I would have made him stay. I *assumed* he got permission.

"I... I..."

For the first time in my life, Elijah was at a loss for words. My grin slowly faded as his mouth open and shut repeatedly. Guilt ate at me, and I slowly got up and walked over to my sister-in-law.

"Blame me, Emersyn," I said softly, and she turned to me. Elijah's brows furrowed, but I smiled softly. I owed him everything after tonight. *This was nothing.*

"I begged him to come," I lied, looking to Emersyn again, "and we were out of time due to the storm. I told him to leave you a note so you knew at least, and then I commanded my brothers to shut down our bonds so nothing would distract us. It was a safety measure, but I wasn't thinking clearly when it came to you. I am truly sorry, Emmie. I wouldn't have been able to save my mate or my children without him though."

CHAPTER 49

Emersyn softened then, and she looked over to my unconscious mate. She crossed her arms muttering, "Just so you know, I would have let him go. I would have never stood in the way of saving Shanely. I just wish he would have told me first. He didn't even say goodbye."

Elijah dropped his head, shifting on his feet as he stared hard at the ground. I patted him on the back, pulling him from the pit of shame he didn't need to be in.

"From now on, he will," I said, giving her a kiss on the cheek. "Your mate is a hero though, and he needs you. Please, just hate me and forgive him."

Elijah slowly opened up his arms, and she immediately rushed into them.

"I am sorry, Emmie," he whispered, kissing her forehead.

"Just don't do that again," Noah muttered, slugging my brother's arm. Elijah gasped as he rubbed the spot Noah struck. "It's near impossible to wrangle these two when they get *that* upset. You have no idea the headache I have from tonight."

I grinned and left those four alone. While my brothers and I have our own deal with our mates, Elijah was in a special union with Esme and Noah too. I had done my job, and he could figure out the rest. I collapsed next to Shanely, perfectly content to watch my daughter wrestle with Caleb.

"He's lucky he has us," Cade muttered quietly, and I grinned, placing my finger to my lips.

Bay came through the back room with two bottles in hand. I didn't even see her come in the room earlier, but she smiled as she came over to us.

My sister didn't get through the attack unscathed either as a long scar ran from the side of her head across her eye and down her cheek slightly. She felt Abraham's heart race when they stole my daughter from him, and thankfully they were close enough to the castle that she could reach them easily in her wolf form. All she told me was that she barely pulled Abraham out before his truck exploded, sending a piece of metal flying across her face. Aerith was long gone by the time the two of them woke up here in the medical bay. I tried not to think about that when I see her scar now.

Bay gave me a warm bottle and passed one to Cade before sitting on

Abraham's lap.

"Good to see you're all alive," she said with a grin.

"What about that prick?" Abraham asked.

"Which one?" Caleb muttered as he joined us.

"Eliminated just as we were instructed," Cade answered.

"Two to the chest, and one to the head," Elijah continued, pulling the rest of the gang over. "Exactly as we were taught. Played their own game and won."

Cassia walked over with one of my boys and handed him to me saying, "This is your first born."

I smiled looking down at my oldest son. I didn't really feel like talking about what happened tonight. I still hated guns, even though they were necessary tonight. Leaving the others to discuss tonight's events, I focused in on my little one. He was perfect and looked just like my mate with her soft features and nose. His light brown hair even had a hint of red in it too.

I chuckled as I gave him the bottle. His little tongue immediately shot out, eager to latch on and eat, but he struggled with it for a bit. I gave him a moment to figure it out, and soon he latched on and started to eat. My poor baby was starving, and I watched in awe as he gobbled everything up. *He was going to be my brute,* I thought to myself. *I just had a feeling he was going to be the one that kept me on my toes.*

Malin brought my other boy out and passed him to Cade. Cade beamed down at the little guy, and I peeked over to get a better look at him too.

"He looks just like you, Bastian," he said, giving my son his bottle. This one had no issues latching and was just as greedy as his older brother. My youngest was definitely the smaller of the two, but his sharp features and dark hair showed the Fenrir bloodline. It just screamed a cunning wolf, and I couldn't be more proud. They each seemed to take a side of us, and that one was the spitting image of me. I had a feeling that Shanely and I would have our hands full as they grew up. *If they were anything like my brothers and I then we were in for it.*

They filled their bellies and fell fast asleep once more. The trauma of tonight wouldn't even be a memory for them, and I was grateful. They

CHAPTER 49

created a spot in my heart I didn't know existed. Now that everyone was safely back with me, I felt complete. Whole again.

"Yeah, it's uncanny," Cain said as he looked to my little one. He slowly stole a peek to the closed curtain on the otherside before sighing.

"Let's give them some space," Cassia said quietly to her mate. She gently placed her hand on his arm. "We can at least sit by the curtain."

Malin looked pale and exhausted as she did a final check on the kids and my mate. It was physically draining to heal others, and she used up a lot of her strength tonight. More than ever before. I gave her a soft nudge.

"Go," I said softly. "Get some sleep, Malin. You were a hero tonight. Thank you for everything."

The corners of her mouth rose slightly as she carefully tucked the flyaway strands of dark hair behind her ears. "Anytime, Alpha Bastian. Please let me know when anyone wakes up. I'll just rest in the spare room down here."

I gave her a nod and watched the incredible healer stroll to the back rooms. Aerith jumped up on the bed between her mother's legs. Her snout went straight to the boys, and I chuckled as I leaned forward so she could see. Her little nose scented them like a true wolf. We grinned, watching her little tail wag furiously before she finally settled in on Shanely's belly. *She would be the best big sister they could ever ask for.*

"Aerith," I said softly, and she turned to face me, "are you ready to switch back?"

Her wolf cocked her head to the side but did nothing except yawn. She didn't answer me, not even through the link, and I frowned slightly.

"If you are ready, I can help you shift back."

Her eyes flashed gold, and I knew she heard my link. She always had been able to before, but she still wouldn't answer me. I looked nervously to my brothers. Aerith was just mute, and my brows furrowed as a thousand different reason as to why she was like that flashed before me.

"Just tell her how, Bastian," Bay said softly. "She'll shift when she's ready."

I sighed but nodded my head anyways. *I wouldn't force a shift from her.* I would *never* do that.

"Aerith, if you want to switch back and forth between your forms," I said as I gently scratched behind her furry ears, "then just focus on who you want to be. When you start feeling things move, don't be afraid. Just let it happen, even if it hurts a little. You don't have to right now but soon, okay? Mommy will want to talk to you when she wakes up."

Aerith's tail stopped wagging. Even in her wolf form, I could see the sadness in her. She merely laid her snout on Shanely's stomach and ignored the rest of us. No amount of playfulness or gently prodding could get her to move off Shanely, and when her little eyes began to droop, we finally just let her be, and she fell fast asleep.

It shifted the mood in the room, watching Aerith shut down like that. All the horrors we saw since finding them, and I still had no idea what else happened to them. My wolf stirred inside and even my bear was agitated within me. Our family was alive, but they were not healed from this, and I didn't know if it would be something I'd ever fix.

Elijah opened the cabinet and finally pulled out a clean shirt. He swapped the bloody one out, and Emmie immediately clung to him once he was changed. The events of tonight went through our minds as the room grew quiet. Everyone seemed to be processing it differently, and I cleared my throat to get their attention.

The group looked to me, and I sat up a little straighter, even though the control I normally had was shaky at best right now. *I just had to get this next part out. It was the last thing left to do.*

"Thank you, guys," I said, my voice shaking silently under the pressure, "for everything. You all saved my family. Never once questioning what I needed or what I asked, and you all took my temper and brashness in stride. I can't thank you enough. I owe *each* and *every* one of you a debt."

"Our family," Abraham muttered, and I turned to him. "We saved *our* family."

"Yeah, and we'd do anything for family," Cade chimed in, passing my youngest to Caleb. The corners of my mouth rose slightly.

Bay clicked at me, and I nearly snorted when she snapped her fingers in

CHAPTER 49

my direction, gesturing me to give up my baby boy. Chuckling, I carefully passed him off to her. She and Abraham looked smitten as they gently rubbed his little hands and feet. *It wouldn't surprise me if they had one of their own soon too.*

"Well, you all mean the world to me," I said, gently rubbing my mate's cheek. "To us."

Noah pulled another chair up and snuggled in with Esme. Elijah had somehow made his way on the foot of the bed with Emmie, and I laughed. Three large Alpha males all managed to cram themselves next to Shanely with Aerith on top of her. It was a good thing these beds were made for shifters because I don't think that *this* was what they were intended for. My brothers needed to be near Shanely as much as I did, it seemed. *Well, everyone really.* When I pulled on the pack bonds, I could see most weren't too far from the medical bay and a lot were running a patrol around the castle itself. My heart swelled at the respect and loyalty they gave my mate. I didn't even command that from them. They just did it *for her.*

Emersyn leaned against her mate to lay her hand on Shanely's, and I could see the baby fever written all over her face as she watched Bay and Abraham hold my youngest.

I grinned, nudging Cade, who smirked at them. His eyes lit up at the idea of kiddos running around, and my grin grew even wider. *I liked the thought of that too.* Our family growing even more and being there to shower everyone with love and support. *To raise our kids the right way,* I thought. *Better than the way we grew up.*

I laid back against the headboard, feeling every bruise and aching muscle I abused tonight. My eyes grew heavy, so I shut them, letting everyone continue to talk and laugh around me.

Soon, I drifted off to sleep.

* * *

Pain shot through my arm as I sat up in bed. I clenched my left hand into a fist and shook, waking it back up, and trying to get blood flowing again. The room was entirely dark and quiet, and I blinked furiously as my eyes adjusted. *The medical beds were just not made for multiple people.*

My eyes drifted over the room as feeling finally came back to my hand. Everyone was still roughly where I last saw them. Abraham must have pulled up another bed because he and Bay were passed out on my right with Caleb sleeping in their chair. Noah and Esme were asleep in the chairs at the end of Shanely's bed, while Elijah and Emersyn were passed out in the bed to the left of us. They had pushed it right up against our bed and were passed out cold. Elijah's wolf must have not been able to leave the room either, and Cade never left his spot by Shanely. *He took his role of Beta well*, I thought, grinning softly. *I'll give him that.* His arm was on Shanely's stomach, and he was currently drooling on her pillow. I rolled my eyes. *At least it wasn't on her.*

I straightened in the bed, trying to shift my hip to a more comfortable spot, when I realized the curtain to Mercedes's bed was open. She was still asleep in the bed, but Daniel wasn't with her. I slowly sat forward and looked around. It didn't take long to find him though, and I made my way to his side.

Daniel smiled as he gently rubbed my son's cheeks. "Got any names yet?"

I shook my head and whispered, "No, sir. I'm waiting on my mate to wake up before even trying. I figured she'd be pissed if she woke up, and I named them already."

Daniel chuckled softly. "You're probably right."

"How is she?" I asked, nodding towards Mercedes.

"She hasn't woken yet," he answered, "but she's stable. I can feel our bond, and it's strong, so I think she will be okay."

The look on his face didn't sit right with me, so I decided to keep him talking. Distract him for a moment, I suppose. Something was eating at him, but I figured if he truly wanted me to know, he'd tell me.

"She's a force to be reckoned with, sir. You weren't kidding when you said she was a large powerful shifter," I muttered quietly.

CHAPTER 49

His eyes went to mine, widening slightly with surprise. "You saw her wolf?"

"I *fought* her wolf," I answered, crossing my arms and flashing him a grin. He wasn't amused. "The disconnect had been too long, so it took some time to get her to submit. Actually, Aerith was the one who brought her back."

Daniel said nothing as he looked to his mate. Tension rolled off him, and I felt bad stressing him out like that.

"She's massive, Daniel," I said, pulling his attention back to me. I gave him a smile, hoping to ease his pain. "She saved our lives at the end too. Cade found her in that house, and they somehow found a way out of that basement. With everything going on, I really haven't had a chance to ask him about it, but I've never seen someone with her ability before. I have *never* seen a shield."

The corners of his mouth rose as he relaxed. Pride pulled through his voice when he asked, "She's a shield?"

"She is, sir," I answered, grinning again. "It was incredible to see it happen. It blocked everything out. Not even the wind or rain got through."

"She always wanted to surprise me, but I never knew," he replied. His hand gently reaching for the twin's hands. My oldest never once stirred, but I smiled as my youngest gently gripped his too small fingers around Daniel's.

"Calvin snapped after that," I said quietly. "Mercedes shredded him shortly after."

"He's lucky I didn't find him first. It would have been a slow death," he gritted through his teeth.

"I think she needed it, Daniel. Her wolf took over at that moment," I said, shaking my head as the memories flashed before me, "and she fought me *hard* when I commanded her to shift back. Like really, really hard."

Daniel chuckled saying, "Yeah, that's not surprising. She always was a stubborn little thing."

I laughed before quieting myself. The only one who stirred was Elijah, but he drifted back to sleep once his eyes did a quick sweep of the room.

"Well, now I know where Shanely gets it from, and good lord, you weren't kidding when you said they looked alike! It's uncanny!"

He smirked as he drifted his gaze to my mate now. "It's why it was so hard with Shanely at first. She looked so much like her mother that it was hard to keep my pain at bay."

"I'll bet," I whispered, looking over to my mate too. She was still sleeping so soundly, and I smiled. *God, it was good to have her back.*

"Thank you for saving not only my daughter and grandkids, but also my mate," Daniel said, pulling me from my thoughts. "You and your brothers didn't leave her to her fate. You didn't even stop to consider the risk, and I will never forget that. You risked your lives for her too. To have Mercedes here with me again... It's surreal, and I can't thank you enough."

Daniel had tears in his eyes when he held out his hand to me. *Screw that,* I thought and pulled him into a hug. I can't imagine spending nearly 25 years apart from my mate. The fact that he's still sane and not lost beyond reach was incredible. *Shanely also got her strength from him.*

"I will do everything to protect my family," I replied quietly. "My *entire* family."

He gave me a firm pat on the back, and I left him to sort his thoughts on his own. I gently fell back in the only spot left on the bed and wrapped my arm around Shanely. Her chest inhaled sharply before she turned into me. Her nose went to the crook of my neck, and I grinned, kissing her softly on the forehead.

They were safe, I told myself. Shanely and Aerith were safe. My twins were safe as were my brothers and family.

And I could finally rest.

Chapter 50

Shanely

I stirred.

Something tickled my cheek. I slowly lifted my arm to scratch the annoying sensation, but I couldn't move. Heavy weights seemed to hold down both my arms, and even my legs had a weight on them. I groaned, trying to pull free to no avail. *What had Patrick done to me?*

My chest tightened as I pulled against the restraints. *I had to get out,* I thought as panic rose in my chest. *I had to find Aerith.* My eyes fluttered open to a dark room, but then suddenly something stirred within me. My shifter abilities rushed to the forefront, and then I felt her.

My wolf.

My brilliant wolf was back, and so was my bear. My lips puckered as relief and pure joy filled my heart. *She was back... They were both back. How?* That question rattled my mind as I took everything in. The room was so loud now that I had my abilities back, but I didn't care. The empty space where they belonged was finally whole again. I no longer felt incomplete or alone, and the two warmed my soul as they settled inside me. *Right where they belonged.*

My power rose as my wolf pushed against my skin, demanding to be released to run free, but then I felt something else. Another heartbeat. It stayed in time with my own, growing louder with each beat, and soothed me to my core.

Bastian.

Suddenly, my last memories rushed to the forefront, and the joy I was feeling vanished. My heart stopped as I remembered *everything*. Bastian standing before me in full tactical gear. *I didn't recognize him at first.* Then the explosion... The gunfire... Patrick's face flashing before me as my heart thundered in my chest. My Alpha power rose with my fear as I watched Patrick's death replay over and over in my mind. The sickening sound of bullet piercing flesh. The way his head snapped back when Bastian took the shot. Patrick's body falling to the ground.

Bile rose to the back of my throat, and I pushed against the heavy weights holding me down. *I needed out,* I thought as my chest began to heave. I couldn't get enough air, and I tried to pull my arm free. I was pinned down and tears filled my eyes as those memories plagued my mind. *I was trapped under this heavy weight... No, not a weight,* I thought as I struggled to catch my breath. *A body.*

The outline of a nose appeared in the dark, and I gasped when Patrick's bloody face was suddenly there.

"Shanely??"

I blinked, and Patrick was gone.

Bastian sat up abruptly, rubbing his chest as he struggled to wake up. My arm felt tingly and numb but finally free from that heavy weight, and I shook it abruptly. Hot air blew across my face, and I about had a heart attack when I turned to find Cade's face smushed into my pillow. *They were both here,* I thought as my heart continued to pound. I struggled to pull my Alpha power back. It seemed to rise with every roll of anxiety in my stomach, and my wolf snapped her jaws wanting out. *She felt threatened,* I realized, and that scared me because I didn't know why.

But when my eyes drifted to my swollen belly, I had finally figured it out. Because it wasn't swollen anymore. It was flat...

Overwhelming panic surged through my veins as my hand touched my stomach. I yanked on my left arm, causing Cade to shift off the bed, and I shot forward. *My boys... My sons! Where were my kids?!* My eyes darted back and forth searching for them but stilled when I saw a wolf pup between my legs. *Aerith...*

"Ouch..." Cade muttered before clutching his chest. "God, what is that?!"

CHAPTER 50

"Whoa, baby," Bastian said softly, pulling my face towards him. "It's okay! You're okay. Everyone's safe, I promise you."

My eyes widened as fear rushed through me. *Calvin... Oh, God. No one is safe!*

I tried to get off the bed, but Bastian blocked my path. He frowned, and I knew none of this made any sense to him. *He didn't get it,* I thought as my Alpha power rose again. I winced in pain as I stopped it from spreading out around me. *He has no idea the danger we were truly in though.* My chest began to burn as my wolf grew more and more agitated inside me. She wanted out *now*.

"Where are my boys?!" I demanded as my eyes turned gold. *I had to know.* I had to know they were alive and okay before I ran. I wasn't going to lead Calvin right to us.

Bastian frowned, opening his mouth, when a figure shot up in the dark. He clutched his chest too.

"Shanely's awake!" Cade shouted, slamming his hand on the wall and illuminating the whole room.

Everyone shot up, rubbing their eyes from the bright light, and my heart hurt when I saw them. *They had been through so much,* I thought as I looked long and hard at Bay's nasty scar. I shut my eyes as my power surged again. It hurt to keep it inside and fear gripped my heart because I didn't have the control I once had. *I had to go.*

Elijah was at my bedside in seconds still holding his chest. "Is that from her?" he asked.

Bastian nodded grimly, and I shifted my legs out from Aerith. *She was so beautiful,* I thought as tears filled my eyes. This time she'd be safe with her father. *Calvin will hunt me, and as long as I stayed away, he will never find her again.*

My heart broke at the thought of leaving my children, my family, and my mate. But I never found the tracker Patrick put inside me. As long as Calvin had a way to track me, I was nothing more than a death sentence to the ones I loved so dearly. *I got a miracle once already,* I thought as my power rose with every worry. *I won't just hope I'll get another one.* But with every fear and worry that ran through my mind, my Alpha power grew, and soon it became so overwhelming inside my head that I was struggling to rein it in.

"Good lord. We don't even get the full force," Cade muttered.

"Breathe, baby," Bastian said, forcing me to look at him again. "Guys, grab the boys."

My eyes followed Cade and Elijah out of the room. *They were okay?!* I thought as my heart thundered inside. My wolf pushed to shift again, needing to find the boys herself, and it was all I could do to stop her from shifting. I couldn't even ask the question. I couldn't do anything but wrestle with my Alpha power and stop my wolf from shifting. *I'd take one peek*, I told myself. *Just one and then I'm gone...*

"Look around, Shanely," Bastian said, pulling me from my thoughts. "You recognize this place?"

I slowly took another look. Between everyone's smiling faces, I saw multiple beds against the wall. One with its curtains closed, but then everything suddenly clicked. *We were in Abraham's medical wing. We were at Abraham's home.* Everyone smiled at me, but I just wanted to scream. My heart thundered in my chest. *We sent the pack here. Everyone left of McCoy pack was here, and I just led Calvin right to them.*

I had to go. I was their Alpha, and I couldn't be the reason they're all dead. I had to leave right now! I thought and turned to the IV in my arm. My eyes widened when I saw the bag of saline was nearly empty. *I had been here awhile*, I thought as panic surge through my veins again. I had been asleep. I had been asleep for God knows how long and... *Calvin could already be on his way. He could have gathered another army by now, and this time he could actually succeed in killing* everyone I love. Bastian flew back as I shoved him aside and kicked the blankets off me.

"How long was I out?!" I demanded.

Cade and Elijah slammed to a stop as they entered the room, their arms full holding my baby boys. The dam broke at the sight of their little hands moving, and one was sucking his thumb. My heart shattered into tiny little pieces, and I covered my mouth, forcing a sob back down my throat. I

CHAPTER 50

quickly looked away as a tear fell down my face. *I couldn't stay to see them,* I realized. *It would be too hard.* My wolf whined hard, snapping her jaws angrily at me, and I wanted to scream. I wanted to scream because this wasn't fair, but there was no point. Their safety mattered more than what I wanted.

"What?" Bastian asked, cocking his head to the side. He narrowed his eyes as I pushed past him and the bed.

"HOW LONG?" I bellowed, and the whole room stilled.

They all looked confused, and I nearly shook trying to keep my animals at bay. My bear wanted to run. She didn't want to ask questions or wait a second more. We were a danger to our loved ones, and she always put them first. But my wolf wanted justice. She wanted to protect our family and slaughter Calvin when he came. I clutched my hand over my ears as if it could somehow silence them, but they continued to roar inside my head. My Alpha power thrummed against my skin, slowly leaking out around me. I always trusted my wolf, but I wouldn't risk Bastian or the kids. Not now, not ever.

I was going to follow my bear.

"About four days," Bastian said quietly, and my heart stopped, "but what..."

I may already be too late, I thought to myself. My bear roared so loud I winced in pain, and I moved my feet to settle her. To our dismay, Abraham blocked our path.

"Shanely, calm down!" Abraham said firmly. "It's okay..."

"I can't..." I shouted back. I dug my nails across my skin, hoping I'd just find the stupid thing and destroy it. I could move my pack and keep them hidden from the wicked humans who just ruin *everything*. My wolf snapped her jaws angrily, but I pushed her aside and let my bear guide me. Power leaked around as I took a step towards Abraham. My eyes turned gold.

"Move Abraham," I snarled. My nails dug further into my skin finding *nothing.*

Bastian gripped my arm, flipping me around to face him. He glared saying, "Hang on just a minute. You can't leave!"

A sob escaped my lips as everything became too much. I couldn't catch my breath as I bawled before everyone.

"YOU don't get it!" I cried out. My power began to seep through my skin. "I have to go! It's not safe. It's not safe, Bastian!"

Bastian's eyes widened, and I felt his grip loosen on my arm just a tad. It was enough to yank my arm away, and I stormed towards the door again.

Abraham blocked me again, and I skidded to a stop. My cheeks were already stained wet as my nails dug deeper in my arms. My fingers trailed up my neck, searching for that blasted tracker, but I couldn't feel anything. *It has to be here!*

"Please..." I begged, but Abraham crossed his arms defiantly. His eyes flashed gold, and I knew he'd shift if he had to. *They didn't understand,* I screamed inside my head. *I had to leave now.* The tracker was in *me,* and Calvin would chase *me* until his dying breath, knowing full well Aerith would be with me. He had no idea Bastian was still alive or that he rescued me. *I couldn't lose Bastian again. I couldn't lose my family again!*

My bear surged forward, and her white fur came through on my arms. I lost my grip on my Alpha power to pull her back in, and it struck everyone. Guilt ate me alive as my family fell around me. Everyone except Bastian. He stood firm against each and every wave. His eyes were blood red.

I tried to stop, tried to pull it back in, but I couldn't. Once the dam had broke, more and more poured out of me. My chest felt like it had split in two, and the more I hurt my family, the worse I felt and the harder I cried. The more I cried, the more power seeped from my skin, and I couldn't stop *any* of it. My wolf wasn't helping any either. She wanted Calvin's death. She wanted vengeance for what had happened. I just wanted to save my family.

"I don't think so, *mate.* Turn it off," he growled. His steps slow and calculated, and I watched as Cade forced himself to his feet. My Beta winced in pain but moved opposite to my mate, shaking with every step. *I knew what they were doing. They were trying to pin me in,* I thought as I stepped back. Blood trickled down my neck as I continued to search for the tracker.

"I can't!" I bellowed back as another wave hit everyone. My heart was

CHAPTER 50

breaking as I took another step. I sobbed, while my wolf snapped her jaws at me. My bear roared in my head to run, and that's just what I was going to do. "I'll come back when it's safe! Please, Bastian! I can't lose you again!"

Bastian skidded to a stop as if I struck him. He looked stunned, and I didn't blame him. All I wanted to do was run into his arms and never let him go. *God, I loved this man more than anything, but I would not risk him.* I made that mistake once before when Calvin offered us the deal before, and it nearly cost me everything. *That won't happen again.*

A sickening feeling twisted my stomach as I said, "I'm sorry."

I turned to run but slammed into an invisible force. I stumbled backwards, my eyes widening as I searched for what hit me. My bear roared again, and I stood on my feet. I ran forward again only to hit the same wall. Suddenly, it glistened white, and I slowly turned around.

My mother strolled towards me, her eye solid white and hands raised. *This was her...* I thought anxiously to myself. *She was keeping me in.* Those in the room relaxed and slowly got to their feet. Elijah shoved himself forward, while Cade and Bastian circled me. I turned to my mate, finding him staring at me like I was a monster.

And maybe after everything, a monster is what I had become, I thought as pain gripped my heart again. *But my mother didn't know. She didn't know, and I was not going to be the cause of everyone's death!*

I pushed against the wall, trying to step through, but it held firm. Gritting my teeth, I tried again. It wouldn't budge, and my eyes widened. *What if I can't get out?* Another sob burst forth as I slammed my fists against the wall. I screamed as panic filled my chest, and my Alpha Power surged to new heights. *They didn't get it,* and I hit the wall again.

"Let me go!" I demanded, but no one listened. Mother held the wall, and I glared at her. "He can find me! Calvin will be able to track wherever I go, so please, run before it's too late! He will kill you all! He won't stop..."

The memories I had buried from that fateful day surged forward, and just like that I was reliving everything again. So much death, so much loss, so much suffering. I could feel the bullet wounds Bastian received all over again, and my bear roared inside my head. I clutched my waist as Patrick came to view. The creative ways he'd punish me for stepping out of line. The ability to summon such utter destruction in a moment's notice... I couldn't breathe. *Calvin would storm Abe's place with another wave of armed forces and slaughter everyone. My daughter would be lost. My mate and family dead.*

And I don't think I'd survive it this time.

I fell to my knees in pain as I sobbed uncontrollably. Tears continued to fall as I whispered, "You don't understand. He will find me. He..."

I looked to my mate, hoping they'd understand and let me go, but blinked when I saw his mouth moving. No sound came forth, and I narrowed my eyes. He had dug his hands in his hair like he always did when he panicked, while shouting orders at those in the room, but I *couldn't* hear him. Panic gripped my heart. *I couldn't hear him. Does this mean they couldn't hear me?!* I shot to my feet abruptly. *He had no idea what I just said.* I *had* to move. I *had* to protect them. I was the White Wolf, and this time I would keep them safe.

My bear surged forward, and I felt my canines enlarging. My vision turned blood red as my nails sharpened, and I struck the wall. Everyone jolted in the room as they turned to face me. My tears had stopped flowing as I let my bear guide my every move. She always protected our loved ones. She protected our kids and our mate most of all. *She wouldn't fail me.*

I rose my hand towards the white wall caging us in and focused on my ever-building Alpha power. My bear helped me pull everything in and funnel my power to one pressure point on the wall. I had never controlled it like this before. I had never *felt* it like this before. Pain rippled on my skin as it continued to build, but I waited until she nudge me forward before slamming it against the blasted cage.

The floodgates opened, and the white wall surrounding me began to crack. Everyone's eyes widened as they took a step back, and I screamed as continued to strike the wall. It wavered under my intense power and relief washed over me. *I can protect them*, I bellowed in my head. *I can protect my family!* The wall began to glitch. Mother wavered in her steps, and my father rushed forward to support her.

CHAPTER 50

I didn't focus on their surprise or fear. I didn't focus on anything but getting out of here before Calvin found us. My bear roared proudly as the wall glitched even more. The room began to shake, and the lights exploded above us as my Alpha power seeped through the cracks. *It was nearly there,* I told myself. *My mother couldn't hold it much longer.*

More power surged from my fingertips as I screamed into the void. My family rushed about the room as cabinets flew open and stuff tumbled out. My bear demanded more, and I gave it. I listened to her every wish as she forced herself further into control. Fur grew on my arms, and I felt my bones begin to crack. I held firm, screaming as I sent more of my power to the cage my mother held, when it suddenly shattered.

I stumbled forward to my knees, breathing hard as I harshly cut the power off. My eyes slowly lifted to my mate. Bastian looked terrified of me and pain filled my heart. I never thought he'd look at me like that, but he had to understand I was doing this for him. For him and our kids.

My bear snarled under my skin, and I didn't have the strength to stop her from shifting. Shouting ensued around us as I let her out. It would be easier to run anyways.

Her fur breached my skin, when I heard a rush of footsteps. I blinked, seeing my Aunt Cassia run towards me. My eyes widened, and I shoved to my feet.

But I wasn't quick enough.

I was too exhausted from breaking through the wall that I couldn't stop her hand from reaching me. I didn't have a chance to block Cassia until it was too late.

She wrapped her hand around my arm, pulling instantly, and I crumbled to the ground.

Chapter 51

Bastian

"KNOCK HER OUT!" I bellowed as glass rained from above.

Shanely *shattered* the shield. Shattered it like it was nothing. I didn't even recognize my mate as the room exploded, knocking me back against the bed where Aerith hid. It felt like a truck slammed into me, and the walls shook from the amount of power she had used. My eyes widened.

White fur appeared on her arms as Cassia ran in. There was nothing I could do but watch as my mate was knocked into oblivion. The mate I searched *so intently for,* she had to be knocked unconscious to save the rest of us. *She wanted to leave...*

Taking the only chance we had to stop Shanely, Cassia flung herself on her niece and pulled. Shanely's eyes rolled to the back of her head before she dropped to the ground in a heap.

Cade and I bolted to catch her, but I was a step behind my brother. I was always a step behind when it came to protecting her it seemed, and Cade just barely made it in time to keep her head from slamming onto the tile floor. The whole room stilled. No one moved. No one said a word as the lights flickered in the back.

"Everyone okay?" Elijah asked. The others merely grumbled an answer.

Someone opened the curtains, lighting up the mess my mate just made. All I could do was stare at her. Stare at the shattered remains of the girl I loved. Shanely just laid in my brother's arms, and just like that, I couldn't breathe. *She wasn't happy to see me.* That gut-wrenching despair filled my chest again as I watched my mate lay unconscious before me. *Because I*

CHAPTER 51

ordered it.

"What in the world just happened?!" Daniel yelled as Cain ran into the room. I finally dragged my eyes over to them, and Mercedes's ragged breathing said enough with how she felt. My father-in-law stared hard at me, but I didn't know what to say to him.

"Are you alright, Mercedes?" Cassia asked.

"I'm alright," Mercedes said in a shaky voice. "No one needs to fuss over me. I'm okay."

I didn't believe her.

"I have *never* seen her do something like this before. Are the kids okay?" Cade asked, looking right at me.

Aerith slowly crawled out from under the bed between my feet, looking at me with her head cocked to the side. She seemed alright though, and I looked at my boys, finding them still sleeping soundly in their bassinets near the back wall. They didn't even wake, which surprised me, but I shook my head grateful they were shielded somehow.

"It doesn't even seem like they were even affected," I replied harshly.

"It's because I shielded them too," Mercedes said softly, and I sighed heavily.

Cade lifted my mate, passing by to lay her back down on the bed, but I moved away from them. My wolf snapping at me with each step, but I couldn't look at her right now. I couldn't look and see how badly I failed her. I wasn't there when she was taken, and because I didn't protect her, she ended up utterly damaged and nearly broken.

Her wolf didn't even seem to recognize me.

"How did you even stand that, brother?" Bay asked, pulling me from my thoughts.

"Painfully," I gritted out. This was the first time I had *ever* felt my wife's power before. The blast that crushed Mercedes's shield *hurt*.

I couldn't wrap my head around what just happened though and pain gripped my heart again. *I thought she'd be happy to see me. To see all of us, but Shanely wasn't. She wanted to leave.* My mate was far more broken than I realized because the Shanely I knew would never hurt her family like this.

She about blew the med bay apart. *All to leave me.* My wolf snarled within me, and a scowl formed on my face.

"Dude, stop it," Cade snapped at me.

I turned to glare at my brother, snarling as I asked, "Stop what?"

"I can see it on your face," Cade said, crossing his arms, "but I rather not have to say it. Just stop. You're reading this all the wrong way, and you know it."

"She was trying to leave," I said quietly. The rest dropped their heads. Cade and Elijah were the only ones brave enough to make eye contact with me. The reality of what just happened was killing me inside. *My mate chose to bring down the medical bay and abandon everyone...*

Suddenly, I just snapped.

"What happened?!" I bellowed angrily. My sanity unraveled before everyone as I dug my hands in my hair. "What did I *do* wrong?!"

Tears filled my eyes, but I didn't turn away. I didn't hide them this time. I never cried, especially not in front of others, but I was spent. My body hurt, my heart was in pieces, and I just couldn't take it anymore.

"Bastian, settle..." Cade started to say.

"NO!" I yelled again. "Tell me, Cade! Was I too late? Did I screw her up so badly by leaving her there because we tried to plan this! IS THIS MY FAULT!?"

"That's enough of that!" Elijah yelled at me. I barred my teeth as he took a brave step forward.

"She wanted to leave!" I snarled right back. "My own mate, whom I struggled to save for five months, wanted to run away! And nearly brought down the entire room to do it!"

Cade snarled, shoving off Shanely's bed to storm over to me. His eyes were red as he got in my face.

"We moved as quickly as we could, and you know that!" he screamed. "Do I need to remind you of Ryder?! Do you want to be dead like he is? Because if you had bolted before we could plan something properly, you'd be dead too on those God Forsaken plates!"

Our noses were touching as he barred his teeth in anger, but for the first

CHAPTER 51

time in my life, my wolf and I just weren't able to meet the challenge. A heavy weight I thought I lifted when I rescued her came crashing back down, and I couldn't take it anymore. I was barely holding it together when she was gone. Always out of reach, and I was forced to watch *everything* from the sidelines. All because of those freaking plates! Some of what happened to my girls made me hurl. I went *feral*, and now she's finally here. Safe and sound, yet still so broken. And it was all *my* fault. *I did this*, I thought as a tear slid down my cheek. *I wasn't there to protect her in the first place, and I took too long getting her back.*

I broke my mate.

My wolf submitted first, and Cade's eyes widened in surprise. I didn't want his pity though, and I crashed to the ground, laying my head on my knees and gripping the back of my hair tight. I didn't want to look at him anymore. I didn't want to acknowledge anyone, and I certainly didn't want to watch her try and run again. I don't think I have it in me to see that a second time. To feel such agony, knowing she didn't want to stay. Hot tears filled my eyes, and I squeezed them shut.

My body jerked when Cade's hand landed on my shoulder. He kept it there, refusing to leave me, and soon I felt Elijah's hand on my other side. No one said a word while I fell apart on the floor. It was all I could do to remember to breathe.

"Alright, everyone out," Elijah commanded. "Cassia go find Malin. Bay take Aerith and the boys to the next room. Daniel check on Mercedes. That took a lot out of her to contain Shanely. The rest leave until I say so."

Everyone moved silently, and I kept my head down. Shame filled my heart as they obeyed my brother's command. I should be the one to lead and sort through this mess. I was Alpha next to Shanely, but I couldn't do it anymore. I couldn't do this without her. *All this help from everyone just to get attacked one last time.* Only when the room was quiet again did my brother speak.

"C'mon, Bastian," Cade said softly, "you're stronger than this. I know we don't know everything that happened with her, but Shanely would never leave you or her kids without a reason, so it's time to think. You're the one that always figures these things out, so use that head of yours."

"Something's going on. Shanely loves you, and she loves her family. Whatever it was, it was big enough for her to go full boar on everyone like that. She has never once used that much power before," Elijah countered, and I took a deep breath, trying to settle myself.

"I didn't even know she *had* that much power," Cade went on. The two talked about Shanely's newfound power as their words struck home. I narrowed my eyes as my mind ran amuck.

Her Alpha power had always been tied to her negative emotions, I thought to myself. *But Shanely wouldn't hurt a fly, let alone her family. Was it the disconnect from her animals that made it hard for her to control her power or something else? And what would make her so emotional she'd lose control like that?* Suddenly, my head perked up as it all made sense.

"There it is," Cade muttered, helping me to my feet. "Alright, walk us through it."

"She shouted that she had to leave," I said as I walked over to my mate. "Right?"

I frowned when I saw the red marks and trails of blood all over her. The wheels in my turning as I inspected my mate.

"Yeah, so..." Elijah countered as I reached for my mate's arm. A sickening hunch hit my gut that I really wasn't going to like this.

"What came through our bond primarily was fear," I said, sorting through my thoughts out loud. "At the time, I couldn't figure it out."

"Get to the point, Bastian," Cade sighed, putting his hands on his hips. I shot him a glare as he said, "Always the long road with you."

"I wonder if that prick chipped her," I replied, barring my teeth. "I mean some of these marks are bleeding. I think she's terrified because she knew. Patrick died right in front of her, but she was passed out when Calvin showed up."

My brothers eyes went wide.

"That would make her bolt," Elijah chimed in as he grabbed her leg, "if she thinks Calvin's on his way."

He dragged his nails down her skin carefully, and I quickly moved to the

CHAPTER 51

opposite arm. *This had to be it. This had to be why she tried to run.*

Cade blew out a deep breath and started feeling her other leg. "God, we really have no idea what she went through, do we?"

We both stilled at his words, but he was right. I looked at my sleeping mate, and my heart broke again. I don't know how many times I could stitch it back together before it finally gave out.

"C'mon, Bastian," Elijah said, pulling me from my thoughts. "Focus."

I shook myself from those thoughts and got to work. I didn't even know exactly what we should be looking for as I had never seen a tracker like this before. The three of us trailed her skin with our sharpened nails but were coming up empty handed. *She was going to wake soon,* I thought to myself as I chewed on my bottom lip. I scratched the back of my head. *It had to be here,* I thought to myself. It was the only thing that made sense to me.

I was baffled though. *Where did that prick stick it?* My wolf snapped his jaws inside my head for my lack of progress, and I snarled. I didn't need his impatient attitude either. *This wasn't something I was trained to find.*

I ran my fingers through her soft white hair and sighed. The memories of all the times I played with her hair over the years came to mind. I wasn't sure why, but it was a possessive thing with my wolf. We thoroughly liked having our hands in her beautifully soft hair. It was like a statement to everyone else that she was mine, and I was hers. Other than her vividly green eyes, her hair was my favorite thing about her. It didn't matter to me when it turned white. Shanely was breathtaking, and the fact that she was mine was hard to believe. A small smile curved on my lips as I remembered all the times I teased her over the years. The scowl on her lips when I playfully tugged one of her curls or the moment she'd fall asleep because I gently ran my fingers through her hair. I loved each and every memory, and I forced myself to remember the fact that we had so many more memories left to make. This was an awful stain on our lives, but one I would make sure to erase.

I was lost in my thoughts, when my nail suddenly felt something. I stilled, going over the spot once more just to make sure. At the base of her skull, right at the hairline, was a small bump. So completely small and tucked away under her skin, if you weren't dragging your nails over it like I was, you'd miss it completely. Pride swelled in my chest as I turned to my brothers.

"Guys, I found it!" I said, gently rolling Shanely on her side. They came around the bed to see. I pulled her hair aside and pointed. "Here. Feel this."

"You sure?" Elijah asked, his eyes narrowing on the spot.

"Shift to your claw," I commanded, and Cade shifted first.

He gently ran his claw over that spot replying, "Yeah, it's something alright. But it's tiny."

"Grab Malin's stuff," I commanded. I smacked the light above her bed, groaning when I remembered she shattered them. *This would be a lot easier if I could see,* I thought to myself. Elijah was way ahead of me and yanked out his phone light. Cade grabbed the bag and ran back over.

"You sure we shouldn't wait for Malin?" Elijah asked cautiously.

"I'm not letting that stay in her," I said, grabbing the scalpel.

"It's in her neck though," he countered.

"Yeah, but if she wakes up before it's done, you know she's going to freak and tear it out herself," Cade snapped back, holding her head to the side. He gave me a firm nod, and I inhaled deeply.

I quickly cleansed the area with an alcohol wipe before easing the scalpel down. My hands shook slightly as I got close.

"Breathe, Bastian," Cade said, his eyes flashing red. "You can do this. Just breathe."

I took a deep breath, settling my nerves before bringing the scalpel down and cutting right above the bump line. Blood trickled down her neck as I cut a little deeper. The door to the med bay creaked loudly as I took another swipe.

"What are you doing?" Malin demanded. Her quicken steps hurried over to me just as a small white bead appeared. The corners of my mouth rose slightly. *I was right.*

"Shanely's got a tracker, and I'm removing it," I replied, turning to Elijah. "Get me that metal dish and tweezers, will ya?"

CHAPTER 51

"Do you think Mercedes has one?" Daniel asked from across the room. I turned, finding him on the bed holding Mercedes, who had fallen unconscious again.

"Probably," I answered as I took the pan from my brother. "Start checking her. Shanely's was at the base of her neck, and I had to use my wolf's claw to feel it."

"Careful, Bastian," Malin warned.

I swallowed hard as she hovered even more and shook out my arms to loosen up the tension building in them. *I'm so ready to get this done,* I thought to myself. Cade's brow rose slightly, and I shot him a glare. I grabbed the tweezers.

"Don't even start," I said through the link.

"Guys, I found something," Daniel shouted.

"You can help him, Malin," I said quietly. "I've got this."

But Malin only left after I pulled the tiny device from Shanely's neck and dropped it in the dish. *It was so small,* I thought to myself. *Nearly the size of a grain of rice.* This tiny device brought such rage from deep within, and I wished more than anything I could kill Patrick all over again.

I covered Shanely's neck with gauze, even though she wouldn't need it in a few minutes, and set her back in a more comfortable position. *Hardly any blood loss,* I thought proudly as I plopped down in the chair next to her. The corners of my mouth rose as I smirked at my brothers, and Elijah roll his eyes.

"When you perform a c-section in the rain with only your claw then you can feel impressed," he muttered, and I laughed at him.

"Where did you learn that anyways?" I asked, resting my hands on the back of my head to wait.

"I told you I studied up on some things after Cade delivered Aerith in the woods," he replied, taking a seat next to the bed. He tossed his legs up over hers. Cade plopped down at the end, and the three of us officially had my mate cornered.

There was no running this time, I thought grinning.

"Well, I sure am grateful, brother," I replied. "For everything, you two."

They gave me a simple nod, and soon the room grew quiet again. Everyone stayed out, waiting until they got an all clear, but I wanted to wait until Shanely woke up before letting everyone back in. She needed a minute to adjust to everything on her own, and with her Alpha power so tied to her emotions, the less in here the better.

A few from the pack came in to help clean the room before leaving us again. I gave them a grateful nod and sent a link to Abraham to double check everyone. I wasn't sure who else felt Shanely's outburst earlier, but any major issues he and Bay could handle. They kept their kingdom running smoothly. They can handle the wolves.

Shanely never once stirred. Her chest would rise and fall the way it was supposed to, and that small fact brought me comfort. I just focused on her heart beat, while my thoughts ran amuck. It was all I could do to pass the time. All that was left to do was wait. Wait until she woke up again.

And maybe this time stop her before she tore the castle apart.

Chapter 52

Shanely

I groaned, clutching my head as I slowly opened my eyes. A blinding light seemed to land directly on my face from the setting sun, and I rolled to my side. Everything on my body hurt, and my head felt like it was going to explode. I was too tired to get up and close the curtains. I was too tired to do anything.

But then I remembered where I was, and my eyes shot open. My bear snarled, pushing me to get up and move, and I tore the blankets off again. My Alpha power grew as I scurried to get out of bed, and my eyes widened when I saw the triplets passed out around me

Suddenly, Bastian's eyes opened, and he lunged. I yipped as he gripped my wrists tightly, jumping on the bed and straddling me. His eyes were wide, and his hair looked a mess from sleeping in the chair, but my Bastian didn't glare at me. In fact, all I saw was love and understanding in his eyes, but he was *not* letting me go. My mate pushed me back, pinning me against the bed.

"Please," he begged, "just listen to me before you freak out."

His brothers woke immediately, and Cade shot out of his chair towards the table next to the bed. Elijah closed in on my right side, putting his hands up defensively as Cade approached on my left.

"We understand, Shanely," Bastian said with a tight lip smile. Cade dropped a metal dish in my lap as Bastian slowly let my hands go. This tiny white thing rolled around, and I stilled.

"Is that what I think it is?" I asked quietly. *It looked no bigger than my pinky nail.*

Bastian nodded as he replied, "There's more though. You don't have to run or be afraid anymore. Calvin isn't coming to get you or Aerith."

My eyes widened.

"He isn't going to find you *ever* again," Elijah continued. "He's dead, Shanely."

"He died the same night as Patrick," Cade chimed in as he placed the tracker in the palm of my hand. "We made sure of it."

My shoulders sunk in as relief washed over me. I stared at that tracker. That *stupid* device that connected me to those monsters and kept me confined to that house. It was finally out of me. *Calvin was gone*, I thought to myself. *Patrick was gone. The entire Jennings household was gone from this earth.* And finally I could breathe again. My lips puckered as a tear fell down my cheek.

"Oh, love," Bastian whispered just as the dam broke. The mental box I held onto so tightly these past five months splintered, and I buried my face in my hands as I fell against him. He wrapped his arms around me and just held me while I cried. I sobbed against his chest, soaking his shirt as I let every emotion go. A faint thrum seemed to coat my skin, and Bastian squeezed me tighter. Both my animals settled within me, making it easier to try and calm myself down, but my power was out of control. I would be nothing more than a liability if I couldn't get it under control.

The Fenrir triplets never left my side. *I was home,* I thought to myself. *I was finally home with my mate, and I didn't have to leave anyone.* We were all alive, and the ones who plagued my nightmares were gone. That was a hard one to comprehend honestly. It was hard for me to accept they were dead for some reason.

I finally managed to dry my tears and pulled back from my mate. He gave me a soft smile as I wiped my face off.

"Where was it?" I asked softly. "I looked everywhere."

"It was hiding here," Bastian replied, guiding my hand to the back of my neck. "I nearly missed it, love."

Doubt crept in as I felt the Band-Aid on my neck. *I checked that spot before,*

CHAPTER 52

I thought to myself. *Could I have escaped sooner if I just dug a little further?*

"What happened?" I asked quietly. My stomach twisted at what I was asking, but I needed to know what happened to him. I needed to hear the details of how we managed to get back here and in one piece.

"I killed him," my mother answered, and my eyes widened.

Bastian turn slightly before hopping off the bed altogether. The memories we shared from that house came forward, and I reached for her hand once she sat down.

"You're okay," I whispered, giving her a small smile. It fell the moment I remembered shattering her wall. "I'm sorry if I hurt you."

My mother waved me off.

"I'm alive, Shanely, and it's all thanks to you," she replied softly. My dad joined us, giving me a grateful smile, but none of it made me feel any better.

"I don't know about that," I muttered.

"You sent this one over here," Mom went on pointing to Cade, "and he saved me. I was so terrified for you and Aerith, when the alarms went off. There was so much smoke, and we *barely* found the exit in time. I didn't know if you guys did too."

Bastian turned to Cade glaring. "You didn't tell me that!"

He shrugged, giving us a sheepish smile. "We survived, didn't we?"

Mom dropped another small device in my hand, and the two identical trackers rolled together.

"We're both officially free," she said softly.

My gaze drifted from the trackers to her. Tears filled her eyes, and I dropped the devices on the ground. Not caring that they were lost forever. No one would find them against the white floor now, which is where they should be. Lost.

I pulled my mother in and held her tight. We stayed like that for awhile, and I felt her tears land on my shoulder. It was all I could do not to break again, and I gently pulled away, reaching for my mate.

Bastian quietly picked me up, setting me on his lap, and my father wrapped his arms around my mother. *They looked so relieved to be with one another again,* I thought as I buried my nose in the crook of Bastian's neck. I was glad they had each other like I had my mate. I inhaled his scent, letting it soothe my animals and keep that uncontrollable power at bay. *I need him to ground me,* I realized. *To keep everything in check because the moment I let go of him, everything became too much. But with him... Everything was just easier.*

"I'm sorry I locked you behind my shield," my mother finally said, and I snorted loudly.

"I'm sorry I broke it," I said, earning a chuckle from everyone.

Cade and Elijah went to the other room as I leaned further into Bastian, taking a deep breath.

"I think these guys have been waiting to meet their mamma," Cade said as he strutted through the room, carrying a small bundle with him.

I straightened, feeling excited for the first time in such a long time. Elijah was right behind him, grinning up a storm, and Cade carefully handed me one of my sons. Pure joy flooded through the bonds as I smiled wide at my son. Elijah placed the other in my other arm, and I held both my boys for the very first time. I couldn't contain my grin as I soaked them in.

"Oh, they're just perfect, Bastian. This one looks just like you," I said as I stared contently at my boys. "And this one looks like me. Oh, they're safe. They're both safe and sound."

They had the sweetest little features, and both my wolf and bear beamed with pride. *The one on my left definitely had my nose,* I thought as I took him in. He looked so much like my mother and I, with his slightly reddish hair and soft features. His almond shaped eyes were mine too, and I watched as he looked around the room. Not a care in the world.

I turned to my other son and smiled. He looked around too, but I could see right away how different these two were. This one looked just like Bastian and his brothers. His dark features were different than his brothers, and he would be the one to grow up brooding like the rest of the Fenrir boys. I could scent their animals already and grinned.

Aerith wasn't wrong.

"He's our little survivor," Bastian said as he gently rubbed the cheek of

CHAPTER 52

the little one who took after him. My smile fell as I turned to my mate.

"What do you mean?"

"You were bleeding badly, and we didn't have time to wait for evac to roll through," Bastian said quietly, "so Elijah performed a C-section on you." Bastian said quietly.

My eyes widened as I turned to my brother-in-law.

"I'm sorry if your scar is a little jagged," Elijah said, rubbing the back of his head. "I used my claw, and it was difficult in the rain."

"We think this little one was trying to be born first, when your uterus ruptured and ended up cut off from oxygen during this whole mess. He struggled once Elijah pulled him out, and Cassia said there was an issue with his heart too," my mate said solemnly.

"Poor kid got a double whammy," Cade chimed in as pain pierced my heart.

"We got help to him in time, and Dr. Malin looked him over as well. He seems right at rain now," Bastian said as he grabbed the empty bottles on the table next to us. He started filling them with formula for me, and I could see them already starting to root around.

"Oh, my little one," I said quietly and snuggled him closer. *We had all been through so much. Too much,* I thought quietly. I gave each baby a kiss, vowing right there that I would never let something like this happen to them again. They would grow up to be happy and healthy. They would grow up different than I did.

"Need me to name these two as well?" Cade asked, sliding in next to me. His cheesy grin was spread from ear to ear, and I chuckled. *I had missed my Beta,* I thought as I leaned my head on his shoulder. *He always knew how to ease tension in a room.*

My mother gave us a funny look, and Cade laughed saying, "Long story, ma'am."

"No," I answered quietly. "I think I know, but Bastian needs to be okay with it too."

Bastian brought the bottles over, and opened his arms. "Alright, give me my first born then. What's his name?"

"Barrett," I replied, handing him over.

My dad grinned proudly. "Brave as a bear."

I smiled back. *He understood exactly why I picked it.*

"What?" Elijah asked.

"It's what the name means. It means the bravery and strength of a bear," Daniel explained, nudging my foot.

"Yeah, and he was born in absolute terrible conditions and survived. They both did. He needs a powerful name to match his animal, don't you think?" I asked, looking up at my mate, who smiled wide.

"I agree, and I like it, baby," Bastian said, giving our son the bottle. "Well hello, Barrett. Are you hungry?"

Cade grinned wide as Bastian continued to talk to Barrett in the sweetest and gentlest voice he could make, and my mother smacked him upside the back of his head.

"Knock it off," she said, winking at me.

"Ow, man," he muttered, rubbing his head. "You hit like your daughter."

My eyes lit up as she laughed. It was the first time I got to hear it, and it was just as I imagine it would be. My dad watched proudly from the sidelines.

"What about this little one?" Elijah asked, pulling everyone's attention to my youngest.

I smiled softly. *This name I had been saving for years.* It was just special to me, and after looking down at this little guy and knowing all that he went through, it just felt right.

"Bellamy," I answered. Bellamy immediately latched onto his bottle, and I smiled when his eyes settled on mine. *They were just like mine,* I thought to myself. Bellamy carried the Medvedev family trademark it seemed, and I was proud one of my babies did.

"What does that one mean?" Bastian asked, sitting next to me with Barrett. He peeked over to look at Bellamy, with the biggest smile on his face.

"It means Good Friend, which is exactly what these two will be with each other. Best friends just like their dad and uncles," I said, giving the Fenrir brothers a big smile.

It was odd seeing such strong, capable men look somewhat emotional, and even Elijah's eyes glistened with tears. *These surly brutes of men were just big teddy bears deep down,* I thought to myself.

"Honestly though," I said, nestling further into my mate, "I just love the name. It's been a favorite of mine for some time, and after everything this little one went through just to survive, he needed a special name. One as special as him."

Bastian smiled. "I like it. Barrett and Bellamy."

"You know..." Cade said with a feral grin, "Barrett was *also* an amazing character on that video game you never took the time to play."

"Are you serious?" I asked, barking out a laugh. "There's a Barrett in the game you named Aerith after?"

Cade tossed his head back in laughter, and everyone couldn't help but chime in. Bastian rolled his eyes, grinning wide at his brother.

"He's a really cool character though," Cade went on. "It fits this little one!"

We all sat for a moment, letting the little ones eat. I remembered holding Aerith like this when she was first born. My eyes drifted around the room, and I frowned.

"Is Aerith alright?" I whispered to Bastian.

"She's perfectly fine," he answered, and my shoulders sagged in relief. "She's with Alana and Thomas right now. Last Johnny said she was passed out asleep next to Tommy."

I nodded my head. *I needed to see her soon,* I thought. *She went through everything too.*

"Will you bring her down when she wakes?" I asked, and Bastian nodded.

"Of course," he answered. "We just wanted to give you a second to adjust is all."

I snorted, giving him a knowing look. "You mean so I wouldn't bring the walls down again."

"Well..." Cade teased, and mom slugged his arm.

"Can you please call everyone back in?" I groaned, feeling my cheeks heat. "I need to say something."

Bastian pulled out his phone as Cassia and Dr. Malin offered to burp and change the boys for us. I reluctantly let my boys go, despite every fiber in my being screaming at me to never let them go again. My anxiety rose the second they disappeared behind the door, and Bastian immediately started rubbing my arm.

"*They are safe,*" he said through the link. "*I promise you, Shanely. Everyone is safe.*"

Hearing my mate's voice inside my head settled my racing heart. I gave him a small smile as the doors opened.

Guilt ate me alive as *everyone* looked hesitant to approach me. Other than Emmie, who hugged me the second she walked inside the room, they hung back a bit, and I pursed my lips together. This time I noticed quite a bit more than I didn't before. *Bay and my Uncle Cain looked the worse,* I thought to myself, and my hand covered my mouth in shock. *How did I miss all this before?*

A deep sadness took over, and I was trying desperately to gain complete control of my Alpha power. I couldn't let it out and hurt everyone again.

"*Don't let me go,*" I said to Bastian through our link. His love poured down the bond as I went on. "*Whatever you do, please don't let me go.*"

"*Never.*"

I exhaled deeply, turning to the others. "I am so sorry, you guys. I didn't mean to hurt you all," I said as a tear fell down my cheek. "I was just so afraid and…"

My voice trailed off unable to finish my sentence. I didn't want to burden them with my trauma, when they clearly went through more than enough on their own. I didn't know how to explain it fully. I didn't know what to say.

"We dug trackers out of Mercedes and Shanely's neck," Bastian said firmly. My eyes widened, but he just held me firm. "I'd show you, but they are lost somewhere on the floor. It's why she was so afraid earlier, and why she wanted to leave. She thought Calvin was coming back and would find us all here."

CHAPTER 52

"It's no excuse," I said, shaking my head. "I shouldn't have lost control in the first place. I don't know why I'm struggling with it so bad. I don't know why I can't..."

Pain gripped my heart, and I leaned into my mate. *Bastian would be the key to my control for now,* I thought as my Alpha power thrummed against my veins. It felt ready to surge, but Bastian's touch helped keep me calm. Cade quickly filled the empty spot beside me, and Elijah stayed by my feet with Emersyn in between his legs. Each one keeping a hand on me.

"Don't worry about it, sis," Abraham said, snickering. "Just remind me to *never* get on your bad side."

He patted my feet, winking at me as if it never happened. I stuck out my tongue despite still feeling so guilty.

"I'm still so sorry," I said, taking Caleb's hand in mine. Bay took my other hand then. Both with smiles on their face. The group softened as they swarmed my bed, and it felt good to be reunited again.

"I'll let you talk with your friends, baby," Mom whispered, pulling me from my thoughts. She promptly stood, keeping her eyes glued to the floor as she attempted to scurry out of the way.

"Mom," I said as I grabbed her hand. She looked to me nervously, and I gave her a soft smile. "Please stay. This... This is our family."

My mother shifted on her feet. *She was uncomfortable,* I thought as I tried to think of a way to help her. Thankfully, my father seemed to notice too.

"We can stand here, my love," he offered. "If you want."

She took up his offer and settled in his arms, and I laid back in my seat. I was mesmerized watching the two of them together. The complete love in their eyes whenever they looked to one another. The smile that never seemed to leave my father's face. I snuggled against Bastian. *I'm glad they were reunited.*

"Everyone meet my mother... Well, *our* mother," I said, grinning. "Mom, this is Caleb. I think you knew him as a baby."

Recognition shown in her eyes as he walked over and gave her a hug.

"Hello ma'am," he said, and she chuckled softly.

"My, my, you've grown son," she said, looking up at him. He stood nearly a foot over her, and his handsome grin reached his eyes. "I didn't recognize you when you walked in, but you do look just like your father. All except the eyes, but you are the spitting image of my mate. I can't believe how much you've grown. You're so tall."

"Not as tall as that brute," Caleb chuckled, pointing to Abey.

I giggled as I turned to my baby brother. "Mom, this is Abraham. Abraham, meet your mother."

"We met on the plane," he said quietly. Half his face was covered by his hand, and he didn't make a move to greet her. I narrowed my eyes as my mother anxiously rubbed her arms. She picked up on the tension too. Everyone did.

"That's right," she said softly. "Thank you for helping me that night."

"Stop being a scardy cat, and give your mother a hug."

The awkward silence filled the room as Abraham slowly dragged his eyes to mine. I held his stare, battling it out with my brother, and after a moment he stood.

"Hi, mama," he said, wrapping his arms around her.

"Hello, son," she replied. She stood on her tiptoes to kiss his cheek. "You have grown into a fine young man too, it seems."

Abraham shifted on his feet before returning to his chair quickly. *He was truly afraid right now,* I thought to myself. I frowned slightly, not really sure how to ease that either.

"I think Abraham is scared of his mom," Bastian's voice came through my link. *"Maybe you should move on with the introductions."*

I rolled my eyes and gestured to Elijah. "I'm sure you know Elijah already, but this is his mate, Emersyn. Her sister Esme is behind her, and is mated to your nephew, Noah. Then that leaves Abey's mate, Bay. She's Bastian, Cade, and Elijah's little sister."

"Wow," Mom said quietly, "you all need to branch out."

Everyone laughed, and it felt good to hear again. I hadn't felt this at ease and happy in such a long time, and I laid my head on Bastian's shoulder, taking it all in. But my mom's smile suddenly fell, and she grabbed my father's hand tightly.

CHAPTER 52

"I am so sorry to the four of you," she said softly, and just like that the room quieted. I squeezed Bastian's hand as my mother went on. "I did what I thought was best for everyone, but it was the wrong choice. I wasn't there to raise any of you or be there as your mate. I even missed what few years I had left with my own mother all because I thought leaving was the best choice. The woman who protected me and loved me unconditionally, and I just wasn't there. I wasn't there for *any* of you."

"Mom..."

My voice trailed off as I didn't know what to say. I turned to my brothers, but Abey dropped his head, refusing to look at anyone, and Caleb just stood there with the same doe-eyed look I had. No one said a word, and my Alpha power surged through my veins as pain filled my chest. Bastian held me tighter.

"No, it's true," she said, her voice shaking slightly, "and I should have been there for you all. My father just..."

"Tell us, please," Abey said, surprising me. He leaned forward in his chair, his eyes begging for the truth. "What exactly happened back then?"

My father's shoulder went rigid, but I wouldn't rat him out. If that was a secret he didn't want to admit then I wouldn't say a word.

Mom sighed. "My father somehow found out about my mate being a bear. He asked to speak with me privately one night, but he was so angry by the time I got there. I hadn't even spoken a word, but his rage..."

She shook her head, and I recognized that haunted look. No one said a word as she gained her composure and continued.

"He never said a word before he struck me across my face and clamped that bracelet on me," she said softly. Clasping her hands together slowly she continued, "I lost my wolf, and it was *devastating*. My father said he knew about Daniel, and that he couldn't believe I'd be dumb enough to associate with a bear, let alone be pregnant by one. That was how I found out about you, sweetie."

My mother's eyes slowly drifted to me, and I took her hand in mine. *This wasn't her fault. She didn't deserve any of this.*

"Jack banished me and told me never to return or he'd kill Daniel and the entire clan. He never wanted to even catch a whiff of my scent again, so I ran. To keep everyone safe, I ran," she said, dropping her head. She pulled her hand from mine and played with the frayed ends of her shirt. My heart broke for her.

Guilt hit me hard. Instead of staying to face it together, my mother ran. *Just like I have in the past*, I thought. *Just like I tried to do before.*

"It was Calvin," I muttered quietly. My stomach twisted so hard, I almost couldn't get the words out, but I forced myself too. *They needed to know.* I looked to my mother saying, "He's the one who told Jack about you and dad, and he gave Jack the inhibitor to use on you. Calvin wanted to isolate you, so you'd be easier to capture. He just used the tension between the pack and clan to his advantage."

Everyone stared blankly at me, and it dawned on me that I would have to explain the rest now. I'd have to explain the experiments, Lorelei, and how far up the Division this corruption goes. *I'd have to explain what Calvin was after*, I thought to myself. Nausea crept in, and I pushed back into Bastian's embrace. *Later. I just can't now.*

"I have something to tell you, my love," my father said quietly, pulling me from my thoughts. "You may look at me differently once you know."

Surprise lifted my brow, and Cade shrugged when he caught my worrying glance.

"She needs to know at some point," my Beta said through our link.

"What if this is too much too soon?" I asked.

"Personally, I respect the man more because of it. It will all work out, Baby Girl."

I squeezed his arm as my mother turned to Dad.

"I could never, Daniel," she said, placing her hand on his cheek. He leaned into her touch, taking a deep breath to say what scared him most.

"I killed your father Jack," he blurted, and my mother straightened. The whole room stayed silent as he continued. "When I lost our bond and couldn't find you, I found him instead. I'm so sorry, my love. I smelled your blood on him, and I lost control of my bear. It was the only time I had ever blacked out like that."

CHAPTER 52

Her eyes widened, and she dropped her hand on his cheek. She didn't say anything at first, but soon my mother leaned forward and kissed his cheek.

"My father was an awful man," she said softly, "and I stopped viewing him as family a long time ago. You are my mate, Daniel. Always."

His shoulders slumped forward, and he pulled her into his arms once more. Dad took a deep breath, and I saw a weight lifted off him.

"See?"

I gave Cade a slow grin, nudging him playfully, and he wiggled his eyebrows at me. *I missed him.*

"And somehow after all that you had me?" Abraham asked, breaking the silence. I knew his early years had been eating at him since we discovered the truth, and I was genuinely surprised he hasn't asked sooner.

Our mother nodded turning back to us. "Shanely came early, and by the time I had her, I had run out of money. I bought a basket and put everything I owned inside to help keep you warm. I needed to figure out a place to stay, and get a job, but it was hard to leave my home. It was harder to leave you, Daniel," she said, leaning into him again. "I tried to stay out of my father's sight, but I was terrified to get too close, so I went past his border south of us. I cut through the woods one night, trying to get across town faster, when that tiger found me."

My father growled. He couldn't help it, but my eyes were on my mother. The traumatic memories flashed before her eyes, and I knew she remembered every detail of that night.

Abraham was unholy still. My heart went out to him as he waited for my mother to continue. I wanted her to stop. I didn't want her to relive these moments, and I didn't think he needed to torture himself by hearing it.

But it wasn't my call to make.

"It was so late that night," Mother went on. Her eyes glistening with every word. "Without my wolf, it was hard to see, and I didn't sense the tiger until it was too late. I don't remember much other than his scent and that he was white. I'm sorry, Abraham. I don't know anymore than that."

"I don't care about knowing him," he said, sitting up in his seat. Surprise knitted my brow. "I was raised by an amazing man, and that guy right there is the only other guy that can take his place. I know where I come from. I just..."

"You want to know why I left you," she said, and he froze. Mom sighed and sat down at the corner of the bed. "I need you three to know something. Leaving *all* of you was the hardest thing I have ever had to do, but Abraham, the only reason I took Shanely with me was because of her scent."

My brother was so still, I wasn't sure he was still breathing. I gave Bay a pleading look, and she wrapped her arms around him.

"The war with the Blackwood pack was becoming too great," Mom said quietly. "Their wolves were becoming bolder every day, son. I was afraid they'd scent me and you kids somehow. I already knew I was at risk because of my father, but you two..."

She shook her head sighing. "You both are mixers. I had no idea what would happen if *anyone* found out. The tigers I left you with were good people, Abraham. You scented solely as a tiger, and I thought you'd be safer with them than with me. I removed myself from your life because it was safer for you. Even though it killed me."

Abraham's eyes glistened as he stared blankly at our mother. He didn't say a word in return, but I knew my brother. He was just holding everything in. Compartmentalizing it and over-analyzing everything. I just wasn't sure if he'd ever comment on it though. I doubted he'd ever mention it again.

Mom turned to me then. "I'm sorry I left you too."

I shrugged, feeling everyone's eyes on me again. "It's okay."

"No," she said softly, "it was never okay. I hated myself so much giving the both of you up."

I dropped my gaze and chewed on my bottom lip. A single question rolled around in my mind, but for some reason I was terrified to ask. I looked to my lap, choosing to ignore it entirely. *It was just easier that way.*

"Why did you leave her then?" Bastian spoke, and I quickly turned to him. He winked at me, and my heart warmed as I felt his love pour through the bond.

"*I can be your voice, Shanely. I can always be your voice,*" he said, and I

CHAPTER 52

kissed his cheek.

Mother sighed again. "A part was that I was paranoid. I was so freaked by Blackwood that I was afraid maybe someone would catch her scent and try to kill her. I had no wolf to defend her with, and when weird things started happening at my work, I freaked again and gave her up to be adopted."

"What happened at work?" Dad asked, and mother dropped her head.

"Calvin, I presume, but I don't know. I thought someone was following me from the pack, so I decided to send her away just in case. The social lady helped me find her a family across the country, and promised to watch over her for me, and I left Shanely with her. It wasn't even a week later, and Calvin had taken me."

My father's fingers gripped her shoulders as his eyes fluttered gold. Mom merely reached up and took his hand in hers, calming him down perfectly. I smiled and leaned into my mate.

"I would have never thought you all would be together though," she said, patting my leg. "How did you even find one another?"

A feral grin appeared on *everyone's* lips before we all burst out laughing. Everyone except Abraham. He turned beat red, sinking further in his chair and refusing to look at anyone. I genuinely felt bad for him.

"It's a long story really," I replied, laughing as Abraham covered his face with his hand. He turned to peek at me.

"*I won't tell her,*" I linked him, and he sighed heavily.

I owed him that much.

"Well, I want to hear about all your adventures," she said, smiling wide. "I want to hear everything about you."

"I'll tell you everything," I said, grinning. "I promise."

My smile grew as I thought about everything I wanted to share with my mother. I had a lifetime of stories to fill her in on. I don't care anymore about what happened with our past. My family was truly whole for the first time in my life, and I refused to take it for granted. We were together, and that's what mattered.

"What I'd like to know is what happened that night?" Bastian asked, looking down to me. I lost my smile.

"What night exactly?" I asked as I played with a strand of hair.

"All of them," he replied. "From the moment I lost you."

Chapter 53

I stiffened, dropping the strand of hair I was playing with. I tucked my fingers under my arms as the memories flashed before my eyes. I quickly shoved them out. *Not yet,* I thought to myself. *I didn't want to ruin this good moment between us and just... Not yet.*

"Well, I'd like to know what happened to all of you too," I said softly. I forced a smile to my lips, needing to change the subject, but when the group suddenly looked everywhere but me, a sickening feeling hit my gut. No one said a word, and I frowned. *Was it really that bad?*

"We have things to tell you that won't be easy to hear. Why don't we tell you our story first, and then we can discuss what happened with you. Deal?" Bastian asked.

"Do we have to?" I muttered quietly. The triplets frowned.

"We can talk in private if you rather, but I need you to trust me with some of it. I don't know how to help you when so much of it I don't even know." Bastian said softly. "Please baby? I just want to help."

"Okay," I finally relented.

It was only fair, I told myself despite my wolf snarling inside me. *She didn't want to talk about what happened, and honestly neither did I. But they were going to answer my questions which wasn't easy for them, so I could do it too.* I figured I should just ask the hardest question first and get it over with.

"Did we lose anyone after Patrick took me?"

Bastian went rigid as Elijah answered, "Brody was dead when Bastian and I made it to the river. It was a massacre of his whole team."

I remember feeling his disconnect. That horrendous pain of losing their bonds. Brody was the kindest wolf I knew and had become a great friend to our family and my daughter especially. *She would be crushed when she found out*, I thought. *She may already know.*

"Ash and Deidre fell," Cade continued solemnly, "you and I saw that. But we lost them, along with Mark and the anaconda sisters. We lost a third of the pack actually."

My eyes widened. *A third?!* All those unnecessary deaths. All because Calvin wanted me and my daughter. He wanted the power pulsing in my veins, and I gritted my teeth in anger. My wolf snapped her jaws again. *She wanted out.*

"Ryder saved my life that day," Bastian whispered softly, and everyone lowered their gaze. My mate lifted his shirt, showing the two scars where he was shot. I gently touched them, my heart breaking as I remembered that part too. I remembered feeling him get hit when I rushed to save Emmie. Bastian lowered his shirt and settled back down next to me. He wrapped his arms around me, and I pulled him in closer.

"I felt you get hit," I whispered. Emmie dropped her head. "It's how they managed to hit me with the tranq."

"I felt it too," Emmie said finally looking me in the eye. "I am so sorry, Shanely. I should have never ran. I should have *never* left you."

"Oh, Emmie," I whispered, taking her hand. "I am so glad you did. I couldn't stand anything happening to you either."

"Thank you for saving my mate," Elijah said. His eyes glistened as he patted my leg, and I playfully slugged his arm chuckling.

"You've saved me more times than I can count, Elijah. Chasing after Emmie was nothing," I said with a grin. It fell though as I remembered our conversation. "What happened after you got shot? Patrick put the bracelet on me so quickly, and I lost *everything*."

"We both got ambushed," my mate said quietly. A haunted look in his eyes. "They left two guys to make sure we were dead, while the rest of the team went towards the pack. Ryder killed them both. He dragged Elijah and I out of the way, and we hid in a cave until I could move again. By the time

CHAPTER 53

I managed to get to the pack, it was all but gone. The three of us searched the land, and our house, but *everyone* was gone. Thankfully because Cade was with the pack, we found where everyone was hiding."

"We hid in Dead Man's Hollow while we figured out our next move," Cade finished before looking at his brother. A dark expression flashing on his face.

I blew out a deep breath, rubbing my face as I tried to process everything. "Good lord, you guys. I'm so glad he was there with you that day. Where is Ryder anyways? I haven't seen him or Johnny and Alana yet."

No one answered me. They all looked so sad, so broken, and a sickening feeling hit the pit of my stomach. My wolf whined as I tried to pull on their bonds. I found Johnny's fairly quickly, but Ryder's was *nowhere* to be found.

"Where's Ryder?" I demanded, my eyes flashing red.

"He didn't make it, Baby Girl," Cade finally answered, and my jaw dropped.

No...

Not our Ryder. I pulled forcefully on my pack bonds, refusing to believe them. Panic surged through me as I searched *everywhere* for him. *I must have just missed his somehow. He was here! He had to be...*

"Shanely," Bastian said, pulling me from my frantic thoughts. The others had taken a step back, and I didn't even realize my Alpha power had leaked around me. My chest heaved as I continued to search, but Bastian placed his hands on both sides of my face, stilling me. His voice was firm. "You won't find his bond. No matter how many times you try to look. I am so sorry."

My lips puckered as I stared into Bastian's hollow eyes. His beautifully blue, hollow eyes that just looked so haunted right now. His own pain and agony seeped through the bond, and I finally believed him. *Not our Ryder.*

"Scout found Patrick weeks after you disappeared and the Division finally returned home," Cade said quietly. Bastian never let me go as silent tears fell down my cheek. "We weren't sure if we were going to catch a break honestly, but she managed to track him to the house, and we all came to confirm you were actually here before storming the place. You and Aerith's safety was our main priority, and we needed to be careful, or we feared losing you two again."

"Our first night here, we were scouting the woods," Elijah went on. Bastian tightened his grip on me, and my heart broke a little more. "We decided to split up and... Ryder was with Bastian."

"He ran point," Cade said, and I covered my mouth with my hands. *Oh my God... The plates.*

"We were making our way towards the house, when he saw something off in the distance. He stepped on those plates just seconds before me. He *saved* my life again," Bastian said, his voice cracking slightly.

My eyes widened when I realized Bastian held back part of our bond. Somehow, he put up a wall, blocking me from feeling certain emotions from him. Because for a split second that wall crumbled, and the darkest emotions I have *ever* felt seeped through. I didn't know how he managed to hide a part of him, but I felt sick when his guilt and agony filled my heart. And then just like that, it was gone, and he built the wall back up.

"He just dropped, Baby Girl. He was dead before he hit the ground," Cade said solemnly.

I sat on the bed unable to comprehend any of what they were saying. I couldn't process it. I couldn't accept that one of our closest friends was just gone. *And my mate was hiding such pain and guilt from me...*

My power rose as my wolf howled within me. One of hers was gone too, and she was livid. Bastian felt my lack of control and promptly picked me up and put me on his lap. His touch soothed us, but I still struggled to keep control. It was too much. Everything just hurt, and the one thing I kept coming back to was this was my fault. *It was all my fault,* I thought as the tears began to fall. *Had I just gone with Calvin in the first place, none of this would have happened. They'd still be alive.*

I sobbed into Bastian's chest again. *Ryder was my friend. One of their best friends, and he died trying to save me.* He had been there for us no matter what and had never once found his mate. His mate would never know, and I couldn't even watch out for her. I couldn't do *anything.*

CHAPTER 53

Rage surged through my veins, and my wolf snapped her jaws angrily. She demanded to be released, but I was afraid of going feral if I let her. A familiar sensation covered my skin as my power rose. I stole a peek finding my mother's eyes white as snow.

It wasn't fair, I thought to myself as I leaned heavily on my mother's shield. Wasn't fair in the slightest. We did everything right. *Everything the way we were supposed to.* And yet we still were the ones to suffer.

My Alpha power lessened as my tears dried on my cheek. This was a wound that would not heal. Ever. I felt my mother's shield fall away as I leaned further into my mate for comfort.

"He saved all our lives that night. It's how we found the plates and cameras in the first place. It's why it took us so long to get to you too," Abraham continued.

"He died because of me," I quietly admitted. Guilt churned my stomach as I buried my face again.

"Give her a minute, guys," Bastian commanded, and I heard the shuffling of feet move around me. Cade closed the curtain for us, leaving me alone with my mate.

Bastian wrapped his arms around me and rubbed my back. He didn't ask me questions, or insist I start explaining what happened to me. He stayed quiet, just rubbing my back until I was ready to speak, but I didn't want to talk about this anymore. I didn't *want* to feel better from this. I wanted this pain to stay with me forever because it *was* my fault. No one could tell me otherwise, and I had no desire to talk about it further. Ryder died because of me.

I sat there stewing quietly on my mate's lap. The familiar *thump-thump* of Bastian's heart beating alongside mine was the only sound in my head. *I never thought I'd hear this again*, I thought. *I never thought I'd see him again, yet here he was. Alive and well.* It was a miracle I even got out of that place, let alone return to my mate and family like this.

My mate sighed, shifting in his seat. Anguish seeped through the bond for a moment, and I knew what he wanted. He was trying to be delicate, but it didn't matter how you asked the question. The answer was always going to be painful to hear. I didn't want to hurt him though, and I was ashamed of what I had done. The things I allowed and pretended. I only did those things to protect my daughter and escape, but I didn't want to admit *any* of it to my mate.

"You can ask, Bastian," I said softly.

His shoulders tensed, but after a moment I heard his raspy voice ask, "What exactly did Patrick do to you?"

I snorted as I leaned forward and away from him. My knee-jerk reaction was to be sarcastic. To just snap back; What *didn't* he do? But Bastian didn't deserve that. His gorgeous blue eyes frantically searched mine as I looked back at him.

And the guilt ate me alive.

"I need to tell you something," I said softly as my cheeks reddened, "but before I do, I need you to understand I've hated myself everyday for doing it. I am so ashamed, but you deserve to know. Please, know I only did what I did to help me escape."

"Shanely, you have nothing to be ashamed over," he said quietly, reaching for me, but I pushed further away from him.

"No I do, Bastian. I pretended that I was accepting him. That I was coming around to the idea of loving him and being friends with him. I let him hold me close when we slept, and he kissed me more than once. I couldn't do *anything* when he touched me or held me. And to make matters worse, there were genuine times when I just felt awful for him," I muttered as my chest tightened. *That was a truth I didn't want to admit to anyone.* I pitied Patrick, and there were moments I forgot he was the villain too.

I dropped my head, and my animals were oddly quiet. Like they didn't want to hear it either. I couldn't look Bastian in the eye and see the disappointment in them. I couldn't bare to see the hurt on his face as I explained how far I let things go, but now that I started spilling the truth, I couldn't turn off my mouth.

And he never once interrupted me.

"After Calvin showed me my mother in the labs below," I stammered, needing to fill the awkward silence, "I needed to adjust my plan. *Everything*

CHAPTER 53

I tried to do prior blew up in my face. Only when I started playing nice and stopped fighting him, did Patrick let up. I needed him to drop his guard, and tell me what I needed to know, so I could get the three of us out. I swear I was trying to escape the entire time, but I let him believe we were actually becoming a family, and it's *kills* me every time I think about it."

My pain flooded the bond, and I knew he felt it all. I just hoped he believed me. I hoped more than anything he'd forgive me. Because I hated myself for it.

Suddenly, Bastian gripped the sides of my face, forcing me to look him in the eyes. His face was not full of anger like I expected though. He didn't hate me like he should, and my lips puckered as he smiled softly. Tears filled my eyes once more when he gently kissed my nose.

"Shanely, I know some of what happened to you. We saw bits and pieces through the scope, and I could tell even from a distance that you were not happy," he said, and a single tear slid down my cheek. He gently wiped it away saying, "Patrick was a monster, and I've never once felt like you cheated on me. Even if he had raped you, I would have *never* blame you for that. Understand? I would have wished to dismember him slowly and painfully if he had, but please let go of your shame and your guilt. You are my mate, and that has not once changed on my end."

I couldn't stop the tears from falling, and he gently kissed each one. I didn't deserve this man, and when his lips moved to my mouth, I melted into him. Relief washed over me, and that heavy blanket of guilt fell away as Bastian poured love down the bond. He showered me with love and affection, and I soaked up every bit he gave. *He was my home, and I loved him. I loved him more than anything.*

I gently pulled back, seeing him smiling wide. I ran my thumb across his bare cheek, still not used to seeing him without a beard.

"Bastian?"

"Hmm?" he said, kissing me again.

I pulled back, giving him a firm look. "Why are you concealing part of the bond?"

He stilled. My words were barely a whisper when they left my lips, but he looked as if I struck him somehow.

"You shower me with love after everything I've done, everything that's eating me alive inside," I whispered softly, "yet you won't share what's hurting you."

He sighed. "You've been through enough, Shanely. I'm..."

"You're not fine," I interrupted. "You're not, and it's my job to heal you too. Please let me in."

My mate's eyes softened as he gently ran his thumb along my jawline. My wolf purred at the sensation, and I closed my eyes, enjoying every second of it.

"One day," he finally said, and I opened my eyes. "I promise, I will let you in one day. Just not today. Let my wolf see you are okay. Let us know our mate is healing and then we'll open that part of us again. He won't allow me to share our darkest thoughts and feelings until he knows you're okay."

My heart hurt, but I gave him a small nod. *It must be really bad if his wolf won't relent right now,* I thought as I leaned forward and kissed his cheek. My wolf bristled in frustration that I gave in so easily, but I shrugged her off. *If our mate needed a little time to open up then so be it. I'll still be here to help him regardless of him admitting anything.* I was just grateful to be taking care and loving him again.

"So who chipped you?" Bastian asked, pulling me from my thoughts.

"That was Patrick," I snorted. "He must have done it as soon as he took me, but it was him. It actually saved my life once. I had managed to escape with Aerith briefly, and that tracker alerted him just in time. He caught us before I hit the plates."

Bastian paled slightly. "I remember that day."

"Wait, you saw me?" I asked, my eyes widening. *I had no idea my mate was watching.* My eyes narrowed as I struggled to remember the details of that day.

He nodded grimly. "Once we found you and discovered all the things Calvin had installed around the house, we were stuck. We couldn't really use any of our shifter abilities like we normally would, so Abraham made

CHAPTER 53

some calls. He called in some massive favors to get us the military gear we used. He got us the retired aircraft, vest, night vision, just to name a few, and we had it all within the week. We trained with it all as quick as we could, while Elijah tried day after day to get into the network or control panel. I don't know, whatever he calls it," he chuckled, shaking his head. "He struggled to get through and shut the plates off though. While we waited, we watched, and I just happened to be on the wall that day. You scared the living daylights out of me when you ran."

"He never told me about the outside security until that moment. It was the first real day I started to lose hope," I replied, my shoulders falling again.

"I'm so sorry, my love. I tried shouting your name. I tried everything to get you to stop and see me. You were right there, and I couldn't reach you. I couldn't get you to see me, and I *couldn't* save you. Cade and I tried more than once to signal you too, but it was difficult," he replied. "We never knew if you understood."

"Signal me?"

He nodded again. "More than once actually. We saw him toss you outside in the cage one night, and I was terrified when you curled up and stopped moving. I was afraid you'd fall asleep and not wake up, so we tried to signal you and tell you we were here. Just to hang on a little longer because we were coming."

It dawned on me then. The light I always saw reflecting in the room and when I was in the cage that night. *It was them...*

"The light," I said, blinking once. "I remember that ridiculous bright light annoying me, but I couldn't figure out where it was coming from."

He kissed my forehead, giving me a soft smile. "It was us. We never knew if our message got across."

"I'm sorry it didn't. I had no idea it was you guys. I just assumed it was from one of Calvin's devices that was annoying me."

"Why did that prick put you there anyways?" he growled out.

I sighed, remembering that day vividly. "I kind of lost it earlier. It all started when he tore Aerith from my arms and then hit me when I fought back. I had officially snapped and broke into Patrick's gun safe to try and shoot him."

"Nuh-uh!" Cade shouted as he threw the curtain back, startling me. He hopped up next to me, his large frame rocking the bed, and I nearly lost my balance. Bastian caught me, setting me right again and glared at his brother. I laughed hard then. *I should have known he was listening,* I thought to myself.

"Cade…" Bastian snapped as he pushed Cade towards the edge.

"No, I need to hear this story!" he cried out as he pushed Bastian back.

"You're listening to all of it anyways, dude. What if she doesn't want to tell you?"

Cade gave me a pitiful look then, and my heart melted. "Baby Girl? Please, can I listen to the story from inside the curtain?"

Elijah kissed Emersyn, who waved as she left with her sister, and joined the three of us. Everyone was beginning to disperse again, and by the delicious smells coming from down the hall, I suspected it had something to do with dinner.

"I'd like to hear this story too," Elijah said with a smile, "if you don't mind, Shanie. We were all losing our minds watching you sit in that cage in the dead of winter."

"I don't mind, Bastian," I replied as Elijah closed the curtain back up and sat down on my other side. Bastian sighed, rolling his eyes as the two got comfortable. I giggled again once they were settled. *These boys…*

"There's not much to tell," I said, sighing. "I had already pissed him off earlier when I attacked him for taking Aerith away from me. I spent the whole night in the cage in the garage for that one."

Bastian tensed when I spoke. I could see the anger spread to the rest of the Fenrir brothers as I explained the rest. I just gripped Bastian's hand tighter to soothe his wolf.

"Anyways, I snapped that day and stumbled into his office. He left it unlocked for once, so I grabbed a very heavy gun out of his gun cage. By the time I figured out how to use it, he was there, and I only grazed his arm when I tried to shoot him. He beat me unconscious, and I woke up outside

CHAPTER 53

in the cage."

The boys stayed silent, processing the information carefully before Cade finally spoke up, "God, if I could kill him twice."

Elijah nodded his head. "Just think... Shanely could have ended it all if guns were a thing shifters grew up knowing how to use."

I shrugged, but the look on Bastian's face concerned me. His brows had knitted together, and I wasn't sure what he was thinking.

"I bet you scared the living piss out of him that day though," Cade said, grinning wide and easing the tension brewing. It was contagious, and soon I was grinning too. *Leave it to him to make it funny.*

"I don't think he was expecting it," I said, chuckling. "Oh, that was also where he kept his *shrine* of me at too. I found it all on the back wall that day."

"Shrine?" Bastian asked, raising an eyebrow at me.

I nodded. "Patrick's been spying on us since I moved here. He had thousand of pictures of me on that wall. It was... disturbing."

Elijah ran his fingers through his hair. "Good lord, that guy was really off his rocker then?"

"Calvin treated him horribly. Like I'm not trying to defend him, but he was insanely cruel to Patrick. It makes complete sense why he turned out the way he did. That cage was his when he was a child. Patrick only took the idea from Calvin."

"You're kidding?" Cade asked in disbelief.

"I am not. It was awful learning all about their past together. Calvin blamed Patrick for contributing to his wife's death, when he had to get him from daycare instead of meeting his wife at home. Calvin thought maybe he would have been able to save his wife if he wasn't stuck picking Patrick up, but it was all a mess. Just awful. And the fight they had the night you came for me..."

I blew out a deep breath before shaking myself from that memory. "I was grateful for what he did for Aerith though. He saved her from his dad.

An uncomfortable silence filled the empty space between us before Bastian suddenly snorted. "Yeah well, my father was no peach either, but you don't see me doing any of what Patrick did. I mean kidnapping a girl and then trying to kill her husband. That's messed up."

"Ultimately, it was Calvin behind everything," I said softly, "but he's gone. They both are, and that's all that matters now."

Bastian leaned down and kissed me on my lips, and I melted into him. I inhaled his woodsy scent every chance I got, wanting to ingrain it into my memory the best I could. He pulled back whispering, "I'm still so sorry it took me so long to save you."

"But you guys did save me," I said with a smile. I narrowed my eyes as I thought about that for a moment. "How did you by the way? The power to the house was out, but I know the outside stuff was functioning."

Bastian sheepishly rubbed the back of his head as he turned to his brothers. Cade and Elijah grinned like banshees, waiting for Bastian to answer. *Oh, I had a bad feeling about this,* I thought to myself.

"Okay, just don't hit me when I tell you," my mate said.

I crossed my arms, narrowing my eyes to the three of them. "What did you guys do?"

"We were dropped in," he said with a smirk.

"You were what?" I asked, my brows furrowing. "You mean like from a plane?"

"It's not as bad as it sounds," he laughed. My jaw dropped.

"Yes it is!" I shouted as I slugged him. "There was a big storm that night! How is it even possible?"

"Okay, the storm made it rough," my mate said, putting his hands up defensively, "but we did alright for only getting to practice for a little while. I saw an opportunity, and I couldn't pass it up, my love. It was risky with the weather, so the three of us decided to jump alone instead of with the team."

"Bastian Lee Fenrir! Don't you ever jump out of a plane like that again!" I shouted, smacking his chest a few good times before he caught my hand. A flash of red and gold appeared in those gorgeous blue eyes of his, and I sucked in a breath. My wolf pushed to the surface sensing his. *God, he was beautiful. He was breathtakingly beautiful.*

CHAPTER 53

"I'd do it again if I needed to save you or our kids," he replied, his voice dropping into that sexy smooth voice he did so well. I smirked, shaking my head in disbelief. I knew *exactly* what he was doing.

"Oh no, you aren't going to distract me from the fact that you jumped out of a freaking airplane!" I cried out. I looked to Cade and Elijah, who were so enjoying my little freak out right now. *These three were going to be the death of me.* "I can't believe that's how you got past those plates!"

"If you wanna be mad at anyone, be mad at Cade," Bastian teased back. "It was his idea!"

"Hey! Don't throw me up the bus!" Cade shouted playfully. The two pushed one another.

"You boys will be in huge trouble if you ever do anything like that again!" I cried out before smacking all three of them. It only made them laugh harder.

"I wish you would of seen Cade's first real jump, Shanie. The fool tripped and fell out the back of the plane," Elijah said as he and Bastian lost it even more. Cade just glared at them.

"Oh, ha, ha! You two swore to never speak of it again!"

My eyes widened, and I couldn't stop the smile from creeping up my face. My mate tossed his arm over me again.

"Why do you think his call sign was Tumbleweed? Our instructor gave him the name after that," Bastian chimed in, and Elijah was grinning from ear to ear. Cade, however, did not look amused.

I started giggling uncontrollably, imagining how funny it must have been to see Cade rolled out the back of the plane. I honestly wish I had seen it, but then again if I had been there, *nobody* would have been jumping out of planes.

"I hate you two," Cade muttered, crossing his arms. Elijah just smirked back, shrugging his shoulders.

"Aww, we can't leave my mate out of the inside joke, now can we? Emersyn knows. So should Shanely," Bastian countered.

Cade leaned back against my bed and crossed his arms, muttering something about payback, and the boys lost it again.

I leaned over and kissed my Beta on the cheek. "Don't worry. I won't tell anyone, Cade."

His eyes slowly looked to mine, and I could see a grin forming.

"Well, I guess it was worth it to see you smile again," Cade said, laying his head on my shoulder.

I snuggled between the Fenrir triplets just happy and content again. I was home. I was finally home and *nothing* was going to get in the way of that again. Aerith and I would heal from this, and the boys would never remember. *This would never happen to anyone ever again.* I yawned, leaning further into Bastian. He kissed my forehead gently.

"You should get some more rest, my love. As soon as you're healed, we're going home."

I smiled at that thought. *Home.* I was so ready to go back home with my boys.

"Send in the girls sometime. I miss Alana, Bay, and Emersyn," I whispered softly, "and Aerith. Please send her in soon."

Elijah patted my leg before saying goodnight. I knew he was on his way back to Emersyn, and Cade just winked at me. He pulled up one of the other beds, giving Bastian and I more room together. I was glad my Beta was staying though. I had missed them all terribly so having them close felt right. I snuggled up against my mate, and soon I was falling into one of the best sleeps of my life.

Chapter 54

Nothing prepared me for when I left the med bay.

Walking through what was left of my pack and seeing the damage that was done to everyone just about broke me. I had no idea it would be this bad.

I should have known.

I had gone stir crazy in the medical bay desperately wanting to see everyone. I had healed entirely, and after having one-on-one time with Aerith and making sure the boys were doing good, I was dying to get out. Bastian dug his heels in, making me stay a full week before he finally relented and had me released. The pack needed us though. I was their Alpha, and I felt like I failed to protect them by not seeing what Calvin was up to in time. I needed to see them with my own eyes and figure out what I could do to fix things.

Aerith bounded on ahead as we strolled through my brother's land. Many had visible scars and some were just straight up missing a limb. My wolf snarled at every injury we saw, feeling more and more guilty the longer we went on, but the pack seemed relieved to see us. I didn't understand how they weren't so angry with me. I expected to receive the blame, not all *this*.

Thankfully, everyone we managed to send to Abraham's survived unscathed, although many were grieving their mates or family members. I tried to spend time with everyone and apologized profusely for not preparing better. They simply held their heads high, insisting I wasn't to blame and said how grateful they were that I was alive. Many of the older wolves thanked me over and over for rescuing my mother too. Seeing her again sent a spark throughout our community, and she and my father would get flocked the moment they stepped outside. It was wonderful to see but guilt continued to eat at me. I don't think I'd ever feel the same.

All I could think was that I can't fix this for them. Every bond I discovered missing was just another stake to the heart. It was overwhelming to bear it all. I can't bring their mates, brothers, sisters, fathers, or mothers back from the grave. I can't heal these wounds that only happened because of me. I couldn't help but just feel like a complete failure.

We had a collective funeral for all the shifters we lost now that Aerith, Mom, and I were finally home with everyone. That was one of the hardest moments of my life. I sat in the front row, while Bastian gave the speech, staying until everyone had finally gone back to their rooms for the night before dragging myself back to mine. I slept the day away. Unable to pull myself from the deep despair my wolf and I felt. Bastian stayed with me.

Abraham erected a statue in memory of all those we lost too, which is what pulled me from my bed in the first place. The Division took most of our loved ones away, so there were no graves to be dug. Abey said this was his way of memorializing everyone who lost their lives in this whole mess, and I loved it. I couldn't take my eyes off it. The tall statue of solid blue granite listed every name of shifter we lost in gold lettering. It stood tall in the center of my brother's land, and as soon as it is safe to return home, a sister statue will be delivered there too.

I bawled like a baby when he gave me the news.

The fellas had Ryder cremated since he died in the middle of winter. Bastian couldn't bare the idea of not bringing Ryder home to our mountains, so they did what needed to be done and stuck him on the shelf in Abe's office. Today, we were making the journey home to not only inspect our land but lay our friend to rest. *They waited for me.*

Johnny, Alana, the triplets, and Emmie all made their way down the stairs towards Cain and I. I didn't sleep, so I was ready to go bright and early. Aerith was having therapy with Malin this morning and then my parents were going to watch the kids until we returned. Another issue I was forcing myself to deal with.

CHAPTER 54

Leaving them.

"Are you sure you should be traveling now?" Cain asked, and I sighed.

"We need to do this," I said firmly, even though I was terrified to leave Abe's kingdom. "Ryder deserves to go home, and I need to see our home anyways. We can't stay here forever."

Cain nodded softly as the group filed out the door to a van waiting for us. Bastian waited patiently for me at the door, urn in hand.

"We are going to have to discuss how to proceed, Shanely," Cain said quietly. I looked around the room full of shifters going about their day. My pack needed to return home soon. *He was right.*

"I know," I said softly, "but it can wait another day. Until I figure out how to handle the Division, we are safer here."

Cain grunted, putting his hands in his pockets. "Let me work on that. If we are cutting ties permanently, then we will have to prepare for another war."

My anger flared as my eyes shifted to gold. "But we didn't start anything! This is entirely..."

"Shanely," Cain interrupted firmly, and I gritted my teeth, "do you really think the Division cares if *they* made a mistake? If you are going to permanently pull away from them, then war you will find. Just... Think about that, okay? I'll see what I can do to about this whole situation in the meantime."

I nodded, stepping away from my uncle before I said something I didn't mean. I just didn't have it in me to deal with that situation right now. Or *ever* for that matter. Cassia's been helping me sleep at night for the most part. The nightmares seem to stay away when she drains me, but every so often they still creep through. *If I couldn't deal with my own issues; how in the world was I going to deal with the Division itself?*

Uncle Cain sighed and motioned to the door. "Go. Take care of Ryder, and I'll see you when you get back."

I sulked out of Abe's castle with Bastian on my heels.

"You alright?" he asked quietly before we reached the van.

"It's just never-ending, Bastian," I answered truthfully. We promised honesty with one another, and I planned to hold up my end of the bargain. He was gradually letting me in too. I shook my head from those thoughts. "It doesn't matter right now. Now, it's time to take him home."

He nodded solemnly and opened the van door. We hopped in the middle bench, and Cade drove us home. My nerves were in knots as we left the safety of Abraham's walls and crossed town. The Den was opened once more. Already hoppin' and in full-swing thanks to the new hires Caleb found. Cade drove on, and soon my woods came into view. The familiar winding road that lead to my pack's home was comforting. *I didn't think I'd ever step foot in these woods again...*

But my heart stopped when we pulled into the lodge.

Rage took over as we filed out of the van. My home was broken, and as I stood in the center of where the attack took place, memories flooded my system. My Alpha power was a steady hum around me, and no one but Bastian came near. I didn't blame them. I was getting better but not quite the same as before. I was working on gaining control again.

Bastian took my hand and led the way into the woods away from those haunted memories. We walked slowly, following the path my uncle and aunt took when they buried Aspen. It killed me to know Ash and Deidre were taken by the Division. He deserved to be with his brother in our pack lands, and now the two would be separated forever. *Just another reason to hate the Division. To hate humans.*

We could have shifted and gotten to the spot faster, but I think everyone just wanted to spend some time together. This was our last walk with our friend, and no one wanted it to end. Poor Johnny never took his hands out of his pockets as he dragged one foot after the other. Ryder was closer to Johnny than any of us. *This hit him hard.*

Deep in the mountains, near a massive fir tree on the left of the river that ran through the land, was my Uncle Aspen's grave. His mate lay next to him, and just like that everything became too real.

Bastian stood rigid in front of everyone. A haunted look washed over him, and my heart broke a little further.

"*He watched him die, Baby Girl,*" Cade's voice came through the link. "*It's*

CHAPTER 54

hitting him harder than he's letting on. It's part of what he's hiding from you."

I gave my Beta a grateful nod before stepping towards my mate. I took his hand in mine, snapping him out of his trance. He kissed my cheek before turning to the others.

"Ryder was the best of men," Bastian said, his voice struggling to contain the emotion he was feeling. "He always put the pack first. Never once complained about helping anyone and has saved my life more times than I can count. He was our best friend... *My* best friend, and what happened to him was inexcusable. He will never be forgotten."

Bastian opened the urn, taking a handful of ashes and spreading them around the family tree. My throat bobbed. I was unable to keep the tears from rolling down my cheek. *This wasn't fair.*

"You saved all our lives, Ryder," Cade said, stepping forward, "and I will always miss you."

Cade took a handful then. Alana sobbed against Johnny as Cade let our friend drift in the gentle breeze towards the roots below, and I could barely sit still. My heart was breaking as I listened to everyone say a little something. My wolf whined within me as I struggled to come up exactly what to say myself. *He meant so much to me, to everyone here, and I hated this is what happened to him.*

Johnny and I were the last to speak, but he wouldn't even look up from the ground. He was just frozen in place, holding Alana. I quickly wiped my eyes and stepped forward. *I was his Alpha too, and this was my fault. No matter what everyone insisted, it was the truth.*

I took a handful then, and my heart seized as I slowly opened my fingers to let the wind take him.

"I am so sorry this happened to you, Ryder," I said softly, "but we made sure to bring you home. This is where my family lies, and when my time comes, I want to be buried here with you too. I will miss you, *always.*"

Everyone turned to face me. Turmoil struck the boy's faces, but I meant every word. I wasn't invincible, and when I died, I wanted to rest next to my family. That was who Ryder was. Family.

"Johnny?" Bastian said quietly. He held out the urn as we all turned to him. Johnny didn't move, even when Alana nudged him. He just stood there staring at the ground. Elijah stepped forward again, and between the triplets, they scattered the last of Ryder's remains.

Cade collapsed near the river as Elijah firmly pressed Ryder's urn in the dirt next to Aspen's headstone. I sat down next to him.

"We need to buy him a proper headstone," I said. Cade slowly nodded, and the rest of the group followed suit. All except Johnny.

"We will once we come home," Bastian said.

"When are we going home?" Alana asked quietly. No one spoke then, and I sighed.

"When I figure out what I'm going to do with the Division," I answered truthfully.

"Kill them," Johnny finally spoke, and we all turned to look back at him. "Kill them all."

Alana frowned and went to stand with him. I understood his pain. More than anybody, I understood. His demand wasn't shocking in the least, but Cain's words rattled me. *I didn't want another war. Who else would die because of it?*

"The two responsible for Ryder's death are dead," I said firmly.

Johnny's icy glare angered my wolf, and my eyes flashed red. He held my stare for a moment before finally dropping his gaze.

"We are all hurting," I said in a softer tone, "but more death isn't the answer. It can't be."

"And why not?" Johnny snapped, tossing his hands in the air. "They so easily kill us! Why can't we…"

I shot to my feet and stormed over to him. My Alpha power surged, whether I wanted it to or not as I shouted, "Because we are better than them!"

My voice echoed through the woods, silencing even the natural creatures that lived here. My chest ached in pain, but I knew this was the right course. I held my hands out, pointing to everyone here. This wasn't fair, but he needed to see my point. *He needed to feel it.*

"Who else would you like to bury, Johnny? Elijah? Alana?"

CHAPTER 54

He barred his teeth in frustration, and Bastian growled low. I took another step towards one of my oldest friends saying, "You have no idea how much my wolf and I want to demand blood over what's happened, but who's blood will get spilled? If I start a war, death will follow, and all that matters is everyone surviving. All of us! I mean is this the life we want to give our children?"

Johnny looked to Alana then. No one said a word, and I huffed in anger back towards my mate. "When you come up with a way to bring justice to our nation without slaughtering more people, then I am ALL ears. But until then, we do nothing."

"No," Bastian said, his loud voice startling me, "we plan. That's what we do. We start planning for the future we want for us. For our children."

I gave my mate a grateful smile, and he kissed my forehead.

"I want our kids to have a normal life," Elijah said. He pulled his knees to his chest as he stared out to the water. "I want them to have an imagination. To grow up without prejudice or fear. To have friends, hobbies, or whatever makes them happy."

"I'd like to see them enjoy things typical kids do," Cade continued. "Go to prom, play on a school team…"

"Attend a public school," Johnny said softly. He gave me an apologetic smile as he sat down with his mate. "Not start enforcer training until after school, and let them have freedom to just be kids."

I grinned towards everyone then. I really liked what was happening, and I fished my phone out of my pocket.

"Okay, so open a shifter school," I said, typing the suggestion on a list I made on my phone. "What else?"

"I want a normal Summit," Alana said with a grin, "more than once a year too. I love having all shifter kinds there, and we need to strengthen the bonds we're making now."

"I'd like to rebuild the community," Bastian said with a grin. "Help the smaller shifters out and give them a real chance here. Build us up, make us stronger."

I furiously typed everything they continued to come up with. Every word making me feel lighter and lighter.

Bastian gave me a small nudge then. "What about you?"

"Me?" I asked.

"Yeah," he said, "what do you want to make happen for our future?"

Everyone turned to me as I set down my phone. I thought about that question. More than ever, I needed to get this right. I *was* the White Wolf. This was my job to protect everyone, but every time I thought about our future, I pictured my little girl. How she went from a carefree, bubbly, and sweet girl to a child so serious. So cautious and wary and afraid of everyone she met. I hated that for her. I hated knowing she went through so much trauma that it changed her.

And suddenly, I knew what I wanted.

"I want to be there for the children," I said softly. "For the kids without parents or families. I want to start some sort of adoption program for the kids who are displaced, or those who have been through trauma at the hands of humans *and* shifters. I want to create a safe place where they can get the help they need. Whether it's helping control their animal side or therapy... Just something."

Bastian gave me a warm smile and wrapped his arm around my waist.

"I think that's perfect, my love," he whispered softly.

Chapter 55

I awoke the following morning to a bright and sunny day. I stretched my arms above my head as I turned to find my mate at the mirror, styling his hair.

"Morning, my love," he said with a grin.

I slowly untucked my legs from the blankets and stood from the bed. "Morning, baby. How are the boys?"

Bastian smiled, pointing to the two bassinets now sitting in corner of the room. "Sleeping the morning away."

I smiled as I walked over to check on them. They were just perfect, both cuddled up next to one another instead of having their own spot.

"Cassia figured out pretty quickly that they sleep better and longer when placed in the same bassinet together. Cain brought them in early this morning, when you were passed out asleep."

I gave him a soft smile, grateful he didn't mention the nightmare I had again last night. I didn't get much sleep because of it, and neither did he.

"And Aerith?" I asked.

Aerith had finally switched back from her wolf form to our beautiful baby girl again. She switches between forms effortlessly now, and every time I look at her with my Alpha powers, she still doesn't come up with a pack color. She looks and scents as a human, which just gives her an extra layer of protection, I suppose. Shifters will leave her alone because of it, and anyone who tries anything with her will get an incredible surprise. By the size of her paws right now, she's going to be large like Bastian and I. John said half-bloods are unique in every case. He and my mother spent a long time together just catching up when we paid a visit to talk about Aerith, and I smiled fondly at the memory.

"Went with Cade and Elijah for breakfast," Bastian answered, placing a kiss on my cheek. "Should be back any minute actually."

I sighed contently and let my mate guide me back to bed. I was glad she was busy with our family. It took a little while for her to leave my side, but I wish I could get her to open up with me. We've spoke once since getting rescued, and ever since then she has clammed up, refusing to say another word over what we went through. I often found her in our bed at night, and while I was glad I was able to give her some comfort, I wished more than anything I could help her sort through the rest. Last night I had her bunk with Bay and Abraham as Cassia was exhausted. I didn't ask her to drain me and woke in a sweaty mess from another nightmare sometime around 2 am. We both had issues sleeping.

I snuggled against Bastian, feeling all too tired to do much of anything today, and stared out the open window. The pack and streak were getting along rather swimmingly, and my council and I had worked day and night on the proposed plan to bring to the Council of Shifters soon. I was so excited to start creating our new future together. Our children were going to have the life I never got.

But nothing could start until I dealt with the Division.

"I could just stay here forever, you know?" I said with a grin, shoving every thought of that wicked group aside. "You're just *that* cozy."

Bastian snorted out a laugh. "Is that so? Well, as much as I would love that, we do have another council meeting this afternoon, and we're supposed to meet everyone for lunch too."

I groaned, already knowing full well what that meeting was about. Cain had been working tirelessly on the whole issue with the Division for me. I knew I was being a coward, but I just wanted nothing to do with them. *Ever.* Every time we discussed what to do, or how to lay the charges against them, memories haunted me of my time at the Jennings household. It hadn't been that long ago that I had been rescued, but it still needed to be handled now. We were just hiding away here at Abraham's, and I knew we needed to

CHAPTER 55

go home. It was hard to muster the courage to come out of hiding though. Cain had been deliberating with Hank a few days now, and this afternoon my uncle was supposed to get me up to speed with what's been going on, so I can decide how to proceed.

Fat chance of that.

"Do we have to?" I asked, giving Bastian a look.

"Shanely, we should have gone after them the minute you were rescued," he said matter of factly. "They need to answer for their crimes."

I dropped my gaze and slowly pulled away. *He didn't get it,* I thought to myself. Didn't understand the pure terror I still felt whenever I heard the Division mentioned. Whenever someone said Calvin or Patrick's name, it sent chills down my spine. I had refused Cassia offer of therapy for now, but my time spent with those men had left its mark. While Bastian was ready for justice and blood to spill, I just wanted to run. Run, and never see them again.

"Shanely..."

A knock barely sounded before the door burst open and in came Aerith and Cade.

"Daddy!" she shouted as she plowed into Bastian. He grinned wide and hauled her into bed with us.

"Well, there's my baby girl!" Bastian said, kissing her cheek. "Did you have a good breakfast with your uncles?"

"I did! Uncle Cade let me have whatever I wanted!" she replied excitedly. *By the sticky chocolate ring around her lips, I'd bet anything she had chocolate chip pancakes.*

"I see that," I chimed in, winking at my Beta. She made herself comfortable between the two of us, but it surprised me when she scooted closer to me. Just like she had during our time with Patrick. She's been pretty glued to Bastian, but she shimmed right up against me, and I wrapped my arm around her.

"Well, that's how it should be," I said, kissing the top of her head. "I'm glad you're back now. Want to spend the day here and watch a movie with mama?"

"Yes!" she cheered excitedly. The sound lifted a weight off my chest, and I grinned wide.

"What about meeting the gang for lunch before the council meeting?" Cade asked, and I pursed my lips together giving him a look. He sighed. "You want to bail, don't you?"

"Please?" I begged. "I just... I don't think I'll be very good company today."

My voice trailed off, and I could see a look of pity form on the triplet's face.

"Tell everyone we're sorry, but we'll make it next time," Bastian said, giving me a soft smile, and my eyes widened in surprise. "We'll be there for the council meeting, but we're going to spend the morning here."

I beamed over at my mate as Cade sighed again. "Alright, but you two owe me! Everyone will be bummed."

"Oh, they won't even noticed we're missing!" I exclaimed, and my Beta rolled his eyes at me.

"Yeah, right," he muttered, opening our door. "It will be the first thing they ask. Everyone's going to hound me, wanting to know where you guys are. Mark my words!"

"Just go, brother!" Bastian said, grinning.

My Beta shook his head exasperated with the two of us and was out the door in seconds. Bastian threw his arm over the two of us then.

"Now, what are we watching?" he asked, and I leaned against his arm. *"Thank you."*

"Can we watch Balto?!" Aerith begged as Bastian turned on the TV. My lips puckered, and I quickly shut my eyes, praying I could wash away the tears forming in them. *She wasn't lost after all.*

"Anytime, love."

My mate turned the movie on, and I realized this was the first time the five of us were alone together. There was no one else here. Just the five of us, and it could not be more perfect than that.

Halfway into our second movie, Cade's link came through.

"I told you so."

CHAPTER 55

***

We entered the hall to Abraham's conference center after dropping off the kids with my parents. I dragged my feet throughout the whole process. I changed both of their diapers and made up their next bottle before Bastian finally hauled me out of the room. We were officially late, but I really couldn't bring myself to care about it. But nothing could prepare me for the scent that hit me as we drew near the door.

Human.

Even Bastian was alarmed as we walked in to find a human male standing next to Cain. His gray hair was thinning and looked to be in his sixties, if I had to guess. He wore a simple suit and smiled nervously at me. I could scent his fear from here, and I barred my teeth. I turned to see the rest of my council, looking as equally pissed off as I felt.

"You must be the famous Shanely," the man said, extending his hand out to me.

I backed further away, and he slowed his pace. Looking to Cain for answers, he quickly stuffed his hands back in his pockets. Cade and Elijah made their way to us as Bastian wrapped his arm around my waist.

"Shanely," Cain said sternly, stepping towards the four of us, "this is the man we were trying to contact before everything happened. This is Hank Cartwright."

I didn't move from my spot as my blood started to boil. My eyes flashed red as I stared at the human man from the Division. *The one who failed us.*

"Why is he here?" I asked, irritated to even be in the same room as him. I turned to my uncle then. "You should have told me."

Cain looked uneasily between the four of us. "Shanely, he's here to help..."

"Help?!" I bellowed. "Where was he when his people slaughtered mine? Where was this so-called help when I was kidnapped, leading my family to their deaths in their attempts to rescue me!? Oh, that's right! He was too busy promoting Patrick and giving him and his team a brand new job!"

Bastian snarled as he stepped in front of me.

"He didn't know until it was too late," Cain replied, and I eyed the man behind him.

"I promise, Shanely. I didn't know what was going on in your area until it was too late," Hank said, with his hands up defensively. "I did *everything* I could with the information I had."

I gritted my teeth as memories of Patrick and Calvin arguing over Hank flooded my mind. *I didn't trust this man*, I thought to myself. *He should have never allowed this to happen in the first place.*

"Then why are you here? Come to finish the job?" I snapped back, and he looked mortified.

"Shanely..." my Uncle Cain hissed. I turned on my heels to storm out of the room, when Bastian stepped in my path.

"We deserve justice," he said softly. "You deserve justice, Shanely. This has to get figured out, and that won't happen if we run away because we're afraid."

I glared at my mate. Crossing my arms, I snapped, "I don't want to hear anything he has to say."

"But you must," he said, stepping forward and gently rubbing the side of my cheek. My wolf settled with his touch, and I took a deep breath. I stared up at Bastian's gorgeous blue eyes as my anger quickly turned to fear. Tears formed as he whispered, "If we want our children to have the life we've planned, then we must deal with this problem. We can't hide forever."

"I don't know if I can," I linked all three Fenrir boys. I didn't trust myself to speak. Not without losing control of my emotions, and the last thing I needed was to struggle with my Alpha power right now. I was just barely getting it under control as it was.

"We can do this together," Bastian said softly.

"First sign of anything you don't like, just give the word," Cade chimed in. *"He won't walk out of here alive."*

I sucked in a breath and quickly wiped my eyes. I sighed, giving my boys one last look.

"Together then?"

CHAPTER 55

"Together," they said in unison.

Slowly turning back to the human, I motioned to the empty seats. Hank and Cain visibly both relaxed and took their seats across from mine. With shaky steps, I sat down at the Alpha's chair and motioned for them to continue.

"Due to everything that has happened, I am restructuring the entire Division," Hank said plainly.

"What does that mean?" I asked, raising an eyebrow. Bastian gently rested his hand on my knee, and I took another deep breath.

"It means humans can be just as violent as shifters, and why should we govern you when we're just as bad? I already have approval to get started, but I have some questions for you, Shanely. I want to know why our men did this. You are the White Wolf. The one in charge of shifter kind, and if any of this is to work, you need to approve it," he said, opening the folder he carried with him. A pad and paper sat on the right, and he ready himself to take notes.

I slowly switched my gaze to my mate then.

"What in the world is this?" I snapped.

Bastian shrugged softly. *"I don't know, but I want to know what this will mean for the rest of us. You don't have to answer anything you don't want to, Shanely."*

I sighed in a huff and leaned back in my seat.

"Okay for starters," Hank said, "can you tell me if Calvin or Patrick told you anything as to why they took you and your mother?"

"Patrick was obsessed with Shanely," Bastian started off.

"He thought he was in love with her," Cade continued.

"But he wasn't part of Calvin's plot against you," Elijah wrapped up.

My uncle cleared his throat. He gestured to me then, but I just quietly smirked. *They were so protective, but I didn't mind one bit. The less I had to deal with the man, the better.* I rolled my eyes, when Cain gave me another firm look.

Fine.

"Calvin took my mother when he realized she was a strong Alpha," I said with a clipped tone. "He found out about her being mated to a bear shifter, and with the laws back then, he created a way for her to be banished from the pack and got her wolf taken away, so she could be caught. He gave my grandfather one of your inhibitor bracelets. Calvin's been testing ways to transfer the Alpha power to himself ever since."

"But why? What did he need it for? Is that even possible?" Hank asked in disbelief. *His gaping mouth would catch flies if he weren't careful,* I chuckled to myself.

"Why to kill you all, of course," I replied with a smile. My uncle just rolled his eyes.

"Way to be dramatic, Shanely," Cain said, and I shot him a dry look.

"I beg your pardon," Hank said. He dropped his pen.

"Does Lorelei Jennings mean anything to you?" I asked, toning down my sarcasm.

Hank's eyes furrowed as he sat lost in thought for a moment. "She was Calvin's wife. Lorelei was one of our Head Scientists until she died in a terrible accident."

I snorted in disgust. Leaning back in my chair, I said, "Yeah, you might want to do your research. I watched the video at Calvin's, and it was the Division who murdered her."

"That's not possible," Hank said in disbelief. "She was beloved by the company! Everyone was so upset when she passed. That can't be right!"

"Lorelei was trying to figure out a way to transfer the shifter's healing abilities to humans, so she could cure things like blindness, those who were lame or dealing with illnesses like cancer," I said, ignoring him. "She was trying to help humanity, yet the ones in charge sought something different. *Dennis* sought something different. He wanted the Alpha power to command shifters and humans, but Lorelei didn't feel it was right."

Bastian's grip on my leg tightened. I hadn't admitted any of this to them. Not yet, at least. This was news to everyone, and they all leaned forward to listen.

"How do you know it was Dennis?" Hank asked quietly.

"Calvin told me," I answered, "and I believed him."

CHAPTER 55

Hank stared dumbfounded at me. The wheels turning in his mind, and I wondered what Dennis told everyone when it happened. I wondered what he was saying now.

I took a deep breath saying, "When Lorelei refused to obey orders, things turned ugly. She managed to destroy most of her work, despite knowing what they'd do to her if she didn't give them the Alpha power. Your precious Division killed her because of it, and they searched her labs top to bottom. They found nothing, and the program was lost forever until Calvin managed to find a surviving file. He had been working hard ever since to finish her work, but he was going to take the Alpha power, and then use it to annihilate the Division once and for all."

Hank's jaw dropped, and he slumped back in his seat. He looked truly shocked, and I cocked my head to the side. It honestly surprised me. I thought he was lying when he said he didn't know, but he *really* didn't know a thing.

He looked pale when his eyes met mine, and he asked, "Did Calvin ever figure it out? With the Alpha power, I mean."

My heart stopped as memories from that night filled my head. Calvin *had* figured it out. He and Patrick had both managed to steal the Alpha power and keep it, but it was only because of my little girl. *She would be in danger if I told the truth*, I thought to myself. *Other half-bloods would live in fear if humans thought this was something possible.*

I could never tell.

"No," I answered, earning looks from the Fenrir brothers. "He was never able to make it work."

Running his hands through his hair, Hank blew out a heavy breath and said, "I had no idea any of that happened. I was transferred into this position not long after her death, and Dennis has never been anything but an arrogant man I've had to deal with once in awhile. There are no records of that sort of work in Research anyways."

"So Dennis and Calvin were both fantastic men and never once gave you any indication they were actually wretched inside," Cade asked snidely. "Is that what I'm hearing?"

"Well... yes," Hank said plainly. "When I first met Calvin at one of our conferences, he never gave an indication he had a chip on his shoulder. He's been a quiet but *loyal* Head for all these years, and Dennis is a decorated man. He's been running operations for the US Government for decades."

"I don't know Dennis's motives, but Calvin's been manipulating things since before my mother disappeared. Ever since I came to Diablo, I've always thought it was Patrick pulling the strings, but in reality it was his father. Patrick *was* unstable but believed he risked himself to save me and Aerith from an unjust order. He honestly thought that he saved us from destruction, but Calvin just used his son's obsession of me to get what he wanted. He's been the one behind everything," I said softly, and I could feel the tension thickening in the room. Bastian tightened his grip on my knee, staring at the table before us. *That was another truth I had yet to tell.*

"Shanely, I am so sorry," Hank said sincerely. "I know that it cannot make up for everything, but I had no idea what was even happening to your pack until well after it was done. I've been in Europe for nearly a year, dealing with getting the new center up and running, and by the time I got home and heard, it was too late."

I snorted, shaking my head as I remembered all the times I tried to get in contact with someone. Only to have it blow up in my face.

"You people make it real difficult to even reach you," I muttered. "I called and called. Left voicemail after voicemail, and the one time I actually got through to someone, my entire pack was nearly annihilated almost immediately. Your entire department is corrupt. That much was made clear by the ridiculous outbox message for shifters calling in with a problem."

No one said a word as I glared at Hank. After a few moments, Hank sighed and flipped through the file he brought. "The Division has grown exponentially, Shanely. We have four men in leadership, including myself. Four men over thousands. Each runs a special department, and we delegate a great many things because we are essentially a military facility. The Division is just a branch of the actual U.S. military, and with so many moving parts... Things fall through the cracks."

Hank tossed us a stack of papers. Bastian began flipping through it, and my eyes widened when I saw what was on it. What charges were laid against us.

"This came from Calvin's office. He seemed to have a lot stacked against you," Hank went on. "If Dennis told Calvin to investigate... Well, he delivered."

Bastian held out a photo of them escorting people from the lodge. I recognized the female in the center of the boys. She and another male were in handcuffs, and my eyes widened.

"The shark shifter?"

Bastian nodded, and my stomach twisted in knots. That was back when they had to work for Abraham years ago. *How long had Calvin been watching us?*

"I'm telling you honestly, Hank. Dennis is the man you need to investigate," I said firmly, jabbing my finger against the table. "I don't know about the others, but Dennis *was* involved. He was involved with Lorelei, and somehow he was involved with the demise of my pack. I just don't know why."

Hank gave me a sorrowful look before leaning forward, scribbling furiously on that ridiculous note pad of his. "I'll be looking into this whole issue with Calvin and Dennis, I promise you. Because of what he did, we are at a delicate crossroad between humans and shifters. We will lose the precious balance between the two races if we cannot reach some sort of an agreement. Cain has explained to me that you are in charge here, Shanely. You, and a select group of others, am I correct?"

"I'm not convincing shifters to forgive the Division as if they simply made *a mistake*," I snarled. "You've killed so many of my family and my people! Don't ask me to smooth it over with them because I won't do it! I am done working with the Division!"

I stormed out of my seat with my mate right behind me. I was furious he was even asking that of me. That Cain put me in the position in the first place! My hand gripped the handle on the door, when Hank spoke.

"That's fair, Shanely," Hank said, halting me in my tracks, "and I'm not trying to gloss over what Calvin or Patrick did. I understand the way this Division was set up in the beginning was completely unfair to shifters, and we need consequences for our own actions as well. We are already in the works of sending financial compensation to all the families that lost loved ones, and while I know that doesn't make up for everything, it's something. Something I can do to try and ease their pain, but the biggest thing we need to do is clean out the entire company and start anew. There is a lot of misinformation about shifters out there. It only causes fear and hate amongst the ranks, and Shanely whether you like it or not, we need to learn to get along. We share this planet after all."

"What are you going to do?" I asked sarcastically. "Hire shifters to work for the Division?"

"Actually, yes," he replied, and I turned to him with wide eyes.

"You've got to be kidding me?!" I cried out. *God, I was so spent,* I thought to myself. So done with today, and I knew I had officially lost it when I laughed out loud.

"Listen, Shanely. This might be the best thing for everyone," Cain said sternly, and I rolled my eyes.

"We need shifters in positions of leadership to help us understand one another better, but also to keep things like this from ever happening again. If there was a shifter that Calvin needed to report to; don't you think they'd be quick to go see for themselves if that was true? Don't you think they'd recognize what are normal pack behaviors versus problematic ones?" Hank asked, tapping his pen on the table. "What I've noticed is a lot of the guys in my program are intimidated by shifters. Whether Dennis was pushing this or not, most are nervous around you guys, but I think if we had actual shifters working and training with us as *part* of the same team, then we can merge our two groups peacefully. Then every location can have either a shifter or human as their Head Officer. If problems come up, an honest and balanced solution can be found. For the good of all."

I stared at the Hank, trying to process everything he said. *The picture he's painting was an amazing one,* I thought. Ultimately, I just wanted shifters to be safe, and he was handing me a solution on a silver platter. *But could I honestly trust him?*

CHAPTER 55

I looked around the room to my team then. They all looked surprised by what Hank was suggesting, but no one seemed upset over it. In fact, I saw *hope* in their eyes, and that alone made me walk back to my chair. My gaze drifted to the empty seat on my left. Pain squeezed my heart as I stared at it. Now that Ryder was gone, we had an open spot on our council.

I looked to Bastian, and I could see the pain in his eyes too. He nodded once, knowing exactly what I was thinking, and I linked my cousin Noah.

"I need you."

Another thought dawned on me, and I linked Octavia too. I needed her to confirm everything before I made my choice. Noah came in within a few minutes with Emersyn and Esme right behind him. Emmie went to her mate, and I motioned for Noah to take the empty seat.

"Noah, please sit. We have a seat available since Ryder was electrocuted by Calvin in the security measures that the Division paid for, and I want you, the future leader of the clan, to take it."

"Shanely..." Bastian whispered in warning.

"No, Bastian. This man," I said, pointing to Hank, "needs to know exactly what happened to our best friend, our council member, and fellow pack mate. You want to work with us, then you need to know our pain. You need to know exactly what happened to him and everyone else here. You cannot just use money as a way to seek forgiveness. You need to *understand* it."

Hank didn't say a word. He took in the room, the anger on everyone's face, before giving me a small nod. He scribbled away in his notebook as Octavia came in.

"You called for me?" she asked, scenting the room. Her eyes narrowed towards Hank before slowly coming to me.

"I did," I said quietly. "I need you to listen, cousin. Please."

She studied me a moment before standing behind Caleb on the other side of the room. Noah took his seat with Esme on his lap, and I leaned forward on the table.

"Alright, before anything starts, I need to remind everyone that this is an official pack meeting and remains private until I say so. Hank here has some new information for us and a plan to restructure the Division. Care to fill our guests in, Hank?"

"Umm... well sure," he said quietly. He looked to Noah then. "I am deeply sorry for what has happened to you and your people. I was not aware of anything going on until it was too late, but I want to fix the issues with the Division before anymore problems arise. As I explained to Shanely, our relationship with one another hangs on a delicate balance. I propose we clear out the whole Division and hire shifters to work with us. That way when problems arise within our collective community, it can be properly handled for the good of all."

Noah gave me a look of concern, and I shrugged. *I don't know how to feel about it either,* I thought to myself. Octavia inhaled deeply, and her normal composure gave me some comfort.

"I will now open the table to you all," I said. "Ask any questions you may have."

"How are you going to get the rest of the humans on board with this?" Caleb asked. "Who's to say they will even cooperate?"

"Because this will be a national security issue if we do not. I don't want a war anymore than you all, and neither does our President. We made this mistake, and it's our job to fix it. All he wants is it to be done quietly. I am not happy, but it will give me what I need to fix this. I do not want to work with anyone that's willing to do something as wicked as this. I already have approval from the government, and I've been appointed to change what's necessary. Even if it means cleaning house," Hank said firmly.

"And what will happen to the men who were present during the attack on our pack?" Cade asked, his eyes narrowing. "Will we simply be forced to work alongside them too?"

The room stilled. *This was the issue I was having with the idea of working with them.* I wanted nothing to do with the Division, and I wouldn't push *anyone* into this either.

Hank finally sighed. "We will investigate everyone assigned to the team for the mission, but some of those men were just following orders. Some of those men might be allowed to stay."

CHAPTER 55

"They killed our people!" Johnny snapped angrily, and the whole room erupted. Hank looked nervously to me, but no matter how many times he tried to speak, no one will let him. *This wasn't working.*

"Silence!" Bastian bellowed loudly. He straightened his shirt, glaring at everyone. "This is not how we will handle ourselves! Now, we have ways of determining who was simply following orders versus those who harmed us gleefully. You all know this. I expect the men who fail our test will be removed and punished correctly. Is that clear?"

Everyone grumbled, and I leaned forward again. "Is that clear, Hank?"

Hank nodded once. "I think that is acceptable. We have lie detector tests we will set up, and we will question everyone in the Division. Not just the ones involved in the mission."

"You mean massacre," Johnny challenged, and I glared at him.

"Do not forget we killed them too," I said firmly. Johnny barred his teeth, and my eyes turned red. I lashed out my Alpha power, hitting him in the chest. "Don't. We killed them too. If they are to accept us, we need to accept them."

I pulled back, and Johnny exhaled loudly. His gaze slowly drifted to me.

"I'm sorry. I'm trying to control my wolf."

"I know."

I turned to Octavia, letting Johnny be for the moment. I needed to know if Hank was genuine. "What's the verdict?"

"He's being honest," she replied before turning back to her manicure. I snorted. *She always looked bored in meetings. Well, in everything she did.*

Hank looked at her and then to me.

"We have ways to make sure you're telling us the truth too," I answered.

"I wasn't going to agree to anything unless I know my shifters will be safe."

His eyes widened. "Then will you agree?"

I leaned back in my chair. "All those who want to try this new way of working with the Division, raise your hand."

Most in the room raised their hands. Johnny took his sweet time, but he slowly put his hand in the air. I noticed the Fenrir brothers kept their hands down though. They were all looking at me, waiting for me to decide first.

I sighed before raising my own hand, and the boys followed suit. In reality, I wanted nothing to do with the Division anymore, but Hank's suggestion was a good one. It would be better in the long run for everyone. Hank seemed to visibly relax as did my uncle.

"This is great news, Shanely! I think you'll like the headquarters and your new position…"

"Wait, what?" I asked, confusion knitting my brow. Panic began to creep inside, and I shrunk further in my seat.

Hank looked at me nervously. "Well, I assumed since you're the leader of the shifters, that you'd take one of the four positions."

I shook my head. "I'm the leader of the wolves, and while I work with the other shifters, I am technically not their leader. No matter what anyone says in this room, I cannot speak for everyone. Not like this. Now, I can help you find good candidates for those positions, and I can help with the applications for shifters to apply within the organization, but I cannot accept any role at the Division."

Just thinking about it made me sick. I wanted to run. My wolf wanted out and was sick of being in the same room with the human. I was done with this meeting and gripped the handles of my chair harder.

Hank looked dejected saying, "I just thought…"

"She said no," Bastian replied gruffly.

"I'll go," Caleb spoke up.

I turned to my brother, surprised by his offer. A little piece of my heart broke then. *I didn't want him to go.*

"Caleb, you don't have to go," I pleaded. "It doesn't need to come from my council or pack."

"I know, but look at it this way, Shanely. I'm part of your council, and I will continue to be. If I take this spot, then I'll be there to help make sure things go the way they should. You will know what's going on without having to deal with it directly, and honestly out of all of us, I'm the most available. Cade and I are the only ones without mates, and he's your Beta. He stays here, so it leaves it to me," he said, crossing his arms.

CHAPTER 55

"I'll miss you, Caleb," I said softly, emotion pulling through my voice. *This felt wrong. So very wrong.* "How can you live so far away from everyone and your home?"

"It doesn't mean I'll never be around, Shanely, but I like the idea of one of us being in that position. I can help make real change for everyone," he replied, and I felt something squeeze around my heart. My throat bobbed, and I could only give him a small nod in return. I couldn't speak right now, but I wouldn't stop him if he really wanted to go.

Caleb turned to Hank. "I want one of the top positions though. I'm not doing some second string crap just because I'm not Shanely. You are to remove everyone else in the meantime. When the time comes, you and I will decide who else gets the final two remaining seats. Like Bastian said, all ground troops will need to go through a test to see where their thoughts and feelings towards shifters lie. If they fail that test, then they are to be removed immediately, and it doesn't matter if they are an amazing solider. Dennis gets Court Marshaled. No exceptions. Do we understand one another?"

"What kind of test?" Hank asked him. I had to give it to Caleb. *He seemed to have more confidence with this than I did.*

Caleb turned back to me. "I'd like to take Octavia with me, if everyone's okay with it."

I nodded and looked to her. "If she's okay with it. Noah needs to approve as head of the clan for now, since she's a bear."

"I'll go with you, cousin," she replied, and Caleb turned to Noah who nodded his approval. Caleb muttered a thanks before he turned back to Hank, who just looked confused.

"If we are honestly going to trust anyone at the Division, we need everyone to go through the lie and intentions test. Octavia here can literally sniff out lies and ill intentions. Those who fail are fired or transferred out of the Division immediately and are banned from ever working with shifters again," Caleb went on.

"And consequences should be given to those who deserve it," Bastian snarled.

"Well, alrighty then," Hank said, folding his hands in his lap. "I didn't even know that was an option, but it would be better than the lie detectors we have. And faster. Who else do you recommend to take the other positions?"

"It should be even down the middle. Two humans and two shifters," I chimed in, gaining odd looks from my family. "Look, if we don't make this fair across the board, then we'll be creating problems for ourselves later on. If we are truly to blend together, then it needs to be even."

Hank smiled to me. "Cain said you'd be fair even after everything. I see why you are the leader, Shanely. Are you sure you won't reconsider taking the other spot?"

"I can't," I said, more emotionally than I meant to, "but I can recommend someone instead."

He nodded his head in understanding and asked, "Who would you recommend then?"

"My Uncle Cain, of course," I replied as my uncle looked shocked.

"Shanely, I'm sure there are..." he started to say, but I interrupted.

"You are the most logical person to take up a position like this. You know Hank well, so between the three of you, I believe you can choose the final human to take the last place. You know shifter law inside and out *and* all the hardships we've gone through. You have also been greatly affected by what happened. Who better to help create something new and fair for everyone than you, Uncle?"

He looked at me and then to Hank, who smiled back.

"I know I wouldn't mind one bit having you around, my friend," he chimed in, forcing a smile from Cain.

Cain chuckled, and I could see a slight blush form on his cheek. "I have to talk to Cassia, but if she's alright with it, then I will accept. We can change everything together, old friend. I will still be checking in on you though, my niece."

He raised one eyebrow, and I spat out a laugh.

"I wouldn't have it any other way. Now that we have that settled, I suggest we end the meeting here. I will be moving my pack to rebuild our

CHAPTER 55

home within the week."

Hank stood to meet me at the door. He extended his hand saying, "We will make this better, Shanely. I promise you. Thank you for taking the time to speak with me."

I accepted his hand this time and gave him a small smile back. "I hope so, Hank. I really hope so. You let me know what comes of your investigation."

I left with my three boys right on my heels.

Chapter 56

"I give it a week," Cade said as he scrubbed my kitchen floor.

"I give it longer than that!" Elijah went on. He was currently replacing every broken light in our cabin. "A month tops."

"Would you two quit!" I said, laughing. "Caleb's going to do just fine at the Division!"

Caleb's been gone two weeks along with Cain and Cassia, and they've already cleared out half the Division. Dennis was indeed Court Marshaled and is now serving time behind bars. A certain secretary came clean about the whole thing concerning me and my pack, I guess. The evidence was lost in the fire concerning Lorelei, but when the small woman stepped forward, pulling out documents of correspondences between Lorelei and Dennis, the trial was swiftly decided, and the judge gave a harsh punishment. With how old Dennis was already, I don't see him ever getting out before he dies. While I felt a more permanent solution was required, humans had a different way of handling things. *At least he was being punished.*

My brother sounds exhausted whenever we talk but genuinely excited about his job. I was relieved because having him in the center of our enemy just about pushed my wolf over the edge. I nearly went after him to bring him home more than once, but Caleb seems to really enjoy what he's doing. He's never been this excited over the family bar or any leadership role here at the clan. I wouldn't take that away from him.

"Please!" Cade laughed. "He's been texting me on and off this past week how Octavia's driving him crazy. She throws up constantly, and is in such a pissy mood that *no one* wants to deal with her. I give it a week before he can't take it anymore and begs to come home."

I chucked my rag at my Beta. "Give her a break! How would you feel if you were in her shoes? Just be grateful she's doing the job for us."

He grinned wide, picking up his mop bucket to dump in the sink. We spent most of our time cleaning the lodge and surrounding area, so it would be safe for the pack to come home. My dad and his construction crew were already drawing plans up to fix it, and then he was coming our way, so we could build onto the cabin yet again. Now, we were finally home and scrubbing the place of its awful memories.

"I'm just glad he's there and not us," Bastian said, carrying my oldest boy with him. "Here. This one's clean and hungry, but I got another waiting for me."

I quickly washed my hands before taking Barrett from him. "Hi, baby! Oh, mama's missed you! Elijah, will you grab me the formula?"

I grabbed a bottle from the rack and managed to unscrew the cap with one hand. Barrett just cooed before rooting around. "He's getting so big. I mean look at his little feet!"

I couldn't contain my grin as I played with Barrett's toes. At almost two months old, Barrett had grown tremendously. Bellamy was a little smaller than his older brother, but both boys were happy and healthy. *Just how I liked it.*

Elijah took the lid of the formula off and added a scoop to the water.

"He's going to a brute, let me tell ya," he said with a grin. Emersyn bounded on the porch then in her sleek black cat and shifted.

"Hello, family!" she said with a grin. She kissed her mate before beaming over towards Barrett and I. "Aww, can I take him?"

I stood there frozen in shock as I stared at my sister-in-law. *I couldn't believe my eyes. I couldn't...*

"Shanely?" Emmie said softly. "Is everything okay?"

I rushed over to her and wrapped her in my arms. I just held her and did everything I could to keep my tears at bay.

"What's going on?" Cade asked quietly, and I chuckled. I pulled back and handed Emmie my baby.

"Nothing," I said, wiping my eyes. I took the bottle from Elijah and handed it to her. "Nothing at all."

The Fenrir brothers didn't look too convince but followed Emmie and Barrett over to the couch. Bastian walked in with Aerith and Bellamy and froze when he noticed them too.

"Is she..."

"Yes," I answered softly. I linked arms with my mate as we watched our family from here, "but let's let them find out on their own."

Bastian's look of surprise soon turned to a massive grin. "Perks of being Alpha, I suppose."

I giggled and rested my head on my mate's shoulder. Aerith tugged on my shirt then.

"I see him, mama," she said, pointing to Emmie. "He's as strong as Barrett."

I grinned wide.

"Well, of course he is! He's a Fenrir, after all."

Epilogue

Five years later

"Boys! Let's go, we're already late!" Bastian hollered up the stairs.

I chuckled as I finished braiding Aerith's hair. She left it long, only trimming it slightly over the years, and now that she was 10, it was well past her waist. She wore the same reddish-brown hair I used to have with pride and looked just like I did as a kid.

My hair was still solid white, but I had grown mine out as well. Not as long as hers, mind you, but it was close. *I would never have short hair again.*

We were all headed to the lodge for our annual family cookout and trying to get everyone ready on time was tricky for a family this size.

Aerith looked adorable in her floral dress and denim jacket with her brown cowboy boots. It was the girliest outfit she owned as she threw out anything pink and purple a long time ago. But she was out of the tactical gear Bastian bought her, when she started going to work with him, so I took the win. *She looked like a little lady,* I thought smiling. I just wore a simple pair of jeans with a white flowy shirt, and Bastian wore his typical jeans and blue t-shirt. The only ones we were waiting on were our twin boys. *Who had probably gotten distracted in their room and had yet to even get dressed,* I thought, shaking my head.

The boys were growing up too fast and had already shifted into their animals. True to Aerith's word, we had one grizzly bear and one very strong wolf.

Barrett was our grizzly, and he looked a lot like my father when he shifted. It was my quiet Bellamy who had the cunning wolf. His wolf was solid black, much like my mother's, but his paws were white as was his left eye. *At least something passed on from me,* I thought. *Although I wish Barrett got it too.*

They were the best of friends but complete opposites. While Barrett was a goofball, and loud at times, Bellamy was quiet and observant. He was a little smaller than his brother, but he never seemed to mind or even notice.

Barrett was rowdy and careless, while Bellamy was patient. He'd wait until the right time to strike and would win against his brother almost every time when they sparred or wrestled. They were so similar in their looks, other than the hair and eye color being a little off, but they were still so different in other ways. Each having qualities and strengths different from one another. When it was time to pass the torch, Bastian and I knew without a shadow of a doubt, they'd do just fine as long as they were together.

That close knit bond was beginning to get them in trouble though. Cade had told them about switching places with his brothers growing up, and now they've decided to try it amongst themselves. I have never wanted to smack my Beta so hard as I did when he gave them the idea. They've fooled some in the pack already, so we're keeping a close eye on them. Especially since Cade started the prank wars.

And then there was Aerith. She had grown into such a beautiful young lady, but she was quickly becoming a pro with her wolf. She started following Bastian to work with the enforcers years ago, trying to train right alongside them. It made me nervous honestly. She was so small and too young to be doing this sort of work, but no matter what I suggested, she'd continue to follow along, doing whatever Bastian put the others through. To the point she stopped acting like a kid though. It worried me to no end. She immediately threw away all her dolls when we came home from Abe's and had little interest in anything in her room other than the drawing pencils she got from Elijah one year.

It wasn't normal, but she refused to talk to anyone. We put her in therapy with Malin since coming home, but she never really answered her either. We all tried our hardest to talk to her about what happened at the Jennings house, but the more we tried, the more she pulled away. I finally told everyone to leave her be. That we would be there for her when she was ready. A few days after we backed off, Aerith finally admitted that she was going to be an enforcer someday like her dad, and that she'd never be helpless again.

My heart broke when she told me. It was the only thing she ever admitted. I knew how she felt and instead of peppering her with more questions, I started to train with her. I had never seen her smile as much as she did after our first official lesson.

As the years went by, Aerith confided in me a lot more. I never pushed and never pried. I let her open up when she's ready, and we are close because of it. It's how she needs to operate to be okay, and that's okay with me. She traded therapy with Malin for drawing, and she talks to me when she wants. I give her space, and every so often she lets me go through her sketch book. It's like a door kicked wide open into her little mind, and I am forever grateful she allows me to see her work. She still has yet to allow Bastian or her uncles to see, and I get why. Every so often, I recognize Patrick or some part of that house. It's really hard to deal with.

Aerith's a prodigy with her wolf though, and I think she's developing her ability a bit more. She senses everyone's shifter animal and their strength now and uses it to her advantage. Aerith's incredibly smart, and I'm anxious to see what else she can do. The boys have yet to show a special ability, but that could change any day really.

"Boys!" Bastian shouted before two sets of loud steps thundered down the stairs. They were both grinning wide, and I just knew they were plotting something for today.

"What are you two up to?" I asked as they followed their sister out the back door.

They both grinned. "Nothing."

"Uh-huh. I'll be watching you two today. No pranks!" I said, and they groaned.

"C'mon, mom!" Barrett cried out.

"Uncle Cade gets us every year!" Bellamy chimed in.

Bastian laughed behind us. "Oh, let them go, babe. They're not wrong. Cade's been laying it on thick with these two."

I laughed. "Alright, but don't complain if you get it worse. Just don't hurt anyone, please!"

They grinned and took off down the trail. I laughed as Bastian grabbed my hand.

"They've been plotting this for weeks," he whispered in my ear.

"What?"

"Those two have been plotting off and on for weeks before bed. They've got a brilliant idea, and I, for one, am anxious to see if they can pull it off," Bastian grinned wickedly.

"You all are going to start a war. Hopefully, it's not another food fight like last year," I replied as we walked down the path.

"Hey, I'm pretty sure Abraham was the first one to throw a hot dog. Speaking of the Tiger King, are they still coming?"

"Yup! He, Bay, Spencer, and baby Nathan should be there already. They said they would get here around 1 so…"

"How old's Spencer now?"

"She just turned four, remember?"

A blank expression covered his face.

"This is your blood niece," I chuckled. "How do you not remember her age?"

Bastian shrugged as he grinned again. "I can barely remember my own age, let alone everyone else. We have so many little ones running around now, it's hard to keep count."

"Yeah, that's true. We have Abey and Bay's two littles, Spencer and Nathan. Then Elijah has Ryder, who's nearly five now. Then of course there's Johnny and Alana's little cub, Thomas. He's just older than the boys. Oh, and I can't forget Lincoln. Noah and Esme's 4 year old little girl."

Bastian shook his head. "See! Too many to keep track of. Can you imagine when they get to be teenagers? We're going to have our hands full, my love."

I laughed again. "We'll be fine! I mean you and your brothers turned out alright!"

He snorted. "Yeah, and we nearly died like a thousand different times, and we're only 30."

"That's a good point," I said, pursing my lips. "You're right, we're

EPILOGUE

doomed!"

Bastian playfully pushed me as the lodge came into view. It was full of shifters and a select few humans from the Division. Ever since Caleb and Cain got into leadership positions, things changed drastically for everyone. We're still hidden from most of the human population, but everyone that works for the Division now has been educated about us properly. The selection process is carefully run by Cain and Hank, and it's very difficult to get into the program now. Once you got in, you were there for life. It's starting to become a sought out program in our shifter community though, which is pretty cool, all things considering.

But there isn't the fear that there once was, and we've rebuilt trust between the two groups. Well, for the most part. Hank stayed true to his word and investigated all those that were running things before, and many have been arrested and are now serving time behind bars. Humans handled the punishment, and we stayed out of it, but they did send financial help to all those who lost someone in the attack Calvin and Patrick instigated. The smaller shifter groups aren't struggling anymore, and because we lifted the rule that says we can't mix with one another, we've had a great amount of new matings. The upswing has caused joy amongst all shifters, and I think it's had a play with passing our abilities down to our offspring. We haven't had a case where a child didn't receive the ability to shift like their parents in a few years.

Bastian and I got approval from the Shifter Council to start choosing locations for an all shifter school two years ago, and the first school has opened its doors this past spring. This fall all kids from ages kindergarten to 12th grade will now attend public school. The entire faculty are shifters on the off chance we have a kid lose control and shift, and every student will be free from worry of keeping that side of them hidden so fiercely. Their peers will understand because they will all be going through the same thing. Bastian and I created rules to keep everything running smoothly, and the construction for the Diablo shifter school starts next year. Soon, my children will get to attend school too.

We also opened a facility that handles shifter children who have no home or place to go. Sort of like an adoption agency but with those qualified to help the kids with their animal side and assist in helping parents who have no mate. Our goal is to keep families thriving in our community, and I couldn't bear the idea of anyone going through what Aerith and I had. Bastian and I cut the ribbon to officially open the Ryder Home for Shifter Families. Now, no child will be without a home.

Everyone's been so busy these last few years that I rarely see my family, and I seriously missed them. Caleb and Cain come home as often as they can, but the Division keeps them very busy. Most of the council meetings we have, Caleb has to be on the big screen. It makes it tricky to just catch up with one another.

Abey and Bay have been busy with their kids as well, and they have their hands full helping rebuild the panther population. Abey graciously gave part of his land to Emersyn and Esme's claw, and now the panthers live with his tigers. Their father sold their land and moved in with them, and the girls are grateful they weren't in a position to chose between their mates or their dad. Now, it's just a short drive to see him, and the panthers and tigers are getting along really well. But I still miss my brother and sister-in-law.

My father and mother disappeared for some time after we were rescued, and I was glad. They needed to heal everything between them, but they've been bouncing between my brother's place and the lodge ever since they got back. Mom's been catching up on all our lives, desperate to know everything about us. We've honestly been doing the same thing with her. I gave her my necklace back too. It didn't feel right keeping it, knowing it was my father's engagement ring for her. She tried to insist I keep it, but I refused. I secretly had Bastian make me another one, but I wanted her to have the original. She has yet to take it off.

Today was going to be a good day though as everyone was coming home for our annual barbecue. The Summit was coming up at the end of summer, but this was our time just as a pack and family to be together, and I was thrilled to see the lodge full of all the people I loved. Even Caleb was coming home.

"Nana!" Aerith called out as she ran to my mother.

"There's my girl! I was wondering when you'd all get here!" she responded, hugging her granddaughter.

"Blame my brothers," she replied before jumping into dad's arms.

"Hey, kiddo! Where are your brothers actually?" he asked.

"Plotting, I'm sure," Bastian replied, giving my mother a kiss on the cheek and shaking dad's hand. I greeted my parents, and we made our way around the back towards the big red barn. Plenty of tables were already set up and some sort of game was already going for the kids.

"Baby Girl! There you are!" Cade shouted. He plowed into me, picking me up and spinning in a circle.

"Cade, you're gonna make me sick!" I screamed as he set me back on my feet laughing.

"Where's the boys?" he asked as he put his arm around my shoulder.

I shrugged. "Don't look at me! I have no idea!"

Cade slowly grinned at me. "Aww c'mon, Baby Girl. Don't leave me hanging! Tell me what's going on."

The group chuckled as Bastian pushed his arm off me.

"Oh no, no," Bastian said. "This war is between you and the boys. Don't be cheating by going to mom."

Cade laughed and kissed my cheek abruptly. "It's alright. I can take'em anyways!"

He grinned wide as he trotted back up to the lodge. I giggled as Bastian rolled his eyes. My mate led us down to the barn, and Aerith took off to find the other kids her age in the pack. I was glad she was branching out a little. *Finding friends for her had been difficult,* I thought to myself. I said hello to my whole family at one of the large picnic tables before realizing someone was missing.

"Where's Caleb?" I asked, frowning. *I really hope he wasn't bailing again.*

Uncle Thomas shrugged. "He and his team should be here soon."

"His team?" I asked.

"He's been assigned a team. They've been traveling around looking into an issue that's come up, I guess," my dad responded, handing my mother and I sweet teas.

"What issue? Why haven't I been told anything?" I asked, taking a long sip. *God, this was good stuff.*

"Because you turned down the job!" Cain's voice bellowed as he pulled me into a swift bear hug. I laughed as tea ran down my arm.

"Doesn't mean I don't want to hear all the gossip!" I said, laughing. Dad handed me a napkin, and I wiped my arm.

I hugged my Aunt Cassia next. *She looked good!* I thought to myself. *I think getting out of pack land's was the best thing for her.* She needed a lot of time to heal after losing her brothers. She's the last of the McCoy siblings now, and I know that's been hard on her, but she thinned out some and wore an adorable pair of overhauls with a black flowery t-shirt today.

"Well, at some point there will be a meeting, but we're giving Caleb and his team a chance to contain this quietly," Uncle Cain said to me. I raised an eyebrow, and he shook his head. "Don't even bother asking me about it, Shanely. I don't know all the details unfortunately. Caleb and Hank have been working primarily on it. Hey, guys!"

Cain waved at one of the older couples sitting at another table. He gave me a soft smile then. "Don't worry. When Caleb gets here, you can ask him all about it. C'mon, Cassia. Let's say hi to Hillary and Steve."

And off they went.

I plopped down at the picnic table and stole my nephew Nathan from Bay. He was two, so not far behind the rest of the kids, but he was such a cuddler. More than any of our kids combined. I loved holding him because he'd just snuggle with you for hours. He was the laziest kid I had ever met, but I loved it. Since Elijah had to perform a hysterectomy on me after delivering the boys, I wasn't going to have another baby. I had to get my baby fix through everyone else now.

Abey plopped down next to me. "Hey, little sis! There's my big boy! Did you catch his scent yet?"

"I did actually," I said with a grin. "He's finally picking an animal it seems. Following in his daddy's footsteps?"

Abey grinned proudly. "Seems like it! While that one over there might

EPILOGUE

just end up being the Mor'du heir."

I smiled, looking at my niece. Spencer ran around with the rest of the kids. Not letting her age or size get the better of her, and you could see she was faster than the rest. My brother looked on proudly as she bested the other kids.

My mother plopped down in front of us. "Hello, son. You forgot to kiss your mother when you arrived, you know. That's going to cost you."

He grinned sheepishly before standing up from the table. He gave her a kiss saying, "Hello, mother."

My mother just shook her head. "What punishment am I going to have to give you? You know my rule. You come say hello the *minute* you see me."

Abe rubbed the back of his head, while I laughed. "My apologies, mother, but I think the kids are hollering at me."

Abraham took off towards the cluster of kids, and she shook her head at him. "You're just running cause you knew I was going to smack you!"

He turned and grinned wickedly before shifting and jumping in on their game of tag. The kids squealed, excited to see his white tiger coming out to play.

I laughed. "You know mom... If you really want to get him back, you could always ask him about the story he never wants to tell you."

Her head whipped to mine, narrowing her eyes as she gave me a look. "What do you mean?" she asked. "Is there something he's keeping from me?"

"Oh yeah, big time. He made us all swear not to say anything, but it's been so long now that I think it's time you knew," I said with a grin. I was being mischievous, I knew that, but I didn't care. Seeing the look on her face was so worth the trouble I was about to be in. *This was way too funny*, I thought to myself.

Bastian covered his mouth, shaking his head at me as he tried not to laugh. I only grinned wider.

She looked to Bastian, who was failing at staying quiet, and then back to me. "What's the story then?"

"Oh, I can't tell you," I answered, taking another sip. "Abey has to be the one to do it. Just sometime today, ask him about the time he made Bay and I... Umm well, work for him."

Bastian suddenly lost it, and my mother looked so confused.

I couldn't contain my laughter as the rest sitting at our table started to chuckle. "Just ask. I promise you, he will squirm, and it will be adequate punishment. Just don't let him run away when you do."

She shook her head, exasperated with the both of us now. "I really don't like the idea that you two were helping him with those deals of his."

Bastian couldn't breathe now, and everyone else sitting at the table has officially lost it. I only grinned wider.

"You are so dead," Bay muttered, grinning wide.

Mom's brows knitted as she turned to dad, who just shrugged.

"Don't look at me! I don't know everything either," he said, and a determined look appeared on her face.

"Oh, I'm going to figure this out!"

I grinned wickedly, leaving my family at the table. I was still the White Wolf after all and needed to say hello to the rest of the pack. My stomach rumbled loudly as I said hello to a few of our new families, and I made my way to the food. Bastian was behind me in seconds, wrapping his arms around me tight and pulling me in.

"He's going to kill you!" he teased.

I laughed. "Let him try! I can still squish him like a bug."

He laughed and grabbed plates for the both of us.

"Already starting trouble, Shanely. Can't be a family barbecue without a little drama, right?" he said before popping a deviled egg in his mouth. I grinned wickedly before stealing one for myself.

"Exactly," I replied. "I mean, did you really think the boys got their pranking skills only from Cade?"

Bastian snorted but said nothing as we filled our plates to the brim with every option laid out on the table. We made our way back, and I kept my eye out for Abe. One way or another, he would be coming after me, but I would be prepared. Time trickled by as we ate and caught up with everyone. It was amazing to see everyone again. *I seriously missed this.*

Halfway through my meal, I scented Caleb. My head perked up, seeing him head down the hill with 6 other Division members I didn't recognize. I jumped up from my seat to greet him.

"Caleb! You finally made it!" I said, plowing him over.

"I wouldn't miss our annual family barbecue!" he said, and I slowly raised an eyebrow. He grinned. "Again, alright? I wouldn't miss it again."

I laughed and hugged him again. I was so glad he was here, but our reunion was quickly interrupted. Whispers came from behind us, and I scented the air. *Human. Entirely* human, and I slowly pulled back. *Why was Caleb's team solely human?*

I took a peek over his shoulder and saw nothing but a group of wide-eyed men and women who scented like fear. *You'd think this was their first time around shifters*, I thought to myself, and then I heard my name. Everything started making sense. I giggled, giving my brother a funny look.

Caleb cleared his throat, silencing them.

"Guys, she's an elite shifter. She can hear you," he mumbled, and they all turned red. My brother looked back to me, shaking his head. "They're new in a lot of ways."

I shrugged, not able to contain my grin. "It's fine. Just not something I've dealt with in a *long* time. Just surprising there are still some who are excited to meet me."

"Hi," I said to the group, "I'm Shanely Fenrir. Not White Wolf or Queen or whatever title Hank's been trying to throw on me. Just Shanely."

They smiled, relaxing a little, and returned my hello. There were two girls on the team with four fellas, who looked passed Caleb and I excitedly. They were eager to join in on the fun, and I smiled, liking the fact they wanted to be here. The shorter of the two girls seemed extra uptight though, and I narrowed my eyes to her. She had shoulder-length dark brown hair with brown eyes and wore a flannel shirt with jeans. I wasn't sure what division of the army she was in, but when I scented her, I picked up on her human scent mixed with something else. I wriggled my nose around, trying to figure out what that extra scent was and turned to my brother for answers.

He sighed heavily as he noticed the confusion on my face. "We need to talk later, but first I have an announcement. C'mon."

Caleb gently guided me back to the table, and his team followed. Bastian inhaled the moment everyone got close, picking up on the funny smell too. He looked to me for answer, but I shrugged my shoulders as I sat back down next to him. *I didn't know either.*

Caleb turned to his team then. "Guys, you're off duty so go mingle. Get food, and have fun! No one here will bite, I promise."

"Speak for yourself," Cade jumped in without missing a beat. He winked at the new group before plopping down next to me.

My brother's team laughed and waved goodbye before making their way to the food. Everyone, but the short girl. I looked at Caleb and raised my eyebrow at him.

"What's with the funny smell?" Cade asked, and I shrugged again.

Caleb ran his fingers through his hair nervously. *Well apparently, this was a big announcement,* I thought as his eyes went from us to the girl again.

"Alright, there's no other way to say this, and everyone needs to know, so I'm just going to say it. Everyone meet my mate, Billie Hayes."

My jaw dropped. No one said a word as we stared at the two of them. She looked uneasy at us and took a small step back, while Caleb sighed heavily. I couldn't get my mouth to work. I just stared at the two in disbelief, and my brother gave me an irritated look.

This was the first mating between a shifter and a human that any of us had *ever* seen. John, the tiger shifter, was the only one that even knew about it, and it was only because of his family records.

This was so rare.

My father and mother stood abruptly to congratulate them, and everyone seemed to snap out of their surprise.

"We are so happy for you both!" mom said smiling. She kissed Caleb's cheek and went to hug Billie, but she pulled further away from her. Mom's smile fell, and her hands fell to her side. I went around her.

"Congratulations, brother. Why didn't we feel the connection to her though? Is it because she's human?" I asked, and she snorted behind him.

"It might be because I have yet to complete the bond with her. Well, at least that's what I'm assuming, but we honestly aren't sure. I was hoping to speak to John today about it. Is he here?" he asked, and I nodded.

"He's around here somewhere," I replied, giving my brother a small smile. "Let me know what he says, please?"

"Why?" the tiny voice snapped behind Caleb.

My brother winced slightly as I turned to face Billie. She stood there with her arms crossed and didn't look very happy with me. Something about her rattled my wolf. I couldn't quite put my finger on it, but for my brother's sake, I wanted to smooth things over. *Yes, I was blindsided, but I was genuinely happy for them. Caleb deserved to have a mate.* He had waited a very long time for this, and I was glad he found someone.

"Congratulations on your mating, Billie," I said, stepping towards her. "I would just like to know what John says about it because we've not had something like this happen in a very long time. I'd like to be prepared if we get anymore cases like yours. I'm sorry if we didn't seem more excited about it earlier though. We were all just a little shocked."

She rolled her eyes then, and I bristled. *Like actually rolled her eyes at me!* I turned to my mate as my wolf barred her teeth inside my head. This girl actually cocked her hip to the side, with an arrogance I hadn't seen before, and I narrowed my eyes to her. *Yeah, this was going to be a problem after all. I don't deal well with attitude issues. Not anymore.*

"Look, whatever this is," she said, gesturing between her and Caleb, "it's between Caleb and I. I'm not reporting anything back to you, and honestly I don't even know what's going to happen between us. Let's just keep it civil between us until I figure out what I want to do."

Caleb swore as my temper flared. *Okay, now I'm pissed,* I thought as I glared at her. Bastian finally stood, his eyes narrowing at her as he made his way to me.

Billie's arrogant gaze went from me to my mate. We were still the Alpha pair, not only to this pack specifically, but the entire world of wolves. *We deserved more respect than that.*

Bastian stepped forward to correct this issue, but I held my hand up, halting him instead. Caleb looked utterly distraught, and I could see how this was going to play out already. *If I snapped the way I wanted to, Caleb would only get hurt.* I didn't want to make anything worse for him. He held his breath, waiting for my answer, and I could see his pain clear as day. *His heart was breaking.*

I cocked my head to the side and sighed. "Actually, that's not how this works..."

"It's exactly how it works because I believe you turned the job down to work at the Division, correct?" she snapped, crossing her arms. "Which means you are not my boss, and I don't report to you. I don't feel like having you meddle in this, when I don't even know *what* this is. I didn't come here for anyone's approval, and it seems pretty clear I wouldn't get one anyways."

Snarls ensued behind me as Caleb tried to interject. I raised my hand again, silencing everyone.

"Let me explain something," I said, stepping forward, "because I really don't think you've been informed correctly. The Division works hand-in-hand with shifters now, and while yes I turned down the job to live and work there, who do you think Hank, Cain, Caleb, and Mitchell meet with every month? Hmm??"

She looked uneasy between Caleb and I as she muttered, "The White Wolf."

"Exactly, and you do realize that's me, correct?"

She glared back at me.

"And besides the fact I am the *actual* ruler of the wolves, after everything got restructured with the Division, I became the official spokesperson for all shifters. If there's a problem, concern, request, or whatever you can think of, they call my mate and I. If you're looking at who's in charge of the shifters, it's us. If you want to pull the technicality card then go right ahead. I'll call a meeting with the four Heads right now and get it cleared up who exactly is your boss, but just so you know I was pulling the sibling card in the first place. In case Caleb hasn't told you when the bond sets in fully, you will feel a connection to my mate and I."

Her eyes went wide. "You're his sister?"

EPILOGUE

I snorted. "You tell her nothing?"

Caleb looked exasperated with me. "It's been difficult, Shanely."

I nodded slightly, turning away from her. "Yeah, looks like it."

Cade suddenly stepped in my view. He gave me a pointed look, and I rolled my eyes.

"No."

"Baby Girl..."

"Don't ask me..."

"Your brother needs this," Cade said firmly. "Help him."

I growled. *Agh! I know he was just being a good Beta, but seriously?!* He turned me around and pushed me forward. Caleb gave me a look that begged me to smooth things over with her. Bastian turned to me.

"How do you want to play this?" he said through the link.

"I don't want to play at all," I answered, sighing.

Billie looked at her feet, her face entirely red from embarrassment, and I felt a little bad. *I wasn't trying to embarrass her,* I thought. *She just frustrated me.*

I sighed and took a step closer.

"Look Billie," I said in an even tone, "whether you like this or not, this is happening. I'm not a bad person, and neither is anyone else here. We'd like to get to know you because Caleb is really important to us. I want this to work, okay?"

She nodded slightly, and Caleb let out a deep breath. He mouthed a *thank you* to me before guiding her to the food.

Bastian came up behind me then. "I'm proud of you, babe, but I seriously think you were going to make her piss herself if you went much further."

I playfully slapped him and watched my brother guide her through the pack and clan. Everyone looked surprised to see him hold her hand, but it only made her look more and more uneasy with each step. *What was I going to do with her?*

For once, I had no idea how to help those two with their bond.

* * *

I slumped back in my seat.

"Well, that wasn't what I was expecting him to say," I said nonchalantly.

"She doesn't seem to like us very much," Cade continued, sitting on my right as Bastian sat back down on my left.

"She must be new because she doesn't seem to know much about shifters either. How did she get through the training and exams to be a Division enforcer?" Elijah asked, and my father shrugged.

"Either way she's apart of our lives now. We need to welcome her and support Caleb. He seems stressed about this whole thing as it is," my Dad said.

"And going all White Wolf on her might not be the best way to go," my mother pointed out, giving me a look.

"What? She was being rude!" I interjected. "She seemed more concern about the job than meeting his family."

"I think she was afraid, and our reaction probably wasn't the one Caleb told her she would have. We were all so shocked to hear of a mating between a human and a shifter, that we lost sight of the joy that someone in our family *found* his mate. We should be excited! But we all stayed silent, and it probably made her feel like we were upset with it in the first place," my mother continued, and we all fell silent.

I didn't mean to give her that impression, I thought to myself, *but my mother was right.* I looked over at my brother, and he was already in another serious conversation with the girl. It didn't look like it was going well at all. Guilt ate at me, and I groaned as I stood up.

"Where are you going, my love?" Bastian asked me, raising his eyebrow.

"To fix this," I said, throwing my hands up.

I gently pushed my way through the pack, and Caleb spotted me coming his way. I could see him whisper something before she turned around to me.

"What's up, Shanely?" he asked. She simply stared at me.

"Look, I think we got off on the wrong foot here. We were all just shocked to hear of a mating like this, but it was *not* because we aren't happy with it. A mating like this is just extremely rare," I said, and her face softened

EPILOGUE

some.

She looked at Caleb, and he gave her a small smile, making me wonder if this was something he had told her before.

"We are thrilled to hear Caleb found you, and I'd love to get to know you better. I'd be happy to help you understand what happens with a mating, so it's not unexpected or overwhelming for you. I know our ways are very different from humans, and I understand how you are feeling right now."

"Look, I don't mean to be rude, but how could you possibly know how it feels for me? This is all overwhelming, and I just don't feel like I belong here," she replied, and Caleb looked dejected. His whole demeanor fell, and I sighed again.

"Did you seriously tell her nothing about us?" I asked, trying to lighten the mood, and he shrugged.

"There's been a lot going on lately. Most of what the new recruits know are just rumors about the elite shifters. I've been a little busy with..." he looked at her, and I saw the unspoken words rattling around his head. He sighed, choosing to keep it to himself. I understood completely.

"Elite shifters, huh?" I said, flashing him a toothy grin. "Is that what they're calling us now?"

He rolled his eyes. "Don't let it go to your head now."

I laughed. "Me? Never!"

I turned back to Billie as she watched our interaction. I gave her a genuine smile, placing my hand on her shoulder. "You seem like you like honest blunt answers, so I'm just going to give it to you straight, alright?"

She nodded her head, and Caleb shot me a nervous glance. I waved him off. *She had stopped glaring. That's a win.*

"There's no backing out of the mate thing. The way you feel for Caleb is only going to get stronger from here on out, especially once you complete your bond."

Her eyes widened, and Caleb looked straight up pissed with me, but it was the truth, and she deserved to know.

"Don't go jumping ahead to the worst case scenario, alright?" I said with a smile. "Finding your mate is a rare and extremely special thing. Caleb is your perfect other half, and he will compliment who you are inside, Billie. It's like a best friend and soulmate all wrapped up in one. This is something to be celebrated, not run away from. I know how you feel because I grew up as a human. I didn't find out about shifters or my family until I was almost 20, so we can deal with everything together. I promise! You are more than welcome to bring your parents here too if they know about us. If they don't then bring them anyways, and I promise we will all act as normal as can be."

Her face hardened, and a darkened look glazed over her eyes. "I don't have parents. It's just me."

Now it clicked. *It was all clear now,* I thought as my wolf softened inside. *I understood why she was so guarded with all of us now.*

I gave her a small smile. "I grew up without parents too. I bounced from house to house in the system before I was finally able to flee from my old life."

"Your parents are right over there though. You still got them at least. Mine are never coming back, so it doesn't make us the same," she said, and I rocked back and forth on my feet.

"No it doesn't, but it does mean we've had similar upbringings. I may have found my parents, but you've just inherited them when you mated with Caleb. Do you really think they aren't going to treat you like their own now that you're with Caleb? I mean, look at that big guy talking to my mother right now," I said, pointing to Abey. "That's my biological brother, but technically he's not Caleb's brother. The three of us are siblings by choice. Someone attacked my mother, and she gave birth to the big guy. Caleb's dad had him from a previous relationship, and I'm the only one in the middle. When my parents finally found one another again, they just claimed the three of us and our mates as their own. I think you need to get to know your new family and learn a thing or two about shifters before you determine that this is a bad thing."

Before she could respond, my entire family erupted with laughter. The three of us turned to see everyone losing it. All but one. Abraham glared at me. *Uh-oh.*

EPILOGUE

"SHANELY!" Abraham bellowed before my mother pulled his chin, forcing him look at her. I could see him struggling to glare at me, while our mother lectured him.

"Uh-oh," I muttered with a chuckle. I started backing away slowly.

Caleb gave me a look before smiling. "What did you do now?"

I laughed nervously. "I... Uh.. I might have told mom to ask about when Bay and I worked for Abey back in the day."

I heard my mother gasp loudly, and then she started wailing on him. He blocked and winced as she hit him repeatedly. I could hear her shouts from here, and everyone else was still lost in their laughter. Abraham's face turned bright red as he snapped his head back to me.

"I think you better run," Caleb whispered.

I slowly backed away. "He wouldn't, would he?"

Caleb laughed harder as Abraham yelled again, "Shanely! You are DEAD!"

"Mate?" I shouted nervously. My mother still had Abraham in a death grip as I weighed my options.

Bastian laughed and shouted back, "Oh no, mate! You're the one that spilled the beans."

I glared back at him grateful my mother was still smacking Abraham. "Beta?!"

Cade grinned wickedly. "I don't know if I'd want to get in that guys way, Baby Girl!"

Suddenly, a loud roar bellowed across the yard, causing everyone to turn and look. Abey finally shifted and roared in my direction.

"Crap," I muttered as I turned to run. "Think about what I said, Billie!"

I took off across the yard towards the barn, shifting into my wolf midstride. I could feel my brother hot on my heels, when I quickly redirected in the grass, and he skidded behind me into the barn. The new recruits who came with Caleb all had their mouths wide open, surprised to see us running in our furs. I ran back to my mate, shifting back. I was laughing so hard I struggled to breathe.

"That was a close one," I muttered, when Bastian quickly threw me over his shoulders.

"Bastian!"

"Abraham hurry up," he shouted as I smacked his backside. "She's squirming!"

"You traitor!!!"

Abey's white tiger flew out of the barn, and he shifted to a stop in front of me. He quickly grabbed me from Bastian, and I squirmed, trying to get out of his death grip. I punched his rock hard back, hurting myself more than I hurt him.

"Aww Abey, c'mon! She was bound to find out eventually! Let me go!"

"She was not, and you know it! She made me tell her *everything!* You know that's a humiliating time for me," he said, stomping through the crowd.

I couldn't help it. I started giggling uncontrollably and couldn't stop myself. Everyone around us were chuckling, amusement in their eyes.

"C'mon, Abey! It's funny!"

"To you all!" he said as he stomped on the pier. I stopped laughing then. Panic slowly rose as he made it to the end.

"Oh no, no, no, Abraham! Don't you dare throw me in the river!"

He shook me, causing me to squeal even more. "Oh no, Shanely. You broke your promise. You can't skip out on the punishment."

"Technically, I didn't promise anything. I just kept quiet when you..."

Abraham launched me high into the air, and I screamed before plunging into the cold water below. *That jerk!* I thought as I started towards the surface. He was laughing hard, and suddenly I got an idea.

Time for a little payback.

I swam to the bottom of the pier and held my breath. I couldn't see him anymore, but I could hear plenty of voices on the pier now. I swam underneath it further, waiting until there were multiple splashes in the water. I quickly swam out from under the pier, making my way out of the water.

"Shanely J! Are you alright?" Mama shouted as I walked up the beach dripping wet.

"I'm fine! Wet, but fine," I replied, when more people shouted behind me. I turned and watched the boys frantically searching the water. Not once did they look back to shore, and I stopped my mom from shouting to them. She just shook her head exasperated with the lot of us.

I put my finger to my lips, but it was Bastian that noticed me first. *The cheater used our bond.*

"Shanely! You did not just fake drowning!" he shouted as he slowly made his way out of the lake.

Abey, Caleb, Elijah, and Cade all turned simultaneously, their eyes meeting mine. They were not amused.

"I have no idea what you mean!"

"Good God, Shanie! You gave me a heart attack!" Elijah shouted, throwing his hands up.

"Baby Girl, that wasn't very nice!"

Abey was suddenly moving towards me quickly and catching up to Bastian. "You done did it now, Shanely!"

I squealed and took off running again. The others scrambling to catch up. I now had all five of them chasing after me. *This was so not fair!*

I ran towards the barn and snuck around the backside of the food tables, pulling one back against the corner. Bastian and Abey about crashed into it, and they both had a wild look in their eyes as they grinned wickedly at me. I couldn't contain my laugh as I struggled to keep the table between us.

"Now wait, just one second," I said, laughing again.

"Oh no, I don't think so, *mate*. You gave us all a scare, and I think that deserves more punishment," Bastian replied, and his eyes flashed gold. I winked, hearing his wolf pull to the surface as he growled.

"I don't know, Bastian. Let's hear her last words," Abey said as the rest finally caught up.

My eyes widened. *The outcome was not looking very good for myself.* I was pinned behind this table, with my back against the barn wall and five *very strong and very fast* shifter males, blocking my path. All looking at me with the same devilish grin, and I could only imagine the trouble they'd put me through if they managed to catch me.

And I began to sweat. *I really think they will this time,* I thought as I scrambled to figure my way out of this.

I looked around, trying to sort out my plan of getting past them, when I spotted something above my head. My twin boys were grinning down at me through the slots of rafters above, and Bellamy gave me a thumbs up. They had a massive bucket with them, and I grinned. *This was my way out.*

"Well," I said as I drug the table back a little closer to the wall. The fellas took a step, arrogantly thinking they were going to win. *Their mistake,* I thought gleefully.

"You see it's not exactly my fault," I continued, dragging them back just a tad more. Cade smirked as he followed me.

"Oh, really?" my Beta asked. "Who's was it then?"

"Theirs," I said, pointing up.

The fellas simultaneously looked up to see a large bucket of what looked like runny red jello pour out from above. It covered them, hitting Bastian, Cade, and Abey the most. I bolted, flying over the table and past them while they were too busy wiping their eyes.

"Nice shot, boys! Thank you!" I hollered, making my way back towards the lake. I knew I wasn't going to get out of this now, and sure enough, I could hear their thunderous footsteps behind me again.

"Run, Shanely!" my mother shouted in between giggles as I hit the pier.

I tried to slide to a stop at the end, but those heavy footsteps told me I was caught. I barely turned around before my mate dove into me, grabbing my waist as we flew back into the water. He was really the only one who could keep up with me, and he did not disappoint today. Multiple splashes hit the two of us as the other boys jumped in as well.

Bastian pulled me in close, refusing to let me go. He was still slightly covered in goo, and I couldn't stop giggling at the sight of him. His skin was stained slightly red, and his eyes narrowed on me.

"You done laughing?" he said, rolling his eyes.

I couldn't stop though. "That couldn't have been better timing. Oh babe, your skin!"

Bastian tried to look at himself and groaned. "The boys filled it with dye, didn't they?"

EPILOGUE

I lost it, watching him scrub his skin in the water only to make it worse.

Abey scooped me up while I was distracted shouting, "I still can't believe you did that!"

He launched me high in the air, and I screamed before hitting the water again. I shot to the surface and splashed him.

"Stop launching me into the sky!"

He splashed back, and it soon started a war. Suddenly, I heard my twins hollering, and we all looked to see Cade carrying them each by one foot upside down. He looked stern but gave a small smile as he walked on the pier.

"Can you swim?" he shouted.

Barrett hollered before Bellamy could answer. "Yes, we can! We aren't babies!"

"Shut up, Barrett!" Bellamy hollered.

Cade raised them higher to look them in the eyes, giving them that typical Fenrir devilish grin.

"Good."

It was all Cade said before he threw them in and jumped in himself. Soon, the entire pack was running towards the water, and even some from the Division joined in. I laughed as the boys tried to scrub their skin, but the goo left a pinkish tint on every one of them. Even Abey's hair wasn't his normal white anymore. *It was just going to have to fade over time.*

My boys swam up to me, and I high-fived them. "Nice shot, boys!"

"Thanks, mama!" Barrett exclaimed, jumping on my back.

"We were only going to get Uncle Cade, but when we saw them gang up on you we had to save you," Bellamy said, making me smile. I gave him a big kiss on his cheek, which he wiped away immediately.

"Oh, I see how it is! This is war now. You know that, right?" Cade chimed in, making the boys grin even wider.

"Oh, it's on!" Barrett yelled before jumping on Cade. Now the three of them were wrestling, and Cade started throwing them in the air. Soon, he was surrounded by all the other kids wanting a turn. I turned to Caleb, who's attention was on a certain someone on the pier. She didn't get in but watched from afar.

"What am I going to do, Shanely?" he whispered.

I sighed, not exactly knowing the right answer for him.

"Give her time and as much info as you can. She needs to learn to trust shifters more than she does right now."

"It's not just shifters though. God, she doesn't trust *anyone* and getting her here today was like pulling teeth. I almost gave her an order to come here today. She just doesn't let anyone in. I don't know what to do, but *this* is killing me and my bear."

My heart broke for my brother. This was something meant to be exciting and joyous, but he was already fighting every step of the way just to make it happen.

"She was made for you, Caleb," I said softly, "so the best thing for her is you. Just listen to your bear and give her love and attention. I'm getting the impression she hasn't had much of that."

He nodded, nudging me before leaving the river. I watched him pull himself on the pier, sitting down next to her. He shook his head, spraying her with water and making her squirm. Caleb laughed, and I watched the two of them talk quietly amongst themselves. *They'd figure it out,* I thought to myself.

I was about to turn and give them privacy, when I saw her shake her head no *adamantly*. Then he grinned. Caleb was up on his feet in seconds, and he hauled her up in his arms and then into the river with us. I about hit my forehead, groaning out loud. *That wasn't what I meant,* I thought to myself. *She's going to chew him out and dump him. God, he's a freaking dead man now.*

Billie rose to the surface, moving her hair out of her eyes before suddenly laughing hysterically. She splashed him, and I let out a huge sigh of relief. Bastian pulled me in close, kissing my cheek.

"I love you, Shanely," he whispered.

I smiled, leaning back into him. "I love you too, mate."

Our beautiful moment came to a crashing halt, when Hank shouted from the beach.

EPILOGUE

"Caleb! Shanely! You need to come in now!"

He was waving a phone around before turning to talk into it again. Caleb paled, and he and his team were *running* out of the river. *Something was up,* I thought to myself, *and they all knew it.* Bastian and I were right behind, with the rest of my council and family.

"What's going on?" I asked.

"There's been another mark found," Hank said before going back to the call.

"Is it human again?" Caleb asked, and my brows furrowed.

"Human?" I asked alarmed. "Caleb, what is going on?"

"It's what I needed to talk to you about later today. I just thought we'd be able to have some fun before all this crap."

"Guys, suit up! We're done here!" Billie shouted, leaving Caleb with the rest of us. *He didn't correct her.*

"Someone start talking right now," I shouted, completely pissed off. Whatever was going on had been going on for awhile now, and I was left in the dark.

Completely in the dark.

"Human female, age 20 to 25, found in Scotland. Discovered by the local pack, and they have the body in their HQ there. Bite mark found on the ankle," Hank said, shutting his phone, and Caleb ran his hand through his hair.

"What did you just say?"

"This is the tenth body we've found, Shanely," Caleb answered as sorrow filled his eyes.

"A shifter?!" Bastian asked, and Caleb nodded his head yes.

"It looks like someone is trying to convert humans. We've been tracking him or her, but they're smart, and it's why I created a task force," Caleb explained. "Looks like I'm heading to Scotland."

"You can't go to Scotland!" I cried out, grabbing Caleb's arm. *What if he gets hurt by this monster?!*

"Shanely, I have to go. We need to find this guy! You know converting a human to a shifter is dangerous! Most people don't handle the DNA change, and we still don't know why he or she is doing it in the first place."

"Then I'm coming with you," I said, pushing forward.

"No, you are not!" Caleb hollered as Billie came down to join our group again. "You have been in enough danger to last a lifetime, and you know it! You have children, Shanely, and I won't risk it."

I glared at him. "I'm not letting you walk into danger alone, Caleb. You need help!"

"He has help," Billie stepped in.

Suddenly, my bear surged to the surface, snarling loudly in my head. Fear gripped my heart as my eyes flashed gold.

"Does he now?" I shouted. "And who exactly will be helping him? You?"

She bristled at my comment but stood firm before me. "Yes, me. He has me to watch his back."

I shook my head, turning to my mate.

"It's not enough," I said through the link.

"Caleb can handle this," Bastian replied. *"He knows what he's doing, and if he needs us, then we go.*

I looked to my mate, my temper softening as he gave me a reassuring nod. I kissed his cheek before turning back to my brother.

"Listen to me, Caleb," I said in a low, commanding tone, "because I will only say this once before I start handling everything as an Alpha first and sister second. You call me the minute you need help. You don't hesitate ever. Bastian and I will be there in a moments notice. Do you understand?"

"Shanely, I won't risk the boys or Aerith growing up without a mother..."

"Wrong answer," I said as his eyes widened.

"Don't you dare..." he started to answer, but I cut him off, throwing out my Alpha power.

"Caleb, you are to call me for help *if* you need it. You are to tell me *everything* that happens with this mission, and you are to ask me to join if you feel in over your head. Or if you and your team are in danger at any point. You will not deviate from my command, and you will keep yourself and your team safe. No risks," I said before pulling everything back.

Caleb rubbed his chest, and he started breathing heavy as my Alpha command coated his skin and caged his bear.

"What in the world was that!?" Billie shouted, but everyone ignored her.

"Why would you do that!?" he shouted at me.

"Because you're my brother, Caleb! I won't let you go unless I know you'll call me if you need me," I shouted right back as tears filled my eyes. "I can't lose you."

His face softened, and he reluctantly pulled me into a hug. "Don't ever do that again, but I get it. We'll be okay."

Caleb kissed my forehead before I pulled back, wiping my eyes.

"We need to go," Hank spoke, gesturing up the hill.

I stomped over to my new sister-in-law as my temper returned. I *hated* letting them go. I *hated* not going with them. And I *hated* that I had to trust this girl to keep Caleb safe.

"You say you're enough?" I snarled. "Well prove it, Billie. Don't you dare leave him, especially over a stupid thing as being afraid to be his mate. Don't abandon my brother."

Her eyes went wide. I could feel the concern rolling off my mate and brothers as I glared at Caleb's mate. My bear roared as the team hollered up the hill. *It was time to let them go.* I suddenly needed to get out of here. I couldn't stay and watch them walk away without me. I turned to Caleb then.

"You better come back to us," I whispered before finally giving in and shifting.

Billie took multiple steps back as my paws slammed onto the ground. My beautiful white fur of my bear shown brightly in the sun, and I chuffed as I pushed past everyone and disappeared into my woods. I needed calm, and I honestly I needed faith. I was scared to death for my brother and his mate.

She was already a problem for him, and I was terrified about letting him to go Scotland without any of us. His whole team was composed of humans, and they were going up against a monster.

What will happen to Caleb if he *finds* this shifter?

But then another thought hit me.

What will happen if he doesn't?

The end.

Series Order

Shifter Series
Shifter Awakened
Shifter Prophecy
Shifter Deliverance
Shifter Sacrifice
Finding Shanely *(A Shifter Novella)*

Nightlocke Series
Realm of Darkness
Island of Horrors

Are you not ready to leave the Shifter Series?

Do you need **more** from Shanely and Bastian?

Are you dying to **keep reading?**

Here's a sneak peek at the upcoming Shifter novella, ***Finding Shanely***.

Bonus Chapter

Bastian

I groaned as I came to, clutching my stomach and trying not to hurl. Everything hurt on my body, and I was struggling to breathe. I lifted my hand in front of me.

Yeah, that's blood. A whole lot of blood, I thought to myself. My mind was reeling, and I tried to sort through my memories, but good God the pain in my stomach was excruciating. I focused in for my bond with Shanely, but my eyes widened when I couldn't find her. Suddenly, my wolf howled in pain, and I felt empty all over again.

She was just... gone.

"Shanely..." I gritted through my teeth as I tried to sit up.

"Whoa Bastian, don't move! You were shot more than once!" Ryder shouted as he pushed me back against the rock wall. We were in some hidden cave on pack lands, and I could still hear the gunfire way off in the distance. Pain coursed through my veins as another member of my pack, *my wolves,* fell at the hands of our enemy. *My pack was in danger. Shanely was in danger.* She was missing again, and I was just sitting here. *I had to go. I had to hurry and save them!*

"Ryder, get out of my way," I snarled, trying to sit up again, when Elijah spoke from behind.

"Bastian, enough! You and I both want to help, but you were gunned down and aren't even able to move properly. Ryder managed to hide us, but we need to hang tight for a moment. You won't be able to save Shanely if you die trying to reach her."

Blood trickled down Elijah's arm, and Ryder had a good size slice near his eye that kept it swollen shut. I looked down at my stomach, where two bullet holes were slowly closing up. *Too slowly.*

"We can't just sit here, Elijah," I muttered in pain, watching my body heal itself. Guilt torn me up inside.

"We're not. We just need to be able to move through the woods swiftly," he replied, holding onto his shoulder. "And we can't do that now."

"How did we get here?" I asked with a clipped tone. "The last thing I remember was... Brody."

Brody was slaughtered by the time we found him in the back of our property. I gritted my teeth at the massacre we found. *They must have killed him and his whole team right after he made the call to me,* I thought to myself, which was looking more and more like a decoy. *And I fell right into it.* This whole thing was planned perfectly, and all I could think was how foolish I was for thinking I could protect them. I thought I could protect my pack and my mate, but I failed.

I failed them all.

I gritted my teeth, knowing there wasn't anything I could do. Even with Elijah and Ryder, there were so many guards, with weapons I had never seen. That too familiar burning sensation pierced my back twice, and I hit the ground hard. The overwhelming pain... The blood loss. *It just happened so fast,* I thought. I blacked out after seeing Elijah's wolf fall. I had no idea Ryder managed to slaughter them alone. Thunder rattled the cave as the rain came crashing down around me.

Ryder was quiet, sitting on a rock near the entrance, and Elijah didn't respond. Pain and horror stayed in his eyes as he watched me. *Waiting for me to blow up, I'm sure.*

"Thank you, Ryder," I gritted through the pain. "You saved us, didn't you?"

He looked up to me and gave me a small nod. "Always, brother. Although, now we're officially even."

Ryder gave a small grin, but I couldn't smile back. Too much pain. Too much guilt. Cracking jokes just didn't feel right when everyone was dying around me. When Shanely was just gone, and I had no idea where she was. *Or if I'd find her again.*

I exhaled deeply as the pain ebbed and waned finally. The deaths seemed to stop, and for that I was grateful, but I was still stuck in the woods with no way to my family. *And that was pissing me off.* I wanted to rip their hearts from their chests for what they did to my pack, and I wanted to kill Patrick *slowly* for taking Shanely. Because that was what this was about. Shanely. *It was always about her for some reason.*

And I was the fool who thought we could take them.

"Storm's moving fast," Elijah mentioned, and I looked outside. The cold rain fell rapidly, and the sun had already set. *This was going to be a long night.*

"Have you reached out to Cade?" I asked.

"In the beginning, I managed to reach him. He said the Division was annihilating the pack, and he was running to the cabin. He was following Shanely's scent," Elijah replied quietly.

My eyes went wide as hope blossomed inside my chest. *If anyone could track her, it would be either myself or my brothers, and Cade was one of the best.*

"Did he find her trail?" I said, trying to sit up again. "Our bond is quiet again, which means she's got another collar on."

Elijah slowly leaned against the wall and slid to the ground. When he looked to me solemnly, I just knew it was bad news.

"He tracked her not far from the cabin, but she's nowhere to be found," he said as a haunted look flashed over his face. "Emmie... Emmie said Patrick took her. She's just *gone.*"

I swore angrily, picking up a rock and hurling it against the wall of the cave. Pain rippled through my abdomen as I felt my wound tear open slightly but nothing compared to the pain in my chest. *How was I outsmarted by this stupid human?!*

"How do I keep losing her?" I asked, unable to keep my voice even. Silence answered me.

"Where is Cade now?" I demanded.

"The Division found him, and his snarls were the last thing I heard through the link. It's been quiet ever since," Elijah muttered, closing his eyes.

"So, we're just going to sit here?" I snapped. "That's our great plan?!"

I know I shouldn't be taking my anger out on my best friends, but this utter hopelessness was too much to bear. The love of my life was gone, which meant so were my boys. We had lost so many in our pack, and it was all my fault. I was the Alpha, and I let everyone down.

"You got a better idea?" Elijah answered without opening his eyes.

I grunted as I sat further up. My stomach had stopped bleeding, but it was just barely stitched together. *It was good enough for me though,* I thought. *I had to move. Had to start tracking where that prick went with my mate.* Rolling onto my knees hurt more than I wanted to admit, but I kept going. My brother opened his eyes as I swore softly.

Elijah glared at me before yelling, "I swear to God, Bastian, if you don't lay back down right now, I'll knock you out cold!"

"I can't just sit here, Elijah! My whole family is out there somewhere in danger, and I'm just hiding in this freaking cave!"

"You're not hiding!" he yelled again. "I mean, what do you really expect to do here?! You are barely stitched together right now, and I can't move my shoulder. We can't fight, and we're just going to get Ryder killed trying to protect the both of us. Don't you get it, Bastian! Shanely wasn't the only target tonight!"

Thunder echoed in time with my brother, who had never looked so angry at me before. My brother's eyes were gold, and with his heavy breaths, I knew he was struggling to keep his wolf at bay. *But he didn't get it,* I thought as my own wolf snarled for me to stand. *My own animals were pushing me too. They wanted their mate back just as much as I did.* I forced myself to my feet, ignoring the pain and dizziness that followed.

"You can stay if you want to," I snapped with an icy rage, "but I'm leaving!"

My brother moved with lightening speed as he shot up and slammed me back against the wall. My head snapped back as a rock dug into my back.

Elijah gripped my shirt tightly, getting right in my face as he shouted, "Don't be dumb, Bastian! Patrick put a target on your head specifically!

Going after the pack like this was just his excuse to kill you and take Shanely. Our pack, our family, *my mate*, just got caught in the cross-fire! So, you are going to sit back and get some sleep because I AM NOT LOSING ANYONE ELSE!"

Elijah snarled at me, and my eyes widened. I had never seen him lose his temper like this before. His wolf was at the surface when his eyes flashed red like mine. *One Alpha challenging another.* And I would never go after my brother like this. I put my hands up slowly, and he finally relented.

I didn't move as he stomped back to his spot and slid back down the rock wall. "We'll move out in the morning and try to figure out what to do from there."

Guilt twisted my stomach, and I felt like such an idiot. I was so consumed with losing my own mate and children, I didn't think about Emersyn. *That's not our agreement, and I should have thought of her long before this moment.* Sighing hard, I slid back down to the ground as carefully as I could and looked over to my brother.

"Elijah, I'm sorry," I said quietly. "Is Emersyn okay?"

He nodded once before dropping his head on his arm. "Our bond's strong, and I can feel her heart beating, but she's scared. She's hiding in the woods far away from the lodge, and Esme and Noah are with her. They got her out, I guess."

"Good. I didn't feel a disconnect from anyone but Shanely, and I wasn't trying to put your mate on the back burner. I'm sorry, brother," I said, genuinely sorry for doing that to him and her. *She was just as important as Shanely.*

Elijah shook his head firmly. "It's fine, Bastian. We may all be drawn to care for our brother's mates, but our own mate comes first. Always. Emersyn was fleeing the woods by the time you came to anyways, so the only mate in danger right now is Shanely."

"It still doesn't make it okay. I'd do anything for Emersyn too, you know that?"

My brother nodded again, but he still looked a little hurt.

"I do," he said, looking at me, "and you can prove it by staying put and letting your super shifter abilities heal yourself. Then tomorrow we can find my mate before we look for yours."

I raised an eyebrow at him. "Super shifter, eh?"

He rolled his eyes, chuckling softly under his breath. "Your mate shared far more with you than you did her. But yes, your *super* shifter abilities. You two heal way faster than anyone I know."

"It's true," Ryder piped up. "Shanely is crazy fast with healing."

I almost forgot Ryder was still with us. He stayed so quiet as Elijah and I spat back and forth that I didn't even hear him breathe.

Accepting defeat, I leaned my head back against the rock wall and shut my eyes. *I needed my mate, but Elijah was right.* I'd struggle even if I managed to catch up to her and Patrick, and I can't save her if I'm dead. I forced myself to just focus on the rain hitting the earth outside, hoping to keep my wolf from spiraling out of control. I'd do anything to shut my mind off and keep my thoughts from becoming too loud. Because Shanely wasn't here to help me.

I was exhausted and overwhelmed and struggling to contain my animals. My wolf and bear were going crazy inside, needing to find our mate. They didn't understand why we were hiding out in the cave when she was in danger and with another male. They only saw in black and white, and I seemed stuck in the gray. Keeping them from shifting was taking all my energy, and before I knew it, I passed out.

Bonus Chapter

Bastian

A very bright ray of sunshine blasted me in the face, and my eyes slowly fluttered open. The woods were beautiful now. No more nasty storm or strong winds but bright unyielding sunshine with so many birds and other animals moving about the forest. Like a massacre didn't just happen the day before.

I groaned as I sat up. My body felt stiff and sore from not only being shot, but also from sleeping awkwardly against a rock. I lifted my stained shirt and sighed in relief. While I'd still be a liability in a fight, the wounds were closed and healing quite nicely. I needed to take it easy for awhile yet, but at least I'd be able to move around today and hopefully shift.

I *had* to be able to shift.

My brother and best friend were still passed out on the other side of the cave. Ryder's mouth was wide open. I smirked, knowing full well he ate plenty of spiders in his sleep last night.

My animals whined within me. *It was time to go.*

I kicked Elijah's boot, and he shot up in a panic. His adrenaline was still sky high, and with his solid gold eyes, I could see he was instantly in fight mode. *Typical,* I thought, but that's just how me and my brothers were. *Always in fight mode. Never flight.*

Seeing it was just me, he settled back down, grumbling at me. I slowly stretched, giving my body a chance to adjust some before I smacked Ryder awake.

"Time to move, boys," I said.

I continued to stretch, trying to see how healed my body was before making my way to the mouth of the cave. I listened to the woods *carefully*.

I had no idea if any of the Division's army stayed behind to make sure we were gone or not, but I wasn't taking any chances. Thankfully, other than the forest waking up with the sun, it was quiet.

Elijah stood at my right, peering out into the woods as well. He inhaled deeply, and I waited to see if he could scent something I couldn't see. It would be better if we had Cade here as well, but we'd make do. *I still needed to find him too.*

"You okay to move?" Elijah asked, his eyes still glued to the forest in front of us.

"I have to be," I replied. "I've already sat for too long as it is. Patrick could be anywhere with her. We need to make our way back to the lodge and then to our house. I need to see where Cade found her and hope to God he missed something. Then we need to find Emmie. I still feel my connection to Cade too, so we'll follow that when the time comes."

Elijah nodded as Ryder came out of the cave yawning. His blonde hair mashed to one side, he gave me a sleepy grin saying, "Ready when you are, boss."

I gave my brother a look, and he nodded too. We stepped out of the cave, and I *painfully* shifted into my wolf. It was clear my body wasn't ready to make the switch yet, but I didn't have a choice. I needed to move quickly and quietly through the woods. Plus winter was nearly here, and it was getting cold. We already had snow far up the mountains, and by the scent of air, I'd say snow was just around the corner. I carefully shook my fur out. *Yeah, this was a much better choice*, I thought to myself.

I took a step, wincing as skin and muscle pulled at my wounds. Giving myself a moment for the pain to subside, I took another step. It hurt, but I was adjusting to it. I soon felt my brother and Ryder's wolf brush against me. Concern filled their eyes, but I forced myself past the pain. Past the stiff muscles and exhaustion. Past everything that stood in my way.

"*Let's go.*"

We took off into the woods. My body slowly loosening up along the way, and between me and Elijah, we kept an eye on our surroundings. The woods were quiet though. No unexpected visitors or men with guns. I was grateful to say the least, but the anger burned inside my veins as we drew closer to home. I could scent it from here. Blood. And lots of it. It didn't take long to reach the lodge, and I stumbled on my feet.

Unable to look away as the remains of the lodge smoldered. It was nearly ready to collapse in on itself. *They lit the whole thing ablaze,* I thought as my eyes widened. *And for what?* The back half looked somewhat in tact still, but I can only imagine the damage inside.

It was ruined.

Entirely ruined, and I knew it was only going to get worse from here. We ran around to the front, and that's when I felt sick to my stomach. I shifted again, not even noticing the pain this time, and tried to keep whatever was left in my stomach inside.

Elijah swore, and Ryder emptied his stomach. There were so *many* bodies scattered around the lodge and the blood... It filled the air with the scent of death. A combination of my pack and the Division lay before me, I stood there in shock just staring at everyone.

A large lion lay off in the distance surrounded by multiple Division men who were all tore up, and both of the anaconda sisters were dead near the lodge. *I asked them to come here,* I thought as my stomach twisted. *To protect my family and here they lie dead. They are never going home to their families again, and if I hadn't asked for support, they'd be home right now.*

Ryder continued to heave as we stared frozen in our spot. Every time he looked at the massacre again, he started dry-heaving all over again. I couldn't take it. *All of this was* avoidable. *None of this needed to happen.* One man's greed and lust killed *everyone* here. I gritted my teeth as my rage grew, and soon my vision had grown entirely red. My power pulsed in rapid concession as I made a solemn vow. "Patrick's days are numbered."

Suddenly, I heard the familiar sounds of tires crunching on gravel, and my head shot to the driveway.

"Someone's coming," I said as I grabbed Ryder and forced him to move.

We hid in the brush and waited for whoever was here to make their way up the mountain drive. I prayed fervently it wasn't those girls selling cookies again.

Multiple vans pulled up with the Division's logo on the side. I nearly snarled out loud, ready to eliminate them all, when Elijah put his hand on my shoulder.

"It's not the time, brother," he whispered softly.

Even though I knew he was right, I was still pissed and jerked my arm away. I gritted my teeth as I watched the group step out of their vehicles.

In dark tactical gear and assault rifles slung on their backs, the Division team stretched once outside the vans. An even larger box truck pulled up then and backed up to the mess in the yard. They laughed and carried on, while I sat there watching them in agony.

Each officer was armed to the teeth too, and I glared at the guns that hung off them. I hated those cowardly weapons. They would never last one-on-one against anyone in my pack, and they took the easy way out with those guns. I was proud my pack never kept the stupid things. *Shifters don't use guns,* I thought to myself, and my wolf agreed. We watched closely as they talked to one another and lifted the back hatch of the box truck.

What happened next about *broke* me though.

They started grabbing all the bodies, our pack and friends included, and hauled them into the truck. My eyes widened as they picked up Ash and tossed his wolf in carelessly. They filled that truck up quickly, throwing the bodies on top of one another without care or any dignity for the fallen. Not even for their own...

A sickening realization hit me. We would never be able to give our friends a proper burial with their families. We would never see them again, and I didn't even get a chance to say my own goodbye as their Alpha, let alone their families who were safe at Abraham's. I couldn't stop my feet from moving and both Elijah and Ryder lunged.

"Bastian stop!" Ryder hissed.

"It isn't right!" I snapped, barring my teeth, and they both let me go.

"None of it is," Elijah said firmly, "but there's nothing we can do about it now. Let's check the cabin, so I can get to my mate."

I sighed, glaring one last time before forcing my feet to move in the opposite direction. We moved slowly, creeping away from the lodge and towards the last place anyone scented my mate.

"Cade said it was right around here," Elijah whispered as we stepped into a clearing. *What was Shanely doing so far away from everyone?* I wondered as I looked around. *And why did she leave Cade?*

There wasn't much here, I thought as my frustration grew. All tracks had been washed away, and I couldn't catch her scent. Anger welled inside as my wolf snarled within. I shifted.

I walked the dirt path back and forth, looking for anything out of place. Elijah and Ryder shifted and started copying me.

"*Over here,*" Ryder said through the link.

I bolted to my left where Ryder dug at the ground. I shifted back. Sticking out of the muddy dirt was a small dart with a red tip. I reached down and pulled it free as my brother approached.

"A tranq dart," Ryder said, and I nodded. And just like that, the image of Shanely getting hit stood before me. I could picture her dropping, her body becoming weak and tired before she finally passed out. I pocketed the dart and forced myself to look away. My wolf pushed to the surface harshly, and it physically hurt to keep him from shifting.

"I can scent, Emmie," Elijah said softly, his voice shaking slightly. I abruptly turned to him, and he pointed to under the large tree behind me. "Over here. Her scent is mixed with Shanely's. Emmie was here with your mate, brother."

I swore under my breath. *Was Emmie the reason Shanely was so far away from the lodge? From her Beta?* I rubbed my face anxiously.

"She's okay though, right?" Ryder asked, and my brother nodded his head.

"She's with Noah, but she isn't saying much," he replied.

I sighed. Worry and shame seeped through my bond with Elijah, and I turned away before he tried to apologize.

"Let's just see what's left of our cabin," I said, moving to the path ahead. "We're this far, we might as well see if there are any tracks to pick up. Patrick must have come in from somewhere."

No one said a word as we made our way to my cabin. I should have expected what I saw, but it still blew me away. All the windows were smashed on the ground floor, and the door was completely off its hinges. It was like they destroyed everything just for the sheer entertainment of it.

Glass crunched under my boots as I walked up the back stairs and into my home. I inhaled deeply, and Shanely's scent was still here. It was thick in the air and mixed with my own. I walked into the destroyed living room and could see even Aerith's toy bin was broken. Not a piece of glass in this house was sparred, and I was honestly afraid to look in my bedroom. But God, Shanely's wild honey scent gripped fiercely around my heart. She was everywhere, and another piece of my self-control snapped within me. I felt... lost. Disconnected somewhat as a piece of my sanity drifted away. My wolf's instincts were taking over. I could feel my eyes shift and turn red as everything looked sharper and glossed over. I couldn't help it. Couldn't stop it.

Suddenly, Elijah shot in front of me, gripping my shoulders. He felt the shift in me, as did Cade I'm sure, and he shook me hard.

"Bastian, I need you to focus!" Elijah snarled, and I blinked. His voice sounded different almost. "You won't find your mate if you go feral on us. Stay with me now."

Elijah snapped his fingers in front of my face, and I blinked furiously trying to get away from him. I rubbed my face, feeling my normal self return and wolf recede within, and when I dropped my hand, my vision was back to normal too. Worry seeped through the bond at what just happened. At what *nearly* happened.

Elijah's eyes glossed over, and I knew it was Cade checking in. If I was truly feral, a link wouldn't go through anyways. I gave my brother a grateful nod before going to the front door. No point searching the house as she wasn't here and looking at our memories and her things would only set my animals off even more.

I stepped out to the front porch and sighed. Not like I expected anything different, but I wished there was some sort of trail to go off of. I walked to my empty drive and knelt down. Other than a few tire marks in the dirt where someone turned around, there wasn't anything here.

"It's really faint, brother," Elijah said, walking up to me. "I can't catch much of anything really."

I nodded and pointed to the tracks in the mud. "He drove his Jeep here, which means there's no trail to even follow them. The road's paved, and anything that would have been there was washed away."

"Do you want to head to town, and see if we can pick up her scent somewhere there?" Elijah asked, and I slowly stood.

"I don't know what to do, brother. Patrick thinks we're all dead, and I bet he's got Shanely hold up somewhere around here. If we spook him, he might bolt with her again, and I may never find her. I'm afraid to risk going into town, and it's a long shot anyways. I highly doubt he stopped anywhere before making his way back to wherever he went," I countered.

It was killing me to not make my way to town right now. My wolf wanted to do this his way, but these people always seemed to be a step ahead of us. *Were we that predictable?* I wondered. I shook my head. I needed to think differently and not spook him in the process.

"I'm sorry, Bastian. I promise you, we will find her," he said quietly. I felt his hand pat my back in reassurance, but it just made me feel like more of a failure. *Some wolf I was if I can't even track her. Some mate I turned out to be.*

Ryder came running from around the back. He gripped our shirts and started to drag us into the woods. "Guys, we need to move! They're coming here!"

My eyes widened as we took cover in the brush. Ryder wanted to keep going, but I yanked my shirt from his hands. I put my finger to my lips, and we blended into the shadows. I needed to see what was going on. *Why were they coming back here? There was nothing left but remnants of a broken home.*

It didn't take long to hear the crunch of their boots as they walked around my home and in it. The men were all relaxed and joking around with one another, like it was just another day at work. Rage filled me and my brother's eyes as we watched them come through.

"There are no bodies here, boss. Can we wrap this up?" one of the men asked, kicking the tire to my truck.

"Yeah, I'm freaking bored, man," another said as he kicked one of Shanely's flower pots over. It broke on the driveway.

Their Commanding Officer took a slow look around. "We just have to make sure. We lost some of those freaks in the woods and orders are to make sure they are dead."

Someone groaned. "Are you telling me we have to hunt them in the woods now?"

My eyes widened as I looked to Elijah. He looked utterly panicked at the thought of the Division combing our woods. *If they continued the hunt on our lands; what would happen to what's left of the pack? Could we find them before the Division did?*

"I have no desire to go hunting in this weather," the C. O. said as he crossed his arms. "As far as I'm concerned, we got them all."

I exhaled a sigh of relief as a black van pulled into my drive. The C. O. walked to it as one of his men shouted, "So, we're done here?"

"Boss says to leave the house," the C. O. replied, "but he didn't say anything about the freak's trucks. Have fun, boys!"

My heart stopped as the group grinned wide. Each one took out their knives and slammed them into the sides of my truck's tires. They smashed the windows and headlights before popping the hood and cutting everything they could reach.

I couldn't contain the growl that emitting from my throat, and Elijah clamped his hand over my mouth saying, "It's done. We'll fix it later, but for now let's just find my mate and then our brother. There's nothing more here but pain and rage."

I glared one last time at the pricks in my yard. *I'll find them again*, I promised myself. *And I'll gut them with my bare hands.* Frustrated with not being able to do anything to them, I followed Elijah and Ryder back towards the lodge.

Thankfully, the Division was gone by the time we got back, and we quickly bolted across the lodge yard and into the woods again. My body was still sore, and I needed to rest soon.

I turned to Elijah once we were safely across. "Lead the way, Elijah.

Follow your bond."

Elijah took point and started moving fast. *I didn't blame him. I'd be running if it were Shanely too.* He stayed in his human form though, so I assumed she must be close. My heart broke a little more with each step, knowing I was going in the opposite way Shanely probably was. It felt wrong not leaving to find her right now, but I was glad to reunite my brother with his mate. I was glad she was safe.

My brother slowed a bit, inhaling deeply before turning to the right. We went down a small path that wasn't used very often, and I spotted her climbing down a tree as fast as she could.

"Elijah!"

She about knocked my brother over, plowing into him as her sister and Noah climbed down after her. I walked to Noah, giving Elijah privacy with his own mate and shook his hand.

"Thank you for getting the girls out," I said, and he nodded.

"Anything for our family. I'm sorry about Shanely, Bastian. You have my support in finding her again. We won't stop until we have her safely with us, and that... What is it you guys say, *douche bag*? Yes, that douche bag will die for this."

My grin didn't reach my eyes, but I liked his choice of words. "Sounds perfect to me. He's crossed the line this time, and this is the second time he's tried to kill me."

I lifted my shirt, showing my brand new scars on my back and stomach. Noah barred his teeth in anger as Esme covered her mouth. Tears formed in her eyes as she looked to me with pity.

"It's time to take matters in our own hands," Ryder said, pushing his hair out of his eyes.

"No more playing by their rules. We end this now. We handle this the shifter way, and this means war," Elijah said viciously, and I grinned seeing their own thirst for vengeance. I pulled Emersyn from Elijah's arms, giving her a hug as well.

Her lips puckered though, and I knew what was coming. "Bastian..."

I ruffled her hair but shook my head. "Not now, please. We can discuss that another time."

She looked to me with such a broken expression, and I kissed her cheek to ease her pain. I knew she spent Shanely's last moment on pack lands with her. I just couldn't hear the details right now. I was barely holding onto a thread as it was. I gave her a genuine smile before looking to the others.

"I appreciate you all and what you've done for this pack and our family," I said, and Emmie dropped her head. "First things first, we need to find Cade and see what's left of our pack. We regroup, and then we try to find a way to call Abraham. I need to check in on my daughter before we start tracking anyone else."

I pulled on my sibling bond with Cade, and it was very far away. My gaze drifted in his direction, and Elijah soon followed. I groaned, knowing exactly where my brother went. *It was a death sentence in the winter, but maybe that's why he chose it.* The Division would *never* find us there.

"What's wrong?" Ryder asked, seeing my worry.

"I know where Cade is," I replied, running my hands through my hair. Elijah shook his head angrily and pulled Emersyn even closer. He was pissed, but there was nothing we could do.

"Where did he go?" Esme asked quietly. She gripped Noah's hand so fiercely her knuckles were white. *They weren't made for this kind of combat,* I thought to myself. Frankly none of us were, but I felt awful pulling the girls into this. I couldn't lose anyone of my people or my family.

I gave her a soft smile before answering, "Dead Man's Hollow."

About the Author

M. L. White is an award-winning Fantasy Romance writer who is obsessed with wolf shifters and all things dragon related. She loves to read and actively seeks out books that suck her in and make her feel like their world is better than reality, and she is determined to spread that same joy to others with her writing. Her books are like movies in your head with characters you can't help but fall in love with.

When M. L. White is not writing, she's chasing after her three children and taking care of her wonderful husband. They're her whole world so she's pretty busy spending as much time with them as possible. You can find her walking the trails with her two dogs or gaming with her husband and son in her free time as well!

You can connect with me on:

- https://www.authormlwhite.com
- https://x.com/Author_MLWhite
- https://www.instagram.com/author_mlwhite
- https://www.tiktok.com/@author_mlwhite

Subscribe to my newsletter:

https://dashboard.mailerlite.com/forms/1169872/137001126070322601/share

Also by M. L. White

* *Trigger warnings*- No sexually explicit content or graphic violence can be found in any of M. L. White's books. All four available books do contain violence and death, grief and loss, and some abuse or mentions of abuse. Realm of Darkness is darker in nature with fantasy monsters and may be disturbing to some readers. Shifter Awakened has pregnancy/birthing moments and kidnapping but are not in grotesque detail. Shifter Sacrifice also has kidnapping, physical and verbal abuse, and violence. No foul language or graphic themes can be found in any of M. L. White's books. These books are written for YA/NA age range. Read at your own discretion.

Shifter Awakened

How would you feel if it were illegal to simply exist? That's a question Shanely Thomas has had to ask herself ever since she discovered she is more than human.

After growing up bouncing between foster homes, Shanely thought the biggest challenge was the mysterious grandmother who left her a cabin. But that is nothing compared to the night a large wolf runs her truck off the road and tries to kill her.

After she is rescued by the local pack of wolf shifters, Shanely learns that her grandmother was the Alpha Female before she died. While Shanely finally understands who her mother is, no one knows her father. But it's clear it's not someone from the pack.

Shanely's scent is off. Shifters do not mix, and the children born of two different shifter kinds are considered to be illegal. A threat to both shifters and humans alike. Mixers must be slaughtered at all costs.

Bastian Fenrir, the Alpha's enforcer, is assigned to watch over Shanely and help her navigate her new world while hunting the wolf that wants her dead. Something pulls him towards her. The mate bond hasn't snapped in place, but he can't help the way he feels about her. It doesn't matter to him that Shanely's father isn't a wolf. All he knows is that she belongs to him, and he must keep her secret.

Twilight: New Moon but without the vampires. Shifter Awakened is a perfect shifter romantasy for those who love werewolves, soulmates, and foretold prophecies.

Shifter Prophecy

Nothing else matter when someone threatens to hurt your family. Not even going head-to-head against a crazy Tiger King who slaughters any wolf he finds.

Life is good for Shanely, Bastian, and their family. The only thing that could make it better for Shanely is finally unlocking her wolf. But until she figures out how to do that, Shanely's just enjoying her quiet and peaceful life.

Unfortunately, all that is about to change when Shanely discovers that her sister-in-law, Bay, has made a deal with sadistic shifter known as the Tiger King. And there's nothing she can do when he takes her and her two cousins, Octavia and Alana, hostage.

Now the race is on for Bastian and his brothers to complete the Tiger King's list of demands to rescue their girls from his clutches. As the boys work nonstop to pull them out alive, Shanely begins to see a new side to the Tiger King. One that he rarely lets others see.

Things come to a dangerous head as Shanely and Bastian struggle to navigate this new threat while trying to find a way back to one another.

Foretold prophecy mixed with Femme power; SHIFTER PROPHECY is a story about knowing your worth with Damsel out of Distress vibes.

Shifter Deliverance
Everything's about to change.

Shanely has finally done it.

She's found her White Wolf, but by doing so she has accidentally taken control as Alpha of the McCoy pack. Every wolf in the world has felt the White Wolf emerge, and now it's time to take control of the World Council.

But they aren't so willing to let their power go.

Now it's a battle between the two as Bastian and Shanely try to save everyone from the Council's wicked ways.

Meanwhile, things are getting heated with the Division back home. The Division Head for the McCoy pack isn't happy with the change in leadership and begins changing the rules on the Fenrir family, making demands he has no right to make.

Can Bastian and Shanely battle it out on two different fronts? Or will the whole White Wolf business permanently split them apart?

"I'm just as afraid as you are Shanely... just promise me at the end of the day you keep getting back up. You dragged me into all this, so don't bail on me now."

Realm of Darkness

What would you do if the shadows were alive? What would you do if they were trying to kill you?

The darkness is a dangerous place, and it's all because of the Nightlocke. Born of shadows and King of all things wicked and evil, the Nightlocke is a monstrous beast seeking those to torture and kill.

The kingdom of Odemark is barely surviving because of it. The land destitute, the Queen murdered, and no Lightspark to save anyone. The kingdom *needs* a Lightspark. The only person able to heal the land and the people within. But the Nightlocke made sure to kill her long ago.

But Kymra has a plan. A plan to save her family from starvation and death. And everything's going well... until she comes face to face with the Nightlocke himself.

To her surprise, he steals her away instead of killing her on sight. Now she's a slave to a new master and has no idea how to escape. But as she starts to see the Nightlocke in a new light, she begins to wonder if she even wants to leave now.

Maybe she's crazy. Maybe she's officially lost her mind, but one thing's for sure. Everyone's might just be wrong about the Nightlocke.

Beauty and the Beast meets dark fantasy. This enemies to lovers story is perfect for those who love dark romance or villain gets the girl tropes.

www.ingramcontent.com/pod-product-compliance
Lightning Source LLC
LaVergne TN
LVHW091652070526
838199LV00050B/2150